Wizardream

BOOK III

The Wizards Way

Wizardream

BOOK III

The Wizards Way

Bruce Chatfield

Press

Published by 99% Press,

an imprint of Lasavia Publishing Ltd.

Auckland, New Zealand

www.lasaviapublishing.com

Illustrations by Bruce Chatfield

Marbling by Bruce Chatfield

Edited by Rowan Sylva

Designed by Daniela Gast

ISBN: 978-1-99-118987-5

To Joanne

Foreword

The Wizards Way spectacularly completes the Wizardream trilogy in what is probably the best of the three books. Mysteries from the lore are resolved, battles are fought, and plot twists are revealed in this climatic work of high, epic fantasy. When completing the first drafts of Wizardream, Chatfield was emersed in the magical of world of his creation, sometimes cosplaying as a wizard with a staff of kanuka. The Wizards Way was not just an idea for the book but also for a board game, in which players moved High and Lesser Wizards along Wizard Lines to occupy Wizard Seats. The board was laid out as an eight-pointed star, and game play, a combination of skill and chance, was determined by the roll of an eight-sided dice. Sadly the knowledge of how to paly the game passed with Chatfield's death shortly before the publication of his books. The Wizards Way also contains a minor character based on myself as a child. Chatfield writes: "Sometimes Roan would spend a whole day working at his writing, which, though something of a scrawl, was filled with wonderful children's fantasies of magical creatures and high adventure." Fitting perhaps that I would indeed become a writer and editor, and to many years later edit this very book.

Rowan Sylva

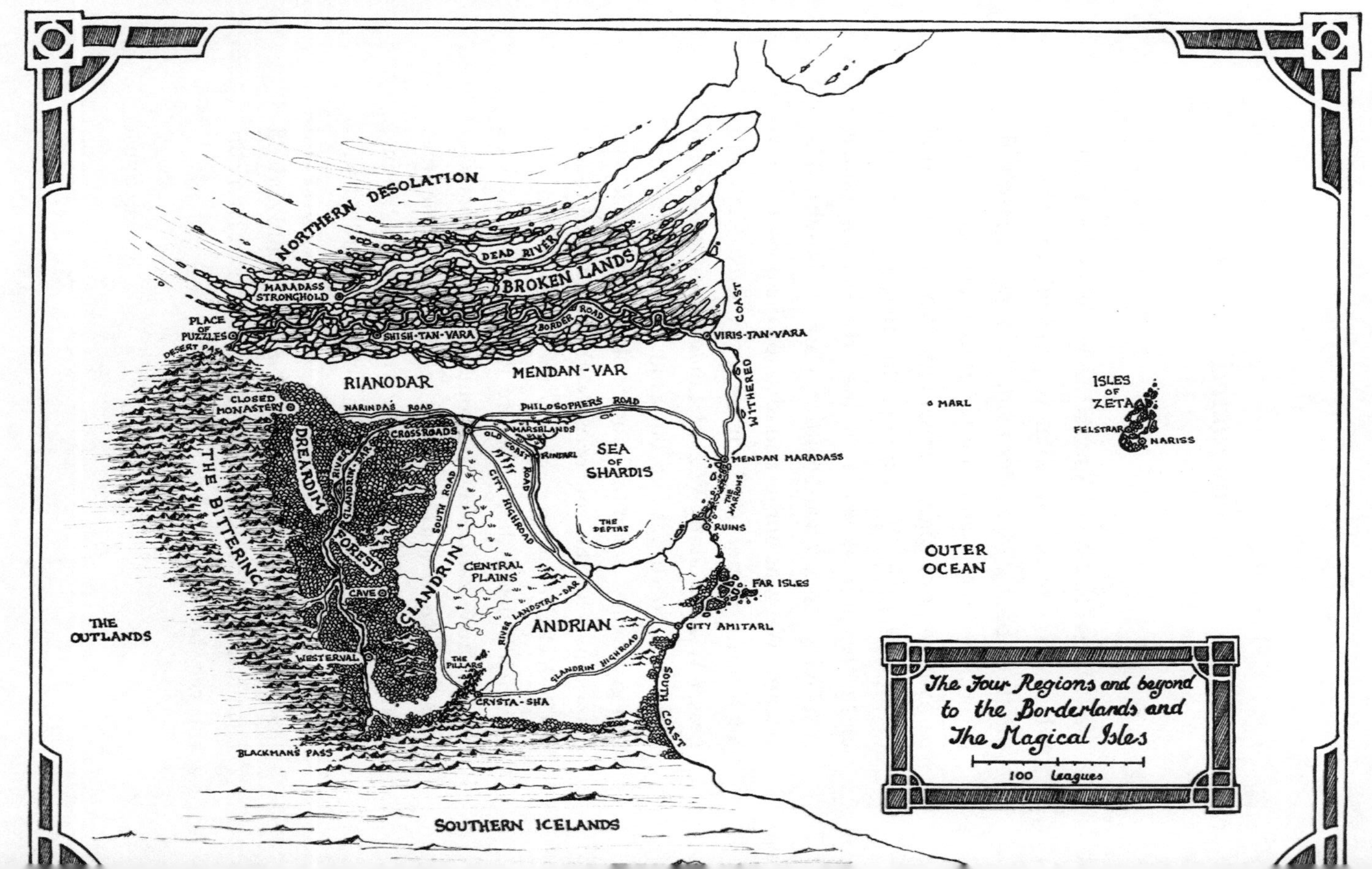

NORTHERN DESOLATION
DEAD RIVER
BROKEN LANDS
MARADASS STRONGHOLD
PLACE OF PUZZLES
DESERT PASS
SHISH-TAN-VARA
BORDER ROAD
VIRIS-TAN-VARA
COAST
WITHERED
MENDAN-VAR
RIANODAR
ISLES OF ZETA
MARL
FELSTRAR
NARISS
CLOSED MONASTERY
NARINDA'S ROAD
PHILOSOPHER'S ROAD
CROSSROADS
MARSHLANDS
OLD COAST ROAD
RINDARL
SEA OF SHARDIS
MENDAN MARADASS
DREARDIM FOREST
RIVER GLANDRIN-VAR
SOUTH ROAD
CITY HIGHROAD
THE DEPTHS
THE MARROWS
RUINS
THE BITTERING
CENTRAL PLAINS
FAR ISLES
OUTER OCEAN
CAVE
GLANDRIN
RIVER LANDSTRA-DAR
ANDRIAN
THE OUTLANDS
WESTERVAL
THE PILLARS
CITY AMITARL
GLANDRIN HIGHROAD
SOUTH COAST
CRYSTA-SHA
BLACKMAN'S PASS
SOUTHERN ICELANDS
The Four Regions and beyond to the Borderlands and The Magical Isles
100 leagues

Contents

Author's Note

Though the lands are not as we know them I have used our own planet's night sky including Earth's moon and stars in this novel. The Six Sorcerers is the Constellation of Crux otherwise known as the Southern Cross, with the addition of the nearby stars Alpha and Beta Centauri, sometimes known as The Pointers.

Manzanee's Cave

Kerran walked in dreams of shadows and darkness. Thin blue fiery tendrils reached through the blackness, licking, burning. He cried out within the dream and flung out his arm to protect himself. His hand struck hard stone and the physical pain drew him slowly from the darkness. Kerran held his grazed knuckles to his mouth, sucking the pain from them. He felt bruised and battered and his head ached; the darkness remained complete and unknown. He reached out and touched rough stone beside him, easing himself to a sitting position. He could not for a time remember where he was or what had happened. He began to recall the sounds of battle, and then the words of the Black One began to return to his waking mind.

Tolth had been driven back to the cave mouth, unable to combat the might of Zard. Kerran remembered that he had held his own fragment of the Seacrest, imploring it to give him strength, to wield its power, but there had been nothing. He recalled now where he was, reaching out in the total darkness his hand came upon something that he did not expect. He had held it so many times that the tattered ancient book of wizards was like an old friend. He did not remember picking it up as he had dashed to the rear of the cave, and with difficulty climbed into the narrow cleft that served as a chimney for the cave. He had found the way too narrow to reach the light above, but a shelf of rock had offered itself as a place to hide. Kerran looked up, remembering the narrow shaft where daylight had earlier been, a single bright star shone now in the darkness above him. Kerran suddenly knew that something terrible had happened. He remembered the sound of Tolth's voice as the old Amitarl had been forced backwards into the cave itself. Zard had followed him, the very air alive and hot as the fire of their struggle exploded into the enclosed space.

There had been a final blast of white-green light, and Kerran remembered being lifted violently by the force of it and thrown against the rock wall behind him, then his memory was shattered. All had gone dark until the evil fire of Maradass had begun to enter his waking mind. It was night now, the air chill and dark, and Kerran made his way slowly to the rock floor below where a faint light showed the cave's mouth against the greater blackness within. When he emerged into the starlight the valley was dark and the army of Zeta had gone. He missed the small twinkling fires and the hum of the quiet army. Kerran felt terribly afraid. The worst that he could imagine was perhaps less to be dreaded than the truth. He returned to the cave after drinking from the stream, and unable to find a blanket he pulled his jacket about him and huddled in a narrow corner to await the dawn.

A fog lay upon the valley when Kerran emerged the next morning. There had been little left in the cave. His travelling pack and blanket were gone, along with everything else. Kerran, though colder, took warmth from this. The army of Zeta had left in an orderly way, collecting all belongings. Tolth he knew could not be with them, for the old Amitarl had once spoken of the narrow chimney as a place of hiding and possible escape. If Tolth was alive and with the army then Kerran would have been found and would be with them also.

Though the valley floor showed little sign of the departed army apart from the sad burial mounds, Kerran could see that they had surely marched to the north. If he moved quickly he felt that he may eventually rejoin them. He looked to the sky, hoping to see the spread of white wings, but there was no sign of Storm. The blue of a clear day had begun to break through the fog, and many small birds began to explore the valley floor, hoping for a few crumbs left behind by the soldiers. Kerran was hungry too and thanked the presence of his sling, which was in the pouch at his waist along with his flint, and the smaller pouch which contained the silver sculpture of Rishtan-Sta. His knife hung at his belt and the ancient manuscript he tied carefully into a torn green shirt, one of the few things which had been missed in the army's departure. Kerran touched the Seacrest fragment beneath his tunic, almost to reassure himself that all was not yet lost. He climbed the hill behind the cave and began to walk at a fast pace to the north and a little east. The fringes of the forest where it met the plains would be easier to travel through than the rocky outcrops and valleys deeper within Dreardim. He had thought of returning to Westerval, but knew that he and the Seacrest must go to the north and seek out the army of Zeta.

Kerran soon found that he could not match the speed of the green and brown army. Days passed in his struggle, with hunger as a constant companion. He ate berries and fungi that he knew to be edible. He did not waste time stalking rabbits, but eventually two had fallen to his sling and stones. He had just begun a new day's march when to his great delight Storm flew down from above and glided over the tree tops. Kerran realised how alone he had been when he felt tears of gratitude come to his eyes, and a burst of joy race through him. It was late afternoon when the white hawk suddenly flew beneath the upper limbs of the overhanging canopy and landed directly in Kerran's path. Storm took to the air briefly, flying deeper into the forest, and then returned again to land before Kerran. The white hawk spread its wings and gave a harsh cry. Kerran stood looking at Storm and knew that the bird wished him to follow. Again the hawk took to the air, diving through the trees into the dark heart of the forest. Since Kerran had first left his home on the journey to Zeta, he had begun to realise the gift that Storm had become. He did not know what to expect but without fear he turned from his path and followed his companion deeper into the forest. The day ended and Storm came to rest nearby as Kerran ate a little, and drank from a small stream.

Sleep came slowly, the bright light of the moon playing tricks with the shadowed trees, as a gentle wind blew through their leaves. Eventually he slept and weariness softened his thoughts into dreams, from the darkness came the red glow of fire but Kerran knew where he was and felt no fear. The face of Manzanee leapt from the darkness as the flames grew suddenly brighter, the cave walls dazzling and clear.

"Welcome Chel-a-Sta," came the gleeful greeting. "You are lost in the wilderness and know not what you seek. Come dance in the moonlight and regain your knowledge." Manzanee suddenly leapt to his feet and swirled into a wild abandoned dance. "Come! Dance!"

Kerran felt himself rise and begin to move to a quick rhythm that leapt from the earth in an increasing pounding beat. He saw phantoms of others who moved around the fire, and then he lost himself in the heat and movement of the dance. After a time the cave slowly faded and Kerran watched Manzanee's maniacal smile disappear as the darkness became complete, the silence throbbing in his ears. Kerran woke with a start. The moon shone down upon his face. It was one day from full. He returned to his dreams and slept until first light.

Storm led Kerran further into the forest. The way became difficult at times, the land sloping upward towards tall broken escarpments. He discovered a way to the cliffs above and eventually found himself on a high narrow plateau which led him to the north. Finally he came to the far side of the plateau where the view was of further bush clad slopes and tall escarpments, a wide valley stretching below, spreading far to the western hills.

Storm suddenly flew close above him, the beating of his wings causing Kerran to bend quickly. He watched the white hawk as it flew high into the air to become a disappearing speck to the north. Kerran wondered what this could mean and where Storm was leading him. He paused, looking afar, hoping to see the bird returning, but there was no further sign of him. Kerran felt suddenly lost and alone. His eyes looked to the path ahead and it was then that he saw the small waterfall. Amazement suddenly rushed through him as he began moving quickly along the escarpment, leaping through the scattered trees where the forest held back from the cliff's edge. He reached the tall familiar rock, where he knew he would find the beginnings of the pathway down the rock face, and then for a moment he thought he must be mistaken. A large tree grew upon the top of the cliff, hugging the edge where the path should begin, its roots clinging to the very brink of the rock face. Kerran held to the trunk and leaned far out, though the tree had not been there in his dreams, still he could see the overgrown way down the side of the glistening waterfall. With the help of a tree root he was able to reach the narrow ledge and began to make his way down the steep path. Water from the falls spraying him, refreshing him, causing him to laugh aloud.

Kerran entered Manzanee's overhanging cave and knew instantly that much time had passed between the period of his dreams and the present. The cave floor was deep in dust and dry leaves, small birds chirping angrily flew from their nests that were lodged in the cracks of the overhanging roof. Water had seeped in at one side of the cave and small ferns and mosses grew there. Kerran moved forward into the strange eeriness which surrounded the cave. He scratched for some time at the earth where he knew the fire had been. Far below the layers of dust and leaves he came upon the black evidence of an ancient fire. Nothing else in the cave showed any sign of the Black Wizard, though Kerran knew that he had been led here. He decided that he would remain the night and see what the full moon might bring.

Kerran collected a small store of firewood, and after cleansing himself in the chilling waters of the falls, he made a fire where Manzanee had set his own, and for the rest of the day he studied the old book, though he learned nothing more of its secrets. There were so many pages missing, and countless unknown words amongst the text that Kerran eventually laid it aside in frustration. He waited for he knew not what and the night came slowly, the moon would not show above the escarpment until well after sunset.

Kerran fed his small cheerful fire without fear. He was some distance within the forest now and no spies of Maradass had need to come this far into the ancient wood. To the west lay the impenetrable darkness of Dreardim, only the denizens of the forest might see the winking of firelight high above on the escarpment face. Kerran sat beside the warming flames and ate sparingly of his last small rabbit and handful of nuts. Though he waited into the night, expectantly, nothing happened until the moon peered down upon him from above the cliffs. He felt a sudden presence about him. The fire swirled a little in a breeze that was not there, sparks spiralling upwards to the ceiling. Kerran stood. There was movement in the cave as if unseen figures danced around the fire. There was the soft sound of feet beating a rhythm in the dust, and then without thought Kerran joined the dance.

It was as it had been in his dream the night before, yet he knew that he was fully awake now and danced with ghosts of an ancient spirit world. The night grew older and he danced until he could no longer stand. His clothes wet and hot from the heat of the dance. The moon had passed far to the west when Kerran moved from the now silent, empty cave and stood beneath the cold invigorating fall of sparkling water. His mind was clear and wondrous. The moon and the forest below shimmered with the clarity of his vision, and the sounds of night birds came drifting to him from the valley far below.

The moon had set and to the west and south the constellation of the Six Sorcerers twinkled near the horizon. He smiled at the thought of the many different stories he had heard of those stars, the beautiful constellation had always captured the hearts of storytellers. Its four stars in the form of a cross and the two that travelled with them, pointing to their companions, following them around the sky. Kerran had known it all of his life, within it was the means of finding directions in the night. His father had shown him how. Kerran returned to the fire, drying his clothes before the flames. His mind continued to remain clear, without thought for explanation. As he fed the fire and stood before its benevolent heat he found that the exhaustion of the dance had now gone and it was much later that he slept. It was then that Manzanee once again entered his dreams.

"Welcome young Chel-a-Sta," the words came from beyond the fire. The Black Wizard's face smiled, teeth flashing in the firelight. "It has been a very long age since we truly met," he said. "Now is the time for all knowledge to gather and form. The game has begun in earnest and you must learn the nature of it before all is lost to you."

Kerran could speak no words, and he sat silently as Manzanee continued.

"The game known as the Wizards Way was devised by Rishtan-Sta the White," he said. "Though he learned to hate his seemingly harmless invention." There was a pause, and the Black Wizard's eyes grew wide as though an old memory of fear passed through his mind. "I did not play the game," continued Manzanee, his voice most serious and yet drifting, as though lost in another time. "I did not play but I remained one who observed," He paused, gazing into the fire for a time. "The stars shine bright tonight, do they not?" smiled the Black Wizard. "What do they show you I wonder?"

Manzanee chuckled now and looked up as though he could see the sky through the rock ceiling above them. "The game has been found again and you must learn its nature," Manzanee repeated. "Only then can you hope to win. Few possess the knowledge to enter the game. You are not one of them yet, but the means is within your possession. Learn the nature of the game. Explore the Wizards Way. It may be your only way of helping the land and its peoples." There was a pause, the Black Wizard smiling with closed eyes. "I have said more than I should," continued Manzanee seriously. "Much rests in your hands now young Chel-a-sta, if only you can discover the key to the Way."

With a strange penetrating stare the Black Wizard looked one last time into Kerran's face, then suddenly the fire burned low. The embers glowed for a moment then fell to ashes.

Kerran woke to the sound of the small birds, which scolded him for sleeping in their home before they flew to the sunlight beyond the overhanging rock above. Kerran ate the last of his food and plunged again beneath the icy waters falling from above. *The nature of the game*, the words rang in his memory.

"What is this game?" he said to himself.

His mind, though clear and light, now became perplexed by this question and he returned to the cave in puzzlement. Kerran looked to where he had placed the old book the night before and was surprised to find that it was gone. Startled, he quickly searched around the cave until in the dim light he could see it lying open on a shadowed boulder. The large stone sat on a flat shelf of rock to the side of the cave's entrance. He remembered well that he had bound the book inside the green shirt the night before. As he retrieved it from the dust and leaf covered ledge. He found it lay open at a page he knew well.

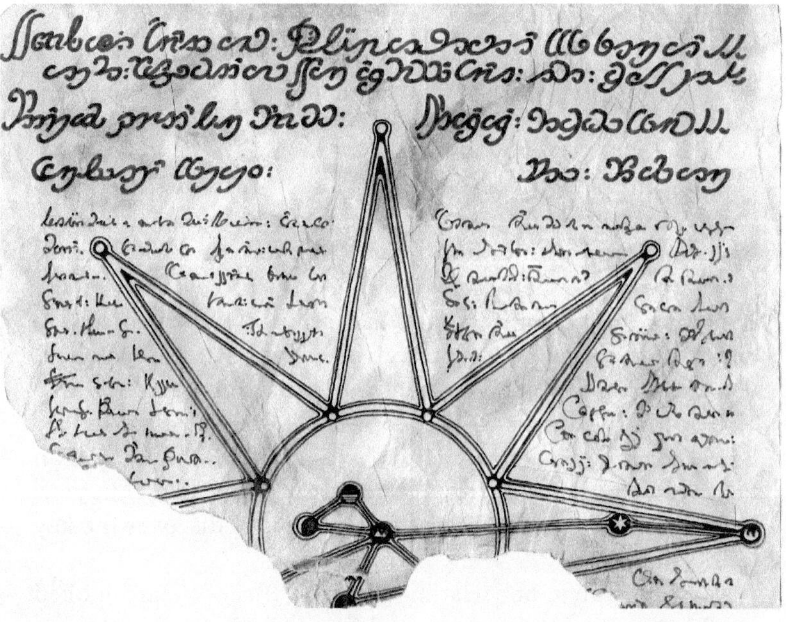

Segment of a page from the ancient Book of Wizards

Kerran picked the book up gently, and returning to the fireside, he began to study once again the torn and smudged leaf before him. Drawn there was the partly disintegrating pattern of the eight pointed star. Within the larger circle, faded and aged with time there were three tiny circles, each with a small symbol at their heart. There were two other circles of similar size that had been drawn further out on the right arm of the star, one at its very point. Various lines had been drawn between some of the symbols.

There was something within the pattern of circles which had always seemed familiar to Kerran, but he could not say why. Taking a charred stick from the fire, he took the book to the flat ledge beyond the cave's entrance. The sun shone warm and inviting, and on a clear area of rock he drew a much larger copy of the diagram, as closely as he could to the original scale. Then he stood back and studied the star and the six points within its boundaries. Still nothing emerged to tell him of their meaning. There was a network of interconnecting lines that had no symmetry to them, three of these lines disappeared into the lost section of the page.

He was in the process of drawing these in when he gave a startled cry and leapt to his feet, looking intently at the diagram. He walked around it for a different perspective then returned to his original drawing position. He knew the pattern but it was as though he saw it in a mirror. Before him on the stone lay the reversed image of the Six Sorcerers. He could not be mistaken. Within the boundaries of the eight pointed star lay the constellation of true stars which had hung in the night sky all his life, and which he had so often gazed upon in wonder. 'The nature of the game' the words seemed to whisper to him from the darkness of the cave.

He bent down to complete the drawing of the lines when suddenly he was no longer sure if he was correct. Most of the lines connected with others of the small circles, including the one that was just visible at the bottom of the burnt page, with many converging on the symbol at the very centre of the star, but there were three exceptions. One line left the central point, and though the bottom part of the page was missing Kerran had no doubt that, with the accuracy of his drawing, the line would meet with one of the valley points of the star to the left side of the page. Though he had no explanation for this line. It did not confuse his idea that he was looking at the reversed image of the Six Sorcerers. The problem was that there were another two lines that conflicted with his idea. One of these lines left the central point, while the other left the bottom most circle. Both lines converged on a missing segment of the page and must surely mean that another small circle had once been drawn at their meeting point.

Kerran sat back on his heels, puzzled. He pictured the night sky in his mind and again saw the bright constellation of stars. With the vision of an artist he could see that, though in reverse, the scale was perfect. He could not be wrong he thought, though doubt still nagged at him. He drew the lines in tentatively but did not represent their meeting point with a circle as he had the others. He changed his thoughts for a time, considering the outer points of the star. These were shown as still smaller circles. He counted them and found that without the outer point to the far right which was covered by a symbol, and without the inner point where the line from the centre must reach a valley point on the boundary of the large circle, there were in total fourteen smaller circles.

'The fourteen Lesser Wizards' he thought and something told him that he was correct in this. The answer somehow seemed obvious to him and with a relieved sigh he returned to the puzzle of the two converging lines within the large circle.

Kerran remembered back to when he and Tolth had decided to interpret some of the book's words as 'Wizard Seats' and 'Wizard Lines,' then another connection was made, though how he truly knew this he did not understand. The six points, and perhaps the seventh that was missing, he called 'High Wizard Seats.' The fourteen he called 'Lesser Wizard Seats,' while 'Wizard Lines' were all of the connecting lines of the eight pointed star. Something of the nature of the game was beginning to emerge and he grew excited, though the puzzle of the two converging lines still bothered him. Could there have once been seven stars in the constellation? If so, then the ancient tales must be wrong, for it was always told that only six High Wizards came to the land. Was there another wizard who was unknown? Kerran paused a moment in his thoughts. Was Manzanee the answer? Perhaps he was to be counted as the seventh High Wizard, though he had said that he only observed and had not participated in the game.

Kerran began to remember the names of the six. The small, finely drawn symbols may give a clue as to the accuracy of what at times to him seemed pure assumption. There was Orlandi, one of the female wizards, who had been married to Lardan-Mor and whose name meant Moon in the old language. Kerran had already seen that the symbol to the left of the pattern surely depicted a small moon, three quarters in shadow. That had been easy. He had never before taken a lot of notice of these symbols as Tolth had been interested most in deciphering the text of the book. The symbols were pale and faded with time. The one to the extreme right, on the outer point of the star seemed to be white trees, or perhaps a flower. He looked more closely and then he knew what he was seeing. On a dark field was depicted a small fire, a number of flames licking at the darkness.

"Cranda-Sta!" exclaimed Kerran, startling a large dark lizard which had come to the ledge to bask in the sunshine. Kerran thought for a moment of his hunger but he let the creature go, so excited was he by the beginnings of his understanding of what Manzanee had called the Wizards Way.

"Cranda-Sta, Dark Fire Star," said Kerran, nodding to himself; the Red Wizard, and the one who was said to have begun the final downfall of his gifted brethren.

Kerran looked now at the top star of the six, within the small circle he could see that the upper half was black, while the bottom half was less dark, cut across by three thin horizontal lines. He could not decide which wizard this may represent. The other star which lay on the arm nearest Cranda-Sta at first appeared to be just a small circle on a dark field. Kerran had never studied it so closely before but when he held it very near to his eyes he could see that it was a small six pointed star.

"Drinda-mira-Sta," he said to himself.

The Evening Star; and he knew that another piece of the Wizards Way had fallen into place. She had been the sister of Orlandi, and wife to Cranda-Sta. Kerran did not yet turn to thoughts of what it could all mean, he was happy for now to be discovering something that must be of use, it had to be. The bottom most High Wizard Seat was only just visible on the edge where the page had been torn and lost. A smear of ancient dirt or soot had all but obscured it and if there was a symbol drawn within its dark circle, Kerran could not see it.

He leaned back and stretched his shoulders, then suddenly leapt to his feet. He could not be mistaken. A strange whispering voice had reached him from within the cave. A startled bird flew out and Kerran slowly walked beneath the rock shelf, an excited fear entwining him within its spell. Nothing stirred. Nothing had changed, and whatever voice had called him, there was now no sign of its owner. Kerran was about to leave when he saw a small black beetle scurrying across the floor. One of the birds in the cave flew towards it, a tasty morsel for its young. Kerran suddenly waved the bird away and went to look at the creature, which was having trouble surmounting a pile of dust and leaves. He had never seen one of its kind before and wondered at its dark shell, which though black, seemed to reflect a multitude of colours as he took it into the sunlight.

With a sudden buzz of wings that Kerran had not suspected, the dark creature flew from his hand, and as he followed it with his eyes he saw it land amongst the ferns and moss covered rocks at the foot of the waterfall. He thought then of Manzanee, and of the dream where he had seen the Black Wizard and Rishtan-Sta complete the forging of the Seacrest. A small black bug had appeared in that dream vision and he looked again towards the falls and wondered.

Returning to his drawing Kerran inspected the dark circle again at the bottom of the pattern. The image of the bug came before his eyes and he heard the voice of Manzanee come from his dreams. *I did not play the game but I remained as one who observed,* the wizard had said. *The Seventh Wizard?* Kerran questioned himself, but he could not say for sure.

The wizards had each taken a part of their identity from a

star in the constellation to play the game, of this Kerran was now sure. The converging lines indicated the point where a seventh star should lie, so where in all the darkness of the night sky was that seventh star? Kerran wondered if a star could die.

With the point of the blackened stick, he now drew a circle where the two Wizard Lines must meet. Kerran scratched at his thin beard and sat for a time perplexed, caught in a tangle that he knew he must unravel. His mind drifted to other thoughts, and he began to wonder about the real nature of the game. Manzanee had said that the game had been found again, and then suddenly Kerran knew what the Black Wizard had meant. The attack at the refuge he had only heard from within the cave. It must have been a large force which had invaded the valley that day, and yet the Elbrand had not seen the enemy until they had been almost upon the refuge. Some must surely have died in the conflict but where had been their dead? There was a great magic in such a thing and Kerran knew that the first play of the game had been at the hand of Maradass. Kerran wondered how soon the Evil One might strike again, while he sat scratching at the surface of the unknown Wizards Way.

He thought then of the name Rishtan-Sta, White Winged Star. None of the remaining symbols looked to show such a sign. He decided that the top point of the cross could be Lardan-Mor, Ocean's Dark Light. The three horizontal lines could well represent the moon's light upon the sea. He looked closely at the central symbol within the circle, the page was much faded and creased and at this point the paper felt ready to crumble. Two small triangles, one overlapping the other, showed against a dark background. The simplicity of it suddenly made Kerran laugh out loud. The High Seat of Ma-dran-Thara, the Brown Wizard, and Mountains of Night in the modern tongue, stood at the very centre of the eight pointed star. Kerran looked over the drawing again and knew that he must be correct, and so the point where the two mysterious lines converged could belong to no other than Rishtan-Sta, the White Wizard. Kerran leaned back and pondered what it could mean.

Hunger would not allow him to continue and he made for the pathway so as to hunt. He would gather food until the late afternoon and then return to continue unravelling the mystery. He had not reached the beginning of the climb when Storm dropped from the sky above. Held in the bird's talons was the body of a small rabbit. The hawk let fall his catch and then flew upward to be lost against the clouds.

Kerran was astonished and much pleased. He skinned and cleaned the rabbit quickly and soon the fire had been rekindled to slowly roast the small carcass. He thanked Storm with his thoughts and again wondered at the hawk's mysterious ways. Returning to his drawing Kerran felt a sudden knowledge that the markings on the stone were correct but not yet complete. Something underlay the pattern that he could not see.

Going back to the fire Kerran could wait no longer and began to gnaw at a partly cooked hind leg and returned to the sunlight. The day had almost passed and the last rays of light playing on the forest below shone briefly between low clouds towards the western horizon. He determined to continue his search for answers into the night and quickly drew the diagram onto the green shirt, and then returned with it to the fire, which he built higher once the rabbit had cooked well enough.

Fascinated, he returned then to the eight pointed star, all sense of danger and time were lost to him and he knew he would remain at Manzanee's cave until the answers came. He had been led here, and would not leave until he understood why. It was far into the night when Kerran found he could think and focus no longer. Sleep called him and he obeyed reluctantly. For a short time his gaze fell upon the fire. It was restful to watch the small flames slowly die into glowing embers. Kerran's eyes closed and he slept peacefully until dawn.

A grey light filtered into Kerran's waking mind. A dense mist hung like a shroud at the wide entrance to the overhanging cave and Kerran shivered as he woke. He was stiff from the cold. The fire lay in ashes beside him and he stood up and moved about quickly to warm himself. The fire came to life with some dry brush and soon he was warm. With a piece of rabbit in hand, he looked again at the diagram on the spread cloth of the green shirt. As the morning crept towards noon the thick blanket of mist turned to a wet haze, trees dripping with moisture. Kerran stretched. He felt stiff and in need of exercise. The symbols on the shirt retained their mystery and a walk would clear his mind for the concentration that he needed to continue his search.

He reached the narrow overgrown path, his thoughts on the possibility of food, and was about to begin the climb when he felt the presence of great danger above. He leapt back quickly and looked up the narrow slope, coiled on a boulder, no more than two or three strides up the path, lay a large black snake; its yellow underside told Kerran of its fearful and deadly nature. The snake lifted a wedged head from amongst its coils, the small forked tongue licking at the air. Kerran retreated further and returned to the fire. The presence of the snake he took as an omen, and he returned to the diagram with no more thought for hunting, or stretching his legs.

The sun grew brighter and Kerran found it now more pleasant to sit outside rather than by the warmth of the fire. His drawing of the day before had all but washed away and he spread the shirt on the flat stone and sat on a round boulder gazing at it intently. For a long time he remained motionless, trying to will the meaning from the dark lines and circles before him, but the answer did not come. In frustration he moved about the rock ledge, he picked up a stone and hurled if far out into the valley below and watched it fall until, without a sound, it disappeared amongst the trees.

Kerran stood silently, looking below at the forest. The sun became obscured by cloud. It would rain that night, Kerran thought, as he began to turn back to his task. Rays of sunlight flooded through a gap in the cloud and caught his attention, on the roof of the forest below a pattern of sunlight played. Something about the spread of light seemed familiar. For a moment he thought that the pattern was there to tell him something, but then it was gone. Dark ominous clouds brooded to the south where flickers of lightning struck upon distant hills within the forest. He looked up the path but the snake had gone, and then decided that the remaining rabbit meat would suffice until the morning. He returned to the cave as the first heavy drops of rain began to fall and the storm broke with great violence upon the forest below the cave. Kerran stood and watched it arrive. Lightning shattered downward, bringing the rolling drum of thunder pulsing through the air.

Kerran realised the strangeness of the cave all in one moment, though the wide entrance faced west and south, little or no wind reached beneath the overhang. A great storm now lashed and blew at the trees of the forest, but hardly a breath reached Kerran as he stood beneath the shelter of rock. Stepping a pace beyond the entrance he was suddenly buffeted by the gale and quickly returned to the shelter of the overhang. Leaves blown on the wind would enter then fall softly to the floor, Manzanee had not used the cave for an age yet his power still protected the comfort of his ancient shelter.

Kerran built up the fire and without thinking of the Wizards Way for a time, he sat staring into the flames. A feeling of quietness and peace came over him slowly as the fire seemed to draw his thoughts from his mind and cleanse them in its flames. It burned down to embers and still Kerran sat, his eyes closed now, a warm tranquillity surrounding him, until a small shiver of cold ran through his body. He slowly opened his eyes to find that the fire had burned low. Though the storm had not entered the cave the chill of the night remained in the air.

He reached over to place more wood on the soft glowing coals that remained, and then he paused and stared into the embers. From the centre of the fire there was a glow much brighter than the sparks and ashes around it. Only for a few moments did it hold its shape, and then it fell apart into small fiery pieces. The brightness of the glow was what had caught Kerran's eye, but it was the shape of it that had retained his gaze. For a second time the familiar yet unknown sign which he had seen spread in sunlight upon the roof of the forest had come to him again. Throwing more wood on the fire Kerran drew the shape as best he could on a corner of the shirt. He leaned back and looked at it but still it remained a fleeting mystery, hidden somewhere deep inside his sleeping memory. The peacefulness he had felt was now slowly evaporating and he began to feel discouraged. The same questions rolled through his mind again but no answers came. Tired now, he lay down to sleep, the storm continued to sweep across the forest and Kerran's last thoughts before he slipped into dreams were of Piata and the Isles of Zeta.

Kerran woke and yet knew that his waking was not complete. He could see and hear, yet his body remained asleep by the fire. He floated from the cave within his shadow and into the dark and stormy night. Quickly, faster than at any time before, he raced across the lands to the north and east, the forest falling away as he sped above the plains. There was no sense of wind, only the rapidly increasing speed as the land and sky turned to a blur and rushed by. Far to the east the first glimmerings of day began to lighten the grey distance. He flew on until he could see the two converging roads of the Southlands. The Crossroads suddenly fell away below him as his shadow was suddenly lifted high above the lands.

To the north lay the vast open plains and the Broken Lands. To the east he looked upon the Sea of Shardis, its sweeping curve running to the south and far to the east. To the west and to the distant south the forest cut a dark line against the Central Plains. Upward he sped, the pattern of the land below becaming more distinct as its details blurred into insignificance. Cloud covered much of the lands below, and the mighty Outer Ocean spread to the distant curve of the horizon. His vision now encompassed all of the Regions. Into his memory came the clear picture of the map of the lands that he had often studied. There was a pattern here, familiar yet strange, but as it began to form in his mind a sudden darkness fell. A black looming presence engulfed him and he was bound as though in stone, struggling against the darkness Kerran saw the first wispy tendrils of blue fire reaching out towards him.

"Enter my domain at your peril!" said the evil voice from the fire. "No longer can you play the wizard and escape my powers."

Slowly, in the heart of the flame, the face of Maradass emerged, his fiendish eyes delving deeply into Kerran's shadow. The flame grew stronger, thin whispering arms of fire flicking at Kerran's mind. Maradass now stood amongst the fire, his crouched malevolent presence leering at Kerran from the flames. "Fool!" he cried. "Do you not see?" Maradass held out before him two fragments of the Seacrest, the last time that Kerran had seen the second piece Tolth had been in possession of it. "Mine!" the Evil One gloated as a painful blinding fire engulfed Kerran's being.

He cried out but there was no sound.

The flames withdrew and again Maradass hung before him, his evil smiling face now questioning. "Come to me before I come for you," Maradass said quietly, coaxing. "Bind your part of Ma-Zurin-Bidar to me now and together we will live long in glorious power. Deny me, and nothing will remain to tell of your memory!" The flames burst upon him again.

"Come to me," said Maradass through the fire. "Come."

The image flickered suddenly and the blue cold lost much of its power, a sound beyond it came harsh and insistent into Kerran's mind. The flames retreated as though a spell had been broken. Darkness returned, and then again the call entered his dreams. Kerran opened his eyes, the pain a receding memory. Storm cried out one more time to ensure that he was awake, and then flew from the cave, leaving behind the limp furry body of another dead rabbit.

The Wizards Way

Kerran rose slowly, remembering his dream. He now feared for Tolth. The evil face of Maradass swept into his waking thoughts for a moment then fled. There was nothing that Kerran could do for Tolth even if the old Amitarl was still alive. The sun had reached its zenith and he stood under the cold falling water as if bathing the memory of Maradass from his body. Then he pictured again the lands of the Four Regions as they had lain far below him, and a wider awakening shone suddenly like a bright star in his mind. In great excitement Kerran entered the cave and scooped up a burnt stick and the green shirt from beside the fire, and then returned quickly into the sunlight.

He began by drawing on the rock surface the outlines of the lands, with a keen eye for detail. The map finally lay before him, and here again he saw the shape that had been so familiar to him the day before, the pattern of the sunshine on the forest and later in the embers of his fire. A feeling of wonder gathered inside him. Spreading the shirt beside the map he stood back, looking from one to the other. He began to draw in the places that he knew, Amitarl City and Mendan Maradass, Crysta-Sha and Viris-Tan-Vara. He included the Crossroads, and to the north and west he drew in Narinda's Sanctuary, the

Closed Monastery. He looked for a pattern amongst the small circles he had drawn but nothing showed any similarity to the pattern of stars which he was sure now must overlay the map.

"They would be ancient places, perhaps long turned to dust," he said aloud to no one but himself.

He had learned much of the land's history from Tolth and the Library on Zeta and he now rubbed out any signs he had made for places he knew had been built after the breaking of the Seacrest. Crysta-Sha and the City Amitarl he knew to have been built in the Philosopher's time, the city of Mendan Maradass had risen where a fishing village was said to have been, and so it too was taken from the map. The history of the Crossroads was ancient, as was that of the Closed Monastery, Kerran's thoughts returned to Redrah, the jovial man had told him of Rianodar and its ancient magic.

"Tis an old place," Redrah had said. "Three tall rocks stand far above the forest. They are said to be hollow but I do not know. Wizardry formed them tis said, but none who go there ever return."

Viris-Tan-Vara was ancient he had read, and then he paused in thought; Shish-Tan-Vara must also be included, although it was not in the Regions it had been a sister city to Viris-Tan-Vara on the coast and so must be an ancient place. As he drew in this small circle he saw a pattern beginning to emerge, in excitement he leapt to his feet to stand above the black markings on the rock. He put a second circle around Shish-Tan-Vara, and then he circled the Closed Monastery and the Crossroads, the three signs called to him but the answer remained elusive.

He spent time preparing the rabbit and suddenly longed for simple bread and cheese. Returning to the drawing he drew a tentative circle south and west of the Crossroads. If the pattern were true a Wizard's Seat must have been somewhere near or within the edge of the forest; and then Kerran laughed aloud and did a skipping dance almost as Manzanee was want to do. The answer was so very simple, for he now stood at the High Wizard Seat of Manzanee, the Black Wizard, within the boundaries of Dreardim Forest. Kerran drew in the double circle and smiled.

Now the four points which formed the cross of the constellation were in place. Far to the east he measured the distance with his eye and felt a shudder pass through him, the High Seat of Cranda-Sta, the most feared of the ancient wizards must surely be found on Zeta. He remembered Felstrar where he and Piata had climbed to the ancient ruins and knew that he could not be wrong. Now only one point of the constellation was missing, the High Seat of Drinda-mira-Sta appeared to fall upon the open ocean, until he remembered the mysterious island of Marl with its temple and deaf priests. The isle of magic which few could find and none could leave unchanged, before he and Flindas had landed there under the protection of the Seacrest. Again he drew in a confident double circle, though in truth he did not know the exact location of the island.

Now only the High Seat of Rishtan-Sta was missing and all indications convinced Kerran that the two converging lines from the Crossroads and Manzanee's cave must surely come together where that High Wizard's Seat had been. On the map the two lines joined at a point in the south of the Sea of Shardis. There seemed little doubt that if Rishtan-Sta had once built his home on solid earth. The remains of that seat of power now lay at the bottom of the deep circular sea. Tolth had thought that in some long passed time the world had been struck by a mountain falling from the stars, thus creating the circular Sea of Shardis. Kerran now had another thought. Rishtan-Sta had stood on a hilltop near a tall and beautiful city, and there, high above the armies of the warring wizards he had drawn on the powers within the Seacrest and destroyed himself and all those around him. Kerran thought in horror at the power which he now knew had destroyed the wizards, and with awesome violence had carved the Sea of Shardis from the very land. Kerran knew that he could not be wrong, the land was no longer there and the Seat of Rishtan-Sta had vanished. He wondered if at the same time a distant star had burned and died; then without doubt he drew in the last double circle.

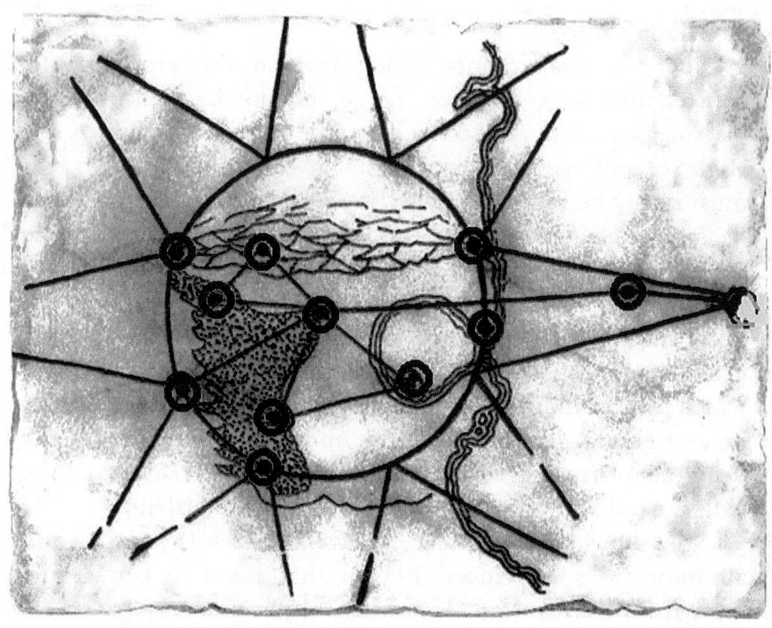

**Kerran's drawing of the eight-pointed star, overlapping the
map of the Regions and beyond**

On the map Kerran then drew in the large circle and arms
of the eight pointed star, many of its points were cast wide,
far beyond the known lands, and far beyond his ability to fit
them onto the shirt. The seats of the Lesser Wizards which
Kerran felt they must be were almost all beyond the Regions.
Only five valleys of the star's arms fell within the known lands.
One was obvious, to the north and east, the ancient city of
Viris-Tan-Vara corresponded exactly with one seat of a Lesser
Wizard, which one, he thought he may never know. A second
Lesser Wizard's Seat lay near the northern point of Eastern
Andrian. Somewhere, on a place above the ocean, Kerran
knew there would be ruins, or traces of some ancient place.
To the north and west, near the Desert Pass he remembered
Tolth telling him of the ruined wizard's castle known as the
Place of Puzzles. He drew a circle around the corresponding
converging lines. The fourth Wizard's Seat he did not know

of at all although he had ridden that way with the army of Zeta. Tolth had said nothing of ruins on the wide plains of the Southlands near the River Lanstra-Dar. He drew no circle here. The last Wizard's Seat he had known as he had drawn it in, but he now returned to it at last.

"The Seat of Chelasta," he said aloud with awe.

There had been times since learning of his heritage that Kerran had not believed that it could be so, to be a descendant of a wizard had been like a tale from some children's story. "Chelasta," he said to himself and stood up facing the sun, looking out far to the south and west to where he knew his home lay.

Of all the families in Westerval he knew that his own had the oldest history. It was said that his ancestors were woodsmen and had cut much of the timber which eventually went into building the town.

How long? thought Kerran. How long had Chelasta been there between forest and river, and how old had been his father? Thousands of years had passed since the age of the wizards. The time spread behind Kerran like a tapestry of intriguing visions and dreams. He turned again to the drawing on the rock, then realised that though he had deciphered much, still the nature of the game still eluded him.

The smell of burning meat suddenly returned him to the present and he rushed into the cave to find that the small rabbit had fallen into the fire. After scraping it clean Kerran returned it to the tripod above the glowing embers and went back to the drawing on the rock shelf, the taste of rabbit lingering on his finger tips.

"The nature of the game," he said aloud, and he spent the day trying to understand its meaning. He used the Seacrest fragment, willing its power to work for him but it was of no use, and he passed the night without learning any more of the game's mysteries.

On waking the next morning Kerran noticed two things. It was raining heavily, and just inside the cave he saw the body of another dead rabbit. Kerran looked from the entrance at the rock surface and saw that his drawing from the day before had been washed away completely during the night. He was not concerned for he knew the diagram well, and as he ate he began to look for somewhere out of the wet to draw the eight pointed star once again. The floor was deep in dust and leaves but the flat shelf of rock near the entrance looked an easy area to clear of debris, and the light was better there. The large boulder on which he had mysteriously found the opened book was near its centre, but there was enough space around it so that he need not bother shifting it. There were a number of smaller rocks scattered on the stone surface and in his cleaning Kerran picked one up and threw it aside. He began to sweep the rock surface again and it was then that he saw a small hollow place carved into the stone surface where the small rock had covered it.

For a moment he stood without breathing. Carved deep into the flat stone surface were two straight unnatural lines which converged upon the hollow. In wonder he looked about the rock face at the scattered stones. Several had fallen, perhaps brushed aside by some forest animal that had ventured into the cave, but enough of them remained in place to show Kerran that he was not mistaken, the larger rounded stone stood near the centre of the rock shelf. Kerran went to it and quickly brushed away the dust from around its base, here he found that two carved lines radiated out from it.

With a gleeful laugh that seemed to echo the Black Wizard's mirth, he continued to clear the area outward from the stone, carved lines and hollows appearing as he worked. He carefully replaced each stone as he went, and those that had been shifted he moved to the nearest point that was missing one. The star as it appeared was oriented to the north as closely as he could tell. When he came to the most eastern point, the one which he now knew represented the Isles of Zeta and the High Seat of Cranda-Sta, the converging lines did not finish in a small hollow. Instead, before they could touch, the two lines reached the wall of the cave as though they would only meet within the rock itself. The ancient magic protection that Zeta still possessed seemed represented here, and Kerran marvelled as the answers to the mystery continued to unfold before him.

Finally the work was done and he gazed upon the eight pointed star carved into the smooth rock surface. It was almost four paces across and had been formed by the most careful of workers in stone or, as Kerran suspected, by the magical arts of the Black Wizard himself. Kerran stood for a long time, turning as he did so and studying the star pattern. He sat down on the large rock at its centre and mused at what he had before him, then he realised that he truly sat on a High Wizard's Seat. Now that he had the board to play on and a High Wizard's Seat to sit on, what was he to do with them he wondered? Somehow Maradass had sent an army to the refuge and Kerran wondered if he could now do the same? The eight pointed star of Manzanee did not have any parts of the land shown, so Kerran collected a burnt stick from the fire and spent some time drawing in the outlines of the lands as accurately as he could. He thought again of the enemy which had attacked the refuge, and wondered at the news of the Stone Army which had disappeared as they marched through Andrian. Kerran had not seen the attackers in the forest, and the strange thing was that though the soldiers of Zeta had buried their own, where had been the dead of the Maradass army? He wondered if Maradass had created them to play the game, or perhaps that only these strange troops could be used by Maradass to appear at will.

Kerran looked again at his map, noting the place that the Stone Army had disappeared was close to the curved grooved circle of the star, and then with a feeling of sudden chill he saw that the refuge must have been very close to the curved line as well. Had Maradass been able to send his invisible Stone Army along the curve of the circle? Somehow they were hidden within the game, and then they had appeared from nowhere to attack the refuge, could Kerran do the same if he was able to unravel the mysteries of the game?

Kerran found few answers that day. He tried sitting and simply wishing to be somewhere else but nothing happened. He held the Seacrest, for he felt that it must be a part of the game, the key in fact, but without success. For a time he returned to the old book to see if he could learn more, but most of the words and symbols remained a mystery to him. Kerran felt his eyelids drooping and he could keep awake no longer. After placing the book beside his bed of leaves he lay down by the fire and quietly slipped into dreams.

Into his sleep came a vision of a place so wondrous and fair, that never in any dream or waking moment had he ever imagined a city so beautiful. The tall spires of white stone seemed to pierce the high cloud above. An inner light glowed from the stone and sunlight reflected from the many towers of glass. Though the city of Crysta-Sha had been wondrous to behold, it was but a shadow of the place that had now entered Kerran's dream world. Thin silver arches spanned great distances across the wonderful city, while water in abundance cascaded from above to feed the wide parklands and streams that flowed between the buildings.

Kerran's shadow began to move closer until he could see the unhurried people who populated the city. There were many amongst the parklands, black skinned and white, either sitting and enjoying the marvellous day or moving amongst the tall spires. They entered and left by high arched doorways that gave access to the inner city and its towers, some moved along the sweeping graceful arches that joined many of the buildings, without needing to descend to the lower levels. The city itself was built upon a range of low hills and overlooked a wide valley of farms and fruit groves. Kerran's shadow moved still closer until he was circling the very central and tallest spire of the city. Then, as if the walls were not there, Kerran passed through the stone and glass and entered a vast chamber where people were gathering. A half circle of seats spread upwards almost to the curved ceiling. A great many people were seated there, as more continued to enter from several doorways below.

Kerran had been watching for some time, and almost all the people were seated, when applause broke out from those gathered there. From above, Kerran watched as a tall man dressed in white entered by a small side door. His hair was long as was his beard, and he strode purposefully towards a low dais where a simple high backed chair stood. Kerran recognised

Rishtan-Sta immediately, and as the people rose to their feet he knew that the applause was for none other than the White Wizard. Rishtan-Sta climbed the dais and before seating himself he gave those gathered a low bow. Though Kerran understood the words that Rishtan-Sta now spoke they were in a language that he had never heard before. The White Wizard told the people of a wonderful thing that he had discovered. It was a means by which he could communicate directly with all other wizards in the lands. Not only was he able to speak with other wizards, he was now able to join the others at their own seats of power. Soon he hoped to make it possible for any number of people to travel this way, visiting far flung relatives and friends at will. The audience applauded the amazing new magic and then Rishtan-Sta stood and applauded them.

"You have made this possible," he called to them. "With your hands and your hearts you have built this fair land where we now prosper. All things come from goodness." Rishtan-Sta held a book aloft. "All things are written here for you to see," he told them. "The magic is not for wizards alone. It is a wizard's duty to serve those whom we can teach and bring to an understanding of life and happiness. We are the bearers of great power, but it is you who must decide its use."

Rishtan-Sta said much more to the people which Kerran would remember always, and then, when the speech had ended, the White Wizard laid the book open on a large table by the dais, then he left the chamber to the applause of all those in the great hall.

The many white robed figures began to leave the chamber, each one pausing by the table and looking in reverence upon the book. Some reached out and touched it as though it were something that was much loved. Kerran felt his shadow taking him downward and as the last person left the hall, he looked upon the open page. There lay the complete diagram of the eight pointed star, the pages new and unblemished. He looked upon the words and symbols and found that he now understood them. He could read it all and nothing was missed or hidden. There was a sound and the small side door of the chamber swung open. Rishtan-Sta appeared and walked towards the table, while Kerran's shadow moved away and hung in the air above the open page. Rishtan-Sta closed the book and put it under his arm, and then, before he left the room, the High Wizard looked up directly at Kerran's shadow. Kerran looked back into the wizard's light green-blue eyes which smiled for a moment, then Rishtan-Sta turned and left the hall as darkness came slowly and Kerran slept peacefully until first light.

As his eyes opened Kerran remembered his dream, he lay still, afraid that if he moved, the meanings of the wizard's language would disintegrate before he could bring them to his waking mind. From the shadows of his dream the words became firm in his memory. Leaping up, with thought for nothing but the phrases and symbols. Kerran took the book into the grey daylight; he was elated when he found that his memory had grasped most of the ancient writings. Some of it seemed written backwards and at times the meaning of a line would not be clear, but Kerran persevered and by noon he had almost deciphered the meaning of this one damaged page. There were just two lines that puzzled him, each word or symbol he had translated, but their meaning escaped him:

TO BEGIN
THE WIZARD'S SIGN
TO THE STONE ONE'S SEAT MUST GO
A WIZARD LINE WILL TAKE THE BEARER ON THE
WORLD

He understood it all except for the Wizard's Sign. There was something which must be placed on the rock at the centre of the eight pointed star. This central rock was the High Seat of Madran-Thara whose symbol and power was with the element of stone. He thought for a moment of the Seacrest fragment but did not expect it to work as the talisman had been formed by Rishtan-Sta after the words had been written. He tried all the same but was only mildly disappointed when nothing happened. He looked at the stone on which he sat. The cave was the Seat of Manzanee and perhaps beneath the stone lay the answer. He tried to slide the boulder but it would not move, working his fingers into the carved grooves which disappeared under the rock Kerran braced his feet and lifted.

Straining with all his might Kerran managed to roll the heavy stone onto its side, and in the rock surface beneath he saw the converging lines come together at a much deeper and wider hollow than the others. The hollow was filled with dust and leaves, and as he bent to look, something dark moved amongst the debris. He started back fearing a snake, but it was no dangerous reptile which emerged to peer at the sudden intrusion of light. The large black beetle waved its front legs rapidly in the air then scuttled back beneath the leaves as Kerran approached. Gently moving the leaves aside he came upon a family of the beetles scurrying about for shelter. Kerran searched carefully for anything which might be a Wizard's Sign but his fingers sifted the dust in vain, as he lowered the rock with a final thump that he could not avoid, he hoped that he had not disturbed the family of beetles too much.

He returned to the book. Perhaps the sentence could have other meanings, but he found none. The words and symbols were clear to him but their use was not, he sat for a time in silence, his eyes closed, trying to empty and clear his mind. His thoughts wandered and strayed, taking him away from the quietness which he tried to create. The answer came when his mind had drifted to his mother and he saw her passing a small leather bag to him as he sat beside the fire of their home.

Kerran's eyes opened with understanding and his hand reached quickly into his pouch, drawing forth the small bag which contained the silver sculpture of Rishtan-Sta. It had lain almost forgotten for many days now, no more than a wonderful trinket and a relic of times far in the past. Kerran stood up from the Wizard's Seat taking the small silver piece to the stone which represented Madran-Thara at the Crossroads of the lands. He lifted the stone which seemed much lighter this time and placed the sculpture beneath it. Slowly, and with much trepidation he returned and sat on the seat of the Black Wizard. He still did not know how Maradass had sent his troops to the refuge, but he knew now the way in which the wizards had communicated. Making himself comfortable on the stone, and facing towards the Crossroads, Kerran slowly closed his eyes and said an ancient, almost forgotten word. A feeling like the soft sprinkle of fine mist tingled across his skin, and he knew that it had happened as his vision cleared.

Kerran's shadow hung above the Crossroads and he could see the massed army spread below, he watched and listened for a long time, then in his thoughts he formed the word again and his eyes flickered open to the familiar walls of Manzanee's cave. Kerran sat stunned; truly he had not expected it to happen. He had felt that there must be further barriers to frustrate him, but no, with the ancient word and the piece of silver sculpture, he had now entered the Wizards Way.

He returned to the book for a time, though the steps were clear before him they were numerous and he felt he must be as sure as he could before going any further. The day passed, and after eating and building up the fire, Kerran prepared to enter the game once again. For a reason he could not understand Kerran would always prefer the night to enter the Way, as though to hide the invisibility of his shadow even further. No matter where he chose for his shadow to go he must first pass through the Crossroads. The word came easier to his lips now, as though he had once known and then forgotten it. Again the ruined castle lay below him, the fires and torches of the enemy spreading into the darkness.

Kerran had already chosen his next Wizard Line, his vision moved to the west and a little north, he formed the word and for a brief moment his sight darkened, and then it cleared. Below him he could see through the darkness of night a place where forest met stone hillsides, three towering rocks on a tree clad hill stood high above the lands below. The Closed Monastery, containing the power that had once been a High Wizard's Seat, lay bathed in the soft starlight. A feeling of awe came over Kerran, and he now felt certain of the intense change that had come over his shadow since entering the game.

Kerran returned to the Crossroads and looked to the south and west, but not to a Wizard's Seat this time, then he formed the word. His vision cleared and he saw below him a mountainous place of rock and ice. Directly beneath him Kerran could see an area as big as a small town which had been levelled and carved from the mountains of the Bittering There was no sign of ruins here and Kerran had not expected any, for this was the Meeting Place, the communicating point between the High and Lesser Wizards. Looking to the south and east he formed the word but nothing happened. His shadow remained suspended above the Meeting Place. He tried again but to no avail.

Kerran was puzzled and returned to the cave where his true body had remained seated upon the stone. A late moon shone in the western sky and he stood on the ledge looking out across the forest, reflecting on what he had learned. He knew now that within his shadow he could go at will to all but one of the High Wizard's Seats, though he had yet to visit them all he understood that only the seat of Cranda-Sta on Zeta was closed to him. Something still barred him from travelling from the Meeting Place and further into the game. Kerran was thinking on this when sleep beckoned him. He lay down beside his small fire and gave over to its call.

At dawn Kerran woke with what possibly could be a very simple answer to his dilemma, the thought had come as his mind had woken. After going to the cold running falls and dashing the clear mountain water onto his face and neck, he returned to the cave. Kerran sat on Manzanee's stone and re-entered the Wizards Way, his unease concerning the daylight being overcome by his curiosity and desire to understand. It was not long before he discovered that his waking thoughts had been correct. Though his shadow could not instantly take him to the seats of the Lesser Wizards, he found that he could will his shadow to fly along the invisible lines of the eight pointed star. It was simple and he wondered why he had not thought of it the night before.

The land became a blur as he sped to the south and east. He found that he could slow his flight, and for a time he flew gently above the forest, watching in silent wonder as it slipped by beneath him. Then again he flew as fast as his shadow would allow until finally he reached the valley of Westerval, where he hung suspended for a long time, watching. He found that he could move downward to the ground but not beneath its surface. It was strange seeing the world as a mouse must see it. When he willed it, his shadow could fly no more than eighty or perhaps a hundred paces to either side of the Wizard Lines. At a certain point an invisible barrier allowed him to go no further. His own family home lay within this narrow corridor as he knew that it must.

Kerran was tempted to see his mother but he did not, for something told him that time and the game did not allow any waste of its power. Eventually he continued to the east until he came to a point above the plains of Andrian, nothing showed below, the grass of the plains covering what Kerran knew must be the site of another Lesser Wizard's Seat. The sun now stood high above, for it had taken most of the morning to reach this point. He did not know if there was a limit to the power he possessed and there was a place he still wanted to see. Something that he had seen earlier during his first drawing of the map had told him of this possibility. If his drawing of the land was as accurate as he hoped it was, then the curved Wizard Line would pass near or through the city of Mendan Maradass. He felt a tingle of anticipation as he sped now to the north and east.

The land flowed by, the dry plains turning to more fertile lands. The troops of Maradass were everywhere and Kerran sped onward toward the blue ocean, until he came to a high point above the sea. Waves crashed against the many islands and rocks which spread to the north. Kerran saw signs of an old fortress. Here a broken tower looked down upon the raging sea below. Kerran's shadow could not smile but he felt an increasing sense of wonder and exhilaration at the power he now used. He sped to the north, following the tightly scattered islands of the Narrows which held back the fury of the Outer Ocean. The sky was dark to the north, storm clouds hanging over Mendan Maradass.

The city lay below him as the sun sank beyond the Sea of Shardis, and lights began to glow from many buildings around the large port. The old city hugged the steep hillsides above the harbour and mounted higher to what Kerran had been told was the ruined fortress of Maradass. What he now saw was not a ruin but the tall ramparts of a dark and forbidding castle, its towers and battlements reaching into the menacing clouds. The power of Maradass had returned to the dark stronghold which, as Kerran had hoped, lay directly on the Wizard's Line though it was not a Wizard's Seat. Kerran moved closer until he looked down on the fortress and the armies camped beyond it, their fires lighting the darkening night.

The menacing storm which had been threatening suddenly burst upon the land. Kerran's vision blurred, but there was no other sensation of rain that disturbed his shadow. He moved still closer to the castle until the tall central tower lay below him. There was something which Kerran had yet to try that he had thought on during his magical journey on the Wizards Way. He could not pass beneath the surface of the earth, but he wondered if he could penetrate the walls of buildings. He descended to the tower where several guardsmen stood looking down upon the lands about, there were many troops guarding the battlements. Kerran lowered to the stone surface of the tower and passed, without sensation, through the stone and into the chamber below.

Again Kerran marvelled. He had not expected it to be so easy, if even possible, but here was his shadow within the dark tower. The room was lit by diffused torchlight from beyond a closed door. There were no windows in the chamber and as his vision adjusted to the dim light Kerran saw that this was a place of imprisonment. Chains and manacles hung from steel spikes in the walls. He was about to explore the castle further when he saw that the room was not empty. In a dark corner, on the cold stone, lay a person covered in a ragged blanket. Kerran moved closer to the unmoving figure until he hovered above him. Kerran knew who it must be even before he saw the long white hair and beard of his old friend Tolth. The patriarch of the family Amitarl lay in chains in the topmost chamber of the Evil One's tower.

Kerran had no way of waking Tolth. Something, almost a warning, told him that he must return to Manzanee's cave soon.

He looked down upon his friend lying asleep in the shadows, the chain and manacles at his ankle surely a vindictive gesture on the part of Maradass, for no one could escape from this windowless chamber, high in the dark castle. The feeling of urgency became stronger and he left quickly, racing across the vast lands to the south. The sun had just risen when his eyes opened to find he had returned safely to the Black Wizard's cave. His body was stiff and when he rose he found that his legs were numb. With a laugh, as much in pain as in pleasure, he forced his dead limbs to move. Soon the tingling of returning sensation began to work its way through them, plunging under the cold torrent he cried out as the chilling waters woke him to the new dawn.

Kerran ate and then slept the day away, though he had seen Tolth locked in the tower of Maradass Castle, a feeling of peacefulness had come upon him. Tolth was alive, and though not a master of the game Kerran was now sure he had discovered a way to observe the workings of Maradass. Soon he would go north to find the Elbrand. They must know of his new ability to help with the final victory that they all sought. He slept long, and it was not until after sunset that he rose and again sat on the Seat of Manzanee and uttered the ancient word. He flew to Mendan Maradass without pause and the sun had not yet risen when he once again looked down on the dark walls of the castle. There was something he felt that he must try. All else had been made to happen that he had thought impossible, and he could but experiment with the limits of his new-found powers. Tolth he hoped would be asleep, and Kerran had decided that he would try to enter his old friend's dreams, and speak with him.

Tidings from the Forest

Flindas and his companions made their way down a steep bush clad slope. The trail to the north and east lay clear before them now, rugged and broken. The River Glandrin-dar could be seen far away as it tumbled from distant falls to the valleys below. They could not rejoin the river before nightfall and so they made camp on a high bluff, where any attackers must come from below. During the darkness they heard a ferocious beast growling in the forest. Rark howled a defiant reply in warning and nothing more was heard that night. When the travellers regained the river it was still turbulent and they followed its course until nightfall, when it began to slow and widen once more.

The four companions camped close to the river, a tumble of rocks for shelter. Here the dark forest stood well back from the riverbank, giving a wide open area, across which they could see the approach of any attackers; they built a fire as the darkness of night spread across the lands. Rark was uneasy and ever watchful of the forest. It was overcast and there was no moon, and beyond the fire and boulders all lay dark and silent. It was much later that they heard the snarl of the creature and from further away it was answered by a second. Rark stood beyond the boulders and growled menacingly into the darkness.

"There are at least two of them now," said Flindas.

He built up the fire and they sat alert, waiting for the attack which they were sure would come soon. Apart from the knives which each of them carried, they all held sharpened staffs prepared that day to meet any attack. It was not long before their fears were realised, with a roar that was answered by Rark, three large creatures charged from the forest towards them. In the light of their torches the companions saw the fast lumbering animals cross the intervening distance. The beasts came on quickly, their long matted hair almost yellow in the firelight flowing wildly about them. They ran on four legs but when Rark leapt towards them they reared up and prepared to meet him, claws flashing in the darkness, a snarling mouth of huge curved teeth.

Rark had met these creatures before, and had learned not to close with their raking talons. At the last moment of his charge the great mountain dog swerved and then lunged sideways at one beast, catching a swinging foreleg, his momentum dragging the creature to the ground. Rark tore at the beast's leg and then leapt away before he could be caught. He howled through the blood which flecked his jaws and then charged again. Two of the creatures turned and made for the fire, their gleaming eyes catching the light, then one suddenly spun around as Rark rushed at it from behind. The creatures were fast but the mountain dog had fought many battles in his life and already knew these animals well. He avoided one beast and leapt upon the other animal's back. It screamed as the mountain dog's weight bore it to the ground, flailing behind with its vicious claws as Rark leapt away again, blood trickling from a shallow wound in his side. The other creatures had reached the boulders now, but were wary of the flames which the companions held before them. The beasts' coats looked like they would burn.

Rark howled again and crashed into the side of one animal but he was not quick enough this time. The fallen creature raked at the dog's back and Rark roared in pain. Flindas suddenly leapt forward between the boulders and before the animal could rise, his sharpened staff passed deep into the creature's body. It screamed and leapt away, and then stumbled and fell. Another of the creatures, one foreleg torn and limp, made to leap upon Leana and was impaled on her sharpened tree branch. The beast screamed and tore away as Tris thrust upward with all her strength. Her spear passed through the creature's throat and hot blood splattered the stones as it reared back and then fell. Rark rushed at the last creature but it had lost the will to fight. The mountain dog harassed it until it disappeared into the forest. The others seemed to be dead, and when Rark sniffed at them the animals showed no signs of movement. The mountain dog was bleeding badly from a number of injuries and he limped to the fire, lying down as though asking for Flindas to dress his wounds.

Flindas was almost in tears as he gently cared for his friend. Rark lay back and patiently waited as Flindas cleaned the wounds, applying ointment sparingly, as there was now little left of his supply. Two deep gashes in Rark's back worried Flindas, for them to heal Rark should move as little as possible. Flindas scraped the hair from around them with his knife and then reached into his pouch. Amongst the other necessary small items he carried was a sewing kit. Rark barely moved as the stitches were applied, only lifting his head once as though to ask if his friend had finished. Flindas stayed beside him for the remainder of the night and Rark slept. The flickering movement of his legs and jaws told Flindas that the dog still fought the beasts in his dreams.

By morning Rark could no longer stand, his many wounds causing him to cry out and fall back to the sand. One of the creatures, which Flindas had thought dead had disappeared, a trail of blood leading back into the forest. He had never heard of such beasts and would always remember the snarling fangs and the yellow, strangely human eyes. He thought that perhaps they were related to the creatures that Duragor had called Dreedow which he had met roaming the Mountains of Maradass to the far north, but these beasts of Dreardim had been more ferocious and much quicker in their movements. The river still flowed swiftly at this point, but they decided to build a raft. They could not carry Rark and the choices were to build a raft or wait until the dog had healed. They decided to chance the current.

The few logs and branches they found which were suitable took the rest of the day to collect and build into a floating platform where they could all sit securely, though not completely dry. They waited until morning. The creatures did not return, and by first light they had lifted Rark and carried him to the raft which now floated partly in the water. With a final push they leapt aboard as the ungainly craft joined the current and floated quickly downstream.

The river broadened during the day, entering a long valley which spread to the north and east. Flindas knew that the end of the forest could not be many days ahead, but what then? Somewhere within the vastness of the lands the Elbrand army would be in camp. Leana had said that the forest was the most probable place, but even then they could not be sure. The current slowed considerably during the day and the raft which was lying low in the water was sluggish, so they began to use the long poles which they had cut that morning. Rark had the driest part of the raft and would look up occasionally to see the river bank pass by, then drop his head again as though exhausted.

Before nightfall they built a fire on the shore and ate, then returned to Glandrin-dar and travelled through the night, hoping that no hidden dangers lurked on the river. At times there seemed no current at all and their arms ached with the continuous work. By morning they were ready to fall from weariness and they rested for a long time on a small boulder strewn beach. Rark had been able to make his own way from the raft, though he walked slowly, gently easing his wounded body across the sands. He ate little and when they returned to the river he lay down, his pain causing him to groan loudly as he sank to the deck of the raft.

Days passed as they continued their slow journey down the River Glandrin-dar, which now flowed more to the east than north. Again they had begun to hear the creatures of the forest. There seemed to be more of them now, so the companions rarely left their floating refuge. Rark could no longer leave the raft at all, and one of the deep cuts in his back had become infected, its poison entering the dog's bloodstream. Flindas was greatly worried for his friend and with his gaze turned forward. He looked desperately for the end of the forest. There were villages beyond that he knew of. If Maradass had not destroyed them, healing potions could be found that may yet save the mountain dog's life.

Some years before Flindas had come up the river from the east. He had not gone far but he remembered that perhaps three leagues into the forest the wide current had been cut in two by an island, its western end a tall buttress of rock. He watched ahead hopefully as each painful day passed and the current seemed to lessen further. He had almost despaired of ever reaching the edge of the forest when early one morning he saw the sunlight casting its colours onto the tall rock face which was the island he sought.

"We are almost through the forest," he said with great relief to the others and pointed ahead. "Here we must decide what is to be done," he continued. "Rark is near death and I would save him, but I cannot put you in more danger."

They were nearing the island, discussing the possibilities, when Flindas heard a high pitched bird call from the island. It was answered by another on the southern river bank.

"Elbrand!" said Leana excitedly and returned the call, loud and strong. "They are here!" she cried smiling and pointing ahead.

She almost leapt from the raft in her hurry to go to them. On the distant southern bank of the river Flindas saw a man step from beneath the trees, the green and brown clothing he wore Flindas had often before seen on Zeta. He poled towards the shore, still not completely convinced that these were truly Elbrand who awaited them. Maradass may have guessed that they would attempt to follow the river north and set a trap. It was only when Leana began to speak across the waters to the man on the shore that he relaxed, and a feeling of relief and great weariness came over him.

Leana could not wait and dived from the raft, swimming

strongly and reaching the shore well before the others. She was soon speaking quickly. Questions flowed from her as she held the man's hand and then laughed at his reply. The raft, with a last thrust of the pole, reached the shoreline. Flindas and Tris stepped ashore to be welcomed by the Elbrand.

"Greetings once again, Flindas," said the man. "Though I doubt you remember me, I competed against you in the games. My name is Var. Most welcome return."

"Greetings, Var," said Flindas taking the offered hand. "I remember that your bowmanship was not far astray."

Var smiled and turned to look at the small dark woman whose face was crossed by two livid scars.

"I am Tris," she said smiling. "I have been looking after these two for so long that I am very glad to meet you."

Leana kept asking questions of Var as Flindas tended to Rark. They learned that a force of Elbrand was no more than three days march from the river, and that Brook and Teaker were amongst their number. A runner would be sent ahead and horses could reach them by the next evening. Flindas also learned that the main force of Zeta was well to the south, at a refuge within the forest. They had won a great victory, Var told them. Tolth was there and so was the young hero who it appeared was nothing less than a descendant of wizards.

Flindas looked at Var in surprise. "It is Kerran you speak of?" he asked in wonder.

"Yes," replied Var. "I do not know all the things he has done, but the stories are that he has wizard's dreams, and his power increases as he and Tolth study together."

"When I lay wounded by Zard in the southern forest, somehow I knew this," said Leana. "I gave him the quest and I understood that he was important in some unknown way. It was truly no accident that he was there."

Flindas shook his head in wonderment. He remembered the boy that he had found mauled by dogs on the Old Coast Road and their dangerous quest together. His picture of wizards had nothing to do with a ragged boy in a smelly rabbit skin coat. Kerran had carried a piece of the Seacrest and had been able to use its power at times, but he had thought the magic of such a thing as the Seacrest would come to any who held it. Then he remembered that he too had carried a fragment for some time and had still gone hungry.

"Stranger than strange," he said to himself as he again opened the stitches on Rark's infected wound and began to clean it.

Rark did not stir, his breathing was shallow and his eyes no longer opened.

Var asked the question that Leana knew must come. "What of Elfhand?" he said. "Does he remain in the north?"

Leana looked sadly into the warrior's eyes."Landin is dead, Var," she said as tears welled in her eyes. "He died to save us." She took the Seacrest fragment from beneath her shirt. "He passed this to me so it would not be lost."

Var's face showed shock and disbelief."It is grave news you bring," he finally said. "How can one such as Landin come to die?"

"He faced the power of Maradass to save me, but could not save himself," replied Leana.

Var turned away quickly and disappeared into the forest. It was some time before he returned. "The runner has gone," he told them. "He takes the news to Torian."

"Why do you watch the river?" asked Flindas. "Has Maradass moved into the forest itself?"

"No," Var replied. "It was Chelasta who told us that you were on the river."

"Chelasta? Who is Chelasta?" asked Flindas.

"Kerran, the young hero, or young wizard," replied Var. "He seems to have acquired a number of names. It was he who told us that he saw you chased by horsemen into the river near his mother's home. I have heard it said that he flies at times in the body of his white hawk."

Flindas remembered the bird's magical ways and smiled in wonder.

"It was Chelasta who told us that Leana was alive," continued Var. "He saw you at the Desert Pass."

Again Flindas remembered the white hawk flying above them as they had run from the horse soldiers of Maradass into the desert, and his wonder increased.

Flindas made a soft bed of grass for Rark and they laid him on it. The great dog was limp and did not stir as they moved him. During the day they talked much with Var, hearing about the sea voyage and the landing in Andrian.

"The Governor told Tolth to leave the city," said Var incredulously. "We could have taken it but Tolth would not allow that. Now the Governor has an army of black troops sitting at his doorstep. I doubt that his tax collectors have much work to do now. It is said that he is your father... you do not look alike."

Flindas laughed at the jest.

Var lit a small fire as evening descended and though his supply of food was limited to a mixture of oats and nuts, and whatever he could find or catch, it was a small feast they made that night to celebrate their return. Var soon had his supply of oats reduced to a few crumbs in the bottom of the bag. They had not eaten even plain oats in a long time, and their bodies seemed to come alive with the sudden change from lizard and rabbit meat.

The horses arrived late the following day with an escort of twenty Elbrand that would take them to Torian's camp within the forest. Flindas watched with concern as Rark was placed on a stretcher that would be towed by a horse, with Elbrand in attendance to see that the other end of it travelled easily. The dog's breathing had almost faded completely, his mouth and nose were dry. Flindas feared for his friend as he had not done for any person in his life. He mounted his horse and followed the litter as it was drawn through the forest. There were healers at the northern camp, and Verardian was there, he had been told.

It was almost two days later when the group of riders began to wend their way up a high craggy hill amidst tall smooth barked trees that soldiers of Zeta began to come from the trees to greet them. News had travelled through their ranks and as the travellers mounted a final rise and looked down at the large encampment on the hollow hill top, the small army of Zeta all stood and watched their descent. There was no cheering or gaiety, for all had heard of Landin's death. Torian welcomed them and Verardian came forward as Leana rushed towards him and threw her arms around her brother.

"Welcome back dearest of sisters," said Verardian into her hair "It has been too long."

They stood there for some time holding each other until Verardian turned to Flindas.

"Greetings, Flindas, I hear you have a patient in great need of the healers." Verardian came to the litter where Rark lay unconscious. He laid his hand on the dog's chest, then rose to his feet. "Take him to the healer's area quickly," he said to the man who rode the horse, and then Verardian turned to his sister and held her hands. "I would greet you more fully but the beast is in great need," he said.

"Go!" said Leana. "Do what you can for him. I would not see him die for the want of your kind hands."

Verardian turned and left them quickly.

Torian took them through the camp to his fireside. The stories they had told Var had been retold and expanded. Tris was a great curiosity for the soldiers of Zeta and she was soon drawn away from the others to retell their tale over and over to the eager ears of the troops. She was at first embarrassed by this popularity but soon began to enjoy it, and the story she told grew much with the telling. Though the troops grieved for Landin, they insisted on hearing of his death. Here Tris told them all she could remember, and in their sadness the troops held silent and listened to her tale.

Flindas and Leana sat and ate at Torian's fire, where they were joined by a number of the Elbrand captains, and it was here that the travellers heard the strange news from the Crossroads. Some days before, on horse and riding alone, Zard had passed through the Crossroads and ridden the South Road into Glandrin. Leana shuddered as she remembered the Black One's brutal laugh as he had stood over her in the forest.

"It is a good day when an Amitarl dies," came his dark voice into her memory.

"Can he then defeat an entire army?" asked Torian, who knew of Zard's power, but also knew that Zard could be vanquished.

"I fought him with the power of the Seacrest and the magic of my heritage," said Leana. "He defeated me and was it not for the white hawk it would have been me who died in the south of Dreardim, not Zard."

"It would take Zard a long time to fight all the Elbrand," Torian smiled a little. "That is if he could find them," he added.

"I must go to Tolth," said Leana suddenly, and stood as if to leave immediately.

"Rest," said Torian. "The way has been long and hard for you. Zard cannot reach the refuge unless Tolth allows it."

"You do not know the power of Zard," she replied. "There may seem no possibility of his taking the Seacrest from my father but the Black One does nothing without reason."

She would not rest until Torian gave orders that a troop of Elbrand prepare themselves to accompany her through the forest into the south. Flindas stretched beside the fire and ate another bowl of the hot soup. He would not go south yet, the Elbrand now guarded Leana and their long journey had taken a great toll on his strength, to sit a few days eating and resting was all he desired. Also he wanted to know that Rark would recover before joining Tolth and Kerran. When Leana was about to leave she came to Flindas where he sat beside the fire.

"I will never be able to thank you, or repay you, for all you have done," she said. "All Zeta and the Regions owe you much."

"I did it not for reward," said Flindas. "We will all play our parts in the times to come. Give my greetings to Tolth and Kerran and tell them I will be with them soon."

For a moment Leana looked into his eyes, a question on her lips which she did not voice. "Until we meet again," she said and was gone.

Later Flindas joined Verardian in the glade where the healers worked their magic. Rark was very ill and Verardian was amazed that the dog had not yet succumbed to the poisonous infection.

"He is a very strong beast," said the healer as they stood beside the litter where Rark lay. "The infected wound has been cleaned and will heal, but there is much poison in his blood. I cannot say yet if he will survive."

Flindas returned to Torian's fire where he remained for most of the day, talking with the Elbrand captains and the army commander. He learned more of the victory won in the south and of the skirmishes and running battles that were being fought nearby on the edge of the forest. He also learned that Brook and Teaker both did battle now at the eastern border of Dreardim, and would not return to the camp for several days. The army of Zeta, though grieving at the death of Landin, were much heartened by the safe return of Leana and the Seacrest fragment. Now with three pieces of the old magic talisman, and a young wizard as well, there was a sense of hope in the camp.

It was late in the day when news came from the Crossroads, that morning many thousand of the strange foot soldiers of Maradass had marched to the forest, joining the other troops who fought there. Meanwhile the black horse troops had withdrawn and begun to move quickly down the South Road, more than two thousand riders and a great many Marauders went to join the Black One.

"Horse troops are of no use in the forest," said Torian when he heard the news. "I do not know why they travel the South Road, but they dare not enter the forest mounted, it would be like giving us their horses."

Over the next days the fighting on the edge of the forest was joined by yet more troops of Maradass who had come from the Crossroads. They seemed to be intent on keeping the troops of Zeta occupied at the edge of Dreardim. The Stone Soldiers were used to push the troops of Zeta from place to place. They could do battle in a slow methodical way but it was in their numbers that their strength lay. Not one of the soldiers of Zeta had yet fallen to their spears.

Rark improved a little each day and Verardian was pleased to tell Flindas that his friend would recover. Flindas had been in the camp for several days and he was with Verardian when the news of an attack on the Southern Refuge was relayed through the camp. They ran to Torian's fire to find the messenger retelling her story.

"Zard came into the refuge and Tolth faced him," Flindas heard her say as he arrived. "Then the Stone Soldiers came up out of the ground, just grew like evil weeds. Our troops were forced from the refuge. Mantris was with Tolth but the battle swept him away from the cave. None saw what happened, but when they returned to the refuge, Tolth, Mindis and the young wizard Chelasta were gone, the pieces of the Seacrest with them."

The news cast a deathly silence on those who heard it.

"The Stone Army disappeared into the ground just as they had come, even their dead," continued the woman. "Later, horse troops of Maradass were seen to be riding north at speed. Zard had joined them but there was no news of captives."

Later that day a message came from the Crossroads. Zard and his horse troops had returned there and many, including the Black One, had taken the Philosopher's Road towards Mendan Maradass. Again there had been no news of captives. A pall of fear came down upon the army of Zeta. They awaited further news from the south, and when it came it was confirmed that Tolth, Mindis and Kerran were missing, and that Mantris was bringing the main force north, as the Southern Refuge was no longer safe. Leana had not had time to reach the refuge before the attack, she was said to be continuing south to join the troops under Mantris.

Days passed before the troops from the south eventually joined Torian's camp. The battle at the edge of the forest had almost ceased, the foot troops of Maradass having pulled back to the Crossroads, their diversionary task done. Leana spoke to no one and when Flindas saw her it was as if she was again entwined in a dark spell of silence. Even Verardian could not help her, though he felt her pain as his own. He tried to speak to her but it was as though she did not hear. Two days later Tris, who was now well rested from the journey, sat with Flindas on a hilltop overlooking the forest and the troops scattered amongst the trees.

"What will happen now?" she asked as she idly scratched patterns in the dirt with a twig.

"That is what Torian and Mantris must decide," replied

Flindas. "All futures seem grim now, Maradass has three pieces of the Seacrest and many more troops than we do. These Krags, the Stone Army, are a force that is powered with evil magic. It is hard to say this, but I fear the war may already be lost. Maradass holds too many pieces in this game."

The day was clear and Flindas looked out across the forest to the south, far away, on the edge of sight, he saw a speck in the sky. Standing and shading his eyes, he watched as the white hawk flew towards the camp. No mention in the messages from the south had been made of Storm's whereabouts.

Again Flindas wondered about the hawk. What magic did this strange bird carry on its white wings? Storm flew directly towards them, unswerving, his goal clearly in sight. With a turn on the wind Storm fell from the sky to land on a rocky ledge nearby, then immediately took to the air again and flew towards the south. Flindas stood and watched as Storm returned and repeated the manoeuvre.

"He tries to tell us something," said Tris, following the bird with her keen sight.

"Yes," said Flindas. "I have learned to trust this creature. He flies to the south and I would go and see why he calls us."

"I will go too," said Tris, camp life had become dreary since the news had come from the south.

"Come," he said. "We will tell the commanders."

They returned to the fire where they found Mantris and told him of the hawk's arrival. Elbrand were offered to go with them but Flindas declined as he felt there was no need. After borrowing small packs and collecting several days rations of food, they left the northern refuge together and began to travel south through the forest. Flindas again carried a long bow, a well made sword, and several knives. Their clothing had been in tatters and had mostly been replaced by the green and brown of Zeta. The smallest boots in the camp were still too big for Tris, but a man amongst the troops who was a master cobbler had fashioned some for her from a larger pair. He did not have with him his fine array of tools but had managed, and Tris found them comfortable enough as Storm led them further to the south.

Kerran sat at the cave entrance watching the early dawn spread across the forest. He still could not believe what had happened the day before. Tolth had slept and Kerran's shadow had entered his old friend's dreams. Tolth's sleeping mind had woken instantly to Kerran's presence. It had been as though their minds were one. Kerran had felt the pain within Tolth, his physical pain of imprisonment in chains and his fear of the tragedy which had befallen them. Kerran had tried to reassure the old Amitarl that all was not yet lost.

Back at Manzanee's cave Kerran was deep in thought when he heard the familiar cry from above, and Storm flew out beyond the escarpment in a slow glide. He had not seen the bird for some days and was a little disappointed to see no rabbit or lizard in the hawk's claws. Storm returned, circling on the air currents. Kerran watched for a time, and then forgot the bird as he returned to his thoughts. Storm fell from the sky and landed on the rock shelf before the cave. Kerran watched the bird as it again took to the sky. Following the hawk with his eyes as it flew near the waterfall Kerran saw two figures standing above on the cliff's edge. He stood in amazement; Flindas and the small dark woman from his dream visions were standing beside the large tree which marked the trail down to the cave.

Kerran waved his arms and called out but they did not seem to hear. Kerran called again but still they did not see him, though their eyes seemed to look directly at the cave for a time and then searched elsewhere. Kerran could not believe it when they turned and disappeared from sight, he leapt towards the pathway to give chase when something told him to take with him his belongings from the cave. Quickly he gathered the book and his few possessions and ran for the pathway. Flindas would not have gone far. He still could not understand why they had not seen nor heard him.

The fine spray of water drifted against his face as Kerran climbed the last overgrown ledge and came to the old tree on the cliff top. He went quickly around the large trunk, balancing on a root and scrambling to the level above. Kerran called his friend's name several times as he stood anxiously by the tree, for he did not know which direction they might have gone. Storm burst from the tree line screeching, flying low straight at Kerran; then from the forest Kerran saw Flindas and his small companion emerge into the sunlight. Overjoyed, he ran to meet them and in turn Flindas strode towards him.

"Tis about time," called Flindas. "I was beginning to think that bird of yours was trying to get us lost."

Kerran smiled broadly, unable to contain his happiness at the return of his warrior friend. They embraced and Kerran could find no words.

"I declare you have grown in my absence," said Flindas looking at Kerran as he stood back from the young man. "No longer a boy in a smelly coat on his way to Zeta. I see that wizardry has turned you into a man now."

"It is so good to see you," Kerran finally found his voice. "There is so much to tell. How did you not see me when you looked down at the cave just now?" He pointed back to the tree and small waterfall.

"I saw no cave," replied Flindas. "There seemed a trick of the eye and Storm vanished for a moment, but I saw nothing of a cave. Show me." They were about to turn when Flindas realised he had been remiss and he laid a hand on the young woman's shoulder. "Kerran, meet Tris from the Broken Lands. We have travelled a long hard road together."

Kerran now looked for the first time into the dark eyes and scarred face of the young woman he had known only in his dream visions. "Greetings, Tris," he said with a small bow "I have seen you before, in my dreams."

"You might call them nightmares," grinned Tris. "I have heard a lot about you. We must have a contest of slings one day. I believe you know the art."

Kerran smiled, instantly liking this small but indomitable young woman.

"No magic to assist you either," she added as they turned back towards the cliff's edge.

Kerran looked down in astonishment, where the overhang had been easily visible from beside the old tree he now looked at a sheer cliff face. The cave had disappeared. Leaning out around the tree Kerran saw that the narrow pathway had also vanished. There was no way now to descend, and the stream fell in an unbroken glistening veil to the valley below.

"It was there," said Kerran pointing at the rock face below. "I have been there for many days and now I cannot return."

His voice grew softer as the full realisation came to him. The High Seat of Manzanee was no longer accessible to him, and he did not know how to otherwise enter the Wizards Way. The look on his face told of his distress.

"What is it?" asked Flindas, placing a hand on his young friend's shoulder. "You look as though you have lost a loved one."

Kerran began to tell his companions of the Wizards Way, and they were astounded by the story of ancient magic and the nature of his shadow.

"It is true then that you are a wizard?" asked Tris looking at this young, softly bearded man who was no older than herself, but who possessed an ancient history of wizardry.

"I doubted it for a long time myself but no longer," replied Kerran. "My father did not have the time to tell me of my heritage, but I cannot now deny the truth of it." He looked wistfully at the sheer rock face where the cave had once been. "What I have learned here must be put to use. Maradass often speaks with Tolth, this I know, and I have already learned some useful things of the nature of that dark man and his family. All is not yet lost."

The three companions now turned as one and began to make their way towards the edge of the forest. Over the next few days, as they travelled north to rejoin the army of Zeta, they heard much of each other's adventures. Kerran learned of the death of Landin and the rescue of Leana. He felt saddened for Tolth, remembering the last vision of his old friend as he lay chained in the dark tower of Maradass Castle. One night by their small campfire, Kerran showed the others the small silver sculpture which he told them was the key to the Wizards Way. Tris turned it slowly in her hands, rays of firelight catching the fine edges.

"I know this," she said surprised, and passed the sculpture to

Flindas. "The centrepiece," she indicated. "Do you remember old Trontar showing this to us?"

Flindas nodded slowly. "It is the star which the old wizard showed us in his magical dome," he said.

"Not a star, but a planet," Tris corrected him and laughed as a false scowl crossed his face.

"I was the one who spent all his time trying to solve the puzzle that the wizard set," Flindas said. "I did not have time for such things as magical domes and stars, or even planets."

He balanced the silver sculpture in his hand for a moment then returned it to Kerran. They had told him of their time with Trontar and Kerran knew now that he was not the only wizard in the lands, and in truth, the scribing of an old book on Zeta had already told him so.

It was a bleak windswept day when the travellers entered the northern refuge. Many welcomed them, surprised and very pleased to find Kerran amongst their company. Commander Mantris drew them to his fire where Leana sat quietly, and Flindas again felt that the residue of the old spell held her in its grasp. The capture of Tolth just days after they had returned had driven her spirit deep within. She welcomed them with a smile full of tragedy, then her eyes came to rest on Kerran and suddenly they were alive. She stood quickly, her heavy cloak falling to the ground, coming forward around the fire Leana stood in Kerran's path.

"You have news of my father," she said with certainty.

Kerran looked into the sad and beautiful face which he had first seen in the southern forest almost a year before. "Yes," he replied. "He is alive, but captured by Maradass. The Seacrest fragment which he carried is also in the Evil One's hands. I have spoken with him in a manner."

At these words Leana and the others around the fire looked at him in wonder.

"How is it you spoke with Tolth if he is in the hands of Maradass?" These words came from Mantris as he looked with disbelief at Kerran.

"I have gained knowledge of an ancient wizardry," Kerran replied. "These last days, in a cave that is no longer there, I learned of the Wizards Way. Originally it was a means of communication between wizards. Finally it became the means of their destruction. I have gained much knowledge, yet there is a great amount that I still do not understand. I can travel with my mind, more than my mind in truth. With Tolth I called it my shadow. It is the part of me that flies. I spoke with Tolth where he lays in chains in Maradass Castle. I heard his thoughts. He has spoken with Maradass who enjoys mocking Tolth, and so now I too know something of the Evil One's designs."

They stood warming themselves by the fire, Leana keeping her eyes on Kerran as he spooned a delicious soup into his mouth, followed by large pieces of bread torn from a crusty loaf. He spoke further of his experiences as he ate.

"Maradass boasts of his coming victory," he said. "Now with two pieces of the Seacrest he believes that none can stop him."

"I fear it may be true," said Mantris looking at the young man who, though lean from his time alone in the forest, seemed to have grown much from the ragged boy who had arrived on Zeta not so many moons before.

"Maradass holds the cities and the best crop lands," continued the Army Commander. "Dantas is managing to bring us some stores from the south, but if we must spend the winter in these lands it will be hard on the troops. Maradass holds all the pieces in this game."

"Not all," said Leana, who reached around her neck and drew forth the fragment of the Seacrest which Landin had carried into the north. She looked at it for a moment and then held it out to Kerran.

"It belongs to you," she said. "I cannot wield it. With both pieces perhaps you will find a way to help us, and the land."

"It is I who should return this to you," said Kerran as he took the other from his pouch. "It is by right yours to carry."

"No," said Leana stepping forward and placing the piece in Kerran's hand. "I can see who you are. I was even told to expect you." She looked intently into his young eyes. "Take it and help us to achieve the victory that we all desire. Go to my father again and tell him of my safety."

"It may be that I can never return to him," said Kerran sadly. "A spell was broken when I left the magical cave and I could not return, but I will of course try."

Kerran looked at the second fragment of the ancient Wizard's Bane and he removed the cord and metal clasp. When he had once before held two fragments they had been those of the Past and Future, Tolth had told him that they were opposite quadrants of the original circle, their rough edges never quite aligning. He saw that these two pieces had a common edge and with an almost idle gesture he brought the fragments together in his hands. They came together perfectly and Kerran could hardly see the fine line where they met. For a moment he felt a light tingling sensation emanate from the Seacrest and then a soft white light began to flow from the strange metal. Those around the fire stepped back in awe as the light grew, soon to become much brighter than that of the fire. The two pieces, though still showing the fine join, held fast to each other. All the weariness and hunger Kerran had felt seemed to fall away from him, and he watched in wonder as a deep scratch on his hand slowly vanished before his eyes. The words of the ancient book on Zeta returned to him.

IN A TIME TO COME A CHILD OF CHEL-A-STA
BLOOD MAY UNITE THE WIZARD'S BANE

Slowly the light faded and Kerran saw the two pieces fall away from each other once again.

"Yes," said Leana, the only one not surprised amongst the group. "I knew it must be so." She smiled brightly now for the first time since they had arrived, the spell falling away from her eyes.

"Tell us more of Maradass," said Mantris. "I am eager to learn anything which will help us win this war."

"The castle of Mendan Maradass has been rebuilt," began Kerran to the surprise of all. "Much magic has gone into its making, I think. Maradass rarely leaves his chambers, which are in the lower part of the tower where Tolth is held. I could not enter those rooms and council chamber. There was a magic which held me out. Whether a warning from Maradass, or my own secret knowledge keeping me from danger, I know not. I have learned something of the nature of the Stone Soldiers. There are many parts of the land where they may appear, it was by ill fortune that the Southern Refuge was so close to the lines of the Way, some leagues to the north of here is a place where they also could emerge."

Mantris passed Kerran a map of the land. The scale was accurate and Kerran spent much of the afternoon explaining the method and boundaries of the ancient magic, drawing lines with the aid of a good pencil and straight-edge.

"There is much I do not know," said Kerran to a question from Mantris. "During the nights, since we began our walk north, I have tried to re-enter the game. I cannot it seems. I must be at a High Wizard's Seat to achieve this, and the cave is no longer there. I see no other way. The Crossroads are held and the other High Wizard's Seats are closed to me now, or else destroyed."

At this moment Flindas and Verardian rejoined the group and between them came Rark, limping slightly and covered with numerous dressings. Kerran welcomed his large hairy friend, and Rark's great tongue caught at Kerran's beard, the wet nose almost pushing him from the rock where he sat. By late evening Kerran had told his tale and had also learned of the situation at the forest's edge, where Torian and the main force fought off any attempt to enter very far beneath the trees.

Few soldiers of Zeta had fallen during the battles, whereas the Black Army had lost many, and the Marauders would no longer enter the woods. They were seen to turn on their masters if driven towards the trees. The foot soldiers themselves entered the forest with fear in their eyes. The speed and accuracy of the bowmen against whom they fought had made many quail and run in terror, though the power that held them always brought them back to the battle. The Stone Soldiers were almost impervious to the arrows that had at first found many a mark in their tough bodies. The warriors of Zeta no longer wasted their shafts on these creatures, preferring to attach with blade and axe, or stones cast from above.

From the south came news of an uprising amongst the people of Andrian, who had begun to train and then fight against the black troops. The Governor remained in token power, surrounded by his new allies, who took at will all that they wished from Andrian, but as yet had not destroyed the city. No Marauders had gone to the Southlands with the black fleet, though a few had come later with the horse troops accompanying the Stone Army. There were not enough of the dogs to combat the night fighting which Dantas and others were beginning to organise.

News came each day from the south carried by horsemen who brought supplies, mostly from Glandrin which remained relatively free of the Black Army. News too had come from the fleet. Captain Ronsarl remained well off the coast. No ships had been sent against him, and recently a smaller second fleet had arrived from Zeta with a large supply of food and almost two thousand fresh troops, who would remain at sea until needed.

"We could return south and clear Andrian of the Black Army," spoke Mantris. "We would be outnumbered but with the people of the Southlands rising against them they could not hold the land and the city as well. Torian and I have discussed this, though we sorely miss the wise guidance of Tolth. He did not want to take the City Amitarl by force. This we know, but Andrian lies open to us. This war at the forest edge avails the south little. Every day we cause great slaughter amongst the troops of Maradass, but every day a few soldiers of Zeta will fall. Winter comes and the land grows cold. We must decide what is to be done soon." He shook his head slowly. "I would that Tolth were here," he said quietly.

Then he was silent for a time, looking into the flames of the fire.

Understanding the Game

The Army of Zeta settled for the night, though dread had stalked them during the last few days the feeling in camp was lighter now that the young wizard was again amongst them, as were two pieces of the Seacrest. Curled up in a blanket beside the fire Kerran dreamed, though it was not like any previous vision. There seemed no great meaning in it except a feeling of pleasure and freedom. He felt almost asleep within the dream. Kerran was carried by his shadow into the darkening west. All night he flew, and as the first glimmerings of dawn touched the sky, far below him he saw a vast blue ocean as the dream slowly ended.

Kerran became aware of the earth beneath him. One shoulder had lain beyond the warmth of his blanket and was cold. He stirred, pulling the blanket closer around him. The peaceful sense of the dream remained with him and the chill autumn air did not invite him to rise this early, though hot food would be available soon after sunrise. There was a stirring amongst those who had slept around the fire. Flindas slowly sat up, rubbing the sleep from his eyes.

"The strangest dream," he said as if to himself.

He did not elaborate but stood, and with Rark beside him

he made his way to a small stream nearby. The vividness of his dream was startling, yet the overall feeling was one of peace and confidence in the future. He washed quickly in the cool stream where others were coming to do the same. There seemed to be a constrained excitement amongst the first few soldiers to join him at the small watercourse.

"Did you dream last night?" one of them asked him as they arrived.

Flindas looked up quizzically. "Indeed I did dream," he told the man, who smiled broadly at the others.

"And what did you dream if you would care to tell?" asked the soldier.

"I was flying," replied Flindas, the pictures clear and precise in his mind. "A dry land and then a blue ocean at sunrise."

"Exactly," said the man excitedly. "We have all had this dream, or vision. I think your young friend, the new wizard, will know something of this."

Another of the soldiers broke in upon her friend who had first spoken. She was tall and strongly built, an Elbrand warrior, not one of the scouts or runners. "We heard that he has gained much now that he carries the two pieces of the Seacrest," she said. "The dream vision or whatever it may have been could be a sign of his increased power, or perhaps he did not dream at all."

"I am sure we will soon know," said the first soldier.

He pointed to where Kerran was walking towards the stream yawning, wrapped in his thick blanket. When he joined them, the soldiers seemed hesitant. One nudged Flindas and asked him silently to seek the truth of the matter from his young friend.

"Did you dream in the night?" Flindas asked casually as Kerran bent down beside the stream, splashing the cold water into his face.

"I did," said Kerran and looked at Flindas. "It was a dream which told me little. Why do you ask?"

One of the many gathered soldiers spoke now, excitedly. "Did you dream of flying above a barren land with a dry river and beyond to an ocean at dawn?"

Kerran looked at the man in surprise. "That was indeed my dream," he said to the others, who laughed aloud.

"Excuse our discourtesy," the tall woman said quickly. "We have all had the same dream, and our amazement at this has taken our manners from us."

"No need to apologise," said Kerran smiling. "Show me no more respect than you would your friends here. I may be of wizard stock but I am of no higher standing than any amongst you, but please tell me of this dream."

Each soldier now told of many individual memories from the dream vision, small things sometimes that Kerran had already forgotten. Others joined the group and it was soon known throughout the camp that all had dreamed a wizard's dream. All had felt a new inner resolve come upon them, as though time had now gathered its forces on their side. They knew that no matter how long the war would take, they would master all and win peace in the end.

By noon Torian had returned to camp for a conference with Mantris, he brought news of a strange dream that all had experienced the night before and he greeted Kerran with a new respect in his eyes. The large and powerful man, his heavy beard plaited in two braids, suddenly knelt before Kerran who stepped back in surprise.

"Young man or no," said Torian. "You are a wizard and I believe one of good intent. I bow to that power and goodness."

"Do not bow to me," said Kerran still surprised. He took the man by the shoulders and raised him. "Whatever magic gifts I have are ours to use as they are granted." Kerran looked into the commander's eyes. "Only time can tell how much strength will come from my hereditary gifts, and from the Seacrest. Your own powers and those of your troops will count as much as any wizardry in the times to come, so I believe."

Torian looked into Kerran's face. This was not the same boy he had met only a few moons before. The change was startling to Torian as it had been for many who were close to Kerran. Verardian had likened it to a slow flowering which, due to the strife in the land, had begun to quicken its pace, and many were heartened by it. Grieved by the loss of Tolth and Landin they now looked to Kerran in hope and wonder. Kerran feared that they may put too much faith in his ability. He did not understand the power himself, nor could he call on it at will, except within the Wizards Way.

A war council was held that morning. Leana and Verardian were there, though both Amitarl sat quietly and said little. They felt that since the capture of Tolth the two warrior commanders should plan the army's moves, while Leana had decided to join her brother in caring for the wounded. She too seemed a different person, thought Flindas, as he looked at her sitting quietly beside her brother. She spoke little these past days and then softly, sadness still hung about her which the wizard dream had not dispelled. Flindas was called on to give his thoughts. He had been born in the Southlands and now it had become common knowledge in the camp that he was the son of the Governor.

"Will the South truly rise against the Black Army?" Torian asked this warrior, so recently met.

"Under Dantas, men will fight," Flindas replied. "He is a leader and a great warrior. I have not seen him for some years but expect that he has just become harder to chew on as he has gotten older."

Torian smiled at the assessment of the old Elbrand leader he had looked up to as a boy.

"The Governor will aid none but himself," continued Flindas, his words clearly showing his feelings for his father. "I do not think there will be revolt in the city streets. Those who would fight the Black Army will disappear into the countryside. There are few trained men in the land, but there will be many who will wish to fight. Though the Southlands have become corrupt under the name of Demsharl, there are many strong and proud people in the land who will not be prepared to bow to Maradass."

"That is good to hear," said Mantris. "Dantas has said as much, but it is well that you confirm his words. The feeling amongst the troops and ourselves is that we should return to the Southlands before winter comes. We will need the stores there that have arrived from Zeta."

"It would be dangerous to leave the forest," said Verardian, who had not spoken until now. "Though Dreardim has a fearful name it is still our refuge. Our wounded are safer here than in open country."

Mantris spoke in reply. "When last that Dantas was here he told us of another refuge that has been prepared in the coastal highlands to the far south," he said. "For some years the caves there have been a place of sanctuary for those who run from the Governor, and much food and other stores have quietly left Andrian recently to be stored there. Wagons have gone south, deep into the cold. This new refuge would be a bitter place to remain for the winter, but the troops of Maradass would not reach us. Once the snow falls, it will be safe. Our troops are trained for such conditions and will be able to strike north against the Black Army at will. Even if the enemy was to reach that far to the south, the refuge is a high mountain valley with one access only and escape if needed into the mountains further inland."

"Will we stop the northern war for the winter?" asked one of the many Elbrand captains who had come to the Council.

"No," replied Torian. "Should we go to this refuge, which I believe is only part of the answer, the fight should continue here. I would like to split the forces, leaving part of our troops to continue the battle, perhaps even as few as a thousand soldiers and Elbrand, left with enough supplies to last the winter, and with some of the horses. We can keep part of the Black Army occupied here and they will be unable to drive us out. Even a full attack from the entire army of Maradass would see but a withdrawal of our soldiers further into the forest to the south." At these words he turned to Kerran. "Maradass cannot surround us, unless he is able to attack us with wizardry?"

"The Stone Army I am sure is unable to suddenly appear closer than ten leagues or more to the north," said Kerran. "I do not know how far Maradass has penetrated into the game, and I cannot say where the stone army may be now, but I can say where they will not be."

Torian nodded.

"Who would command these northern troops?" asked one

of the captains. "I doubt not that you and Commander Mantris will go to the Southlands."

"Yes," replied Mantris. "I am not so in favour of this northern force, but I can see the reason in it. Torian and I will keep our command in the south. One of you will be chosen to lead the troops who remain here."

One of the captains, a woman with a long braid down her back, now spoke. "There are many amongst us captains who would agree that there is only one who can take that position."

Others of those gathered there nodded as though this was a common piece of conversation between them.

"Brook, who continues the battle and will not rest," she continued. "He inspires the troops with him. Few would be disappointed by such a choice."

Torian looked at the woman from across the dead fire. "You read our minds I think," he said. "Tis true he is the best choice, so long as he will slow down long enough to give orders."

Several of the captains laughed at this.

"It is almost winter," continued Torian. "It is a march of at least thirty days to the southern refuge, probably more. I believe that the main force should leave soon, going through the forest to the south. The troops that remain here must battle on every front for a time. The later that Maradass learns of our movement south the better. We must avoid an open fight in the Southlands, from the refuge we can strike into Andrian, but we must first get there safely. The northern Regions will have to wait for their liberation; I always knew that this would be a long war."

The Council came to an end and Kerran felt in need of some time alone. There was much on his mind that he needed to think on. The effect of the dream on those about him was obvious. They seemed more cheerful and more resolved to free the lands, though Kerran still doubted his ability to help them much with their cause even though he now held two pieces of the Seacrest. He wanted a quiet place where he could think, and slipping away from those who would hold him in conversation Kerran left the hilltop, going down the slope to the west. After a short walk and a warning from a sentry not to stray beyond a certain place, he came to a tumbling stream. Here he paused to spend some time in solitary thought. The day had clouded over, threatening rain.

Kerran saw Storm flying above against the grey sky. In the narrow valley, amongst tall young saplings and sparse undergrowth, he sat down on a log. After a time, a pair of small birds joined him, whistling to each other and dancing in the trees as though to entertain him. The pure joy of living, which seemed to be this small bird's way, caused Kerran to smile and make sounds through his lips to attract them. One came and perched on a branch just above his head. Kerran reached up to this familiar little bird which he had always known as the *Woodsman's Friend*. The small bird twittered, and with a light flutter, landed on Kerran's outstretched hand. He hardly breathed, watching the creature as it twirled and spun on his fingers, amused by the strange branch on which it had landed. The 'Woodsman's Friend' finally rejoined its mate as she hunted for small insects that flew through the air around them. They seemed totally care free, unaffected by trivial things such as war and ancient magic.

A line of ants passed by amongst the stones and grass at Kerran's feet. Even these creatures seemed satisfied with their lot, going about their daily tasks. One day they would die with no thought of death to disturb them, no war of hatred and greed to fight, no evil to be vanquished. Kerran could sense the peace and fate in which the entire world live except for humankind who must struggle against the wickedness of others, and at the same time banish their own inner fears.

"There is no need for evil in the land," Kerran said aloud to the line of ants that passed by his foot. "There can be peace if enough people wish it."

"True," said a young voice from the bushes nearby.

Kerran started to his feet, and then saw Tris come from beyond a low bush.

"Excuse me Kerran," she said. "I saw you leave camp and thought you may care for a contest, but I think your thoughts are today far above any use of a simple weapon such as a sling."

"Not so," said Kerran suddenly pleased that she had

disturbed him. "Perhaps it is exactly what I need to clear my head of its entangled thoughts."

They went to the wide stream bed and began to set up targets and collect stones. Kerran had not used his sling for some time and it was not until he heard Tris snigger after a particularly poor throw that he began to put his concentration into nothing but the weapon, driving all thoughts of wizardry and the future from his mind.

"You improve," said Tris in deference to a series of fallen targets. "How is it that one with magical powers needs a sling to throw stones? Are there not ways that you can use your powers in warfare?"

"None that I have found," he replied as Tris took her turn at the targets. Speed and accuracy were the key, and the whistle and crack of the sling echoed in the bush clad valley. "I have mastered no other weapon," he continued when her series of throws had ended. "I am not meant to be a warrior I think."

"I see that," said Tris. "How could you be a wizard and a warrior all at once anyway? I doubt it is possible. I too had the dream last night. There is nothing but goodness in your intentions. This everyone sees, but without knowing you may have it in your power to do much that is useful."

"What do you suggest?" asked Kerran. "I have experimented with a number of possibilities. If I concentrate I can make things float in the air."

"Float!" exclaimed Tris. "I would like to see that, can you do it now?"

She was delighted when Kerran said he would try, he chose a rock that he could comfortably hold in his hand.

"I discovered this on the ship coming to the lands," he said.

He told her of his experiment with lifting Tolth's books. Since then he had experimented at times until he had found the limits of this power, or until he thought he had. Kerran now held two pieces of the Seacrest and was in for a surprising day. The first rock, as he concentrated on it, rose slowly from the palm of his hand.

"It will continue to rise until level at eyesight," he said.

Tris clapped in wonder as the stone rose to a level just above her head. "How long?" she asked briefly, her eyes held by the floating stone.

"So long as I concentrate," Kerran replied. "If I look away it will not fall, but I must retain the thought of it if I am unable to see it." He lowered his hand and turned to her. "It will fall as soon as I forget it." He cleared his mind and then thought of Zeta. There was no crash as there should have been when a rock hits a streambed.

"It still floats," said Tris reaching out to give the stone a push. It remained totally rigid and unmoving in the air. Nothing she did could shift it.

Kerran looked in amazement as Tris clung to the stone and lifted her own weight from the ground.

"Not expected I think," said Tris, laughing. "Make one go higher, next to this one." She hung from the stone, swinging her small body back and forth.

"I have not succeeded with two at one time," said Kerran, but the surprise at having even one stone float for so long urged him to examine the extent of his new power.

He sent another stone to hang with the first, and he was only mildly surprised when he was able to send it higher than before. Soon there were five stones of a similar size hanging in the air before and above him. Tris, with great faith in his powers, nimbly climbed amongst them, reaching up from one to the next, giggling wildly.

"More," she cried.

All he needed to do was touch a stone with his mind and it would float to any height he chose, in amazement he finally stood back and looked up at Tris who climbed easily amongst the stones, almost to the treetops. She laughed aloud and waved to the sentry who stood further up the streambed. A stunned statue of brown and green looked back at her. Kerran had to coax her down for she did not wish to leave her high perch. When she stood beside him again he was not sure how to undo what he had done, but as he thought it, so it began. The stones, which had been the last aloft were the first to return to the bed of the stream. Slowly, like a soft rain they came to rest gently amongst the other stones. The last one seemed to remain a few moments longer than the others, as though it wished to tell him something, then could not remember and sank to join the others.

"Not at all expected," Tris smiled broadly, her dark eyes twinkling with delight. "What next?" she asked, pushing, wanting to know as much as he did about these new found powers.

"I can make small things disappear, metal things," he told her.

"What about stones?" said Tris hefting a small one in her hand.

"I tried stones before but nothing happened," he replied.

"Try again," she encouraged. "Your powers have increased you say. I say for the good of all you must find out your full strengths. In aid of the land much may depend on you."

Kerran was amazed at the depth and understanding of this young woman. He had heard her tell of her hard life amongst the thieves of the Broken Lands. Always she spoke of her dead father with pride, a man who had given much time and understanding to his thoughtful and clever young daughter.

"Let us try stone," he said smiling, and she passed him a small pebble, an ideal stone for the sling. In moments, from the palm of his hand, Kerran made the stone vanish. "It has probably arrived in Manzanee's cave at another time," he said. "He passed things back to me in dreams."

"Can you bring it back by yourself?" Tris asked, more interested in Kerran's powers than the dark dream figure Kerran had told of.

Kerran concentrated, pleased to let someone else make the decisions on what he should try. As he thought the thought the stone appeared in the air before him. He had lowered his hand and the pebble floated at the exact point from which it had disappeared. He chuckled and looked sideways at Tris, who plucked the stone from the air and held it. When she let it go it fell to the ground as any normal stone should.

"I would like to see if you can manage something that is alive," she said, looking around the stream until she had found what she sought. "Perfect," she said and brought to him a small dark beetle that looked identical in shape and colour to the creatures he had found in Manzanee's cave.

He eyed the beetle, wondering if this might be a message of a sort from the Black Wizard. He held the creature in his palm for a moment and then it was gone. It had disappeared so quickly and easily that it was several moments before Kerran returned the animal to the palm of his hand. The small lumbering creature lurched across the unfamiliar surface and Kerran bent to free it amongst tufted grass nearby.

"What about me?" said Tris all of a sudden.

"No!" he said quickly and more violently than he had intended. "This is not a game we play here."

"I know that," came back her stinging reply. "If you can make a person disappear, and if that person goes to the wizard's cave, then perhaps you can take yourself there?"

The thought had not come to him before. Now, with this obvious increase of his powers, indeed it may be possible. Perhaps from any point in the land he could enter the Wizards Way. Silently he thanked Tris for this insight.

"If I can send myself I need not experiment with you," he said to her and thought he had won. He did not want to endanger his newfound friend.

"True," she said. "But if you can take others to the cave, perhaps you can send yourself and others further into the game, like these Stone Soldiers I hear about."

It somehow made sense of what he had felt for some time. Maradass had limited access to the game it seemed and had not sent human troops to attack the southern refuge. From his dreams and visions Kerran knew that in the past, humans had travelled along the Wizard Lines of the game. Yet he was fearful, should it not work it could take him and Tris to somewhere, or some time, from which they might not be able to return.

"That is why you should try it with me first," she said, knowing that her sound reasoning had won out. "You should not send yourself to begin with. As you say there may be danger, and the land does not want to lose its only free wizard just yet." She smiled at his wordless expression then continued.

"If you can send me then I am sure you can bring me back. Learn to trust yourself, who knows what other conjurer's tricks you have unfound."

"Conjurer's tricks!" he exclaimed, laughing at the same moment that his pride was nudged. "No," he said, "I fear it and I will not dare."

"Try another animal, something bigger, a rat, or a rabbit," came her exhorting reply.

"I will do it now on myself and be done with it," he said. "In the past I have tried and failed at any attempt to place myself elsewhere. I do not believe I have the power."

"Try then," said Tris defeated. "If it works for you then you must try to take me when you return."

Her hopes swung on this new reasoning and Kerran looked at her for a few moments.

"Agreed," he finally said, and after sitting on a flat stone in the streambed he concentrated, his eyes closed, willing himself to the old wizard's cave. When he opened his eyes Tris still sat before him looking at him quizzically.

"I said it may not work," said Kerran, almost relieved that the experiment had come to an end.

"Wait," said Tris as he began to rise. "Try it again with your eyes open."

"Eyes open?" he questioned her as he returned to his seat.

"When you made the other things disappear your eyes were open. Here," she said passing him a stone. "Make this disappear with your eyes closed."

He tried and then heard Tris laugh.

"You had best do better than that, young wizard," she said.

He opened his eyes and saw the stone still in his palm.

"Now," said Tris. "Eyes open as you did with the others."

Kerran looked at the stone for only moments and it was gone.

"Exactly," said Tris. "It is when you first blink that the disappearance happens. Bring it back now with a blink and I will observe. As I thought," she said when the stone reappeared in the air a short distance above his hand.

He took it and let it drop to the ground. "And you think I

will disappear when I blink?" he asked her incredulously.

"Yes," she beamed assuredly. "Try it and see."

"But I blink all the time and do not keep disappearing," he said with a strange smile.

"Think and then blink," she chuckled. "Concentrate on the cave and then blink."

He looked her in the eye and then concentrated on the cave of Manzanee for a brief moment, and then he blinked.

Flindas had remained by the fire as the last of the captains drifted away to their various duties and needs. Rark lay beside him, almost fully recovered, though still stiff along his back muscles. Flindas knew that he would go south with the troops of Zeta, for he wanted very much to visit his sister, if he could, to assure himself of her safety in the occupied city. He had little fear of being detected should he enter the City Amitarl, unless it was totally overrun by the enemy. For now it seemed that Maradass had chosen not to destroy the city. He played a strange game of which only he knew the rules. Flindas hoped it would remain so. There were many ways in and out of the city that did not require a gate or a pass. He had told Torian and Mantris that should the need arise he could probably get a small force of soldiers, undetected, as far as the base of the rocky buttress on which stood Castle Celisor. Dantas knew the ways as well as Flindas and a few others. Flindas knew that he would fight beside the Elbrand until the end, though he had not committed himself to the command of Torian and Mantris. He wished to remain apart and under no one's rule, and they, knowing Flindas, respected this and counted him a strong ally.

It would be some days before the army of Zeta departed to the south and Flindas rubbed his chin, knowing that his beard would be well grown by the time he needed a disguise to enter the place where he was born. He had no fear of his father, and now with the Black Army inside the city walls he knew the Governor to be a defeated man, no matter who won the war. By late afternoon Flindas had prepared his weapons, sharpening his numerous blades, taking care to replace any damaged flights on his arrows. He was resting, watching the quiet life of the camp when he saw Tris and Kerran moving quickly towards the Council fire. They were in excited conversation and hardly noticed him as they approached. When they did see him they quickly told him the important news. Kerran could now take himself, and it seemed a number of others, to the Black Wizard's cave, and possibly into the Wizards Way. Flindas listened intently as they told him of their experiments.

They had both reached the cave safely, eventually holding hands to make the contact needed. Tris had joined Kerran as they had flickered from the nearby stream bed to the dusty leaf littered cave. Kerran had not wanted to experiment further, he still felt safer to enter the game during the night, and it was yet to be seen if Tris could travel with him along the Wizard Lines. Their bodies, including clothing and weapons, had been transported complete to the cave. This had surprised Kerran most of all. Previously, only his shadow had travelled. Now perhaps his entire physical being could enter the Wizards Way and any part of the eight pointed star. That evening Tris and Kerran planned to delve further into the old magic, but they wanted a third person. Flindas looked at them dubiously.

"If you promise not to turn me into a toad or a flea I will come with you," he said.

Kerran had hoped it would be so.

Around the fire, during the evening meal Kerran told Mantris and others of the Elbrand about his newfound powers.

"Tonight I will try to take Tris and Flindas into the game," he said.

"Is it not dangerous?" asked Mantris. "What if it should fail and the three of you become lost, or locked into a place you cannot leave?"

"Without more knowledge I cannot gain knowledge," said Kerran in reply. With a thought he made one of the stones around the fire lift from its place and hang in the air. Some marvelled while others drew back startled. "Today with the help of Tris I learned many things," he said, as the stone lowered again to its place by the fire. "I must know more if I am to help in the conflict that is to come. At present I can perhaps be a messenger between Tolth and your command. Since receiving the second piece of the Seacrest I realise that my powers have grown, I must seek until I know it all."

Mantris nodded, hearing the truth in the young man's words. "Take care and return safely," he said quietly.

Kerran, Tris and Flindas stood together and held each other's hands. At the fireside Mantris watched as the three vanished before his eyes.

There was a moment of darkness as if the world had blinked. The black shadows within the cave were penetrated by the lesser darkness beyond the overhang of rock.

"A fire," said Kerran and soon a small blaze lit the cave, sending shadows to dance in dark corners. "This is the High Seat of Manzanee," he said as he stood above the lines and stones, and then Kerran frowned. "When we came here today we cleaned dust and leaves from this surface," he told Flindas. "I was surprised that so much had collected in such a short time, and now look here. The dust is as thick as the soles of my boots. This much does not collect in an afternoon."

"Time must be different here," said Tris as she trailed her fingers through the thick dust. "It is perhaps more dangerous than we thought."

"I intend to find out," said Kerran as he took from his pouch the small sculpture of Rishtan-Sta and placed it beneath the stone of Madran-Thara at the Crossroads. He now found that he could lift the stone with one hand.

"First I will try alone," he said as he sat upon Manzanee's High Seat. "I expect only my shadow to leave. My body will sit and await my return."

Kerran closed his eyes as he had done previously and spoke the ancient word. His eyes slowly opened to find that he had not left the stone High Seat of Manzanee, but in sudden fear he realised that the sun was shining from beyond the mouth of the cave. Flindas and Tris were nowhere to be seen, and when he stood, his clothes fell from him, the fabric brittle with age and turning to dust. At the eerie touch of the garments he leapt from the stone, quickly brushing it from him. His boots fell apart, the stitching crumbling to dust.

A haunting disgust shuddered through him and his hand suddenly leapt to the pouch which was no longer at his hip. Searching through the grey dust and rusted metal fastenings Kerran found the Seacrest fragments, untarnished and clean. When he drew his knife from its cracked and broken scabbard the blade snapped with rust and brittle age. Beneath the stone of the Crossroads the small silver game piece was free of any signs of age. Kerran picked it up and held the magical pieces in his hands. He felt afraid and knew that he must find Tris and Flindas again.

Replacing the sculpture he sat on the stone, barely aware of his nakedness. His body had not aged a moment whereas his garments had rotted and fallen apart. Kerran closed his eyes and spoke the word. The familiar tingling sensation passed through him but when he opened his eyes, he found that his shadow hung above the Crossroads. This was not where he wished to be. He felt panic leering at him from the darkness. Forcing it away, Kerran looked at the lands below. It was for certain the Crossroads. The roads were familiar in the half light. What was unusual was the castle which stood tall above the large town and farmlands around. The lights of the town shone upon the castle and the busy streets where people and wagons rambled along the narrow ways. Kerran then lowered his shadow to the courtyard of the castle. Here at the centre of the Crossroads he looked for signs of the ancient game. From the dark courtyard he returned to the night above having discovered nothing. Fear came rushing upon him and he returned quickly to Manzanee's cave, finding the grey dust of his garments had not changed. It was of little consolation to find that he had returned to the same time as he had left.

Discouraged he left the stone and went out into the chill air of autumn where he noticed something. The sweeping valley and hills below showed no signs of age. He even recognised individual trees he had noted in his earlier time at the cave.

"Perhaps only the cave is elsewhere in time," he said to himself and looked to the narrow ledge where he now saw the old and gnarled tree, seeming to be just as it always had.

Another thought caught him now. Perhaps he had returned

to his own time with the dust of his ancient clothing coming with him as a reminder. Then where were Flindas and Tris? Lost in some other time? Departed above? He could not think what to do, as a last resort he would leave and seek out the Army of Zeta, but first he must search for his friends.

He washed himself in the stream, the water cleansing him and easing his fears. He would find his two friends safe he believed and return them to the present time. He was worried now about the possibility of taking others into the game, and knew that he must discover its secrets alone. Kerran shook the cool water from his shivering body and realised that he had no flint or steel to make a fire. The sun dipped below the horizon as he returned to the cave, where to his surprise he saw the flicker of firelight from within, causing him to slow and peer into the darkness. A small fire burned and welcomed him into its warmth. It was not until Kerran came to stand by the fire that he saw, in the semi-darkness at the back of the cave, a mound that had not been there earlier, something lay across a flat rock which stood near the darkest corner. Kerran went towards it and had to smile as he touched, and then lifted the rabbit skin cloak and wrapped it about his shoulders. He suddenly felt no need for fear. He was being cared for, and perhaps guided in his search of discovery into the nature of the Wizards Way.

Feeling warmed by the cloak and fire Kerran returned to the Black Wizard's High Seat. With his eyes open Kerran thought himself to the time when he had left Flindas and Tris. He blinked but remained where he sat. He tried the word again with his eyes closed and his shadow hung above the Crossroads, but now in a far different time. A craggy and lustreless fortress seemed to grow from the very earth below; Kerran did not know why he was so certain that the castle below was built at the Crossroads of the Four Regions, for nothing was familiar. No roads came or went from the shadowed brooding fortress. Kerran willed his shadow upwards into the clear light of day. Upward he flew and saw that the land had changed. The river Glandrin-dar flowed far to the east but met no Sea of Shardis. The forest lay close by the castle but Kerran was certain that the dark forbidding fortress was that of Madran-Thara, the High Wizard, in a time before the shattering of the game. He did not return directly to Manzanee's High Seat, instead he faced to the east and south. The word came unspoken and as his vision cleared Kerran saw, perhaps a league further to the east, the magical light filled city which Rishtan-Sta had built with his followers. It glistened marvellously in the starlight and Kerran rejoiced in its beauty, but it surprised him that the city stood so far off. Below him there were only hills and darkness.

His shadow lowered to the summit of a sharp peak. The top had been levelled by magic and a clear surface of polished stone reflected back the pinpoints of starlight. Here, carved into the rock, Kerran saw the shape of the eight pointed star. Small rounded spheres of polished metal were used to indicate the Wizard Points, and Kerran knew that it was from this hilltop that Rishtan-Sta had shattered the game and destroyed the warring wizards, and a vast tract of land to the north, which much later had become the Sea of Shardis. Kerran turned to the south and west and the direct Wizard Line took him back to the Black Wizard's cave, and he suddenly realised that at any time, Manzanee and Rishtan-Sta could travel between their High Seats without first passing through the Crossroads. They were allies in a game which was to turn from an adventurous pastime into bitter war, the slaughter of humanity, and the final destructive compromise. The fire burned in the cave and the rabbit skin cloak remained wrapped around his shoulders. There was no sign of his friends and the night was slowly making way for dawn, a soft tinge of sunlight caressing the high clouds above.

Kerran was not sure what he should now do. Somewhere within the cave was the time where Flindas and Tris may be. He could walk into the present by leaving the cave, as they too may have done when he did not return. That is, he thought with wry humour, if any time had passed for them at all. The fact that his friends had left no message suggested to Kerran that they were still in the cave. Something must be tried, he thought, and he made his way up the pathway and swung himself on the exposed root to the ledge. When he looked back at the cave it was gone. He had almost expected this. Holding the magical pieces in his hands, Kerran thought of the cave and blinked. Kerran returned there instantly. The fire burned, and as he turned he saw Tris and Flindas looking at him intently.

"Does it not work?" asked Tris.

It came to Kerran that truly no time at all had passed since he had left his friends, and yet at least a day had come and gone elsewhere in the game, and he had travelled some thousands of years into the past. The cloak had gone to be replaced by his usual clothes. The Seacrest was in his pouch, and when he looked under the Crossroads stone the silver piece gleamed at him from the small hollow.

"It worked," he said as he turned to them. "I thought for a time I would not be able to find you."

"But you did not leave," said Flindas, coming to stand by Kerran and placing a hand on his shoulder as if to reassure himself that his young friend was truly there.

"I was gone for at least a day and a night, though no time passed here," Kerran replied.

"But what is this time we are in?" asked Tris. "It is not our own time."

Kerran went to the entrance of the cave. From above, where the small falls tumbled and sprayed, the rocks formed the narrow ledge. Kerran saw that the old tree still guarded the way, unchanged from any time that he had seen it.

"I believe we are in the present time," he said. "All we need do is leave the cave and go above to return to the army, though I do not think that will be necessary. The cave is in a different time it seems, or many different times, and I now believe it may be too dangerous to take anyone further into the game, not until I understand it more."

Tris looked disappointed but did not speak as Kerran continued.

"Perhaps in dire need I would do this but not now. It will take much time for me to know. Time runs through the Wizards Way like a thread through many needles." Kerran looked out on the forest for a time and then turned to the others. "I think we should go back now," he told them. "I see no problem with that now."

Moments after holding each other's hands they found themselves back at the council fire of the northern refuge. Mantris sat as he had before they left. Indeed all those around the fire were in the same positions. Time here had barely moved a moment.

"You were gone," said Mantris in surprise. "You disappeared for a moment and then returned. Did it not happen as it should?" He rose and came around the fire towards them.

"It worked," said Tris, and they laughed at the bemused look on the faces around them.

"It is, I feel, too dangerous for others to use yet," said Kerran speaking to the Elbrand commander. "I will spend more time with this until I understand it better. Somewhere within this game there is a greater power to be harnessed. I feel it but have not reached it yet."

Kerran stretched out on his blanket against a nearby boulder, and if anyone noticed Kerran vanish from the fireside it would have only been for a moment, but in that moment a change came on Kerran that many were to notice the following morning. Though he remained young, a sense of great age had appeared deep within his eyes.

As the days passed Kerran could be seen wandering alone amongst the forests and streams near the refuge. Tris joined him at times but she learned little of his journeys into the Wizards Way. All he would say was that his progress was slow. He played no more frivolous games with his power as he concentrated on penetrating further into the unknown. As the days passed and the time neared for their departure to the south, Kerran was seen less often. His disappearances worried the Elbrand commanders but they understood that it could be no other way.

Flight to the South

The morning of the army's departure arrived and nothing had been seen of Kerran for almost three days. In the early dawn news came from the scouts that Storm had flown south. The troops of Zeta prepared to march. If Kerran did not return soon Flindas knew that he could find the cave again. Brook and Teaker were both there to see them depart. Brook was to remain as commander of the Northern Refuge while Teaker, who had been used as a runner due to his great endurance, was now to join the southern march.

"Take care of our little friend there," said Brook to Flindas as Teaker lifted his pack to his shoulders, preparing to march. "Not that I care for his bedraggled hide but he owes me three days rations and I would like to collect it some day."

"You will never find me paying a debt I do not owe!" exclaimed Teaker over his shoulder. "Tis you who owes me and you know it!"

"Those rations will choke you," returned Brook as Teaker limped from the camp, a leg wound making it impossible now for him to continue as a runner.

He should have been on horse back but had refused, saying that his leg would cure stronger if he marched for a time. Flindas said goodbye to the captains who would remain behind, fighting on as if they were the entire army of Zeta.

"And take care of yourself," said Flindas grasping Brook's hand. "I will see you on some future battlefield and we will tell of our victories."

"Aye," said Brook. "When all is done there will be many a long tale to be told."

Flindas waved briefly to the others and marched from the hill top to join the horsemen and his mount. Tris too had elected to ride, and her dark figure could be seen holding the reins of three horses, her own, another for Flindas, and the last for Kerran who had not reappeared. Across her back Tris now carried a finely made bow of Zeta, and a pouch of arrows protruded from in front of her saddle, though she had yet to master the unusual weapon. Verardian and Leana would also ride south although the healer had been loath to leave the northern command. There were a few whose wounds would not allow them to travel, either by foot or horse. Healers would remain with them and Verardian knew that his own strengths would be needed in the Southlands. Many riders and foot soldiers had already left the camp, disappearing under the dense canopy of Dreardim as Flindas joined the others.

"Should Kerran return here, he will be brought to us," said Mantris as they prepared to ride.

Flindas was just turning his mount to follow when Kerran appeared from the forest nearby and walked slowly towards them. Flindas called to Tris who looked back, and on seeing Kerran cantered towards him, leading the other horse.

"We almost left you behind," she scolded him. "Your blanket and all else is on your saddle."

"Thank you," he said his voice soft as though lost in a dream.

He mounted slowly and joined them on the ride south. Flindas passed Kerran some camp bread and a mixture of cheese, nuts and dried fruit. It was only as he mechanically put the food to his lips that Kerran realised that he had not eaten for a very long time. He had learned much now of the nature of the Wizards Way and he knew also how Maradass had managed to enter the game himself. He almost fell from his saddle as sleep beckoned and Flindas rode beside him, very aware of his young friend's exhausted condition. Kerran looked at Flindas and in a voice strangely hoarse and dry.

"I have been gone a very long time," he said. "Have I not aged at all?"

Flindas was surprised at the question. He looked into his young friend's eyes and saw there a look of aged wisdom in the young face. Kerran looked back for a moment longer and then he began to slip from the saddle, collapsing into exhausted sleep. Flindas caught him and rode close beside the young man's mount, allowing Kerran to sleep as they rode slowly through the forest, supporting him when he was about to fall. By the end of the day Kerran could not be roused. Verardian came to his side as his young friend lay in the deepest sleep, unaffected by all around him. The healer stayed with him throughout the night and it was in the early dawn that Kerran woke and asked for water. The heavy sleep had lifted from him and he dozed gently until the smell of breakfast roused him back to the company of others. He felt weak, empty, and as he remembered his time on the Wizards Way, he remembered with an amazed sense of awe the powers of the ancient High Wizards, and the horror that it had brought on them.

When Kerran had returned to Maradass Castle he found the windowless cell empty. On the floor had lain the tattered blanket in which Tolth had slept and the scant straw which had been his bed. Kerran had then passed into other chambers, lowering his shadow to finally enter the luxurious Council chamber of the Maradass family. The memories of it remained sharp and clear in his mind now, as though scorched there. He had listened as the Evil One spoke of his plans for the future to Tolth, who had been forced to lie in chains upon the floor of the lavish chamber. He knew now what Tolth knew, that Luista had come to Zeta to betray him by leaving a child who would lead Maradass to the army of Zeta once it had reached the Southlands. On its march towards Dreardim Maradass had been able to know exactly where the force from Zeta was, because all along Mindis had been the key. There was something else that Kerran had learned which still remained sharp in his memory. Luista had been able to bring the cruel dagger to Zeta, and with it she had corrupted Davin, to his death.

The treacherous nature of Luista, known by her true name Aluist, and her connection with all of the Maradass men, had also been shown to him in his searchings. The corrupt line of Maradass had much of its evil come from this poisonous woman. Indeed she was longer lived than any member of this ancient dark family. She had been the wife of the Philosopher, and when he had died along with her son Zard, the creator of Crysta-Sha, she had seduced her mad son Darss to produce the twins required for the family to survive. When Zard the Black Knight had been killed by Leana in Dreardim Forest, she had again coupled with her son, the Evil One, the man who now commanded the family Maradass. She was two thousand years old and had retained without flaw her great and commanding beauty.

Kerran's shadow had hung in the ornate room and watched. The twisted dark figure of Maradass sat as though crumpled in a high ornate seat upon a tall dais, surrounded by treasures and many wondrous things. Zard, divested of his dark armour, stood brooding by the large log fire, while Luista sat nearby and nursed the baby Darss. On another seat opposite her sat Mindis, looking as he had always done, his expression blank and unknowing. On the stone floor at the foot of the dais was Tolth, still in chains, and forced to lie prone while two guards stood against the wall nearby. Kerran remembered the overpowering fear of his position. He felt as though Maradass need only look up to perceive his shadow, but it was not so, it seemed. Maradass and the others had known nothing of his presence, and Kerran had begun to listen to the Evil One's words. The memories came. He could hear and see it all clearly once again.

Maradass was speaking."...and you believe that your army can still win? You are a fool Amitarl. You are a slave to your ideas of compassion. One cannot hold power and use it, without burning." He paused, a dark look of triumph on his face. "I feel the power of it," said Maradass victoriously and held the two pieces of the Seacrest in his hands. "Nothing will stand in my way now, not Amitarl or your boy wizard. It is too late for him. He will not learn what I have learned before I seek him out and crush him."

"And what have you learned?" came the voice of Tolth from the floor.

"Quiet!" screamed Maradass. "I said you would not speak and you will not! Speak again and you lose your tongue."

At a signal from Maradass one of the guards struck Tolth a blow across his back with the shaft of his spear.Tolth cried out in pain.

"Why do you beat him?" said Zard from his place by the fire. "He can do you no harm, and if you allowed him to speak we may learn things to our advantage."

"You dare to question me?" screamed Maradass turning to his tall and powerful son. "You, who are but a child, new born but a short while passed, you know nothing of these times and what has gone before. You will not question me. I hold all power. If I commanded you to leap from the highest tower, you would."

Kerran could see that Zard held down rage that boiled within him. He said not a word, and turned quickly back to look into the fire.

"Do not provoke the boy," said Luista, her smooth beautiful voice seeking to calm the father of her children.

"Provoke! Provoke!" screamed Maradass, storming down from his seat towards the fire. "I will provoke," he cried as he stood before Luista and seemed about to strike her.

She looked at him calmly, almost with pity, and Maradass slowly lowered his arms.

"I could have *you* thrown from the tower," he said quietly to Luista. "You are mortal and would not survive the fall, as would our dark son there."

Zard turned to look at his father, a mysterious look on his face, his eyes held something close to hatred for his powerful father.

"It is you dear wife and mother who is the truly evil one," growled Maradass, unable to meet his son's gaze.

Luista laughed then, a lovely sound in the oppressive air of the chamber. "Come, my loving husband and son," she said. "You know that you would not do me harm. Who would truly love you if I did not? Your wife and mother, a man could ask for no truer ally."

Maradass stood for a time glaring at Luista then turned back to his seat. As he walked by Tolth, he kicked the old man's elbow as though it was a piece of rubbish that lay in his path. Tolth suffered this new hurt in silence. For the first time Kerran saw that Tolth was not only chained at the wrists and ankles. A narrow hoop of steel encircled his body at the waist, holding him to the floor. Maradass sat in silence again, brooding over the two fragments of his beloved Seacrest.

"You asked what I have learned," he said now to Tolth, as though the period of rage had not happened. "I have learned much of the old wizards' power. You had no idea that all these books still existed." He waved his arms towards a large collection of ancient books and scrolls that stood in high bookshelves against one wall. "And there are places other than books where old magic and spells of wizardry can be found, if only you know where to look." At these words Maradass looked directly at Kerran's shadow.

Kerran suddenly realised that Maradass knew of his presence there in the castle, the play had been for Kerran's benefit also.

"Yes, Chelasta," snarled Maradass. "I hear you. Your thoughts can be seen. Study what you will, go where you please, but you cannot defeat me. For a thousand years I have waited to become Maradass, to hold this power, and I thank Amitarl for this. My father, the Mad One, would have retained the glory had not Zard unexpectedly died by the girl's hand. What a delightful surprise that was when I heard. There will be no peace!" he suddenly screamed hysterically.

A bolt of blue fire lashed out towards Kerran's shadow but without a thought or movement, Kerran found himself flung from the blast and into yet another part of the game. Kerran's memory had turned away and followed this other path. He had travelled into the past and had seen all that had happened at the Crossroads on that fateful day when Maradass and Amitarl had divided the Seacrest. When the blow had been struck the image of Rishtan-Sta had come to all those present. The White Wizard told them that he had foreseen this act, revealed to him in the past, and knew that it must be so to avoid the horrors that would soon come should Ma-Zurin-Bidar remain whole. Rishtan-Sta told the four bearers of the fragments that they could each live for many years, using the powers which they now held.

"Because nothing will last forever, so it must be that you will all eventually depart this life." Kerran could hear the words of the ancient White Wizard inside his mind. "Narinda, though your future is long, the piece you carry will take you into the Past. Your way leads there and you will follow one who has gone before you. Long life to you and your brother's daughter, for it is she who will carry the piece after you pass. Barthol, it is for you to look into the Future and your way is the most difficult. You will live long, as will your children. The deed here today is well done, though it was best that the Seacrest should never have been found again. None, not even a High Wizard, could hold Ma-Zurin-Bidar and not be burnt and overcome by its power."

In the face of Barthol Amitarl, Kerran had seen the likeness of his old friend Tolth. Maradass the Philosopher had been a tall dark man with robes of night blue, and beside him had stood the lovely Aluist. Their two young sons, Zard and Darss had stood nearby.

"I will not accept long life if my family cannot be with me," said the Philosopher as he held his wife's hand.

He pleaded with the vision of Rishtan-Sta for the immortality of all his family. Finally Rishtan-Sta had spoken, and sealed the fate of the Maradass family.

"Immortality is not possible," the shimmering white vision had told them. "You are a kind and benevolent leader and this I will grant you. Zard will carry the piece that governs Life. Should he choose to be so he could be the mightiest warrior ever known, and though armies might stand against him, they will not conquer him. Only in battle against another solitary opponent can he be overcome, and if he should die he will then return as the firstborn son of his younger brother."

"To you Maradass the Philosopher goes the piece which governs Death. You will never die by another's hand, or by long life. Only should Zard your firstborn be overcome in combat will you too succumb to mortality. At sunset of the following new moon day you will die your first death, but you also shall return as the younger of the twin sons born to your younger son Darss. What memories you may retain of your past life will depend on your own unknown strengths. Darss, your youngest son will outlive you all and become the new head of the Maradass family."

"And what of Aluist?" the Philosopher had cried to the vision. "I cannot live without her. If she should die I too would wish to die, must I kill my own eldest son to end my suffering. A long life without her would be a life forlorn and empty."

"Aluist will be with you until you should die," the voice of Rishtan-Sta had spoken. "So long as she is joined in natural marriage to the head of the Maradass family she will live as long as he, and will not age."

And so the dreadful and flawed pact with the Maradass family had been sealed. None would die but that Zard should die. Kerran had heard the young man's words as the vision of Rishtan-Sta had departed the Crossroads.

"I will not die in combat," he had said. "Not because I will be a great warrior, but because I will be a great leader, and bring only joy to my people. Peace will prevail and none will wish me harm."

And so it had been for a thousand years. The Regions grew under the two families and all was well. There was but one darkness which fell upon the Maradass family. Darss, the younger son of the Philosopher had aged slowly and then had gone mad, a calculating madness which finally forced the family to lock their son and brother into the high tower of Maradass Castle. Few had visited him over the centuries other than family and a few unsuccessful healers.

Kerran's thoughts wandered, but then he pulled his mind back. He knew that he must remember all that he had learned.

What he had seen had given answers to many of the questions of those who sought to find the ways of Maradass. He saw the scene again before his closed eyelids. Zard, the builder of Crysta-Sha, had gone to visit his family at Mendan-Maradass. When he had climbed up to visit his brother in the tower, Darss had at first been rational and calm, but as their time together had increased he had grown agitated and bitter. His peaceful brother Zard wished to calm him and was hit about the head by his insane brother, who cried out that he would kill him.

"I cannot die except in combat," Zard had spoken. "And I do not intend to fight you."

"You think this is not combat?" Darss had questioned, and slapped his brother hard in the face.

For the first time in a thousand years Zard grew angry and leapt at his brother, wishing to strike him. This was what Darss had been waiting for. As his brother's hands came around his bared throat, Darss had taken the long sharpened piece of wood, broken carefully from one of the chairs in the room, and stabbed his brother to the heart.

"Now the Mad One will be Maradass," he had said with glee.

His brother's eyes clung to his own in horror as Darss held his brother in a gloating last embrace. When the Philosopher heard of his eldest son's death, he knew that he and Aluist must die too. He would return he knew as would Zard, though he knew not what may be the true result. His beloved wife he mourned, for she must surely die and be no more. Little did he know the lengths to which Aluist would go to remain amongst the living. At sundown of the following new moon day, as the Philosopher began to feel his life ebbing away, she had left him and had gone to her mad son with whom she joined. She lived on to bear him two sons. Zard, who was to grow quickly into a man and be corrupted by the Mad One, and Darss, the younger son, who would age slowly but inexorably to become the Evil One. Aluist would join with this one whom she called son and husband at the death of the Zard the Black Knight, and once more would bear twin sons. The corruption of the family was sealed, and evil stalked the lands in the name of Maradass.

Deeper into the far distant past went the thoughts and

memories of the young Chelasta. In his time within the Wizards Way Kerran had also learned of the most ancient of histories, but only a little of the story of the wizards before they came to the Great Southern Land. Rishtan-Sta had seen in it a vision. The ancient homelands of the wizards were poisoned and dying when he had led the great journey of wizards and fair skinned people into the southern oceans. They had left behind many who would not go, people and wizards who feared the unknown even more than the evils which had befallen their own lands. Though Kerran had learned much from Tolth on the history of the wizards, he now understood it in greater detail, for Tolth could never have known it all.

With Rishtan-Sta had gone five High Wizards and fourteen of lesser stature and power. After a voyage of many storms and other hardships, the people and wizards had reached the land promised by Rishtan-Sta. A lush green coast and many islands greeted them. There were black people in the land and at first they were afraid of the white skinned people who landed upon their shores. They were fearful that the new people would take their land. The wizards were seen to be all powerful and could do as they pleased, but for a long time the wizards did not wish to harm the dark inhabitants of the land, and soon the two peoples joined each other for the mutual good of all.

The lot of all people was improved by the workings of the wizards. Cities were built of light and air, and the land gave forth an abundance under the guidance of the Magic Ones. Later, Rishtan-Sta had come one day to the ancient forest, for he alone of the High Wizards cared for the overgrown mysterious place. Somewhere within its bounds there was power. Rishtan-Sta had known this and eventually he had met Manzanee. The Black Wizard had been in the lands long before even his black brothers and sisters had entered the vastness from the north. Where Manzanee had found his unique powers Kerran had not learned.

Many centuries passed in harmony. Manzanee and Rishtan-Sta became great friends, their minds flowing together and growing stronger from the experience of each other's wisdom. Together they discovered further powers which had lain dormant within their minds, and as they found this knowledge, so it was given to all. Above in the night sky of the Southern Land hung the constellation of the Seven Sorcerers. The very brightest star of the seven, often seen in daylight, had been a source of wonder to Rishtan-Sta. In delving into the meaning of this most brilliant of all stars, he discovered the great powers which lay hidden within it. For an age he sought its magical uses, eventually bringing forth its great gifts to the land. He had connected and joined the powers within the constellation, and all of the stars combined, to help him discover the secrets that led to the beginning of the Wizards Way.

The High Wizards followed Rishtan-Sta's vision and had built their High Seats across the land as he instructed, the fourteen Lesser Wizards forming the points of an eight armed star. The energy drawn from these patterns of power formed the Wizard Lines, connecting all in mind. Across a thousand leagues, from the Magical Isles to the most western plains, wizards communicated at will. From the Isles of Tarsa in the Deep South, to the lush sultry forests of the north, all had truly become one people. The lands flourished, and the lot of one was the lot of all.

Though High Wizards would often marry, Kerran believed that they could never have children. Nowhere in the histories or in the Wizards Way had he come upon a child of a High Wizard. Of the fourteen there were a number who had offspring although it was a very rare thing. Most of these children inherited some limited powers but were never as powerful as their magical parent.

Cranda-Sta, the Red, was a most powerful High Wizard, a worker in metal and fire. His name translated into the common tongue as Dark Fire Star. Drinda-mira-Sta, the Blue Wizard, was his wife, and later founded an evil sisterhood on the ghostly isle of Marl. Her name translated as Evening Star. Her sister was Orlandi, the Yellow Wizard, of whom Kerran had learned almost nothing as some power greater than his own had held out his probing shadow from her High Seat, which was later to become the Closed Monastery. She took her name from the moon and had helped build the fleet of ships which had brought the wizards and the people to the great southern lands. She was the wife of Lardan-Mor, but unlike her husband Kerran had seen her play no part in the wars that were to come. All others he had seen vanquished and destroyed by the power of the Seacrest, but the fate of Orlandi, alone of the High Wizards, remained a mystery to him.

Lardan-Mor was the Green Wizard and translated as Ocean's Dark Light. Kerran had heard from Flindas and Tris of the vast caverns of bones beneath his ancient home of Shish-Tan-Vara. Though an apparently gifted and highly intelligent being he had become the first to corrupt the usage of the Wizards Way. There was one other High Wizard who came to the Southern Continent with the high sailed fleet. He was Ma-dran-Thara, the Brown Wizard, translated as Mountains of Night, a worker in stone, a delver into the earth, and a key figure in the Wizard Wars. This High Wizard, dark and mysterious, had been the one who would most encourage the wars to be continued. He stood supreme in his position at the crossroads of the game.

Much later it was Ma-dran-Thara who discovered the power within the earth which began the game. Previously the Wizard Lines could only be truly travelled by the wizards; it had now become possible for people to pass along the Lines as well. By travelling through the earth itself, and becoming one with the rock and stone which was their own true element, the people of the land joined in the game willingly. Manzanee warned Rishtan-Sta that the earth should not be used in such a way, but when all knowledge was given to the people and other wizards, there were none who did not wish to use the newfound magic. And so it became a time of wonderful adventure, which developed slowly into a vast and intricate game, the rules of which Kerran knew he had only just glimpsed. He did not know how or why Cranda-Sta had killed the Lesser Wizards, Pelan and Narta. It had happened during the play of the game, and suddenly war had raged amongst the High Wizards, and those of the Lesser Wizards who followed them. Ma-dran-Thara whose High Seat was placed at the very centre of the Wizards Way fought on no one's side, but allowed all to pass through the game, and so allowed the carnage to continue. All had to pay his tolls to pass and he reaped great profits of power for in truth he was the most covetous and darkest of all the High Ones.

The High Wizards could never die by accident, and they also knew that they could not kill another High Wizard, because anyone, wizard or not, would die themselves should they strike a death blow to a High Wizard. Also, if a plot was to be successful to kill a High Wizard, all those involved would also die. It was a thing that was never considered by any of the High Wizards, except Rishtan-Sta.

The wizards began to use the people of the lands to wage their war, binding them in spells to do their bidding. Some of the Lesser Wizards died in the conflict as did many people forced to fight against their will. Rishtan-Sta called for peace but none would hear him, and he could not use his benevolent powers against the other wizard's armies. He could not stop the carnage and his city of Light became the only beacon of hope in an age of grief and fear.

The black people, those that could, left the eastern land and disappeared into the vastness of the west. Rishtan-Sta and Manzanee saw the once fruitful country rent and torn in blasting wars of fearful weapons and magical powers. Over many centuries the lush northlands became a broken waste, poisoned by the destructive battles. To the west the wide fertile plains turned to desert, while in the south, where once had been a golden coastline and an endless blue ocean, now was a vast place of advancing ice. Each year the cold encroached more upon the lands, the fire of the Wizard's Wars doing nothing to slow its inexorable march to the north.

In the east, on the Magical Isles, Cranda-Sta held sway and none could attack and succeed over his mighty powers. It was Rishtan-Sta, who by a clever ruse had drawn the Red Wizard from his home to the Isle of Marl, and then the White Wizard had taken Zeta, but not by force, and though Cranda-Sta fought bitterly to regain his High Seat, Rishtan-Sta held firm and none could overthrow his magic.

Zeta had remained a place of peace and sanctuary while the western lands burned. Many of Rishtan-Sta's followers came there and found tranquillity on the Green Isles. Others remained at the High Seat of the White Wizard on the mainland and tried to bring peace and healing to the battle torn lands. Knowing that they could not kill each other, the High Wizards began to change the nature of the wars they waged. The slaughter became no less, but the wizards themselves had turned it back into an intricate game of pleasure. They were warped by the powers they commanded and cared not for humanity or thoughts of peace. Where before the Wizards Way had been like a most elaborate variation of a children's game, where, *you run and hide and I will come looking*. Now it had become the most brutal game of all, with much of humanity inextricably drawn into its violence and inevitable outcome.

Rishtan-Sta and Manzanee pleaded with the others but the four High Wizards would not be counselled. Instead they turned all of their combined forces against the Black and White Wizards. Dinismar and Arbis, both the followers of Rishtan-Sta, were captured while using the game to ease the suffering of others. They died at the hands of the High Wizards. The shining city of Rishtan-Sta had then come under siege, and it was only his superior powers of peace, and those of Manzanee, which were able to hold the other High Wizards at bay, until all of the White Wizard's followers had left the City of Light and sailed forever into the east. Rishtan-Sta and Manzanee remained on the Isles of Zeta and on the mountain side where Cranda-Sta had made his High Seat, and in the ocean itself, they formed Ma-Zurin-Bidar, the Wizard's Bane, the talisman which held Life and Death, Future and Past within its binding spells.

Alone Rishtan-Sta and Manzanee returned to the tortured lands. While the Black Wizard had gone back to the ancient forest, protected there by a magic older than his own, Rishtan-Sta had entered the Wizards Way, in search of allies and any that should be saved. He held great protection and none were aware of his presence as he slowly moved along the arms of the eight pointed star. He found Trontar, a Lesser Wizard, who had never entered the game and was no enemy to the lands or its people. Trontar was warned by Rishtan-Sta about the coming time of cataclysm. With a scribe to keep the records and ancient history alive for those who would come later, the one called the Follower was given powers to survive the conflict to come.

Rishtan-Sta had at the very end of his travels arrived at the Wizard Seat of Chel-a-Sta, who was also one who had not joined the conflict. This quiet and retiring wizard had always lived within the southern bounds of the forest, desiring only to observe the passing of nature, and the seasons to run as they should. Kerran knew that much mystery still surrounded his ancient ancestor. All was not revealed and Kerran felt that one day he must find the true answers to his ancestor's history. Chel-a-Sta too was given the knowledge to survive the coming time, a great upheaval when the game would be broken.

Rishtan-Sta had returned then to his own High Seat, a high place within sight of his once magnificent city. His presence was felt then by all within the game and the wizards were drawn to him. Rishtan-Sta called one last time on all wizards to end their struggle, or face their own destruction. They laughed and continued to throw their armies into battle about the beleaguered hilltop, cries of war on their lips. Cutting swathes of fire reached towards Rishtan-Sta but were dispersed. War machines and creatures, human and not so human, were forced into the dreadful fire. Then Rishtan-Sta had called on Ma-Zurin-Bidar, and with a final terrible spell had burst through the very fabric of the game.

The wizards on the battlefield and elsewhere throughout the eight pointed star, felt the wrath of the White Wizard and were destroyed. From the hand of Rishtan-Sta, which held aloft the Wizard's Bane, there came a final high death spell which tore the lands asunder. The earth where the armies had fought, erupted and burned, and none lived to tell of it. Rishtan-Sta had died with the others and the Way of the Wizards was at an end. Only in dreams and in visions would he come at times, though few would ever know of him. Only when the Seacrest had regrettably been fished up from the ocean did some of his memory and wizardry return to the lands.

Manzanee, with much of his own powers tied into the

wizard's talisman, could not survive in the lands, and with a power known only to him the Black Wizard had been able to leap into time. Never again could he exist 'now', and he would forever remain nowhere at all and yet in all places at once, coming at will into past or future, observing, and playing his own mysterious games.

Kerran knew that the Wizards Way had been shattered and lost for many thousands of years. It had brought destruction upon the lands and he did not know if he should again bring its knowledge to the people. Maradass used it in a way that did not come from great understanding, and Kerran feared that should Maradass use the game with more care he would gain knowledge that best remained hidden. Just one thing seemed to be gained by Kerran's time amongst the Family Maradass, and that was the apparent rebellious nature of Zard, who seemed to truly despise his father.

Kerran did not know how to judge the time that he had been gone. In this present world it had been but a few days, and yet he had seen an age come and pass within the game. He had seen the history of the wizards, and Kerran now knew much of the inner character of all but one. Orlandi would remain a mystery to him. He saw her shining reflective face but her history was closed. Her story for some reason unknown. Also Manzanee had rarely appeared in his visions within the Wizards Way. The Black Wizard was an enigma, a ghost travelling in other times.

Quietly, Kerran sat by the fire as they camped each night. He would tell others very little of his experiences in the game. His mind was full of ancient memories and it was not yet time. For several days, as the army of Zeta had moved south through the forest, Kerran had spoken little and recovered slowly. He felt weak and constantly hungry, as though the time in the game had not filled some of his bodily needs, and food was one thing that had been missing.

Bitter winds and rain lashed the moving army as they hunched low against the harsh late autumn storms. Eventually the forest had been left behind and for expediency they had taken to the South Road. Days passed and the army of Zeta met little resistance. The road was not a place where the armies of

Maradass lay in camp. One day Kerran looked ahead at the distant mountains. He knew them from the earlier march westward to the forest. They were called the Giant's Pillars, and it was a high buttressed plateau, carved as though by huge sculptor's hands into many gigantic near-likenesses of beasts and humans. As the silent lightning flickered on the high places, Kerran could see the many columns and pillars of this strange land. The road he knew, led almost directly through the hills without much of a climb. Only at one point was there a narrow pass to be scaled. Scouts were spread throughout the Giant's Pillars and there had been no word as yet of any Black Forces in the lands ahead, while from the Crossroads came word of the continuing battle.

It was at their evening camp that news came of a large movement of horse soldiers through the Crossroads three days before. These troops had travelled south on the City High Road and were numbered at three thousand. A large mounted force was also reported to be gathered at the meeting of the City and Glandrin High Roads.

"I think that we are expected," said Torian as they ate their evening meal around the small fire.

"Torian and I have spoken," said Mantris, leaning forward and pushing a small branch further into the fire. "If we turn back we are cut off from the coast and our supplies. It would be hard to support the army in the forest all winter. We have agreed that we will push on to the refuge. It is almost certain that we can win our way through in battle, though at what cost none can say. Once through these Giant's Pillars, and before we reach Crysta-Sha, we will leave the road and keep in the southern foot hills. It may be possible to avoid the Black Army, but it is difficult to see how."

"We will win through," said Torian with a powerful certainty, as others of the captains nodded and murmured their agreement.

"I am surprised that they have not sent a large force of foot soldiers against us," said Flindas as he studied the map before him. "It would be too late now for them to cut us off from the south. How is it that Maradass still seems to know our whereabouts and yet does not push harder against us?"

"I think I may know," said Kerran speaking for the first time since they had camped. It took an effort for him to bring the words forth. "Without Mindis with us I think that Maradass can still sense our presence when our army is on, or has crossed one of the Wizard Lines. A few days ago we would have passed through the Circle Line." Kerran pointed at his own copy of the map which showed the various lines of the Wizards Way drawn over it.

"I see what you mean," said Mantris as he crouched beside Kerran and studied the map. "If that is so, and Maradass knows when we cross one of these lines, then we must certainly give away our southern position when we cross this line." Mantris pointed at the eastern line of the most southerly arm of the star. "The refuge is beyond it," he said. "Towards the coast Dantas has told us."

"Let us hope that the army of Maradass does not like the cold," said Torian.Flindas remained silent, the mention of his old teacher's name taking him back through the years. Once again he saw the face of the man who had taught him all he could of the warrior arts. Flindas had yet to meet the old Elbrand captain since returning to the Regions, though word came constantly from the Southlands of the gathering resistance to the Black Army, mostly the work of Dantas and his close followers. Mantris marked a spot on Kerran's map where the refuge lay, then turned to the young man whom all were beginning to call wizard.

"When we cross the Wizard Line," said the commander. "We must know where it is. If possible we must try and throw Maradass off our scent."

"I know something of the southern hills," said Flindas. "It is not such an inhospitable place as you may believe. There are many hardy folk who live there, high in the foothills of the Ice Mountains. I have friends there. They could not feed an army, but would lead us by the easiest paths. If the snows come early it will be hard on the horses, as well as the troops."

"It is a chance we must take," said Torian. "Once we are beyond the Giant's Pillars there can be no turning back. The hills will be our protection. The refuge is still twenty days from here, even without the Black Army to contend with."

The army of Zeta continued their march in the early light of dawn. A mist covered the lands and the silent troops moved as ghosts through the soft damp haze. News came from the east. The mounted force of Maradass, now perhaps ten thousand in all, had ridden the Glandrin Highroad and by now would be approaching Crysta-Sha, there was now little chance that a battle could be avoided before the green and brown troops reached the refuge. The towering pinnacles of the Giant's Pillars loomed ominously above the mist and the army moved swiftly. As soldiers tired they would take to the saddle of one who was rested.

The road was wide and wound gently through the strange forbidding hills. A soft drizzle fell, finally obscuring the heights above. By nightfall they were well within the Pillars and the army camped, spread out along the Highroad. Having pressed hard all day they ate without fires then eased their tired bodies into sleep. At the war Council that night it was learned that the way before them was held by the mounted enemy.

"The choices are now few," said Mantris. "We retreat and take our chances with the winter to come, or we meet the Black Army and win through to the south."

"There are no other options that I can see but to go on," said Torian. "I do not care to freeze and starve, and let Maradass have his will against the Regions during the winter. We will meet his horse troops and they will fall."

There was no dissent amongst those that heard his words and the meeting soon came to an end.

Rain began to fall steadily during the night and in the cold foggy dawn the army of Zeta returned to the road. By day's end they were within sight of the plains beyond the Giants Pillars. Scouts had reported that the troops of Maradass were camped beyond the last of the foot hills to the east, while Marauders had been seen scouring the slopes to the south.

"They anticipate us," said Mantris to Flindas as they rode together into the darkening gloom of a late autumn storm. "Tonight we will rest and tomorrow some will sadly die.

I wonder sometimes if we can make any change here at all. Maradass can throw many thousands against us and yet deplete his forces so little. To lose a single soldier is for us a disaster."

"It may prove to our advantage that Maradass faces us with horse troops," replied Flindas. "War horses are one thing he does not seem to have in plenty."

"Those have been my thoughts also," replied the army commander. "Our troops are trained well. Each will attempt to gather in a mount as its rider falls, though I believe the black horsemen will be more wary now. Word of our first victory will have made them realise the skill of our foot soldiers."

Flindas turned in the saddle and looked back at the slumped swaying figure behind him. Kerran seemed lost in a dream. "We must protect Kerran," he said turning to Mantris.

"He will be saved though all else perish," replied Mantris. "He has come in a time of great need. It is by no accident that a wizard should come to us now, albeit a young man unskilled in the ancient arts of his calling."

The dawn came slowly to the eastern sky. Rain fell intermittently, the grey oppressive clouds foreboding of war. As the army continued its forward march the high plateau was left behind. The road followed a last small ridge, until far below on the plains the Black Army could be seen spread across the open land, the force dissected by the Highroad.

"We will let them come to us," called Torian as he turned from the road, leading the army along another ridge which the scouts had followed to the south.

A way was being sought that would keep them beyond the reach of the horse troops for as long as possible. As the day passed the black horsemen were seen to split in two. Half of their number rode to the point on the Highroad where the army of Zeta had left the easterly way. These were now following some leagues behind. At certain strategic points archers of Zeta were left to slow the horse troop's advance. Though not many were spared, only where a few could hold for a time against the greater force, and not be overrun.

The other black horse troops had turned south and now rode parallel with the force of Zeta across the distant plains.

At times, when reaching some high point, they could be seen on the dim edge of sight, a dark mass moving more easily than those who passed through the higher country. Marauders kept a constant watch on the green and brown army but never came within bowshot. Scouts had reported that ahead lay a league or more of open ground and it could not be avoided. A towering pillar, placed there absently by a giant's hand, gave the troops of Maradass the battlefield they would be seeking. From the rear came word that the pursuing horse troops were no more than half a league behind, coming on as fast as the terrain allowed.

The troops of Zeta increased their speed, those on foot striding hard and often breaking into a slow run. It was not a rout, but a calculation. The green and brown army would not tire easily, but if the choice was exhaustion or battle, they would turn and face the enemy. Ahead could be seen the high buttress which would force them on to the plains. The horse troops closed from behind and were keeping pace, spread as wide as they could just beyond bowshot. Torian and Mantris rode with several of the captains, speaking rapidly.

"We cannot outrun them," Mantris said. "We must choose our ground here before we reach the open place."

"I disagree," said Torian. "We must push on and meet them in the open. If we remain on high ground they will surround us."

"But open battle on the plain could spell disaster," said Mantris.

"We must do it sometime," countered Torian. "Why not now? The black troops are spread behind us and we cannot fight on two fronts. We must break through those ahead. There is only a league of open plain to cross and then we rejoin the hills. Let us fight with the possibility of safety at our backs." He glanced at the towering rock pillar ahead. "Beyond is safety. To fight here is to court death."

Mantris looked at his dear friend and fellow commander. "I hear your words and understand your thoughts," he said. "I agree to go forward but I fear for our army, though we win a great victory here today the cost may be hard to bear."

They came to the last hill above the sloping plain where the horse troops of Maradass prepared to meet them. Those behind pressed forward, eager for the battle, their evil standards flying on the breeze. For a short time the army of Zeta paused. those on foot secured their packs to the horses of those that would ride. Swords were loosened in their scabbards and bows were strung, while from amongst the horsemen gathered about Kerran the standard of Amitarl was raised. The white hawk on the green field waved defiantly on the wind, and brought a great rumbling cheer from all the army of Zeta. Flindas looked above and saw Storm circling against the grey clouds.

Around the standard were gathered many of the mounted Elbrand. Here also were Verardian and Leana to represent Amitarl. Kerran and Tris also rode within this protective shield of horse troops. Flindas left them in safekeeping, and having passed his mount to another, he and Rark moved to the outer perimeter. The mountain dog had recovered well from his wounds, and though Flindas wished to protect his friend from danger the great dog seemed to know that battle was soon to begin and he would not leave the side of his friend. The march began and the army of Zeta spread wider, flanked by the remainder of their horse troops. The words of a defiant battle song began to rise from some of the green and brown warriors, and it was soon taken up by many as they marched deliberately towards the enemy on the open land below. They were on the flat when a horn blast from the Black Army ahead was answered by those gathered on the hillsides. As one the two forces of Maradass broke into a gallop. The pounding of their hooves could be felt through the earth.

Flindas stood amongst the forward ranks, all of whom now awaited the first charge, arrows notched to bows. He began to make out the individual horsemen but he would not release his shaft until he was sure of his mark. The horses were precious and so too were his arrows. The archers of Zeta waited until the black horsemen were no more than thirty paces from their line, then without command or word, the bowstrings sang and the long straight shafts from the Green Isles were sent on their deadly journey. As though an invisible scythe reaped a terrible harvest, the first line of black riders screamed and toppled from their saddles. Few arrows did not find their mark. As the first wave fell their horses scattered in fear as those behind broke through and stormed down upon the army of green and brown warriors. Flindas loosed two more arrows before the main crush of horsemen were upon them. From the rear the other force of Maradass charged from the low hills. They were met by the same flights of death before their lances and swords were amongst their foe.

Flindas saw the intent of the first rider to reach him, the man's lance poised high in his throwing arm as his mount galloped down upon the tall unarmoured warrior. Easy prey, the man must have thought, and he probably did not even see the throw which sent the heavy knife deep into his chest. Flindas had no time to catch the battle crazed horse, as others of the dark riders rushed down upon him. It was desperate, reflex fighting, and he sent a silent word of gratitude to Dantas as instinct took over. The battle formed on all fronts. The army of Maradass charging time and again, heedless of their losses. The horse troops of Zeta replied with their own attacks, forcing their desperate way to the south. Slowly the green and brown army began to make their way against the waves of black riders, many leaping to an empty saddle, the white hawk standard held high as though an axle of a great moving wheel.

Mantris rode at the southern most point of the army. Twice his horse died beneath him pierced by black lances, and twice he battled for his life and regained another saddle. Torian fought in the rear on foot and held his troops against the great press of horsemen from behind. His high battle cry anchored the line as his mighty sword dealt death until none would come nigh the savage red bearded warrior. Flindas had spent all of his arrows and throwing knives. Only his sword stood between him and death. Once when he was sure that the end had come, Rark had leapt to his aid, tearing at the horsemen who had surrounded his friend. Flindas continued to battle his way up the slight rise, Rark beside him howling his own death cry. In the last furious dash up the low hills to safety some of the rearguard were caught. Many died on the lower slopes in protection of their comrades, and the warriors of Zeta wept openly at having to leave so many of their friends on the red stained earth. Amongst the fallen lay their most fearless of commanders. Torian would never again see the tall mountains of Zeta which he had loved so much, for a black spear had pierced his heart and ended his noble life.

Kerran lay by the fire and watched as Verardian dressed yet another wounded warrior of Zeta, while far away on the plains he could see the fires of the Maradass Army glittering in the night. The army of Zeta had won through, and at no time had those about the standard been under attack. The black troops had learned at great cost the deadliness of their foe. Tris stirred beside Kerran, pushing a small log further into the fire. She felt protective towards this young wizard and had watched over him during the day. She had seen him take little notice of the battle as though absorbed in another world, and she wished to break into that world and understand it.

"Where does your mind wander?" she asked him.

Kerran lifted his heavy eyelids and spoke. "It is not yet time," his voice faltered. "I am tired. Much is clear, yet it helps me little. When I sleep I know that this exhaustion will only increase."

He lifted himself onto an elbow, finding through his fatigue that he did wish to speak a little of his further understanding of the game. As he began to tell Tris of the many wondrous places and times he had been to, his confusion seemed to drift away. He eased himself to a sitting position and began to tell her of the Way. He spoke of ancient times and the dealings of wizards.

"What of now?" she finally asked him. "What have you learned of this present time?"

Kerran sighed and peered into the fire as if he would find an answer there. "In all my time away I have learned little more of Maradass than I knew before," he told her. "Sometimes I can watch him, but after a while I know that he can sense my presence. He is silent and broods much. Perhaps of most importance is the conflict between Zard and his father. I have seen Zard now in three separate lives, first as the benevolent son of the Philosopher, then as the Mad One's black son, and now he is someone different. I believe that his heart is not totally dark. He argues with Maradass sometimes, though his father holds the power to silence him. All is not well in the Maradass household and my wish is to find a way to turn that against them."

Kerran turned now to look at Tris, though his face retained an exhausted expression, his eyes had returned to the present, away from the hollow darkness of time.

"Tell me more," she said and they talked on into the night.

When he finally slept Kerran did not enter the Way, nor did his shadow compel him to search further. For the first time in many nights his mind rested in soft forgotten dreams. The following day the gathered horse troops of Maradass came after them. The land was more broken here but the forward scouts of Zeta had picked their route well. Even at the pace of their slowest, the army of Zeta began to outdistance the horsemen of Maradass.

"Your appetite returns," said Verardian that night as he watched Kerran scooping the last dregs of soup from his bowl.

The healer, after observing Kerran during their journey south, had noticed that his young friend was again eating very little. He had also seen the deep and distant suffering in the eyes of Kerran, and though he could not know the reason he was gladdened by the young wizard's return.

"I must regain my strength," replied Kerran. "I have neglected my body in my search for answers. I need all my powers equally if I am to be useful in the times to come."

Verardian nodded and smiled. "That advice is as good as I could have given you myself," he said. "The body is the bearer of the mind and heart, each a part of the other. If one part is unhealthy then all will suffer."

Over the next few days, as their journey took them further from the clutches of Maradass, Kerran recovered. One night as they camped in a small wood by a gurgling stream, he felt ready to again enter the Way.

"I will go to Tolth," he said to those around the fire. "I do not know how soon I might return."

Even though they knew what he meant, there was a gasp from many as Kerran vanished before their eyes.

The light dimmed before Kerran's vision then he was once again in Manzanee's cave. A small fire burned and the High Seat lay covered in dust and wind blown leaves. After placing the silver sculpture beneath the stone at the Crossroads he sat for a few moments preparing himself. He had told those at the camp that he would speak with Tolth if he could, but this was only part of his intent. Kerran spoke the ancient word and his shadow entered the game. The lines of the Way flickered by quickly as it only took moments now to reach any point on the Wizards Way, only to Zeta was he still denied access. In the dead of night his shadow entered Maradass Castle. Tolth lay in the high cell of the tower and welcomed Kerran as their minds joined.

On a previous visit to Maradass Castle, Kerran had tried to take Tolth with him to Manzanee's cave, but he had not been successful. Either because Kerran was not in his true body, or because they were within the sphere of the Evil One's powers, the magic had not worked its spell. How wonderful it would have been to pluck Tolth from the very tower of Maradass Castle. Kerran felt if he were able to return in his body that perhaps he could make such a thing happen. Thoughts and possibilities had occurred to him over time and not all had yet been discarded. Finally all was told between the two minds and he bid Tolth farewell, not revealing his newly formed intention to seek out Zard.

The Maradass family and council chamber was empty, the fire glowing low in the darkness. Several doors led to other parts of the castle. Kerran chose one and passed through into a long corridor lit by a single torch. Kerran slipped sideways through the stonework and found himself in total darkness. Though many powers had been granted him, an improvement in his night vision was not one of them. He listened for a long time but not a sound came to him from the room. He realised that he could search until dawn and still miss Zard in the darkness. He finally sensed, rather than knew, that the room was empty and passed on further into the maze of chambers and corridors that was Maradass Castle.

The moon was well to the west when he found the place he sought. In the corner of a large bedchamber, lit by the moon, stood the dark armour of Zard. Kerran chose to wait. There was time now, for he felt that much of his strength had returned. He had pushed himself too hard during the past days, delving into the past for answers. To help the lands free itself from the Evil One's grip he needed to know more about the plans of Maradass and his elder son. The past was no longer so important. The first light of dawn crept through the small windows of the chamber and Kerran watched as the tall and powerful warrior woke from his slumber. Wearing a long dark robe Zard crossed the deeply carpeted floor to a washstand on which stood a bowl and pitcher of water. He was quick to wash the sleep from his eyes. Zard looked deep into the mirror for a few moments, then crossed to the heavy wooden doors and left the chamber.

Kerran followed as Zard made his way along darkened corridors until he reached the richly furnished family room. The fire now lay in ashes. The early dawn's light entering through windows high on the walls. Zard, on entering, paused and looked slowly about the chamber, and then with a grunt of satisfaction the large powerful man crossed the room to the shelves of books and scrolls. Reaching up, Zard took a large volume from the topmost shelf and walked with it to a corner behind the elevated seat of his father. A heavy draped canopy concealed a quiet space that was lit by the coming dawn. Zard sat at a table of rich dark wood and opened the book near its middle. He began to read and Kerran moved closer. This was a Zard he had not expected. The dark cold man seemed more human as he sat hunched over the book, his lips moving a little as he read the tightly worded page.

For a long time Zard did not move except to turn the leaves of the book. Occasionally he would study a page at great length, reading it over again until he understood it well. Kerran came still closer so that his shadow floated at Zard's shoulder, where he too could see the words on the page. Kerran began to read what seemed to be a history of the Maradass family, and yet it was not the same history that Kerran knew. The Philosopher was called the 'Deluded One' and Amitarl were continually shown as villains or worse. The section of the book which Zard delved into concerned the times leading up to the wars between Maradass the Mad and Amitarl.

Where does such a book come from? thought Kerran as he read further into the great lie which had been written on its pages.

The Mad One was seen to be an oppressed victim, thrown from the lands by the wicked Amitarl. A piece of the magical Seacrest had been stolen from Zard, its rightful bearer. Kerran began to understand what it must mean, Zard was reading a book which had been contrived for his eyes only, a history which Maradass, the Evil One, wished his son to believe. Kerran came to the realisation that though Maradass held all of his great power to himself, he remained in fear of his own son. If Zard was to learn the true history of the two families, Kerran wondered how it might affect the outcome of the war. Zard, the Philosopher's son had been an open, caring man, loved by his people. The black son of the Mad One had been totally evil and corrupt. Who was this new Zard? The one who sought for answers in the past? And what power did he have over his father, perhaps unrealised, that caused Maradass to deceive him?

Kerran read on for a time but the corrupt story and blatant lies repelled him and he studied instead the dark man himself. Zard continued to read for a long time and took little notice when a man entered the chamber and attended to the fire, which was soon roaring in the grate. The dark clad soldier lit a great many of the large candles around the room, then he departed, not aware that Zard sat in the alcove intently continuing his studies. The morning passed and it was much later that Zard rose from his seat, and after replacing the book on the shelf, he went to join the others of his family. They sat at a long ornately carved table in a heavily furnished dining hall. It was the midday meal and Kerran followed Zard as he walked down the length of the massive room. Maradass was not there and Kerran had been prepared to flee should the Evil One sense his shadow. Luista sat at one end of the laden table. There was so much food that it could have been a feast rather than a meal for so few. Beside Luista was the cradle where Darss slept contentedly, rocked gently by his mother's hand. A few seats away sat Mindis, dark and sallow as Kerran had remembered him. His eyes looked blankly at the table before him and yet he ate of his own accord, which he had never done on Zeta.

"Good day mother," said Zard as he joined her at the table, kissing her lightly on the offered cheek, before taking a seat opposite Mindis.

"You have been studying again," said Luista. She delicately picked up a small pastry from the many before her, and took a perfect small bite from its round crushed edge. Not a flake fell or clung to her exquisitely sensuous lips, where a knowing smile played lightly.

"I will understand," said Zard gruffly, tearing a limb from a lavishly decorated game bird, spilling the artists work across the lush red cloth. A deep anger, barely disguised, lay beneath his cold stern countenance.

"Yes," said Luista. "One day you will understand and it will probably send you mad. Accept what your father tells you. Do not gainsay him, but follow him. He is the truth. To look elsewhere is to be a fool. You are Zard the son of Maradass. You have your duty, and that is to follow your father."

"If Amitarl are so evil, how is it the old grey one speaks such truth when father allows him?" questioned Zard, his mouth full and turning to a snarl.

"They are indeed most wicked, you must believe me," said Luista, her eyes aflame now. "Look here at this son I bore to that old whoremonger." She pointed to Mindis. "I was trapped by that Amitarl beast's spells," she told him. "Taken to the debauched Isles of Zeta to be his slave until I was able to escape, and yet had to leave my son behind."

She smiled benevolently at Mindis who continued to pick slowly at his food, seeming to take no notice of the words. "And now all my dear sons are with me again," she continued.

"And the old lecher is bound in the tower. Do not believe his serpent's tongue, my son. Maradass keeps him from speaking for obvious reasons. Amitarl, should he be allowed to talk, would turn your mind. He will make you see truth in his dreadful lies. Though you are a man, you are but young in this world. Your father's power holds you in its loving embrace. He is a hard man and perhaps most hard on you, but it is only for your good. Try not to argue with him. He is so much older and has seen so much in his long and troubled life."

Zard broke in on her words. "What was it the old grey one said?" then without waiting he answered himself. "He said that the taint in our family came from both mother and father. What did he mean by that?"

"Evil words!" Luista suddenly shouted, her beautiful features torn suddenly into the mask of some wild animal. "He lies! Do not hear his words when he speaks. They will corrupt you. Rather burn in fire than believe any truth in what he says."

She had risen from the table, her anger uncontrolled. After a time she became calm again and smiled wisely at her dark son as she sat down. Kerran could see that she too was afraid of Zard, or feared that he would gain knowledge of the truth and not be a puppet to his father's plans. The new Zard was not who Maradass and Luista had expected, or needed. They both had wanted him to return as they had known him before, wicked and powerful, a tool to his new father's cunning madness. Yet here was someone who was beginning to seek the truth, a man with thoughts and feelings, and on his life hung the future of all that was Maradass. Darss was still a child. If Zard was no longer as ruthless as his previous self, he could perhaps be overpowered by some mighty warrior of Zeta. Luista knew what that would mean. Maradass would die and so would she, unable this time to keep her evil tryst with her youngest son, she would die and Darss would be left to his fate.

Luista did not wish to die. After two thousand years her beauty remained flawless, her physical strength intact, and her appetites insatiable. Maradass, who was her husband and son, had aged to the point of revulsion long before their marriage. Her private apartments were hers alone. Many could only guess at what may happen in those sumptuous dimly lit rooms. Some knew and kept their silence, daring not the murderous wrath of Luista.

All was silent for a time. Zard ate his food greedily, caring not whether he upset the dishes in his haste to feed his hunger. There was wine and he drank quickly, when he spilled a goblet of the deep red liquid Luista rose quickly, anger once again tearing at her face.

"What is this charade?" she cried, her eyes flashing at him down the table. "You act like a child. You were born with the knowledge of who you are and what is expected of you, and yet you defy me and your father." She was almost weeping in frustration, as though she truly believed her own lies. "You are the Black One returned," she said softly. "The most revered and loved leader of the last two thousand years, and have come again to rid the lands of evil. It is your destiny. Believe your father's words. Have no doubt that he speaks the truth."

Zard looked at his mother and in an insolent gesture tore another huge piece of meat from the platter and bit into it viciously. Kerran was fascinated by the scene, so much so that his shadow had drifted in close to the table. Suddenly Mindis glanced up from his plate and looked directly at him.

"Chelasta," the name came whispering from his lips.

Zard heard the word and stopped chewing at the meat. "What?" he asked, looking with eyes wide at his half-brother.

"Chelasta," the name louder this time.

Zard turned and stared with intense hatred at the air about him. Luista, clasping Darss to her breast drew back, fear in her eyes. Now Zard's hard gaze rested on Kerran's shadow. Kerran did not know what these dark brothers could see, a ripple in the air perhaps, or a faint light. Whatever it was, it brought Zard to his feet, lunging across the space between them. Kerran's shadow was quicker, in a moment he was gone from the castle of Maradass. He had not even time to form any thought before he found he had returned to Manzanee's cave. Here, the afternoon sun shone brightly beyond the entrance. There were the sounds of birds from the forest below and a feeling of safety surrounded and protected him.

The Stone Army

Kerran took leave of Manzanee's cave and to the surprise of a small group of Elbrand he suddenly appeared beside the fireplace from which he had vanished the evening before. The army had moved on, leaving these men with a spare horse should the 'young wizard' return there. Kerran was glad of the camp bread and other rations that the Elbrand carried. He ate quickly then they mounted and rode hard through the night and by the following day had rejoined the army. That evening, camped in a wooded valley, Kerran told Mantris and those around the fire of his thoughts on Zard, of how the Black One was led to believe in a false history and was not fitting into the mould of his previous self.

"I wished to enter his mind," Kerran said to the astonishment of several around the fire. "I sense that it could be a most dangerous thing, but it could benefit us much. Maradass has power over his son's mind, but if I could reveal the deceit, Zard may become impossible for Maradass to rule, or use against us."

"And if it is not so?" asked Mantris, fingers stroking his beard. "What can you see as alternatives? Perhaps it would send Zard mad, or in some way even entrap you. Can you see into these possibilities and their outcome?"

"No," replied Kerran.

"I would not choose that you do this thing," said Mantris looking across the fire into the young man's eyes. "Only if Tolth agrees should you do more than observe. It is not my place to tell you how to use your powers, but it is my advice none the less. I am responsible in many ways for all those around me. I fear that your venture may bring the wrath of Maradass down upon us with greater force. The Evil One has been enjoying his war so far. He plays it as a game in which he is prepared to lose many pieces. Should you turn his son against him I fear that he will attempt to crush us quickly. I may be astray in my thoughts on this but it is said that I am a cautious man."

There was a slight turning of heads, and a few smiles amongst the captains.

"Torian and I were perhaps a perfect balance as leaders," continued the commander. "He fired my cautiousness, while I tempered his impetuousness."

Mantris looked sadly into the fire, he was not going to forget nor stop missing his friend. "Do as you think you must," he finally said. "Tolth will counsel you far better than I."

Tris was fascinated by what Kerran had told them and sought him out after the meeting had ended.

"When will you go?" she asked, sitting down beside him and wrapping her blanket about her shoulders.

"Soon," he replied. "Not tonight. Each time I enter the game it drains part of me. This will be a long war they say. I will go to Tolth soon and tell him of my plan. I fear it but feel compelled to try. I do not know how Maradass could harm my shadow, but I cannot be sure that I am safe, so until it should happen I will not know."

"You did not tell all at the meeting, I think," said Tris. Her words were not a question. She had seen untold thoughts behind Kerran's words.

"How is it you know me so well?" he spoke with mock anger.

She gave him a careful knowing look and then burst into laughter at his gruff expression.

"It is plain for all to see who care to look," she told him. "All your thoughts and feelings are shown in your eyes and voice. You cannot tell a lie I think without that I would know. No Kerran, I have lived amongst honest thieves and evil robbers. I know the arts of deception and how to read the truth in another's lie. You have a thought, a plan in your head which is dangerous and important. You will not tell us as you do not think it can succeed."

He looked at Tris in astonishment. "Are you of wizard's blood yourself that you can read so much of my unspoken thoughts?" he said.

"No," she laughed again. "I am no wizard, only someone who has seen a little more of real life than you. To be brought up in a safe home does not lend itself to a life of great experience."

Kerran felt a little chastened by her words. He knew himself to be descended from wizards and that he carried unknown powers, and yet he knew also that she spoke the truth. He had learned little of people, having led a solitary life. He laughed to himself at the paradox of an ignorant wizard.

"It is more an idea than a plan," he said to her, wondering why he felt a spark of apprehension at his disclosure. It was fear, not for himself but for Tris, which stopped him from saying more.

"Tell me," she insisted. "It will help you think it out."

Finally knowing the truth in her words Kerran began to tell her more of his recent thoughts. "There may be a way that I can help Tolth escape from Maradass castle, but there are many difficulties," he told her.

"Tell me of your idea," she said. "From the beginning."

"There is little to begin with or to end with," he said smiling at her. "I believe that if I choose, I can take myself, within my real body, from Manzanee's cave to the outside walls of Maradass castle, and that is almost as far as the plan goes. All I need do then is climb the castle, smash through the walls with magic I do not possess, unheard by the guards of course, and reach Tolth's cell." He laughed at his own joke.

"What then?" asked Tris as though she took him seriously.

Kerran looked at her quizzically for a moment. "Then, if that were at all possible. I think I could bring Tolth to Manzanee's cave and then return him to his place here with us."

"Why can you not arrive within the castle?" asked Tris, looking for other possibilities.

"It cannot be done," replied Kerran. "For reasons unknown I can only take my living body to a place where I am in contact with the earth. I have found no other way."

"Can you take others with you?" Tris asked, her own plans beginning to form.

"I dare not risk others," he replied.

"Tell me, should you decide to try," she said to him. "Do not endanger yourself unwisely," she added

"Yes, I would consult with others before I attempted such a thing," he replied. "It is but a thought and not yet a plan."

"You still do not know if you can take others with you," she said. "Take me back to the cave with you sometime, when you are ready. You need to know if you can do these things. You must take someone and I am willing."

"What makes you so ready to put yourself in danger?" he asked her, wondering again at this tenacious and resilient young woman.

"It is living," she replied. "It is adventure and excitement. I will not lead a life where drudgery is the daily task. I saw the women in our thiefs' camp. Few were able to fight against the dominance of the men. Those who did wish more for themselves than the daily toil were called wicked and ungrateful. My father taught me differently, he told me that the purpose of all people should be to lead a life of their own choosing. I came south with Flindas to discover the places I had only heard of. I do not truly know why I came. It just seemed that I should."

Kerran made an impulsive decision. "Let us try now," he said. "Not to Maradass castle, but somewhere else along the Wizard Lines, somewhere safe."

An excitement lit her eyes as she reached out and held Kerran's hand.

"You are very sure of this?" he asked, and she nodded silently not taking her eyes from his.

No one sleeping around the campfire saw them depart,

only Rark lifted his head for a moment and sensed their going.

It was only a short time later that they stood amongst darkened ruins high above the pounding ocean. The wind, scattered with knives of bitterly cold rain, beat at them from the north and east. Tris stood against a broken parapet, her hand clutching the stone as she leaned out to see the waves crashing far below. Kerran's heart leapt as Tris leaned out still further, the wind rushing up at her from the wall of rock, throwing her short dark hair skyward. He had brought her here because she said she wanted to see the ocean. Only at Viris-Tan-Vara had she seen it before and never in all its fury, and she rejoiced in it.

"We can go below. There is a path!" she called to him over the wind and she pointed, but he could see nothing.

"Come away," he said back to her. "I have had enough of this place. We will return now."

"The night is not yet old!" she called again, but came away reluctantly from the edge. "I wanted to stand by the sea," she said as they stood in the lee of the wall. "Was this truly a wizard's home?" she asked, touching the crumbling stone.

"It was the tower of Valdaris," he replied. "He was a Lesser Wizard and his name meant 'Reflection' in our tongue. He did not survive the wrath of Rishtan-Sta."

"Was it really so necessary that the White Wizard destroy them as he did?" Tris asked turning to Kerran in the near darkness. "Were they truly so evil?"

"I have seen the time of the wizards," replied Kerran. "I have been in their midst, though they did not see me. They were corrupted by their own mighty powers. Rishtan-Sta saved my ancestor and your friend Trontar the Follower, and he destroyed the others and himself so that humanity could be freed. The power of Maradass is small compared to the might of Cranda-Sta and Lardan-Mor, and none were more corrupt than Drinda-mira-Sta and Ma-dran-Thara. The Broken Lands from whence you come were once a vast green country. There were forests and rivers, cities and a great civilisation. If the wizards had continued to wage war I do not think that the Regions and its people would exist now. I have taken my shadow to the far points of all but one of the places in the Wizards Way. There is nothing out there except desolation. Maradass seems to have the same plans, to torture the land until it dies. He would live forever, lord of an empty land."

He sheltered further into the shadow of the wall, sharp gusts of wind catching at his clothing. The storm grew but Tris did not wish to leave.

"I will go down!" she called to him suddenly. "It is not far. Wait for me."

Then she was gone, running across the broken courtyard and disappearing before Kerran could stop her. He crouched back under a broken archway and watched for her return, time allowed but he felt apprehensive. Something in the broken walls and tumbled stonework of this ancient fortress clung to Kerran's mind like a long forgotten memory. He searched into his dreams for a clue but found little of help and returned to the present. He was angry at Tris for running off as she had. Dawn was not so far away, and though he still knew not why, the thought of travelling during daylight along the Wizard Lines brought fear into his mind each time he did so.

He had stepped away from the shelter of the ruins, and was looking below in the hope of seeing Tris, when there was a violent crack of thunder from above. A bolt of blue lightning exploded against the remnants of the ancient tower, close to where he had stood only moments before. Kerran stumbled and fell as the sky seemed to explode above him, the crash of tearing thunder crushing him to the ground. Kerran's eyes were dazzled and it was some moments before he could see much in the darkness. The first thing he noticed was a shimmering blue glow coming from where the lightning had struck the wall. A thin tracery of blue fire was slowly spreading across the stonework.

"Maradass," he said to himself, backing away from the eerie fingers of cold fire.

Above him the dark sky exploded into light once again. The earth shook and the ancient courtyard burst and cracked with the violent impact. Kerran knew now that they had been here too long, Maradass had somehow sensed them on the Wizard

Line and now sought their destruction. He turned to run as another bolt from the skies sent the blue fire shimmering across the ruins. He leapt through the gap where Tris had disappeared just as another shattering shard of lightning crashed down upon the stonework. In fear, Kerran rushed down the narrow stone stairway. He called to Tris but the wind blew the words back into his mouth. The air was split by blue light, then part of the ancient tower fell into the gulf, and crashed to the rocks far below. He knew that Tris was somewhere down there.

Kerran began the steep descent. The path was narrow and overgrown but the stone slabs had been laid well. The cliff top above erupted into blue flame and the very stone seemed to burn as rivers of cold fire trickled over the edge and began to form bubbling pools on the path behind him. Kerran dashed headlong down the stone stairway. Rocks fell from above to shatter on the path about him. He felt an intense cold radiating from the stones. He clambered over them quickly. Once he almost missed his footing and had to reach out with his hand to regain his balance. As his fingertips came in contact with the stone the extreme cold burned into his skin.

Crying out, he tore his hand away and stumbled across the fallen stonework to the darkness below. Looking back quickly he saw that the thin tracery of cold fire was beginning to swell and grow. Bolts of blue lightning continued to rain down on the ancient ruins above him. The very cliff top seemed to be melting. He heard a deep rumbling which shook the earth and he stumbled as a huge section of rock sheered away from the cliff above and fell with a thundering roar to the rocks and ocean below. The upper end of the stone stairway was no longer there, blue fire cascading into the gulf.

Kerran ran on, the way becoming clearer as the light from above grew. Rain lashed at him as he fled the destruction. He was almost to the bottom and could see clearly the rushing and plunging of waves against the rocky shore. The descent was beginning to level out when he heard Tris call to him from beyond the edge of the path. He found her within moments where she sat crouched under a low overhang of rock. As lightning flashed above, Kerran could see that she had been hurt. Blood pulsed from a head wound and her tunic was tattered and bloody.

"You were right," she chuckled through her pain. "We have been here long enough."

Kerran sensed rather than knew that they were still within the bounds of the Wizard's Line, and taking her hand it was but a few moments before he was rousing the surprised Verardian to tend to his wounded friend. The first light of dawn was beginning to glow in the east and Leana, disturbed by the quiet movements about the fire, woke and joined her brother.

Tris was shaken and bruised but her head wound was small. A fragment of rock had grazed her scalp, while others had hit her about the arms and shoulders. She gave thanks to the heavy green and brown tunic which had deflected much of the falling rock.

Tris was reluctant to have the healers tend to the other hidden wounds beneath her clothing, but Leana insisted, for she could see that her young friend was in some pain. Tris sat quietly and grim faced as Leana and Verardian gently eased the jacket from her shoulders, she winced as they drew it down her arms. For a moment all looked in horror at the great number of old scars which crossed and re-crossed her slim body. Tris sat in silence, her eyes glaring into the fire as old memories returned to haunt her. With warm water and a mixture of healing herbs, Leana and Verardian cleaned and then dressed her many small wounds, while Kerran sat with eyes closed, thinking of the great danger they had both just managed to escape. Maradass now had power amongst the storm clouds of the sky he realised, perhaps only above the Wizard Lines, but Kerran knew that in some way the second piece of the Seacrest had increased the Evil One's part in the deadly game. Much greater care must be taken, he thought. The Wizards Way was not a thing to be used lightly.

The army of Zeta began the day's march under dark storm clouds. There was contact with people who lived in the mountains, and for several days they were led by an assortment of men and women who showed them the passes through the hills from one small village to another. Much of their way led through forest and across wide boggy flat lands amongst the hills. Bitter southerly winds blew at them relentlessly from the freezing Icelands.

Kerran huddled into his cloak and turned his face from the wind. His mount followed those before it, an occasional snow flake catching in the animal's coat. He had not entered the game since the near disaster at the ruins overlooking the ocean and had spoken little of it. Tris had not seen much of the dreadful fury which had been released on the cliff top. Soon he knew they would cross a Wizard Line to the east. He had told Mantris that he would find it by entering the Way and guiding them to it. The commander had decided that the army would turn south for a day once they had crossed the line. Mantris did not want Maradass to guess their destination before winter closed his black armies out of the southern mountains.

News still filtered through to them from Andrian. The pursuing army had given up the chase and returned to the plains, but a great number of stone foot soldiers had marched from the Crossroads and had met with another large force out of Andrian. It was estimated that almost thirty thousand foot soldiers now marched west and south along the Glandrin Highroad, most of them Krags.

"It seems that Maradass may now want to push us harder," Mantris said when he heard the news. "He will have to find us first," he added.

It was on the night of the new moon that Kerran went, within his shadow, in search of the place where the army of Zeta would cross the Wizard Line. It was not as easy as he had thought, and it was well into the early morning before he finally saw one of the pre-arranged beacon fires lit by forward scouts which told him where the army of Zeta lay. It was all he needed to know and returned to Mantris with his information. Almost a league beyond the beacon fire, lay the Wizard Line they sought, and by noon the following day they would be there. Kerran was hoping that Maradass had not sensed his shadow on the lines of the Way. He slept uneasily for the remainder of the night, rivers of blue fire haunting his dreams.

At dawn the army began its day's march and by noon had come within sight of the landmarks which Kerran recognised and pointed out to Mantris. As they rode up the last rise and reached the invisible Wizard Line, the army spread wide across the rock strewn hillside then crossed the three or four hundred paces at a run. If Maradass could detect the army's presence on the Way then the more quickly they were across and gone the better. Kerran galloped his mount until he was far beyond the Line and then with the other riders of Zeta he turned to the south. The army followed quickly and many a fearful eye turned back to look at the barren hillside where lay the unseen wizard's magic.

The army had ascended another low hill, no more that a few long bowshots from the Line, when all eyes were drawn to the west by a cry from the rear. Kerran watched in horror as the distant hillside seemed to erupt along the ancient Wizard Line. Rark howled a defiant warning but there were none who did not see the coming of the dark magic. Dust swirled on the breeze, obscuring all for a time. Then the nature of the disturbance could be seen. From the earth, along a great length of the Wizard Line, arose rank upon rank of the Stone Soldiers. Their numbers could not be guessed at, as troop after troop began to move from the clouds of dust and advance on their foe in a fast shuffling march.

Mantris gave the order for their own army to increase its pace, though there was no need for this command, the green and brown army turned and quickly marched to the east, into the cold and barren lands which spread as far as their eyes could see. Kerran caught a flicker of white wings against the grey clouds. Storm too cared not to remain anywhere near the terror that was the Stone Army. So began a long game of the hunter and the hunted. Days passed in the cold and inhospitable hills and still the chase went on. Though the army of Zeta far out-distanced the march of the Stone Army during daylight, the Krags did not stop for nightfall. Even during the darkest moon they advanced, following the unseen path ahead. Neither sleeping nor resting the Krags pushed hard on the heels of the army from the Magical Isles.

It was before dawn, on a cold blustery hilltop, that Kerran heard on the wind the distant sound of the marching Stone Army. The troops of Zeta had rested little that night, the inexorable advance of the Krags had not ceased, and now the soldiers of Zeta had to move again, pushing tired limbs into another hard march. During the past days the green and brown troops had tried to delay the Stone Army. In narrow gullies amongst the craggy hills they had caused many a rock fall, crushing great numbers of the enemy. Arrows were of little use, never penetrating deep enough to more than lightly wound the Stone Soldiers, who would continue their march unaffected. Stone was their element and also the best weapon to defeat them.

Mantris was caught between two evils. If the army of Zeta continued to out distance their enemy it would not be many days before they reached the point of exhaustion and would be unable to fight. The other choice open to him seemed the more deadly of the two, though he knew that he must soon take that option. Although greatly outnumbered, the army of Zeta must turn and fight. Scouts had been sent ahead to discover a place of advantage, a high point which they could defend and escape from should they become overrun. Food was becoming a problem. Though the rivers and streams of this rugged land abounded with many fish there was little time available to catch them, and the dry rations were beginning to run low. To reach the Winter Refuge and the supplies there, they must first destroy or else escape from the Stone Army.

By noon Mantris had made his decision. Scouts had brought news of a craggy highland within two days march where, if it was climbed, a few could hold off many and still escape to the east. Those on horse could pass through a narrow defile and reach the heights some leagues beyond. This narrow place could also be defended from above. There was much loose rock the scouts had said and the cliffs were unstable and shattered, it would not be difficult to cause parts of them to fall. Mantris smiled for the first time in many days.

The army of Zeta pushed themselves hard and by the following morning, with little rest in the night, they came within sight of the cliffs. Mantris studied it as they approached and as the scouts had said it was ideal. The almost sheer rock faces shadowing the narrow way between the high buttressed cliffs were crumbling and riven with cracks and deep fissures. The army split in two, those on horse, including Kerran, made their way eastward through the defile while the strongest remained on foot and quickly scaled the steep rock strewn slopes on either side of the narrow way. The Stone Army had never been seen to deviate from the path of the green and brown army and this, thought Mantris, could be their downfall. From the heights above he surveyed the land to the west, as the entire army, though tired and footsore, began to collect a great many boulders and rocks. It was not long before the edge of the plateau looked as though an ancient wall had once stood there, defending the western approaches.

Flindas and Tris slumped against a large boulder, both tired from the heavy work. The cooks had been busy, and hot food was most welcome. Rark lay sprawled at their feet uninterested in their plain meal. The huge dog could take care of himself in such country. Rabbit was becoming a staple for many of those from Zeta. They had grown accustomed to its strong unusual flavour out of necessity. For to survive they must learn to eat whatever the land provided. As dusk settled on the Southlands the army of Zeta lay down on the cold ground to sleep, the exhausted soldiers not knowing if they would live to see another sunset. Though they held the higher ground, the army of Stone Soldiers was vast and would never give up the fight, or so it seemed.

Flindas was awake long before the call to arms which roused the camp. The darkness was almost complete beneath an overcast sky as the army took its place at the edge of the plateau. In silence they ate a dry breakfast as to the west could be heard the approach of the Stone Army, the distant clatter of steel upon steel and a deep vibration in the earth. From the depths below came running the last of the scouts for they were no longer needed, in the first pale light of dawn the huge army of Krags could be seen as a dark mass moving across the flat land below. As the Stone Army reached the base of the cliffs, the Krags split up, just as the army of Zeta had before them. The main force marched directly for the narrow pass where Kerran and the mounted troops of Zeta had ridden the day before. The remainder, still many thousand strong, turned to the cliffs, and rank upon scattered rank they began to scale the slopes.

The Krags did not climb nearly as well as the troops of Zeta, often taking a longer way around an obstacle, and therefore channelling themselves into narrow places. They seemed ponderous on the rocky jagged slope and it was only their greater numbers and hard nature which brought a fear into those above. Mantris let them come on until the cliffs below were a mass of dark seething lines, crawling forward up the slopes like grey evil snakes. Not until the first of the Krags were pushing up the final incline did Mantris give the signal. With many a straining cry from the soldiers of Zeta, the first of many boulders was sent crashing down upon the approaching enemy.

Tris cried out in wild glee as the first wave of rock fell like deadly rain upon the Stone Army. The Krags could do little to avoid the onslaught and they did not even try to run from the tumbling cascade of rock. More boulders crashed down upon them, and a great many of the strange silent soldiers were swept from the slopes. Dust began to obscure much of the scene below and Flindas paused as, from the narrow pass which the main force had entered, there came a thunderous echoing roar. A huge section of the crumbling shattered rock had fallen into the depths, helped there by the fragile nature of the plateau's rim and the embattled soldiers of Zeta.

There was a long pause as the dust began to clear from the battleground and was carried away by the cold southerly wind which swept the land. From their vantage point the army of Zeta looked down upon the destruction below. In the time it had taken for the pale sun to clear the horizon, perhaps a full third of the Stone Army had been crushed and broken. From the carnage below the Krags who had survived again took to the slopes, many creeping forward on shattered limbs. There were no cries of pain from those that had fallen. The Krags lay in silence as they succumbed slowly to their ghastly wounds.

The day broadened cold and bleak, sheets of hail and snow drift sweeping across the bare plateau. Much of the nearest stone had already been used upon the dark enemy and the troops of Zeta were spreading further afield in their search for boulders to cast down upon the advancing Krags. The morning passed slowly and still the Stone Army came on, Tris and Flindas rested a moment after finally sending a large rock crashing on its way to the destruction below.

"It seems so easy," said Tris as she stood panting and wiping the sweat from her brow. "They die by the thousands and yet they still come on. A fool guides them I think."

"I doubt that Maradass is a fool," replied Flindas, watching the slow advance of the Krags. More boulders crashed into the crawling ranks of the Stone Army, who fell like toy soldiers in a child's destructive game. "Not a fool," he said. "Maradass holds many pieces in this game, and as he throws them against us we are slowly weakened."

During the late morning a great press of the Krags reached the summit and fierce hand to hand fighting began on the southern ridge which Flindas and Tris had helped to defend. Though the Stone Soldiers could not match the green and brown warriors in skill, their greater numbers and durability began to tell on the thinly spread troops at the plateau's rim. A wall of spears marched tirelessly, finally pushing the army of Zeta from the edge. Mantris rallied his troops and signalled for the withdrawal of the southern arm of his force. It was unavoidable if he was to save the many that were soon to be cut off from their companions, but it gave the Krags the foothold they needed.

The Stone Army began to spread wide, attempting to corner this large part of their enemy, and drive them into the depths of the pass. Mantris, with the standard of Amitarl held high beside him, retreated to the east. Many Krags were killed in each meeting of the armies, but always a few warriors in green and brown would also fall as exhaustion began to take its toll. A large force of Krags had managed to escape the destruction of the pass and had scaled the steep slopes on both sides, and soon Mantris found their way to the east was blocked and they were forced back towards the edge of the plateau.

Flindas fought wildly, each blow that he struck sent a jarring pain up his arm as though he truly was striking stone. Tris could do little in this battle except avoid death. Rark, sensing her vulnerability, stayed close to her and protected her with his giant body and savage jaws. Krags lay deep upon the battlefield but eventually the troops of Zeta were forced back, until they were again on the very edge of the plateau. The Stone Army seemingly intent on pushing them into the depths when from behind the ranks of Krags there came the high clear blast of a battle horn. The horse troops of Zeta had returned and thundered across the plateau into the gathered troops of Maradass. The Krags were slow to react to this unexpected attack and fell beneath the hooves of the war horses, or were pushed from the heights by the many spears they faced. Countless fell while others were forced down the slopes to where the troops of Zeta found more boulders and stones to cast upon the grey army. The close quarter battle was over and the day was eventually won. All of the Stone soldiers who had assailed the troops of Zeta had been forced back into the narrow defile, falling, and often dislodging those who still attempted to join the fight.

By early afternoon the battle was almost over, of the horse troops of Zeta only the wounded had been sent on, Verardian and Leana with them. Kerran had been advised to continue to the east but he had chosen to return and was now staring in mixed horror and wonder at the mangled remains of the Stone Army. The Krags continued to climb the slopes, though it seemed to Kerran's eyes that they lacked any purpose, trudging forward slowly or climbing awkwardly. There seemed very little resolve in their movements. In the short space of a morning the Stone Army had been decimated, while the army of Zeta had lost perhaps one hundred of their number. Except for the charge of the horse troops a great many more could have been surrounded and destroyed by utter exhaustion.

Finally the Krags ceased their advance, as one they turned from the slopes and gathered on the flat land below. They seemed without purpose. Some formed into broken ranks and stood motionless looking towards the plateau. Others seemed to have lost all their senses, walking as though bereft of sight and crashing into others of their kind, or falling helplessly where a human would have seen the danger. Kerran watched them with a strange sense of pity and sadness.

"I would see one of these creatures close at hand," he said.

Kerran began to make his way towards the nearest of the crumpled bodies a little way down the slope. Tris and Flindas followed and soon they stood above one of the many Krags who had died under the avalanche of boulders. The man, if man he was, lay wedged beneath the large rock that had killed him, his lower body shattered. There was little blood, and his torn flesh showed a dull red grey. Flindas lifted the heavy steel helmet to reveal a grim, unyielding face. Even in death the stern jaw was held tight. No sign of pain marred the stone-like features. The Krag's eyes were open and dull. No hair grew anywhere on his features and Flindas felt the strange hardness of the flesh. Tris was examining the Krag's heavy steel spear, which had broken with his fall, as Kerran stepped by her to get a closer look. He was staring into the dead eyes when suddenly they flickered with blue fire.

Kerran leapt backward but was not as quick as the cold hand of the ruined grey faced soldier. A stone like grip suddenly held Kerran by the ankle. At the same moment a flash of white-blue light leapt from the contact. Flindas and Tris were thrown violently away from Kerran as the fingers clenched his ankle, and then the Krag began to slowly drag Kerran down towards the blue glowing eyes. Without thinking, Kerran's hand leapt to the pouch at his hip. He saw the Krag's mouth open wide, and here truly was the colour of blood. The beast snarled silently as Kerran was forced to his knees. The other hand of the stone soldier now clawed at his legs, the vice-like grip sending shards of pain shooting through Kerran's body. The Seacrest pieces were now in his hand, and not knowing why he did it, Kerran pushed the two fragments against the Krag's arm, and the stone soldier screamed. No earthly sound could compare with that terrible cry. The eyes of blue fire grew wide with hatred and pain as a deep shudder ran through the stone body. Then it was as if the Krag and his armour began to melt, the creature gave one final terrifying snarl as he and his armour turned to soft powdered sand, crumbling and returning to the earth from whence it had come.

Kerran staggered back. It had taken but a few moments and the others had barely time to rise. Tris lunged forward still holding the broken spear, and as it came into contact with the ground where the Krag had lain a moment before, it too turned to dust and was absorbed. Tris fell forward, striking the ground with a surprised grunt. Flindas almost had time to smile at her before Kerran collapsed to the ground, cold blue flame burning his mind and body with violent pain.

Autumn was coming to a close and the first heavy snows had fallen in the deep Southlands when the army of Zeta climbed the last rise and looked down into the crescent shaped valley that was to be the winter home for many of their number. Verardian glanced at his patient who sat hunched in the saddle, the young man's hood hanging low over his face. Kerran had been in the trance for nine days and Verardian was greatly concerned for the young wizard. Though Kerran had taken food and appeared to sleep well, his mind wandered in a far place that Verardian, with all his healing powers, could not reach. No words had passed the young man's lips, and he comprehended nothing that was said to him. One evening, a few nights before, Kerran had fought an unseen foe. Silently he had thrashed about the fire as Verardian and Leana had tried to sooth his tormented body and mind. At times a faint blue aura seemed to surround the young wizard, and Verardian feared that Maradass held Kerran in a grip which could not be broken.

Through deepening snow the army of Zeta trudged down the slopes of the partly wooded valley, their presence much disguised now by their cloaks and other clothing which, when reversed, showed a white surface to the world. Ahead lay a large two storeyed house built of wood and stone which lay on the western side of a shallow river. The water course flowed north and east to join other mountain streams in their tumble to the distant ocean. Smoke rose from the stone chimney of the house and there were many who came from within to welcome the troops. Some ran out and directed the main force of the army to the high western arch of the valley. Here amongst the trees and broken rock lay the beginnings of a vast maze of overhangs and deep caves carved far into the hillside by wind and ancient underground rivers, with shelters built at the entrances to keep out the snow the army and their mounts would survive the cold of winter without difficulty.

As the army crossed the river and entered the trees, Mantris led the small group of Amitarl and others across the shallow water and dismounted near the house. Dantas was there amongst the Southlanders, and welcomed Mantris with clasped hands. Flindas looked at his aged teacher. The man was older by far than any warrior in the ranks of Zeta, but his stance, and the way he moved, told Flindas that here indeed was a warrior still. The years did not weigh heavily on his old tutor and friend, and Flindas was glad of it. As he dismounted Dantas glanced at the tall bearded man for a moment without recognition, then his eyes grew wide in delight.

"Flindas!" he cried, and strode across the courtyard to welcome his most favoured of students. "It has been too many years." Dantas clasped his hand.

Just then from the top of the stairs which led into the house, a man began to speak. He was tall and slim, thinning blonde hair reached to the shoulders of his dark cloak and a long moustache hung beneath his sharp nose and bright laughing eyes, he spoke as one who was used to casting his voice to a crowd.

"Welcome Amitarl and all who ride with you," he said. "I am Mykal and I am your host for this coming winter. You may fit as many of you in the house as you can. The more severely wounded will find greater comfort here than in the caves. I reserve only my family's room at the back of the house. Enter and let us not tarry with lordly introductions. There is food and warmth inside."

Saying this he turned and entered the arched doorway. Verardian and Leana supported Kerran up the stairs and into a large open room which was both kitchen and living space for many.

"Above there are smaller rooms, each with a fire," said Mykal, pointing to a wooden stairway which led to the upper floor. "Come and eat. I am sure you must want for the warmth of fire and food."

A small woman with a warm amused smile was standing at the fire stirring an enormous pot, while a slim boy with tangled blonde hair looked with shy amazement from his place next to her. A small girl of no more than three or four years was playing an intricate game on the floor with a great many coloured stones and seemed little interested in the newcomers.

"My family," announced Mykal to them all. "This is my sweet wife Ayla," he said putting his arm around her shoulders, a twinkle touching his eyes. "My children, Roan and Solia."

At the sound of her name, Solia glanced up and her face suddenly broke into a beaming smile. It was so touching that several amongst those gathered felt a pang of longing for their own children, far away on the Magical Isles.

"Welcome to our home," said Ayla as she gave her husband a light slap on the hand as he tried to delve with his fingers into the bubbling pot. "It is a great pleasure to have you as our guests," she continued. "Now, before any bother with introductions, please take a bowl and eat, there will be time enough during the coming moons to get to know each other."

There were several other men and women sitting around the pleasing, wood panelled room; the large open space was bare of furnishings except for kitchen benches and a large wooden table, the top of which had been hewn in one piece from some mighty tree. The fire was broad and allowed several logs to burn at one end while the cooking could still be done on embers at the other. Thick rugs covered most of the floor, while woven wall hangings made the large room even more warm and inviting. Indeed the heat was such that those who had just entered were taken by surprise. The aching cold of the last few days began to be driven from their bodies as they gathered at the fire or stood holding a bowl, waiting their turn at the delicious smelling fare. Tris almost sat in the fire as she ladled the hot thick soup into her mouth.

"It is good to feel warm again," she said to Flindas, through a mouthful of crusty bread, as he too came to sit by the flames. "There is never snow in the Broken Lands. I doubt if I could ever really get used to it. It is beautiful but bitterly dangerous, like a golden dagger I once saw which belonged to an assassin.

Gilded winter's dagger
Strikes as bitterly snows.
Assassin's blade
 A dangerous edge
That the frozen beauty knows."

Mykal laughed at his instant rhyme.

"That was like poetry," said Tris, looking at their host with a curious look.

"It was not 'like' poetry," Mykal said, his face creasing into a mischievous grin. "It *is* poetry. For I am, if nothing else, a marvellous poet." He beamed at her. "I am also quite humble," he continued with a wink, then began a long conversation with Tris on the qualities of snow.

Flindas turned to Dantas who had remained near, yet had not spoken further since their greeting. "Tell me of Andrian," Flindas asked his old friend. "How does the city fare under the rule of Maradass? I would go there soon to see Darbra and her family if the ways remain clear. I would take her from there if she is prepared to come."

"The city is not safe," replied Dantas. "But then, when was it ever truly safe? I still pass freely through the gate. They do not recognise me even though they once knew me well. The soldiers of Maradass have kept your father's guards and treat them well. In exchange the guards point out any who may be a trouble maker. As far as they are concerned I am an old hag who has been coming and going through the gate for years."

He paused and looked at Flindas. "You may not be so lucky," he said. "Your height does not allow you the disguise of a woman, and unknown men are stopped and held to account. The city itself seems little changed on the surface.

The Governor still has power, though why Maradass has not ended his rule I cannot guess."

"Are the old ways still open?" asked Flindas through a mouthful of thick crusted bread, dripping with the nourishing soup.

"The walls are too dangerous now," said Dantas. "There are many more guards these days. The Underways are known of course and many have been blocked, but few know them well enough to find all the openings. Your father has kept some open for his own uses. There is an evil stench trapped down there below the city."

"What of the Black Army?" asked Flindas. "Is the city not overrun by them?"

"Not yet," replied Dantas. "No more than a thousand are within the walls. Others are camped beyond the gates, but a great many have joined with those who marched from the Crossroads and now they come south in search of Amitarl."

"I do not think that it is Amitarl whom Maradass seeks," said Flindas and nodded towards Kerran who sat at the table where Leana slowly fed him another spoonful of the soup.

"Much has happened since we left the forest," said Flindas. "Maradass would have what the young man carries at any price, but my young friend is safe for now."

"Do not be so sure," said Dantas rubbing his old grizzled chin. "The Black Army pushes hard and may yet come to this valley before the true snows come. They are but four or five day's direct march from here, but they will have to spend much time in their search before they can find what they seek."

"They will not come," said Mykal with confidence, beginning to fill a long stemmed pipe from a pouch on the mantle. Few people in the Southlands smoked, but Mykal seemed to enjoy the sweet herbal mixture. He did not continue speaking until the pipe was well alight, filling the room with its pungent aroma. "This place is protected by a time and a people more ancient than mere wizards," he told them. "There is old, old, magic here."

"How do you know this?" asked Tris, looking at this strange yet fascinating man, who would turn a phrase into a rhyme and then laugh at his jest, or speak seriously, and at great length, on the wondrous qualities of snow. Mykal leaned back in his chair and for a moment gazed into the fire as he called to mind old memories never forgotten.

> "Old, old magic
> Deep in the ground.
> Burial ground
> Ancient sounds.
> Protection given
> Invisible gates
> Turns back hate
> With their ancient sound
> Hate is bound
> Here
> In the Old Ones' ground
> Old, old magic
> Buried deep
> Deep in the ground.

The caves," said Mykal as though this answered all her possible questions. When she continued to look puzzled he waved his long-fingered hand in the air in mock frustration.

"The black man lived here in this valley long before the ice began to advance from the south. It is an ancient burial ground. Their bones are now mostly turned to dust and are deep within the cave system. Though I have explored there many times over the years, I know that I have only seen a small part of those dark tombs. The water level continues to rise and the burial chambers are slowly being drowned. The black people left behind their dead and also their ancient magic. Maradass will not come here."

Dantas shook his head a little. He was a practical man and talk of ancient magic did not impress him nearly as much as the keen edge of a well made sword. Mykal looked at the doubt upon their faces and smiled knowingly. Solia had come to cuddle into his lap while Roan stood quietly at his shoulder, the boy's quick intelligent eyes seeming to tell those gathered that they should believe his father.

As Ayla spooned yet another bowl from the apparently bottomless pot she spoke quietly, as if to no one but herself. "Maradass will not come here," her voice a soft knowing whisper.

"You have studied the black people?" asked Flindas, his thoughts flying across the great western lands to Duragor. He imagined his friend somewhere out in the desert with his family, perhaps little concerned with the great and evil deeds of the white men to the east.

"I have studied much, including the black man," replied Mykal as he took a small burning stick from the fire and coaxed his pipe back to life. "I went to the desert for a time and lived amongst them."

"Few have ever done that," said Flindas with a new respect for the man.

"Yes," said Mykal, looking with friendly eyes at this quiet spoken warrior. "Few indeed have cared to learn anything about them. Tis a pity, for they could teach us much."

Mykal seemed to be enjoying immensely the new company at his hearth and again began to recite. His memory was prodigious, and during the winter moons to come he planned to enjoy himself even more. As he began to intone his work concerning the black people in the west, the power of his voice silenced all those present.

I walked alone into the west
Beneath a clear white sun.
I heard old words in silence there,
Of all the deeds that were done.
In the ancient times still yet recalled
By ones that wander free
In peace, not troubled by our wars
From burning desert to western sea.

I walked this way where few have gone.
And I heard their ancient ritual song.
Then began to wonder had I come

To hear these words in silence, done.
The war is won, the war is won,
I heard the silence, quietly run.

To the people I came and asked them where
 I could find peace and escape the snare
That bound my people in war and strife
The white one's way, the sword and knife.
And they said I should search to the end of time
And before the end I would find in rhyme
That peace lay hidden in my mind and heart
And I wondered long what could be my part
In these sad times when evil lurks
Like a swampland vile, a sucking murk
That takes all those who will venture there
Dragged down into the dark despair,
For it follows those who take to war
I heard the silence, quietly roar.
Take heed of peace, take heed of time
Take heed of what one calls a crime,
I chose my way and wandered thus
Into the west, the soft red dust.
And I walked there long in search of peace
I asked when war would come to cease,
And they told me then of a place to find,
Within my heart, within my mind,
And reflected seen in a mirror deep
Or found within my dreams and sleep.
And I thanked them and returned to find
That peace cannot be left behind
And my words in silence quiet run
In distant lands neath clear white sun.

For each person in the room, the words of Mykal had
conjured up visions of far open lands, mysterious and yet at
peace with all those who knew them. The meal was over and
for the first time in many days a feeling of warmth and safety
slowly descended on those gathered in Mykal's home. After a

time Verardian and Leana had assured themselves that those in their charge were well cared for. They laid Kerran gently to rest in the main room on a straw filled mattress, which Mykal had brought through from a storage room at the back of the house.

"How is the way between here and the city?" Flindas asked his teacher. "I would leave soon."

"I too return to the City Amitarl," replied Dantas. "There is a war of stealth being waged within the old city and all over Andrian too. I arrived here with the last wagon loads of winter supplies but I will return to that fight soon."

"We can go together," said Flindas and the old man smiled and nodded.

"I would like to see the City Amitarl," said Tris from her place by the fire. Flindas turned to her and saw the stubborn expression that he knew so well, there would be no arguing with her. He turned back to Dantas who was scowling at the small dark woman as though he thought her mad, or one of the enemy. "She will come too," he said with finality to the surprise of his old tutor.

The look on his student's face told Dantas that this was one foe that Flindas could never defeat, and Tris grinned at a battle so easily won. Mantris, who had been seeing to the troops, returned then and came to stand by the fire. He seemed pleased with the refuge.

"There are a great many stores," he said speaking to Dantas. "You have prepared the refuge well."

"There is much here that was stored long before the arrival of your fleet on our shores," said Mykal. "There are many in the Southlands who, for a long time, have guessed at the evils of Maradass. We knew that war would come, and though you did not see them all, there are many from the Southlands within the caves. Families of the fighting men have come south to evade the Black Army, though many more have chosen to remain in Andrian. Maradass may hold the city, but he has not yet crushed the Southlands."

There had been word from the fleet. As soon as the reinforcements heard that the army was to arrive at the refuge, the two thousand men and women on board were ordered to land. They came ashore well to the south so as to avoid detection, and they would join the main force within days. Mantris would soon sit in council with his captains and decide what action should be taken over the winter moons. The presence of the fleet, and the apparent lack of one in support of the Black Army, was an advantage that would not be overlooked.

Verardian sat with Kerran throughout much of the night. Whatever spells lay on the young man's mind, the healer somehow knew that the crisis would come soon. Verardian held his hand on Kerran's chest, feeling the soft life pulsing deep within. Over the last few days he had sensed the battle which raged within Kerran's mind, though the young wizard's body had showed no signs of the conflict. The ebb and flow of life was soft and shallow. Kerran had taken little food that day and his eyes had closed as soon as he had lain on the mattress.

The firelight dimmed briefly and Verardian looked up to see Leana tending to Diris, the most seriously wounded man in their care. He would survive now they had reached sanctuary, but he had almost died in the snow. The full moon cast its light through a chink in the shutters, the beam falling on Leana, and for a moment Verardian saw not his sister but a much older woman. The face was like Leana's and yet not. He had seen a portrait of his grandmother painted many years before his birth, and for those few moments it was she who tended the wounded man. Leana looked up into Verardian's eyes and smiled. A cloud obscured the moon, and when its light returned the old woman was gone, to be replaced once again by his dear sister. Verardian smiled as he watched Leana finish dressing the wound. It was as though his grandmother, the Elveren, had come to reassure him, and he thanked her memory, for she had succeeded in her quest. Verardian lay down on a mattress beside Kerran and for the first time in many days he closed his eyes and slept.

The Southlanders

The advancing troops were barely discernible against the white snowfield below, just as Flindas and his two companions wore the white snow capes and breeches, so did the reinforcements of Zeta who moved on the lower slopes. Though the scouts reported no black troops within two days march, Mantris had still ordered that those moving in the snow must wear the white camouflage clothing.

"They come heavy laden," said Dantas, noting the bulky packs which the troops carried. "The refuge will have more than enough supplies to survive the winter."

The three companions began to descend the snow covered hillside. Again Flindas had been sorry that Rark could not join them, but his great size would be like a sign post to any who saw him. Besides, the mountain dog seemed to be much attached to Kerran recently and always slept near the young wizard. They hailed the approaching troops, and were greeted by those who came on. A tall man with a craggy bearded face recognised Dantas immediately, and after a few moments left the others and came to speak with the old Elbrand captain.

"I had heard that you were once again amongst us," said the man not taking the proffered hand. "It is strange that Mantris should trust one who proved unworthy to be Elbrand."

Dantas clenched his jaw tight, his eyes held smouldering fire as he looked steadily at the Elbrand captain.

It was Flindas who spoke into the cold silence. "If it were not for Dantas and those who have learned from him, the refuge where you go would not exist, and your winter would be a bleak one. Judge a man by all his deeds and not by just one."

The man turned to Flindas and his eyes lit with recognition. "Greetings to you Flindas. I did not recognise you at first." He stroked his own beard for a moment. "If you trust this man then so be it," he said. "But a man is a coward or he is not. I would choose my company carefully if I were you."

"I have chosen well," replied Flindas, recognising the man from the games on Zeta. "Dantas is more than a companion. He is my close friend, and I would rather you spoke no more of this."

The man's face dropped and with a final scowl he left them, returning to his command. The reinforcements passed slowly; the snow, and their heavy loads, causing many to sink to the ground and rest their tired limbs. Perhaps half the troops had passed when Flindas saw a face that he knew, but could not at first remember where they had met. She smiled at him briefly in recognition and had passed on before he remembered her part in the games. Though she was young she had entered the test of endurance, and had gone further than many of the men, and had been the last woman to leave the race. He then remembered something that Verardian had told him. Kerran it seemed had formed an attachment with a young woman on Zeta.

You may remember her, the healer had said. *She outdistanced all but a few men in the endurance race of the games.* Flindas smiled a moment. It would do the young wizard no harm to have another person near who cared for him.

The troops had been left far behind when the three travellers found a dry camp beneath the broken trunk of an ancient tree, which at one time must have stood proudly above the rest of the wooded valley. Evening had come on quickly and snow began to fall from the deepening grey sky. Huddled for warmth against the cold night, they ate their evening meal and watched the dance of flames from the small fire. Tris ate the last crust of the delicious bread baked in Ayla's kitchen as she wondered about the meeting between Dantas and the Elbrand commander.

Curiosity finally caused her to ask. "Why did he call you a coward?"

Flindas heard the question and was shocked by its bluntness. He too wished to know the story from his old friend's lips but could never have asked. After a long pause in which Tris began to think she had offended the man.

"There is little to tell," Dantas said, straightening his back against the tree trunk. "I ran from Zard and left those under my command." He paused, the memory coming painfully to mind. "Some died that night and I did not. It is something I have lived with, and over the years it has become easier to bear. Only recently has it returned to haunt me. I could never return to Zeta after that and so, when I tired of my wanderings in the Regions. I made my home in the City Amitarl." He paused again, his old stern face lit by the flames. "If I were to face Zard once more I would not avoid him," quiet defiance in his voice. "I swore never to run again, and have not turned from a battle since."

There was silence then, broken only by the crackle of the fire and the light wind sighing through the sparse trees. As he wrapped himself deeper into his blanket Flindas thought on how one rash act, or one mistake could influence a person's life forever. How different things may have been if one were able to change the past, but then he smiled briefly at the foolishness of his thoughts as his mind turned towards sleep he knew that nothing could be different than it truly was.

The three travellers continued north on foot, keeping far from the most frequented roads. They avoided contact with the troops of Maradass, often seeing them, and once killing a Marauder when it found their trail. Undetected they left the bitterly cold south, and after many days travel they stood within sight of the City Amitarl. It was late in the evening and the last song of small birds could be heard amongst the tall stand of trees which was less than half a league from the city walls. Dantas stood talking with a number of brown clad Southlanders who had travelled with them over the last two days, while Flindas leant against a tree and looked at the city which had been his home for more than twenty years. Tris came to squat against the trunk and quietly watched the last rays of sunlight strike the high stone walls across the plain. She marvelled at the tall spires and artistry of construction. High above stood the towering castle of Celisor Amitarl, impregnable, yet now conquered by fear and the Governor's own complicity.

As the sun's rays caught the last tower of the castle, the distant gates of the city clanged shut, the sound reaching to them on the light evening breeze. A curfew was now in place from sundown to sunrise, and anyone caught out in the dark of night was quickly put to death, executed with or without the farce of a trial. The law was a genuine Governor's proclamation, but was enforced by the troops of Maradass. Even in the countryside, none were permitted to leave their homes by night, though there were too few of the Black Army to guard all the roads and byways of Andrian. The members of the Governor's court had not been treated harshly it seemed. They were being kept in place by some whim of Maradass. Perhaps to legitimise his invasion of the Four Regions, though why this was necessary none could say.

It was the merchants and traders who were hit the hardest. Many of their businesses were ransacked or destroyed and taken over by the Black Army to aid its own ends. Commerce still continued in the city by many who had given their allegiance and demanded payments to the Governor, and therefore to Maradass also. Those in the countryside fared little better than most within the high walls. Winter was upon them and many granaries and storage houses stood empty. The contents had gone to feed the invading army, with wagonloads going north to Mendan Maradass as well.

The Southlanders had learned that this very night a number of wagons were being prepared to leave the city by first light. A daring plan had been made to waylay the wagons and its heavy guard late the following afternoon. Should the plan work, the wagons would be driven off into the coming night after the black guards were engaged by a much larger force and destroyed. It was hoped to overwhelm the black soldiers quickly and be gone far to the north and east before any word reached back to the city. Nothing like this had been tried before, but food was becoming scarce and the winter would be a difficult time for many. The three travellers had not yet decided on a way to get all of them into the city and so they decided to join the raid. Dantas and Tris could enter the city easily as long as Tris remained silent, and did not speak with her northern accent. It was true that the guards may have been told to look for a young woman with crossed scars on her face, however Dantas knew well the arts of disguise, and the scars would not be seen except under the closest scrutiny; it was Flindas who was the problem.

The night deepened as the band of Southlanders began to travel westward, keeping well away from the Highroad. Much later they were on horse back, travelling quickly towards the empty and desolate village where the attack was to take place. Well before dawn they reached their destination. Several hundred Southlanders were already there and well concealed before the light of morning could expose their scheme. During the long day several troops of black horsemen rode by, both to the east and west. Occasionally a lone rider would gallop through the village carrying messages between Andrian and Mendan Maradass. Eventually word came that the wagons were no more than half a league from the village. The sun was lowering in the west when Tris saw the approaching troops and wagons. She peered through the slit in the broken shutters of the old ruined house where many others crouched in wait, watching the moving column.

The moments crept by slowly as those about her silently strung their bows. She held her own finely worked bow which had been a gift when first she had joined the army of Zeta in the north of the forest. She had learned quickly on targets but had yet to experience the weapon in battle. It was not the cold that sent a shiver through her small frame, but whether it was fear or excitement she could not tell. Tris looked across at Flindas who stood in the shadows of the broken wall, unmoving, his eyes keenly watching the eastern road. Soon there came the sounds of horses and the trundling of iron hooped wheels on the roadway. The soldiers were riding without caution, talking amongst themselves without any fear of danger. The Southlanders would not dare attack a heavily armed troop of soldiers, they thought. They knew the people of Andrian to be weak, with few real warriors among their scattered rabble. Only at night, and as thieves rather than soldiers, were the Southlanders feared. Knives in the dark and stolen horses were their way.

The wagons began to enter the village. Tris was close enough to hear the horse's breath, to smell their warm straining bodies as they pulled their loads further into the trap. For long moments she held her breath. Where was the signal? Her eyes flickered quickly about the shattered house. All was so still that life seemed frozen; except for the troops and wagons beyond the broken walls. Then it came, a sharp blast on a high pitched horn. Tris leapt to a standing position, but suddenly the bow seemed like something she did not comprehend. It was clumsy and foreign to her. There were cries of pain and battle from the street. Horses reared as riders suddenly fell from their saddles. Shafts carrying death flew across the narrow space.

At either end of the village, barricades of old timbers were quickly thrown up to prevent escape. Tris managed to shoot one arrow wide of her mark before she heard the second signal blast of the horn. The sliding of steel from scabbard was accompanied by a great yell as the Southlanders attacked those soldiers who had not yet fallen. Flindas leapt over the wall and was gone as the sounds of battle grew furious. Tris did not join the fighting, but watched from shelter as the black horsemen were quickly overpowered by the greater force. Soon the sound of battle had almost ceased.

On one of the nearest wagons stood a tall and powerful man, the captain of the troop, swinging his great broadsword down upon those who attacked him. His armour was heavy and well made, and it could be seen that no shaft was going to dislodge him. He fought ferociously for his life though his entire troop had fallen. With a muffled defiant yell from within his steel helmet the man swept the head from a Southlander who had tried to jump onto the wagon. Tris saw Flindas and Dantas both near the fight. Surely the man must fall soon, but he did not. Tris saw another man die by the warrior's blade, and then she leapt quickly up the broken wall onto what remained of the roof. Moving lightly, she jumped the narrow space between two buildings and came to stand above the battle, the top of the wall on which she stood was crumbling and broken. Tris bent, and with little effort pulled away a heavy brick. In the Broken Lands she had cast many stones onto unwary prey. Lizards and rabbits could easily fall to a well thrown rock from above.

Tris steadied herself then cast the brick outward and down upon the battling warrior, her aim was true yet the man was in constant movement. The brick did not hit his head as she had hoped, but instead it smashed down upon the great broadsword and the blade shattered as it caught the edge of the wagon. The man roared in frustration and rage. Sweeping out his short sword, he hacked at the hands and weapons which reached for him. In a movement, which Tris saw as the mark of a trained warrior, the man changed the sword to his left hand, still fighting those around him with his less effective blade. A heavy throwing knife seemed to leap into his right hand. Tris felt a sudden fear. Though the man had not looked up, she thought that the knife was meant for the one who had taken from him his most valuable weapon. Tris looked quickly for a way of escape but the sloping roof was intact and she could not drop down behind the walls.

When Tris looked again to the roadway below, she saw the last movement of the man's throw and it was not aimed at her. To her surprise the warrior had cast the knife far beyond those who pressed closely about the wagon. She could not see who may have suffered from the thrown blade and began pulling another brick from the wall, but it was not needed. Men with spears taken from the fallen horsemen pounded at the man until, with a bellow of rage, he tripped and fell from the wagon.

"Save him!" someone called above the noise. "I will not

have him killed."

Tris thought it sounded like the voice of Dantas but she could not be sure. The man had fallen heavily, smashing into the ground at the feet of the many that were prepared to take his life. He moved no longer and could well have been dead already.

Tris climbed down quickly. Already several wagons had left the village as the barricades were pulled aside. When Tris joined Flindas he was gently wrapping the right hand of Dantas. Much blood was already seeping through the cloth.

"Bring our horses," Flindas told her. This was not the time for questions.

She quickly brought the three horses from their hiding place in the village. Dantas could not ride easily and so he climbed aboard the wagon, which also carried the bound, unconscious form of the captured warrior. The man's helmet was gone and the chain mail had been pulled from his head to reveal a savage and bitter face. The dark hair was cut short and his small beard was trimmed in a fanciful design that professed to the man's vanity. Tris and Flindas rode with the wagons, and when the drivers took a side turning to the north of the Highroad, they followed. The men of Andrian who were afoot disappeared to the east and west, leaving only the horsemen to guard the supply of stores. At sundown they did not stop but pushed on as fast as they could along the deteriorating, deeply rutted roadway. The horses drawing the wagons were tiring, when ahead in the misty darkness Tris could see the dim light of a lamp as it swayed to and fro. The Southlanders had planned well. Teams of fresh horses were waiting to be exchanged for the exhausted animals which were quickly stripped of their harness. By the light of ghostly lamps they were led away, their heavy breath visible as puffs of floating mist on the cool night air.

The fresh horses were soon in place and the wagons, with their precious cargo, were spirited northward through the night. Fresh horses were again ready for them the following morning. Though men slept in their saddles, and some left the procession to rest their own horses, the wagons did not slow.

They went along many small roads and narrow country lanes, and by late evening they came to a small forest nestled in a narrow valley. Here lay a secret refuge for the Southlanders, and many hundreds were gathered there, outlaws in their own land.

Tris cared not if Maradass himself was about to fall on them from the sky. She needed food and then sleep, both of them quickly. When a bowl of rabbit and vegetables was passed to her she gulped it down. She wondered at the silent thoughtfulness of Flindas who sat by Dantas and spoke with him quietly as they ate. Tris was curious, but sleep demanded that she succumb to its beckoning call. She slept throughout the night and it was not until late morning of the next day that she heard from a Southlander, one called Shen, about the reason for the strange mood which clouded the brow of her warrior friend.

"Twas one of Dantas's men before, a high warrior that one," said the Southlander, indicating the captured black captain who sat not far off, tied securely to a tree. Shen's long narrow beard waggled as he talked, giving him a comical and likeable presence. "That one, 'e was a friend of Demsharl before," he said. "Flindas that is, your friend. Great friends for a time they was. Then Flindas now, 'e kills 'is older brother, s'pose you know that story. An' that one, Marlto be his name, 'e hunts Demsharl for years. Rewards see! Old Governor 'e wants Flindas's head, alive but. Big reward. Marlto looks for years, but I reckons Demsharl be a might cleverer, always was. Marlto turned against Dantas too, said Dantas knew where Demsharl could hide hisself, an' then 'e makes great friends with Jondarl, Flindas's young brother see. Dantas on the out then, an' Marlto set to kill 'im too. Escaped before they got 'im."

Shen was enjoying the telling of his tale and was old enough to know it first hand. "Marlto becomes terror in hands of Jondarl," Shen continued. "Tax gatherin' and such. Fearful man is Marlto, an' then 'e gets some sort power over Jondarl. No one knows what, but Jondarl gives im all 'e wants, everything. Mysterious. Then Marlto wants Demsharl woman too, Darbra. But she got married to this Alarin 'gainst all wishes, father

Governor's too. Strong minded woman that one. Marlto offered all 'e got, but Darbra turns 'im flat, saying man who wish to kill Flindas Demsharl will never marry Demsharl. The name, that what he wanted supposin'."

"Why do you think he just wanted the name?" asked Tris, fascinated by this insight into the Demsharl family.

"He wants so 'is own son comes Governor some reckon," said Shen smiling. "This be supposin', but many was supposin' that way. 'E marries Demsharl. Old Governor croaks it, Jondarl under Marlto's thumb somehows. Marlto gets all power. Jondarl maybe not take Governor's place, or Marlto could even fix accident maybe. Jondarl got no children. Never likely either with 'is inclinations. Marlto went worse bad for these last years. Jondarl creeps under a rock every time Marlto is about. Big man in the castle guard, though now looks like 'e joins the Black Ones. Always lookin to get higher up was Marlto. Reckon 'e be some low now."

"What happened at the village when Marlto was fighting alone?" asked Tris into the brief silence. "He threw a knife." Flindas had been quiet and long in thought during their ride, saying little to any but Dantas. Tris guessed that something strange must have happened.

"You not hear that?" said Shen surprised. "Mazing thing, most 'mazing thing. Talkin' with my friend Lardris who seen it all, 'mazing thing."

Tris was getting a little annoyed at not knowing what the 'mazing thing' could be, but she did not interrupt, the story would unfold as Shen decreed.

"Mazing thing," the Southlander said once again and shook his head in disbelief.

Tris waited patiently.

"Marlto, 'e was great fighter sometime passed, slowed some now but still high warrior. Swingin his big sword then someone throws a big brick and breaks it. That was good work."

Tris smiled then, realising that perhaps none of the Southlanders had seen who had cast the brick.

"Then 'e up with other sword,' said Shen. "And 'e looks fit to die fighting. Then but 'e spies Demsharl and 'e whips out 'is wicked throwing knife and tries hard to take your ol' friend Flindas with him. Demsharl should be dead now, dead as any I guess. Mazing thing," he said once again and Tris was on the verge of strangling him when he continued. "E caught it," said Shen with a look of wonder on his face. "E caught it," he said again quietly as if to himself.

"What do you mean?" said Tris, her voice now almost threatening the short but powerful man. "Who caught what?"

"The ol man," said Shen pointing with his thumb. "Ol' Dantas there, 'e caught the knife. Ol' Lardris who seen it says 'e never even seen the knife flyin' but Dantas, 'e just leans sideways, an plucks it from the air, sweet as that. Cuts hisself bad I hear, but still most 'mazing thing."

Shen had finished his story and began to tell Tris of his wife and family who were somewhere safe in the Deep South. Tris listened for a time but her mind wandered, and soon Shen was summoned to help others in the building of an enclosed space for the many extra horses taken during the ambush. Tris watched Marlto as one of the young Southlanders came to him with a bowl of food. The dark, angry warrior took one deliberate mouthful of the hot soup, and then spat it back into the young man's face. The guard who stood at Marlto's side made to kick the warrior for his attack. It was a mistake. Marlto, though tied to the tree, saw the blow coming as if he had been waiting for it. As the boot reached his ribs Marlto lunged sideways, and his teeth fastened onto the man's leg just above the knee. The guard screamed and pounded upon Marlto's head with his fists. Blood gushed down his leg as the teeth sank deeper. The man, in agony, reached for the knife at his waist. At the same moment Flindas arrived running and with a sharp well directed blow sent Marlto's mind spinning into blackness.

Tris woke shivering in the early dawn a few days after the attack on the wagons and much of the stores that had been captured were already distributed to the needy. A light frost lay on the open spaces amongst the trees and the air was sparkling with shafts of light from the rising sun. Men and women moved about the camp, rekindling fires as the day's activities began.

On this day, Flindas, Tris and Dantas planned to leave for the city. They had spoken together over the last few days and their scheme to enter the ancient seat of Amitarl was simple, yet dangerously bold. They had discussed many possibilities, and all but this one had been rejected. Dantas spoke against it but Flindas would not be swayed. He knew that the truce between Maradass and his father would not last and he had to try and get Darbra and her family out of the city.

Dantas and Tris were to approach the gate first, preferably in a crowd which would also include Flindas. Dantas would be well armed beneath his disguise, but he did not expect any problems for himself from the guards. For Tris he had some anxiety, and for a time he tried to dissuade her from her course. She risked herself needlessly, he told her, but was met with stubborn silence and a wilful look. He surrendered and told her that he would disguise her appearance, that she must remain silent and to let him do any talking if they were challenged. Flindas was to come some paces behind, there was little that could be done to disguise his tall warrior's body, but his face would be much changed, and the plan was not to avoid the guards at all. Once Tris and Dantas were safely through the gate he was to ask to see the captain of the guard, saying that he had important news to tell. They hoped that the presence of the Black Army within the city had not changed the procedures at the gate. Flindas and Dantas knew well that he should be taken into a large guardroom built just within the city walls, where he would be held until the captain would see him. His face would not be easily recognisable under the disguise that Dantas planned. Few had seen him for many years and he had never worn a ragged unfashionable beard in his younger days.

At the gate they could expect to find soldiers of Maradass shadowing the city guards. Flindas knew that he would eventually be shown in to see the captain after being searched for weapons. He would carry only one, and he knew that it would not be found. If they suspected him to be dangerous there was a chance that he may be in chains, but he did not expect even this to thwart his plans. It was daring beyond anything that Dantas wished but Flindas was determined to reassure himself of Darbra's safety and he would not turn aside. Once he could speak with the captain there was one ally which he knew he could depend on. Above all else, greed dominated the minds of his father's guards and those others in his employ; there was not a man amongst them who could not be bought.

"You will not change your mind?" he asked Tris as she shouldered her pack, preparing to travel. "You could remain here," he said. "The city is strange to you, and should we become separated or discovered I know where to hide and you do not."

"We will not get separated," said Tris stubbornly. "Not unless your plan gets you hung."

Flindas shook his head and smiled. "You risk your neck just for a glimpse of a fabled city," he said as Dantas arrived ready to leave.

"I have left Marlto in the hands of the Southlanders until we return," Dantas told Flindas. "He was once a good man and I would turn him to our cause given time."

Flindas knew of the respect the Southlanders held for Dantas. Though he claimed no leadership over them, their were many in the scattered bands who looked upon him for guidance in these troubled times. Men who had heard of Maradass in their childhood stories, but had never expected him to return in their lifetime. Untrained, and with few arms, they sought to hold off the dark invasion and looked to Dantas for his knowledge. This band, which was larger than most, were loath to see him depart for the dangers of the City Amitarl.

"You would not get by the gates without me," Dantas said to Tris. "And if Flindas is caught I do not intend to see him hung."

Tris looked at the man who seemed to treat Flindas as a son. The right hand of Dantas was still bandaged where the knife of Marlto had sliced him to the bone. Dantas saw her glance at his injury. Suddenly a knife flickered, sparkling in his left hand. It seemed to tumble in space, and then, with the practice of years it vanished before her eyes.

"I did not use my most important hand to catch Marlto's knife," he said smiling. "That would have been foolish."

The three travellers left the camp well armed. Only near the city would they put aside their swords and don their disguises.

After three days of hard walking across farmlands and fields, travelling by night when the moon allowed, they came within sight of the City Amitarl in the early dawn of a cold, windswept day. Sheltering from the wind in a hollow near the edge of the wood, Dantas began to transform them into people other than themselves. Tris became a stony faced mute, her scars almost disappearing beneath a powder which Dantas mixed carefully to a paste. Other layers were delicately laid on until the scars no longer disfigured her face. Indeed, thought Flindas, her young beauty before being cut by the evil hand of jealousy must have been admired by all men who saw her in the ungentle lands where she was born.

When it came to Flindas, Dantas took a great deal of time. First he pushed most of the younger man's hair into a conical hat which was old and battered. Some hair he left hanging and cut off raggedly with his knife. The beard he thinned a little and left a straggling unevenness to the ends, and then he added redness to the otherwise black hair. Around the eyes he worked for a long time, deepening age lines, turning Flindas from a man in his thirty-eighth year, to one who looked to be fifty or more. The nose he shaped with a crooked twist to it and the warrior's teeth he blackened as though they truly rotted in his head. The eyebrows became wild, bristled, and touched with grey. Dantas finished his work, aging Flindas with a final streaking through his hair and beard.

"Now," said Dantas. "Let us see if you can be the great fool you say you can." Tris did not understand the words until Flindas came to his feet, but instead of the tall and softly moving warrior, there stood before her a gangling aged simpleton. His eyes rolled in his head and his mouth hung loose and awry. When he walked Tris began to chuckle.

"Do not laugh overmuch," said Dantas quickly. "Otherwise your face will crack." He watched with a critical eye as Flindas returned to him, drooling with stupidity.

Tris bit her lip.

"Not so much of the fool," said Dantas. "They must believe that you have important news and are not a true madman."

Flindas straightened his face a little and spoke in a wild high crackling voice. "Mus' see Cap'n," he blurted. "'Portant news. Seen wagons, dead soldiers." To Tris, Flindas seemed to be another person.

Dantas had chosen a busy market day to enter the city. Though much commerce had ceased, there were still many for whom life had not changed. Gold was in the pockets of those favoured by the court, and many of those who sold in the markets were too poor for the tax men to bother with. Black soldiers took what they wanted from the impoverished without payment. There were none who could speak against them. The dungeons of the castle and the other city gaol were crammed with those who had spoken out, while hangings had become a daily occurrence under the new powers which the Governor continued to grant himself.

The morning became no warmer and a strong wind swept across the flat plain between forest and city. No great press of people moved on the road, and as rain began to fall, it seemed doubtful that more than a few farmers and gardeners would be selling their goods in the city square that day. It was not until noon that a group of several wagons, together with people on foot, came trundling along the Highroad towards the city.

"This is as good as we could ask," said Dantas and led them from the tree line to intercept the group as it passed.

Tris looked at Dantas and could not help but smile. The old hag with the shuffling walk and bulging eye could never have been recognised as the aging Elbrand warrior. A scowl from the twisted brow and red bloodshot eye frightened Tris a little, then she remembered her part and became a hard faced mute, her features in shadow beneath her hood.

Flindas had dropped back a little to walk with a struggling limp behind a wagonload of green vegetables and village-made cheeses. Talking to no one, he watched carefully as they came upon the broad stone way that led up the gradual slope to the city gate. From his position behind the wagon, he saw that the guards were not checking many who were passing through, but there seemed to be some problem when Dantas and Tris tried to enter. Flindas knew that if they were discovered they would fight their way quickly from the gate. If that was to happen Dantas would probably never be able to enter the city again. Flindas edged forward but could not hear over the crowd, he decided that it was time for his act and began to shuffle forward, pushing people aside in his apparent hurry to reach the gate.

"Guard! Guard!" he called out breathlessly as if he had run a great distance. "Call captain, must speak captain. Gov'nor! Gov'nor, tell Gov'nor!"

The guards at the gate turned at this disturbance and watched with amused sneers as the wild eyed idiot approached, sending a youth crashing to the roadway in his haste to speak with them.

"Bloody murder! Bloody murder!" Flindas gasped as he almost fell into the arms of one of the city guards.

He was quickly pushed away, for Dantas had made sure that Flindas smelled as bad as he looked, ragged and filthy, someone who worked on pig farms to the north.

"What bloody murder?" the guard asked, keeping Flindas at arms length. From the corner of his eye Flindas saw that Tris and Dantas had been allowed to enter the city. The four guards seemed more intent now to entertain themselves with this new arrival. Just within the shadows of the gate Flindas saw black soldiers watching the city guards.

"What bloody murder?" the guard asked again.

"In village," said Flindas frantically pointing west, his other arm flailing at the air. "Soldiers die, many black soldiers."

The guard shook his head and looked back at his friends on the gate who laughed in derision at this apparent simpleton. "We know all about that," he said turning back to Flindas. "Known it for two days passed. Get off now, 'fore you feel my blade."

"I knows where they tooks 'em," said Flindas secretively, holding his hand so as to cover his mouth.

"Took what?" asked the guard impatiently. He had almost had enough of this fool.

"Took the wagons," said the fool knowingly, watching a look of comprehension coming to the guard's face. "Reward yes?

Mus' be reward."

"You know where they are?" the guard asked, suddenly taking Flindas by the collar and drawing the idiot's face close to his own.

Flindas nodded gleefully. "Yes! Yes!" he cried, leaping into a shambling dance while still held by the guard. "An' there be more," he said. "Gold and jools there be, yes, gold and jools."

"Jools?" the guard said the magical word quietly, wondrously. He held Flindas by the arm and after a moment's thought he turned and began to pull the idiot towards the gate. "Captain best see this one," he said to his fellows, and pushing Flindas in front of him they entered the dark way beneath the walls.

From the shadows a figure stepped into the light. "Where do you take him?" said the black soldier, obviously on watch for any irregularities at the gate.

"Take to captain," replied the city guard. "Got some to tell on those wagon robbers."

"What does he know?" asked the black soldier and stepped in the other's way.

"Not asked," replied the city guard, snarling at this usurper within the city. "Captain still be in charge of gate I reckon. He asks questions, not me." He pushed past the soldier of Maradass and dragged Flindas with him. "Come on," he said. "Come talk to the captain."

"Think I may join you," said the black guardsman.

The city guard did not seem able to do anything about the presence of the black soldier, but he spat with venom on the roadway before entering the heavy wooden door not far inside the main gate. In the dim light Flindas saw once again the guardroom and office of the captain who commanded the gate. It was warm inside the large room. Several soldiers of the Maradass army and a number of the city guards were lounging about by a glowing fire, playing games of chance. The guard pushed Flindas to a seat.

"Stay there," he said and rapped on the inner door that was the captain's office.

After a moment a voice called for the guard to enter. The man did so and after a few words with someone unseen, he emerged again.

"Come along," he said to Flindas, pulling him by the arm.

Before they entered the man gave him a cursory search for weapons and then the black guard made as if to follow.

"Oh no," said the city guard with a smirk, "captain says no one else. Captain says you can go about your duty. Not needed see. This one we reckons harmless."

The black guard fumed, but it seemed that the captain and the Governor still held some sway in the city, at least for the present. The city guard chuckled and pushed Flindas through the open doorway. Flindas recognised Narad from his youth; the captain was older than Flindas by a number of years and had been a guardsman then. The faces of the Demsharl family had been known well to all in the city, but Narad did not recognise in this simpleton the outlaw son of the Governor, the man whose discovery would make a rich person of his captor.

"What is it you have come to tell me?" Narad asked as though he did not expect Flindas to know anything of interest to him, or the Governor.

Flindas, without changing his maniacal expression, put a hand to his mouth as though to cough and silently shot the guard in the neck with his small blow pipe. The guard looked at him with surprise as he fell. Flindas grasped him with one hand and eased him to the floor in silence. In his other hand he held the small pipe, a tiny dart already within its hollow stem.

"Do not cry out or you are dead," said Flindas, changing his voice from the idiot's to a more natural tone. Flindas stood over the terrified captain who had remained frozen in his seat. "I am not here to kill you," said Flindas. "Do as I say and you will be a rich man. Reveal me to others and you will certainly die."

"What is it you want?" asked the captain. "What ...?" Then he paused and his eyes widened in recognition. "Demsharl, Flindas Demsharl," he said quietly.

"Yes," said Flindas relieving the man of the knife at his belt. His sword and other weapons stood in a corner by the door. "What I want is free passage in and out of the city until sunset tomorrow," he said with a strange smile.

From within his clothing Flindas produced three small but exquisite gems which he placed before the captain. The man's eyes glittered at the sight of such wealth. Here before him lay more than all the bribes he had ever taken in his life. Jewels such as these were rare even for the Governor to see. The captain could not keep the greed from his voice. The Governor had put a very large reward on his outlaw son, yet here in these three small stones lay enough to double that sum.

"Is there more?" he asked, touching the stones, holding them in his palm.

"There are five more like them," said Flindas. "When I wish to leave the city tomorrow I will come here and you will escort me through the gate, you will have the other stones when I am beyond the walls."

The captain looked at the guard who lay spread across the floor. "And how do I explain him?" he asked.

"He is not dead," said Flindas. "He will waken by nightfall with a painful head. I am sure a few pieces of gold will soon make his pain and his memory disappear. I see you know the value of these stones. It is worth far more to you that I remain alive and that we meet again tomorrow. If you betray me I will find you and you will die. Escort me into the city now and then leave me. I will return by sundown tomorrow."

The captain said not a word but rose slowly, and after dragging the limp body of the guardsman to a recessed corner, he opened the door to the outer guardroom. Flindas became the stumbling simpleton again and walking beside the captain they emerged into the dim winter's light. There were wagons and a further press of people entering the gate and Flindas glimpsed the black guardsman as he turned to watch the idiot and the captain walk up the cobbled roadway.

"Leave me now," said Flindas as they reached a corner far from the gate.

"Tomorrow," said the captain with a leering smile and quickly departed. Flindas watched him until he had passed the figures of the old bent woman and the silent young girl as the two made their way along the street.

Dantas was chuckling when he arrived at the side of his friend. "I see that the quality of the city guard has not changed," he said, looking after the disappearing figure of the captain. "I wonder if he knows that on Zeta those stones are but rarely dug for, being so plentiful and having little use. I will go my own way now. There is much that I need to learn. I will meet you as we have arranged, tomorrow before noon in the south Underway."

He cackled an old hag's laugh and began his shuffling walk towards the city market. Flindas and Tris turned towards the south where lay the more affluent part of the city. For a moment Flindas watched as Dantas disappeared around a corner in the street, and then he turned to Tris.

"We go this way," he said, pointing along a narrow street. Flindas quickened his step a little, for he hoped to be soon greeting his beloved sister once again.

The Occupied City

The two companions walked deeper into the heart of the city. Tris kept stopping and gazing in awe at many of the fine buildings and old gardens from the time of Celisor Amitarl. The castle could be glimpsed between high buildings and the splendour of it made her forget her part.

"Tis much better than in the old wizard's glass," she said quite loudly in her unusual northern accent.

"Quiet!" said Flindas angrily. "Do not speak so loud, if at all. Only one man knows that we have entered the city. I do not want the whole guard and the Maradass army searching for us because they heard a strange accent on a foreign looking girl."

Tris almost burst. Her eyes closed in anger but she remained silent, and after a while she regained the sparkle which had been ignited by the sights of the city. Where she saw wonder and beauty, Flindas saw destruction and the loss of hope. The city Amitarl had sunk further into ruin over the decade since he had last viewed it in daylight. Old buildings fell into disrepair; poverty now struck deeper at the hearts and stomachs of the people. On other visits to Darbra and her family he had come at night through the Underways which were an ancient and disused honeycomb of tunnels deep beneath the city. Few knew those ways, but Flindas had learned from Dantas the major routes across the city as part of his training. It was useful knowledge in the possible defence of the city should it ever come under attack.

Few in the guard had ever bothered with the smelly rat infested underworld of the city. It led nowhere except that in two places, to the west and south, there were small openings low in the city walls where in times of rain much water would flow from the city. These drains had thick steel doors that could be lifted from the inside in need. Some of the Underways were perpetually flooded, ancient dams and water systems that had fallen into disrepair over recent centuries. Celisor had designed great water wheels beneath the city as well as underground gardens where had grown all manner of foods which enjoy near dark and cool places. Now the Underways were a place of damp and darkness. There were some who lived there, disdaining the world above, going up at night to scavenge amongst the squalor of the city.

They passed smelly fetid alleys and mean, yapping, little dogs. One that persisted in biting at their ankles was deftly kicked by Tris as though it were a ball in a game. It yelped as it sailed through the air to land in a deep puddle of mud and worse. The rain began to return as Flindas made his way down several twisting alleys which took them by an indirect route to the bottom of a tall hill. The houses here were especially grand and in better condition than any Tris had seen so far in the city. She marvelled at the beauty and exquisite artistry of the structures. The stone stair which they climbed to reach a higher level was wonderfully ornate, many animals, birds and flowers depicted in the elegantly curved steps. Tris knew that she could never count the number of tiles that had gone into making this marvellous walkway, and yet it was but a small part of the grandeur which surrounded them.

"Here!" called Flindas into her reverie.

She turned to see that he had entered a narrow walkway between two high stone walls. Even these were a feast to the eyes of one accustomed to rocky outcrops and mean slovenly camps. Following him quickly down the narrow way, they eventually came to a wood and iron gate set deep into a high plastered wall. Flindas gave the gate a push but it was locked, with no handle or keyhole to be seen. He smiled, and looking around to be sure that none saw him, he strode back into the alley and then leapt upward, his hand just managing to grasp the top of the wall.

"I put this hold here years ago," he said to Tris as he pulled himself higher, finally disappearing from her view.

The gate opened quickly and Tris entered a many coloured garden which took her breath away. She had never, in all her life, seen a place so beautiful. Tears came to her eyes as she stood in the midst of this wonder of flowers and trees and ferns. A deep pond held golden darting fish and small birds hunted in the trees and amongst the greenery below. Flindas quickly walked up the path which led to his sister's back door. Tris followed slowly, gently touching the strange delicate flowers as Flindas rapped on the door. There was a shuffling from within and the door opened just enough for Flindas to see the flash of steel and an old face within the dark hallway.

"I got cold steel for you if you come in here," said an aged rasping voice. "Get you gone before I stick you."

Flindas smiled and removed his hat, letting his long hair fall to his shoulders. "I hope that an old friend will say hello before he sticks a knife in me," he said through the narrow gap.

There was a pause, and then the door opened a little more. "Master Flindas?" asked the voice in wonder.

"Indeed Samlin, your young bird has returned to the nest."

Tris watched as a small aged man stepped from the house and greeted Flindas with a warm clasping of hands.

"You have been gone such a long time, we thought you dead," he said still holding the younger man's hands. "Someone has certainly been pounding on your face to change it so. Excuse me Flindas, but I think even Darbra would pass you in the street."

Flindas laughed as they turned and entered the house. "The nose is not all mine," he said. "Dantas does fine work with disguise."

"Dantas!" exclaimed Samlin. "So the old rogue is still out

there somewhere, I am glad to hear it."

"I would be glad to hear of Darbra," said Flindas looking around the familiar kitchen where Samlin led them. "Is she not home that you must be the one to ward off robbers?"

"She has gone to the markets," replied Samlin. "We stay living in this beautiful home but it is much harder now. The house remains under the protection of the Governor, but few now believe that he will be Governor for long. Darbra sent the children to safety in the south. She is not able to leave the city, and Alarin is kept a virtual captive by the courts. He works as he always has as one of the lawyers, but they give him very little time with Darbra. Your father knows that they both wish to leave the city, but neither will try to escape without the other. The children were a lucky gamble and left without detection." Samlin rubbed his chin, a look of deep concern in his eyes. "Sometimes they watch the house, but only when Darbra and Alarin are here together," he said.

The old man turned to the fire and set water to boil. During the meal, which Tris ate in small portions so as not to disturb her disguise, Flindas sought news of his mother and received a solemn look from Samlin.

"She has sunk deeper into her silence," he said. "Only the Governor can get a word from her these days, and he has now stopped trying. She no longer sits at his side, but spends her days abed, neither truly seeing nor hearing anyone." A deep sadness was in the old man's voice. "Darbra sees her often, but they can no longer share words or thoughts. There is little time left to her I fear."

Flindas lowered his eyes to the table. He had not seen his mother since he had fled the city. Darbra had told him of her failing health over the years. Alone she lay, now in a high inaccessible chamber of the castle where her favourite son could not go. Flindas loved his mother, and in his youth had watched with great sadness as a creeping illness had slowly invaded her mind and taken her from him.

Late that afternoon they were sitting comfortably in the kitchen talking with Samlin when they heard the front door open. Heavy steps came down the hallway and a large and powerful man entered carrying two baskets filled with produce from the market.

"What this?" he said gruffly to Samlin, eyeing the two shabby figures who sat about the table.

Flindas rose from his seat as his sister entered. Tris could see a likeness in the two, though the family resemblance was not strong. Where Flindas was tall and dark Darbra was much shorter, and as the sunlight from the window caught her hair it shone a soft brown, flecked with gold. Darbra's face was strong and a stern expression held her features rigid as she first looked at the small untidy woman, then at the tall figure who stood against the light of the westerly window.

"Who is this you invite into our home," she asked Samlin, who broke into a wide, silent smile.

She looked again at the strange features of the man before her, and then her face lit with recognition. "Flindas!" she cried and threw herself across the room and into his waiting embrace.

They held each other for a long time, her sobs muffled in his chest as she clung to him and he enveloped her in his arms.

"We thought you dead," she said, finally overcoming her tears, and held him so she could see his features. "You have not got any prettier," she said, looking into the strange face that was her brother's and yet was not.

"Take care of the nose," said Flindas with laughter in his voice. "It is not mine and I must not damage it. There was much work needed to make me look so ugly." She laughed then and slapped him lightly on the shoulder. "You change not big brother," she said, then again pulled him close.

Introductions were made. The large man was called Nold. He was the grandson of Samlin and had come to live in the house when the children were sent to the south. He was immensely strong, yet it was obvious that his mind would never equal his powerful frame. He was slow to understand and did not like change. It took sometime for Darbra to explain that Flindas was her brother and that none should know of his presence in the house. Nold seemed to finally understand, but still eyed the newcomers suspiciously as they sat around the table and told their stories. Darbra could hardly believe much that she heard during the telling of their adventures.

"To have faced Maradass," she said in awed wonder as the tale reached into the Broken Lands.

Flindas told it briefly and missed out much. His concern for his sister had not lessened with seeing her well and not in poverty. They both sensed that their father would soon fall from his powerful seat, and there could be no telling if Darbra would remain safe in the city.

"You must come away with me," said Flindas. "Escape before Maradass takes full power here. No one can understand the mind of this Evil One. Why he keeps the Governorship in place I cannot say, except that with the continuation of commerce he keeps his army fed."

"I would follow you gladly," said Darbra. "I wish to be gone from here, but I will not leave without Alarin. Maradass keeps the people entrapped here. Some fight him but there are others who see him as inevitable or even worse, a liberator. The fools think that Maradass could be no worse than our father."

"His plans are far worse than anything," said Tris, having spoken little during the day. "It is the Krags, the Stone Soldiers that should be feared the most. They live from the land's energy and nothing can grow where they have walked. Maradass intends that all will eventually die, except for his household and the creatures he makes."

"I had not heard overmuch of these soldiers," said Darbra. "News comes but sparingly. Even father does not know what is happening in the Regions. He bluffs his court but I understand him. He is afraid, and does not know what to do except to carry on as long as possible."

"Alarin must come too," said Flindas returning to his earlier thoughts. "You should go to him and convince him of the need to escape. Can he get away from the courts this evening?"

Darbra thought for some moments before replying. "He could get away but he would be followed," she said, finally making her own decision to leave the city. "If Samlin would go and say I am very unwell I think they would let him come home."

"It must be done," said Flindas as the old man nodded his agreement.

"I will prepare for the journey," said Darbra and stood up from her place at the table.

"Do not take overmuch," advised Flindas. "We will need to go by the Underways, and whatever you bring will be heavy with water by the time we leave the city walls."

"The Underways," said Darbra to herself, as childhood nightmares crept into her waking mind.

She left the room slowly, her thoughts already wandering through the wet dark places beneath the city. The afternoon was drawing to a close when Samlin left the house and made for the castle. Nold also left the house to stay amongst friends elsewhere in the city. The home of Darbra and Alarin would not be safe once it was discovered that they had escaped. When Darbra had finished her preparations, she returned to the kitchen with two small packs.

"How will we avoid being followed?" she asked her brother, coming to sit at his side, her hand resting gently on his arm.

"It is not far to an entrance of the Underways," he replied. "When it is darker, you and Alarin will leave as if going for a walk. If you pretend to be weak, the ones who follow will only think that you go to a physician, or need the cool night air. We will wait here until I see how many follow. They will not dog your heels for long."

His matter of fact statement eased some of the fears which had been building in Darbra as the day had lengthened. It was almost dark when the front door of the house burst open and Alarin entered quickly, running for the stairs to the upper floor. Darbra called him from the kitchen, his worried look as he entered turned to one of surprise.

"I was told you were very ill," he exclaimed as he came to her and took her hands in his.

"It was a ruse," she said. "Flindas has come to take us from the danger here. We must go tonight."

Alarin turned to Flindas and Tris who had now removed their facial disguises. They were sure now that they would no longer be needed, as it was through the Underways and not the main gate that they would leave the city. The two men clasped hands as old friends.

"It is good to see you again," said Flindas to the tall wiry man dressed in the dark lawyer's garb. "Will you leave with us? The danger here is great and I would see at least some of my family safe."

"Willingly," replied Alarin. "The city palls on me and these black ones are strangling it even further." He looked at the packs which lay upon the table. "It is little to show for many years work," he said, glancing about the room at all the things which they must leave behind. "Still, our lives, and those of our children are more important than all the gold in your father's coffers. Yes, let us be gone as quickly as we can."

"Did you see any who followed?" asked Flindas, peering through a back window to judge the darkness of the night.

"They always follow," replied Alarin. "At least two, sometimes more. They wait in the shadows across the street, and in the alley behind the house."

"It is as dark as it will be this night," said Flindas returning to the table. "You must leave first. Act as though you are in distress and taking Darbra to a physician. We will follow with the packs and take care of those who lurk in the shadows."

Alarin smiled, remembering the skills of which Flindas seldom spoke.

"It is time," said Flindas.

They watched from a dark window as Darbra and Alarin opened the front door and entered the street. The couple turned right, with Darbra leaning heavily on Alarin's arm, and began to make their way down the dimly lit roadway. Flindas touched Tris on the shoulder and pointed as a dark shadow left a narrow alley across the way and began to follow the receding pair. With great care Flindas quietly opened the door and then they too were in the street, following, but staying well behind. The one who they had seen was soon joined by another shadow from the back of the house. They were not soldiers but would surely be armed with a knife or two.

"If I do not take them both, then it is up to you to get the second," said Flindas to Tris in a whisper; but there was no need for her help.

Those who followed the slow moving pair did not expect to be followed themselves. On quiet swiftly moving feet Flindas came within an arm's length of the two before they sensed him and turned. One man suddenly slumped to the roadway, while the other managed the beginnings of a cry before a fist smashed into his jaw and his mind fell into darkness. Quickly they dragged the two men into shadows then ran to catch up with the others.

"The nearest entrance to the Underways lies not far ahead," said Flindas taking his sister's arm and moving them quickly down the street.

After a short time he took them along another narrow lane and into a small park. At one time it must have been a pleasant place for the local people to pass a fine summer's day, but it was now unkempt and devoid of trees. The grass was long and the many flower beds were overgrown with creeping vines covered in long sharp thorns.

Flindas moved towards a ruined building at the other side of the open ground, and pushing back a thick mass of the thorn covered vines, he clambered through a broken doorway. He stood for a while as his eyes became accustomed to the darkness, the dim lights of the city doing little to dispel the gloom. When he could see better he made his way to the far wall of the roofless building, and after a brief search he gave a small chuckle.

"Dantas has been here already," he said and held in his hands a sword, a length of rope, and a number of torches. "He will not be in the Underways yet but will join us later."

Flindas looped the rope around a sturdy beam and prepared to lower the others into the depths. Alarin went first, and then Darbra. He was lowering the packs when he heard from further within the city the sudden blaring sound of a horn being blown.

"It is an alarm," he said to Tris. "Perhaps for us, or perhaps not."

"Samlin did not return," said Tris. "He may have been questioned further."

"Samlin would not betray us, even if it meant his life,"

replied Flindas.

Quickly he secured the rope about Tris in preparation for lowering her to join the others. Far off he could hear the sound of troops running through a distant street.

Tris reached the bottom of the shaft in darkness. She could see nothing, and it was only the voice of Darbra which gave her any idea of direction. Flindas soon joined them, the rope slithering down into a heap beside him. It took only moments to light one of the torches, and soon they were all able to see the green slimy walls of the old waterway as it stretched away into the darkness to the east and west.

"This way," said Flindas and led them along the western tunnel.

The stone slab floor of the old waterway was slippery with mud, while overhead many ancient cobwebs hung down, often catching in their hair, or puffing into brief flame as they caught in the fire of the torch. The tunnel began to slope downward a little, taking them deeper beneath the city. In places the ancient bricks, which formed the old waterway, had crumbled and fallen into their path. Yet the packed earth and rock had remained solid. The engineers and builders had done their work well, and it was only through neglect on the part of the later governors that water no longer flowed through the city by this masterful system.

"I do not know this part well," said Flindas, his voice echoing ahead of them as they made their way down the slight incline. "Soon we should come to a major tunnel which leads to the south. If I am right we will await Dantas there."

Occasionally a side tunnel could be seen, or from above a pale shaft of light would show where another opening reached to the surface. Though the way ahead appeared straight, it was difficult to tell for sure. Flindas could only guess that their course continued to the west. Then, after a long slow descent, the tunnel levelled out and they found themselves confronted by a widening passage filled with stale fetid water which reached almost to their knees. There was a large hole above them which led to the surface but gave no idea of direction. Long tendrils of a wet subterranean plant hung down, making it difficult to see very far ahead. They moved along the tunnel where rats, frightened by the intruders, swam away before them. A foul revolting smell intruded upon their senses. Flindas entered a new tunnel holding the torch aloft. The tunnel immediately began to slope downward in a slow curving sweep.

"I do not know this at all," said Flindas looking up a long shaft at a few stars far above. "Though it seems to leads us in the right direction."

He took them down the ever increasing slope. The smell did not lessen, though they slowly became used to it. Flindas did not wish to alarm the others but he knew that somewhere ahead there must be something which caused the smell, something dead and rotting. The descent became more difficult until Flindas brought them to a halt.

"It is no longer possible without the rope," he said to the others then turned to Tris. "I will lower you as far as the rope will reach. If it does not level out we will have to find another way."

Tris agreed and was soon slipping down the incline attached to one end of the rope, as the others fed it out slowly. Tris held a torch and Flindas watched as its light disappeared down the shaft. There was little rope left when it went slack in his hand and he heard Tris's voice call to them from far below.

"I have reached the bottom," her words drifted up to them. "It stinks even worse down here." Then she gave a startled cry which was cut off quickly.

"What is it?" called Flindas, preparing to plunge down the shaft to her rescue.

"Rats," came her reply. "Huge cursed rats."

Flindas smiled as he prepared to lower Alarin to join her. Darbra began to speak as she helped.

"Do you remember our childhood," she said. "How Kaylan and Jondarl would chase me with a sack they said had a rat inside? I always ran, even though I never saw the creature. I fear rats more than anything else."

"Do you also remember how they suddenly stopped playing that game?" said Flindas.

"Yes," she replied. "I often wondered why they ceased such

a successful amusement."

Flindas chuckled a little at an old memory. "One night, in their separate rooms, they each found a very live rat beneath their bedclothes," he told her. "Of course they knew it must have been me but they never once said anything, perhaps through fear that it might happen again. They were both too timid to touch a rat. I think they taunted you with a fear that they both held themselves."

Alarin called out that he had reached the bottom. Darbra followed her husband and then Flindas, in total darkness, began the descent. It was difficult, his fingertips wedging into small gaps between bricks where mortar had fallen away. His hands were aching by the time he saw the torchlight below, and he slid the last short distance to join the others. The tunnel branched in four directions and Flindas took the way that he guessed most likely to lead towards their goal. Many rats now scuttled ahead of them, and the stench increased until their sense of smell seemed to override all others.

There were many side tunnels and shafts leading in other directions, but Flindas continued to follow the way he had first chosen. The tunnel began to broaden until the brick work on either side of them ceased and they entered a vast chamber. The smell was overwhelming and their torchlight became dim in the open space, while the floor ahead of them seemed to writhe and move. Flindas walked forward slowly. In the gloom a tall mound of indistinct whiteness rose above them, then he stopped as he realised what lay before him. The movement on the floor was that of hundreds upon hundreds of rats, retreating rapidly from the firelight. The white mound which towered over their heads was the fleshless bones of a great many dead, rags of clothing still covering parts of their horrible nakedness. Those at the top and the outer extremes of the hideous mountain still carried a little flesh which was being stripped by the myriad teeth of the hungry rats. The horror was too much for Darbra and she fell into Alarin's arms, holding tightly, her head buried in his chest.

"Quickly," said Flindas and moved away.

They followed him until they were far from the horror,

though it would stalk their minds for a long time. When they rested Alarin held Darbra in his arms and turned to Flindas.

"Maradass murders the people and casts them into the Underways," he said it with such conviction that he was surprised at the reply.

"Most of those bones have been there much longer than that," said Flindas. "There is only one man who can be responsible for such a thing."

"Father?" said Darbra incredulously, and then realised that it must be true. "But who are they?" she asked. "How is it that we have not heard of so many people missing from the city?"

"We are beneath Dargol," her brother replied and Darbra saw the final truth.

"What is Dargol?" asked Tris, not knowing the city as the others did.

"It is a prison," replied Flindas. "The dungeons of the castle hold only a small number of those that the courts see fit to put in chains. Now I also understand why, even in these hard times, that the city is not plagued by rats."

He led them further into the Underways. An occasional shaft of moonlight from above helped him to find his way, and finally they reach a tunnel with a high curved ceiling, the one which he sought.

The group rested. Dantas was not waiting for them as Flindas had hoped, and the old warrior was the only man alive who had spent the time to learn all of the ways. Even before Flindas had been born Dantas had passed through the tunnels many times, never knowing when his knowledge may be needed. Extinguishing the torch the four companions sat in a narrow side passage, a little drier than out in the much larger tunnel. They waited and in the darkness, Flindas and Darbra spoke quietly of the recent years that had passed. Flindas was laughing softly at a whimsical story which his sister had just told when Tris spoke with a hushed urgency.

"Someone comes," she said. "More than one."

A dim light flickered far up the broad tunnel, sending eerie patterns across the ceilings and walls. Distant voices began to grow louder.

"It is not Dantas," said Flindas as they moved deeper into the narrow passage. "He would not come with such noise."

Indeed, there seemed to be more than a few coming down the tunnel towards them. Somehow, over the stench of stale air and stagnant water, Tris detected a familiar smell.

"Marauders," she said urgently and Flindas knew not to question how she could tell.

"They search the Underways for us," he whispered. "Quickly, we must leave here."

The distant torchlight was still far off and so he took a chance and led them as silently as possible along the broader tunnel. They had not gone far in the darkness when Flindas saw torchlight appear ahead of them from a side turning. There was a splashing and a guttural shout. They had been seen, caught between the lights of the approaching soldiers. A marauder howled, its call piercing the air, echoing, shattering the grave-like stillness of the Underways. From the second group of soldiers came an answering howl, from another of the black dogs.

Flindas cursed beneath his breath. They had waited too long for Dantas and now they were trapped. Both parties of soldiers were rushing towards them, and in the torchlight Flindas saw the first marauder lunging forward on the end of a long leash. There was nowhere to run, nowhere to hide. He grasped his sword, preparing to meet the running soldiers, and then from somewhere in the darkness an arrow whistled through the air. With a scream of pain the marauder stopped its forward rush, thrashing about in the shallow water. Another shaft sank deep into the handler's chest and he fell without a sound. There was a cry of surprise and terror as two more fell writhing. The others turned and fled along another side tunnel, though not before another of their number had fallen. A light flickered further down the tunnel as a torch was lit.

"Hurry!" called Dantas. "They will not hold back for long."

"Well met," said Flindas as they joined his old teacher at a run. "That was a little close for my liking."

"It is still too close," replied Dantas as he handed Flindas a bow and a stock of arrows.

Turning, they began to run down the old watercourse, their feet splashing in the shallow waters, as from behind could be heard the sounds of pursuit.

"This way," called the old Elbrand commander.

He turned left along a side tunnel which began at once to take them downward. Soon the sound from behind was lost in the density of stone.

"Here," said Dantas. "Climb!"

The torchlight had caught the dangling end of a rope which hung from a narrow shaft in the ceiling of the tunnel. The rope was needed though it was not a vertical climb. Dantas climbed last.

"They will not follow us this way," he said as they reached yet another level of the ancient system. "They are combing the city and the Underways, and it is Flindas Demsharl they seek."

They rested for a moment before pressing on.

"They know you are here," continued Dantas. "How, I can only guess. They will increase the guard on the outfalls and close the outlets. We will not be able to pass that way."

"What can we do?" asked Alarin. The concern in his voice told of his fear for his beloved wife.

"We must return above," replied Dantas, standing and preparing to leave. "We could avoid them for a long time down here but not forever. The dogs are the danger. I believe they have brought them into the city just to find us. I heard from friends that they were seen just after dark with their handlers entering the gates. Somehow they learned of our presence here and now we must return to the city above. There are safe places, and friends who will hide us until we can escape. I fear the dogs most of all. We must be careful, and also hope that rain comes soon."

It was not long before first light, when Dantas, after many side turnings, finally led them from the Underways into the south of the city. The sky was dark and promised rain, while the streets were empty and silent. Not far from the exit of the Underways Dantas turned into an unlit street, and then led them to a small shabby house set back a little from the road. It had once had a pleasant front garden but the pathway was cracked and broken, and only scraggly bushes and a lone tree remembered its former charm. Without knocking Dantas entered and whistled into the dark hallway. From the floor above came the sounds of someone opening a door. Soon they were joined by a twisted misshapen old woman who did not speak, but showed them into the small kitchen at the back of the house.

"This is Mira," said Dantas in introduction. "She does not speak, but understands all that you say. We will be safe here."

Mira nodded, smiling a toothless grin. She hobbled to the fire and soon they were drinking a welcome hot tea and drying themselves by the low flames. Dantas stood by the window and looked hopefully at the sky. It was not until much later that he was rewarded. A soft drizzle turned slowly to rain, then a downpour which caused him to smile.

"They will not find us now," he said, a note of relief in his voice. "We will be safe until we leave, though I think we should remain here for a while, perhaps a day or two. With luck they will think we are still in the Underways. The place that we came out is not easily found, though the dogs could perhaps detect it. Even so, it would take them some time, and after that the city is a large place to search."

They all rested now. Mira had dragged two old mattresses in by the fire and soon they were asleep, the dark night in the Underways colouring their dreams.

During the following day Mira left the house to gather news in the city. When she returned she spoke to Dantas using her hands until he knew all that she had learned. Samlin had not been taken prisoner and was now hidden in another part of the city, awaiting his own chance to escape into the countryside. As Mira silently told the last part of her news she made a strange gesture with her hands, as though to ward off evil.

"Zard has come into Andrian," Dantas told them when Mira had finished gesturing.

"That does not bode well for the city, or the Governor," said Flindas.

"What of the search?" asked Darbra. "Do they still seek us?"

"Yes," replied Dantas. "The dogs are all over the city, not many of them, but they move quickly and search for our scent. We must remain inside and not open doors or windows. Mira will go tomorrow into the city and contact a group of Southlanders who are helping people escape. I know some of them and they may be able to aid us. The Underways are heavily guarded now and we cannot go that way. I can see no other route out of the city except over the wall. If horses were awaiting us we could escape, though it will certainly mean an attack on the sentries who guard the walls." He paused a moment and looked at Flindas, who nodded knowingly.

"We must choose our escape route well," said Flindas, his mind travelling along the walls of the city, remembering its corners and towers.

"I know the place already," said Dantas smiling. "It is where the wall turns sharply against the most southern tower."

"So we just jump over the wall and escape," said Tris, a look of doubt on her face.

"It may take a little more than that," Dantas replied. "We will have a great many soldiers on us in moments. What we need most is a night that is not too dark, and some rain."

"And horses," said Flindas.

"Yes, horses," agreed Dantas.

News from the city the following day was not hopeful. The city gate was now even harder to pass. Everyone was being checked and there were marauders there at all times.

"The Southlanders cannot help us as they have some others," said Dantas. "Their only escape routes out of the city were by the gate and the Underways. The dogs know our scent so these are closed to us." He looked out the window at a grey murky sky. "The moon brightens," he said, returning to sit with the others around the table where Mira was laying bowls of hot soup. "If it rains tonight I think we should go. The Southlanders have agreed to help as they can. They said they will wait each night for us until the full moon, and will have horses waiting in the woods as close to the city as they can without being seen."

The storm that had been brewing all day broke upon the city in the early evening, bringing much rain and a gale from the south. To Dantas it was ideal for their purposes. The wind was bitterly cold as the companions left the small snug house in the darkness of night. Rain came fitfully, washing the streets and narrow ways by which Dantas led them, keeping to the darkest shadows. Several times they saw soldiers patrolling the city, torchlight flickering against the broken walls of deserted streets. Once they saw a troop with a marauder but they were going another way and were soon lost in the darkness. Flindas knew this part of the city well. He had passed through it many times as a boy on his way to the harbour, to the freedom of a small sailboat and open waters.

Dantas turned to them and whispered. "The Southlanders are close by," he said, then led them down a narrow lane and entered a roofless ruin of a building.

He gave a soft whistle into the darkness and received a reply from the shadows. They were soon joined by a small number of bowmen. After a short whispered talk they left the building and made for the city wall. They could see it against the darkness where torches flared as the wind caught at them, dulling their effectiveness. In the scattered light they could see the night sentries who were all soldiers of Maradass and should have been standing only a few paces apart on the high parapets. Now most were huddled against the stonework, not caring to look out to the south and into the eye of the wind, or even behind to the silent city. Flindas passed the rope he had been carrying to Tris.

"No matter what happens, you must get this secure and be gone," he told her. "Help my sister and go to the horses in the forest." He turned to Darbra and Alarin. "You will depart with Tris and not wait for us. We will follow as we can."

Darbra reached out and held him for a moment. "Take care brother, and join us quickly," her voice trembled a little.

They moved off and reached the shadows of the wall without being seen. A narrow stairway led to the upper level and Flindas began to climb, followed by Dantas and then the others. In the shadows of some nearby buildings the Southlanders stood, bows strung and ready.

Wind and rain continued to lash at the city as Flindas

reached the top of the stairway. The first black guard only saw a glimpse of movement before Flindas smashed him into unconsciousness. There was a muffled cry as a second guard fell to a blow from Dantas, and then the other sentries were aware of them. There was a cry from one which turned to a gasp of pain as an arrow plunged into his body, the blast of a horn was heard as Tris, who had already tied a loop in the rope, quickly slipped it over the wall and fixed it to the stonework. Steel flashed in the torchlight as black soldiers began to rush upon them. Several fell, caught by the Southlanders' arrows. Flindas and Dantas stood their ground as first Tris, then Darbra, scrambled over the wall and quickly began to climb down the rope.

"Go!" cried Flindas as Alarin hesitated, bending down to draw the sword of one of the fallen.

Flindas struck and felled an onrushing spearman and another screamed as a short stabbing sword slashed across his unprotected face, Alarin waited no longer and was gone. The black soldiers were hesitating. The ferocity of their two opponents and the shafts of flighted death from the shadows caused them to slow their attack.

"Go!" cried Flindas as he saw Dantas rush at them.

"No!" he heard his old teacher call back to him. "You go before me!"

There was a sudden rush of soldiers as three abreast they charged their enemy from both directions. Flindas cast a knife into the throat of one as a spear thrust from another caught in his clothing, a searing pain running across his ribs as the man fell to the thrust of his sword. Arrows continued to fall amongst the soldiers as Flindas turned and swung himself over the edge, there was no time to argue and Dantas would follow if he could. The clash of swords came to him as he dropped down the rope. Then from somewhere on the wall a large stone was hurled, almost catching Flindas as he neared the ground. Other rocks fell past him. Dantas was still above and there was no feeling of another on the rope. The sounds of battle reached Flindas as he dropped to the ground and looked up. Another rock crashed down from above and he cursed, the rope was still, the Southlanders had not been able to stem the rush of soldiers.

Flindas heard a cry from above which could have been the voice of Dantas. He growled loudly. His first thought was to scale the rope and die on the wall with his friend. Then he saw the senselessness of such a gesture and quickly turned to go, to disappear into the darkness. He had only taken a step or two when a large stone thrown from the wall crashed into the side of his head, sending him reeling to the earth. A grey fog clouded his mind and he felt his stomach turn. Pain lanced through his head like fire as he tried to gain his feet, then he fell again to the earth. Flindas attempted to crawl away from the wall but all his strength had flown. He collapsed and lay with his cheek against the damp cold ground, unable to move. The grey fog deepened and his last thoughts were sadness that he would not see Darbra again, then the fog turned to blackness and he knew no more.

Awakening

All was cold blue fire. For an age there was nothing but painful blue light, and within it the maniacal ruinous laughter. Dream visions came, and all were destroyed as the lands wept and died. Forests burned and oceans boiled, and even the earth was consumed. The lands split and fire belched forth, engulfing all that lay in its path. It was the portent of time's ending.

Kerran, the wizard Chelasta, swam against the ice blue flame and was not consumed. Through an age of burning that stripped him of thought, but not of understanding. Kerran learned and absorbed the old power of Chelasta, the memories of his own ancient family finally lifting him above the flames. Though Maradass screamed his vengeful threats, Kerran heard them no longer. Leaving the fear and horror behind, he climbed high into an open dawn, clear and bright, awake and alive.

Piata sat as she had often done in the last few days, curled into a corner beside the sleeping figure that was Kerran. As a runner she was not yet needed by the army and had spent much of each day amongst the wounded in Verardian and Leana's care. She helped where she could and then would return to sit by the young man whom she loved. When she had arrived at the refuge Piata had been told that he had remained asleep since arriving at the poet's home, and nothing, not even water, had passed his lips in almost a moon. When at first she had seen him again, she could barely believe that he was the same person. His thin gaunt face seemed so much older now as he lay on his mattress, lost in dreams. Though they had spent so little time together on Zeta she knew that there could not be anyone else for her. At times she would hold his lifeless hand in her own and whisper softly to him, hoping that he would hear and return to her from his sleeping world.

It was warm in the large living chamber of the house and there was always hot food to be had. Mykal would often do the cooking himself, while Ayla would spend time on rug making, or teaching their children any number of things from their small but varied library. Sometimes Roan would spend a whole day working at his writing, which, though something of a scrawl, was filled with wonderful children's fantasies of magical creatures and high adventure. Solia was a delight to all who came into the home, her warm nature capturing all their hearts.

During the cold bitter days there were often many who would stand around the hearth, rather than brave the colder conditions of the caves on the hillside. Mantris was frequently there when not to the north with his troops, and had made the acquaintance of the young woman, Piata. At first he could not see how someone so small and young could have been strong enough to do well in the qualifying runs which had brought her to the Regions. It was not until Verardian reminded him that the commander recalled her from the Games, and her endurance against the last of the men.

Mantris often sat at the large dining table and listened to Mykal tell ancient tales and poems collected in the man's eventful lifetime. It was sometimes difficult to tell where historical fact ended, and the clever, articulate mind of the poet would take over. He might weave a wonderful adventure with his words, only to say that he had made it up on the moment and would never be able to remember it again. Mykal would laugh uproariously, and then assure them that the next one was indeed a true and honest tale.

In the evenings of the long winter, there was often a tankard of dark ale at Mykal's elbow, and any who wished could help themselves from one of the large barrels that were kept in the basement beneath the house. There were none so unwell that they would not occasionally partake of the poet's smooth but potent brew which he made himself. Few though could drink the four or five tankards which Mykal himself would sometimes consume in an evening. He seemed immune to its affects, while Mantris, when he had once succumbed to the offer of a second, woke the next morning having forgotten when or how he had found his bed. Verardian said that he felt strange even after one sniff and had declined the no doubt wonderful experience, which Mykal assured him would result from *just a sip or two*.

Many days had passed in this way and snow lay deep upon the Southlands, Kerran slipped further into his dream world to a place where none could reach him. Wandering in this dream time his body had lost all need for nourishment. Neither food nor water had passed his lips and yet he had not withered and died. Some force, which Verardian could barely detect, kept the young wizard alive as the long season darkened.

Eventually Piata was called to the army. She stood for a while over the still and silent young man whom she no longer knew, and perhaps would never know again. She had heard much from others of his wizardry and latent powers which had brought him to the understanding of what they called the Wizards Way. She wondered if he could have become all this without leaving much of his past behind. Piata stood for a moment longer above Kerran's bed then left quickly, joining the band of soldiers who were to escort the wounded back to the coast, and the sanctuary of the fleet. Verardian and Leana stood on the stone steps and watched the troop begin their long and arduous march to the coast. Snow was falling gently and the white shrouded soldiers of Zeta were soon lost from their sight.

"She loves him much," said Leana turning to her brother.

Verardian nodded slowly in agreement.

"Wherever his mind roams, I believe she was able to reach him where I could not," he said.

He turned to enter the house.

"Will you never marry?" asked Leana suddenly, though some years earlier they had much discussed this subject.

"No," replied Verardian with a smile. "As I have said before, we both know that we are fated to live very long lives and will age but slowly." He smiled at his sister gently. "What life would it be for a woman who would marry me?" he said. "I have chosen a path of healing and solitary contemplation. I will not stray from that path even though it may mean the end of the Amitarl line. No dear sister, it is you I think who must consider marriage. We will not live forever and we are, after all, almost a hundred years old already. Should you wish the blood of Amitarl to remain flowing in the life of the land and its people, it is you who must take a husband." He looked at her, his eyes kindly and understanding.

"I cannot," she said abruptly. "Not yet or perhaps ever. Amitarl may die with us both. I cannot say."

She reached out for her brother's hand and Verardian held his sister close. "When we are at peace again," she said. "When Tolth has returned and Maradass is no more, perhaps then."

Verardian was about to close the stout hardwood and iron door when there was a flurry of white wings as Storm alighted upon the step. Verardian was surprised, for the bird had not been seen in a long while, having flown to the north after the army of Zeta had reached the refugee. The white hawk walked quickly across the threshold and after a moment took to the air, flying to a rafter above Kerran's bed. The bird looked down inquisitively upon the young man, and then dropped fluttering to the blankets which covered him. For a long time Storm seemed to study the young wizard, walking up and down his body while Leana and Verardian watched in amused astonishment. The hawk scratched gently at the thin pale face with one taloned foot, when there was no response he took to the air and returned to the rafter above the bed where he spent much time over the following days. Most nights would find him perched there, or he would sleep beside Kerran sometimes, close in to the side of the young man's body. It seemed to Verardian that the hawk had come to watch over the young wizard now that Piata had departed. Rark had taken to sleeping very near to Kerran too as though guarding him, protecting him from the dark forces which the young wizard fought.

Though Mantris spent much of his time at the refuge, the war for him had continued unabated. With relief he had realised that the army of Maradass would not discover the snow bound sanctuary before the winter snows made it impossible for the heavily clad troops to advance into the highlands. When Mantris had become assured that the refuge was safe he had sent troops across the ice fields to harass the Black Army. Using their skills in the snow as they had in the forest, the white army had begun to exact a heavy toll on the soldiers of Maradass, and the Black Army had pulled back almost to the plains south of the Glandrin Highroad.

It was from the Crossroads that news was scarce. Marauders were again present on the Central Plains, roaming alone they covered great distances, and several runners had not reached their destinations. Not for half a moon had news reached Mantris from the Northern Refuge, and he was greatly concerned for Brook and his troops. The night was growing long and he was about to leave the room for the quiet of his own chamber when a cold blast of air told him that the door to the white world beyond Mykal's sanctuary had been opened. He turned as a man staggered in and would have collapsed to the floor but for quick hands. He was a runner from the north along the coast, and without relief had fought through the snows for two exhausting days to bring his messages to the refuge. All were hushed as he regained some of his strength and began to tell them his news.

"I know not which I should tell first, for all is bad," he struggled to say. He nodded in thanks as Mykal passed him a small tumbler of deep amber liquid. It warmed him immediately and he continued. "I will tell it all as I was told it myself. First, word comes from Brook in the north. The Black Army there was joined by a more powerful force from Mendan

Maradass. There was strong fighting for many days. The dogs broke through to the refuge, causing slaughter amongst the wounded. They were driven back and a great many killed but it was the shortage of arrows which caused Brook to retreat. The soldiers of Maradass break all the shafts they can find and press deeper into the forest than they have before. Our troops are tired, and have had little time for rest, so Brook has abandoned the refuge and has taken them far into Dreardim, to face perhaps worse dangers than the Black Army."

The man stopped a moment and looked into the fire. "The last words of that message," he continued. "Were from Brook himself, and he asked the first runner to relay them exactly. These are his words as I was told. 'We are living on the edge of darkness. We lack arrows and the black hounds bay for our blood'."

"It is not good news that you bring," said Mantris as he sat by the man who now gazed forlornly into the fire, unaware of the bowl of hot soup which Ayla was offering him.

"That is the least of the evils which I must tell," the runner said and he appeared to be on the edge of tears. "The fleet has been attacked by blue fire from the skies," he blurted the words out quickly.

There were exclamations of dread amongst those who now hung on his every word.

"Tell," said Mantris quietly as the man turned to him.

"They say it was a shower of blue lightning bolts from dark storm clouds," the runner continued. "Captain Ronsarl had decided to take the fleet north to avoid the bitter cold. They were being overtaken by a heavy storm when the sky opened up and burned with blue fire." Tears now flowed down the man's cheeks as he spoke. "Perhaps ten ships have gone. Captain Ronsarl managed to keep Moonchaser out of danger, and when the storm had passed he picked up survivors, but many have been lost." He shook his head sadly. "Three hundred of our sailors, maybe more."

The stillness around the fire was crushing. The messenger was silent for a time and some of the captains turned to leave, wishing only to forget the news for a time in sleep.

"There is more to tell," said the runner looking up into many fearful eyes. "News comes from the plains where the Black Army lies in camp. Zard had ridden south and has joined them."

Mantris spoke into the silence that followed. "There is much in your words that brings me sadness, and much for me to think on. I will call a meeting of the captains for the morning. Until then I suggest that the night no longer belongs to revelry. I go to my bed and advise you all to do the same." He laid a hand on the weary messenger's shoulder. "Eat, my friend, and sleep here warm beside the fire. You will be asked to speak more on this tomorrow."

Mantris rose and left the room, the captains slowly filing out into the cold night air, leaving Verardian and Mykal sitting beside the fire. The messenger ate quickly, and loud snores soon attested to the man's great exhaustion.

"I too must seek my bed," said Mykal, though he seemed loath to move from the fireside. "Sad news," he added as though to himself and looked across to where Leana lay on a mattress in a corner.

She too preferred the large room as a place of rest and seemed to have gone to sleep quickly, though Mykal doubted this. When the messenger had told his news, the poet had noticed Leana grow pale, and he thought for a moment that she would faint, but she had not. Instead, quietly, Leana had laid herself down and spoken to no one. He wondered again as he often had about this silent and beautiful woman.

"Your sister has a sad and lonely heart," he said to Verardian quietly, knowing that she would not hear his words. "She has lost so much that cannot be replaced and her fears for your father weigh her down with doubt. It is perhaps not my place to say, but I think she should return to Zeta. Her heart would be happier there, and her safety as Amitarl, is most important. If Maradass should conquer the Southlands and push your army from the Regions, there must always remain a hope that Amitarl will return, even if it is not for a hundred years."

"The army of Zeta may not be large but it will not abandon the fight easily," said Verardian, looking across to where Leana lay upon her bed. "It is true that we may lose this war and Leana should be on Zeta, but she will not go. My sister no longer wishes to be a warrior and win the war single handed as she did when she was younger, but we have spoken, and she will not leave the Regions while the army remains here. It has taken a long time, but the old healing magic of our grandmother begins to come through her too. She will not leave while there are wounded to tend."

Verardian's gaze moved across the room to where Kerran remained motionless, lost in his world of dreams. "I believe that young Chelasta has yet a great part to play in this," he continued. "Even now he struggles with Maradass. Kerran holds unknown powers, and though the Evil One was able to touch him with his blue fire, and captured his body, I do not think that he has yet trapped Kerran's mind and being."

"The magic of Maradass has become most powerful," said Mykal in reply. "From what we have heard tonight we will need this young wizard soon if he is to help at all. I am no great scholar of war, but now that Zard has joined his army I do not believe that they will bide the winter on the plains, and not come looking in the mountains again. Zard," he spoke the name with a touch of horror in his voice. "The plague of the lands for centuries, and now he again stands upon the soil of Andrian. Only magic can stop the Black Knight. I hope our wizard wakes up in time." Mykal rose then and bid Verardian goodnight.

In silent semi-darkness Verardian sat on into the night, his eyes almost closed, his mind finding a peaceful tranquillity, slowing his breath and calming his thoughts. Verardian did not sleep at all that night. In the darkness, some time in the early morning, he rose and went to kneel beside Kerran's bed. The healer laid one hand on the young man's chest and one on his brow, giving unseen light flowing through himself into Kerran's body. The first glimmer of dawn began to creep through small cracks in the shuttered windows and Kerran had not stirred. Verardian had failed again as he had before in trying to bring the young man's mind back into the world.

Exhausted, the healer lay himself down upon the straw

mattress near where Rark the mountain dog lay in sleep. Looking up for a moment, Verardian saw the white hawk stirring on its high perch amongst the rafters. There was much to think on, including the strange bird, but Verardian did not allow thoughts to cloud his much needed rest. Soon he was lost in a dream of the Magical Isles. He walked on a long sparkling beach under a warm sun. The ocean smelled of salt and was cool to his feet as he walked the deserted shoreline.

Verardian woke much later and instantly felt that something had changed. He shivered as he raised himself on his elbow and looked towards the front door of Mykal's home. It stood ajar and a small snow drift had collected in the doorway. Snow continued to fall and Verardian wondered who could have been careless enough to leave it open. It was not until he stood and looked around the room that he saw that Kerran's bed lay empty. Verardian searched quickly but found no sign of the young wizard. Rark and the white hawk were also missing. Rushing to the door Verardian looked out on a field of newly fallen snow, just faintly he could make out tracks across the white field. Kerran had left on his own legs and was headed north, and beside his trail were the marks of the mountain dog as he had ploughed through the snow. Verardian called out to those in the house. Leana came quickly, followed by Mykal and Ayla from their room in the back of the dwelling.

"Kerran has gone," Verardian said fearfully, pointing to the rapidly fading tracks in the snow.

"We must follow," said Mykal pulling on a heavy jacket and boots which stood by the door.

They moved as quickly as they could through the knee deep whiteness, and it was only when the trail was completely lost in the falling snow that they stopped. Breathing heavily, Mykal leaned against a tree and stared through the falling flakes into the north.

"We cannot follow in this," he said indicating the increasing snowfall. "He goes directly north. Whatever draws him seems to be in that direction. Let us return and organise a party of men more used to this strenuous work."

Mykal was exhausted and Verardian felt the burning ache in

his own legs. Frustrated, the healer saw the sense in the man's words and they returned as quickly as they could to the refuge. Leana had already alerted a captain of the army, and when they arrived back at the house Verardian and Mykal found four strong men preparing themselves for the search.

"We did not find him," said Verardian as he sank down beside the fire. "He goes to the north."

The men finished their preparations and were soon gone, walking on the snow in their wide spread shoes.

"Where does he go?" Verardian asked himself and shook his head, a great fear descending upon him.

Chelasta the wizard stood and looked around himself, a blanket of snow covered all the land, tall trees, heavily laden, stood with their branches bent low. The sky was a soft blue, and high above he saw the slow flight of a white hawk. He thought for a time and then recalled the creature from his memory.

"Storm," he said the almost forgotten name.

Above him the bird turned in mid flight and fell swooping across the sky, until with a flurry of wings the white hawk landed on the snow, almost disappearing, white on white. Kerran heard a sound, and on looking around him. He saw, not far away, the large hairy dog as it dug in the snow in search of food.

"Rark," he said the unfamiliar name and instantly the dog looked up and came to join him.

Though barefoot and in light clothing Kerran felt no cold or hunger. An inner warmth flowed through him, sustained him, and he understood it and welcomed the first true touch of his own wizard's fire. No longer was he a naive young man from the edge of Dreardim, nor was he the traveller and young hero of Zeta; he was Chelasta, a true wizard who had only just begun to know his strengths and powers. He had been seared by the fire of Maradass and had survived. A strange feeling came upon him and suddenly he laughed. Rark looked up with curiosity and then howled in apparent delight, as Storm gave a cry and took to the air, circling the lone figure in the snow. Then the bird turned and flew to the north. Kerran, the young wizard, Chelasta, began to follow.

Though the snow was deep it did not impede him, and now showed no sign of his passing. Ahead of him, to the north, Kerran knew that he could find the one person that may help him, the only man who could turn back the tide of evil and madness which swept the Regions. The Wizards Way was now closed to Kerran, perhaps forever, but he cared little for that. Maradass held sway on the Wizard Lines but he could be vanquished. This Kerran now knew. To the north was the only man who could end the reign of Maradass and that man was Zard. The son must be persuaded to cease his attacks on the south and to thwart his own father's evil plans.

Two days passed as Kerran pushed to the north, though keen eyed Elbrand were scattered through the snow clad hills, none saw him pass. Messages passed between those who watched and others who scoured the hills for Kerran. The search continued, but soon there were many amongst the men and women of Zeta who did not expect the young wizard to be found alive. It was suspected that he, and the great dog, Rark, had fallen into a crevasse and would never be found again. One small grain of hope reached Verardian as he sat downcast at Mykal's fire. The white hawk had been seen far to the north, high above the last hills bordering the southern plains of Andrian.

Zard had come and none could stand in his way. Mantris had rejoined his main force which lay scattered amongst the hills and forests of southern Andrian. Though the conflict continued, to the commander all now seemed lost. The battles could go on for years but he saw no hope for victory. Even if ten or twenty black soldiers should die for each one of Zeta, Maradass would still win. Southlanders had flocked to the banner of Amitarl and yet they were ill prepared for war in the snow. The South Coast was slowly being lost to the army of Maradass and there were not enough troops to quell their advance. The arrow makers could not keep up with the needs of the white clad army, and now the young wizard had vanished into the snow. To Mantris this was the telling blow. For a long time he had felt some confidence with a wizard amongst them.

Now even this hope was gone.

Mantris stood leaning on his sword, the blade chipped and bloody from a recent exchange. Few of the captains who stood about him had escaped injury during the last days. Far below they watched a slowly advancing line of dark soldiers, pushed on by their captains and commanders. There were many such lines scattered for leagues across a wide front. Though a great number had died it was too few to even slow the unstoppable advance south. Mantris felt at a loss. He sorely missed the advice and encouragement of Tolth and his lost friend Torian. Was he to continue the fight until all the pride of Zeta lay waste upon the battle field? Or should he retreat to what remained of the fleet and return to Zeta, hoping that the Magic Isles would keep Maradass at bay? All choices seemed fraught with evil, but in his heart Mantris knew that he would not leave the Regions. He would die on this foreign soil, held by the oath of Amitarl to protect its people against slavery and death. He would not betray that oath, but soon he would give the army a choice. Each soldier must decide to stay or return to Zeta, though both choices led to an uncertain future.

The Black Army was attacked during the day. White clad archers appeared from the snow, loosening many shafts at the struggling advance, and then disappeared over rocky outcrops or into the dense woods. It was mid afternoon and Mantris had withdrawn to the east when a change came over the trudging black troops. Mantris watched as the most advanced soldiers led by Zard hesitated, their lines breaking and scattering. The dark figure of Zard could easily be seen on his tall warhorse against the distant snow. He had ceased to advance and for the remainder of the day he sat upon his horse, unmoving, his men falling back as though by some invisible force. Mantris watched in wonder until the sun set and all was plunged into darkness once again. It was sometime in the early morning that Mantris was woken by one of his men, who explained excitedly that a silent battle of fire was tearing at the land to the north. Mantris came quickly to the high vantage point where the guard had kept watch. A freezing wind pushed at his back as he stood upon the frozen rock and looked down upon a valley of glittering blue and white fire.

A cold and bitter wind swept across the blood stained battlefield, where the Wizard Chelasta stood before the Black Knight. Zard remained seated on his ghostly white steed. He looked down on the young man and smiled.

"So I need pursue you no longer," he said, a sneer on his lips. "Is this surrender? Or do you challenge me? Come, speak! I wish to see the humour in this." His confident words held a laced edge of fear in it, though there were none close enough to hear it except Kerran.

"I do challenge you!" cried Kerran, a power in his voice that surprised Zard. He knew that Kerran could never overcome Maradass with magic. His father held two pieces of the Seacrest and that same power passed unhindered from father to son. Zard heard the bold reply and laughed. "And what weapons do you bring?" he asked. "I see neither sword nor blade of any kind, a pouch that could hold any number of small things, but a weapon, no."

Kerran, his eyes looking hard into the black warrior's face, reached into the pouch and brought forth the two fragments of the Seacrest.

A look of unbridled lust flashed in the eyes of Zard. "Give them to me," he said, thrusting out his armoured hand.

"No," said Kerran calmly, his eyes unwavering. "I challenge you with no other weapons but words," he continued. "If you listen and hear a lie I will give you what you most desire." He brought his hands together, one fragment in each, and held them out before him. "Hear me, for I know that you wish to. I have seen you search for the truth in a book of lies, the truth of your past and the truth that your father has kept from you. Listen and I will tell you only truth." He paused while the face of Zard, hard and bitten by the winter's cold, became like stone.

Kerran knew that the Black Knight fought against his dark other self and the wicked nature of his father, in a search for the truth. Zard was afraid to hear what Kerran would say, and yet could neither depart nor slay the young wizard. Bound in his own fear, he heeded the words in silence. For the rest of the day and into the night he listened as Kerran told him of the true past, of the early times of the Wizard's Wars, the making of the Seacrest, and the final desperate deed of Rishtan-Sta. Zard learned of how the Seacrest was fished up from the blue depths of Shardis, and how it had passed though many hands until the Alliance of Maradass and Amitarl. He learned of Zard, the benevolent Governor of Glandrin for a thousand years, and then his return as the Black Knight, the son of his mad brother. Now he had come again and he must decide for good or for darkness. Zard heard these words and knew the truth in them.

"Your father holds you with his magical powers, but you can defy him," said Kerran softly. "Defy him I say. I counsel you to listen, and be not the same as you were when you last lived. Your father would kill all that is good and leave nothing but darkness. The lands will die and all will be dust, and then only the Maradass family will live on in a world that is poisoned and dead. Why I ask? The Wizard Rishtan-Sta wished for peace and goodness among people. The Seacrest, and the desire for its power, has twisted all of your family. There is more strength in goodness than in evil, so I bid you hear my challenge. Turn against all that Maradass would have you do. Become the benefactor you once were and not again the dark killer. All I have said is the truth and this you know. You must choose now if you are able, if you are not held lifeless and unfeeling under your father's control."

Kerran said no more and there was a long silence. The night lay dark to all eyes who watched, though for Kerran and Zard the darkness was not a barrier to their sight. All could be seen now, for their magic made it so.

"It is in my power to do good or ill," said Zard, finally breaking the cold silence. "I do not know if what you call 'good' can ever be found. My father holds me as you say, yes, but even if it were otherwise I think I would not defy him." These last words were said with a note of sadness in the Black Knight's voice. "I have come to take what you have," he said, pulling himself erect in the saddle and suddenly glaring at Kerran, a blue flicker coming from his eyes. "I will not defy my father and our history," he said defiantly. "You will give the Seacrest pieces to me now and then you may go, unhindered. Return to

Zeta. Take your ragged army and go. I will not prevent you, nor will I pursue you to those lands, on this you have my word, but I must have what you hold, for my father wills it."

Zard spurred his mount forward. There came a sudden blaze of white light which threw a great fear into the beast. The horse reared backwards to escape the brightness and Zard was thrown from the saddle. He rose deliberately with blue fire searing a path towards Kerran. White fire caught it and flung it back. The Wizard Chelasta spoke ancient words of power as the blue flames danced about him in a silent battle of light. Zard came to a standstill and white flames enveloped him. Lunging into the flames, he drew his sword and cried out as the white fire burned him. Unable to advance Zard was held motionless. With great effort he drew a long throwing knife, but it exploded into white flame. His sword burned brightly and then lay melting on the snow. Blue and white fire fought in the air between them until the blue fire finally succumbed and was gone. Zard staggered and fell to the snow as all life seemed to leave his body. Kerran fell to his knees, the white fire flickering for a time before it gently faded.

On a high snow covered knoll, Mantris stood and looked into the darkness. All was still, now that the lights had gone. He wondered what it could mean but found no answer. He had seen only the wondrous lights that fought and then were consumed. The following morning Mantris woke to hear the strange news that the Black Army had withdrawn. Scouts who followed the soldiers of Maradass throughout the day reported that they seemed to be returning to the plains.

"Another strange thing," said the scout, who came into the temporary camp late that evening. "That white hawk seems to be following them too." He paused a moment as if he could say more but did not continue.

"Is there something else?" asked Mantris, sensing the man's hesitation.

"Just a report from the coast," he said. "A lone scout came across dog tracks. Big dog heading north, thought it could be that Rark maybe."

Another day passed and then came the strangest and most terrifying news that Mantris could imagine. He heard in disbelief how Kerran had been seen riding towards the City Amitarl with Zard, and a great many other black horse troops. The woman who had seen this was sure that she was not mistaken. She had been within a few paces of the passing troops. Although the woman had insisted that Kerran was not bound. Mantris was stunned by the news. For a long time he could but stare into the fire, while a great feeling of dread gripped him, Maradass now had all four pieces of the Seacrest and held both Kerran and Tolth captive.

"It is over," he said into the silence as those around him stirred, but did not speak. "It is over and all is lost," he added, the sadness in his voice causing many to turn away from the fire and into their own darkened thoughts.

Would even Zeta be safe now? None could know. A fearful silence gripped the army of Zeta as they looked to Mantris for guidance. He could think of nothing except to save what remained of his army and return to Zeta. He decided that he would speak with Leana and Verardian and if they agreed the army would sail as soon as they were aboard.

News had not reached them from Brook for some time. The land between them now swarmed with marauders and it was a long route that a messenger must take to pass beyond the dogs and the many horsemen on the plains. Brook would be told to come south if he had not begun to do so already. Ships would remain to carry his command from Andrian should they ever be able to reach the coast. Mantris had never felt happy with the danger of splitting the army, but Torian had been convinced of its value. Now all decisions seemed irrelevant since Kerran had been taken.

The following day the army of Zeta began to march south through the bitterly cold land and returned to the refuge, where all had heard the dreadful news. For a long time Leana argued that they could not leave Tolth in the hands of Maradass. She disputed with her brother who agreed with Mantris that there was nothing they could do to free their father. To storm the castle would be suicidal, though the army would certainly attempt it if asked. Verardian tried again to convince his sister.

"We can do nothing now for the Regions except offer refuge to those who can find Zeta," he said. "Though I fear now for our Magical Isles. There are black times to come and perhaps it is the end of all things. We must return to Zeta and hope that the old magic will keep Maradass at bay. I know that father would have wanted it so."

Leana looked at Verardian and finally realised the truth in his words. She sat at the table and wept into her hands. It was Ayla who laid a gentle hand on her shoulder, which seemed to ease her pain after a time.

"It is agreed then?" asked Mantris, and she nodded her head as fresh tears flowed down her cheeks.

All was now at an end and Leana felt that she too must soon shatter into pieces and be gone.

It was a snow swept day when the army of Zeta began its sad march to the coast. Mykal and Ayla had almost decided to go with them but after much thought on it they found that they preferred not to leave their own valley.

"It is protected," said Mykal, with a strong certainty in his voice. "This magic is even older than the wizards. Maradass will not come here."

Verardian was sad to leave behind this new found friend and kindred spirit, over the winter moons they had shared much, and both found it difficult to say goodbye.

"Go now," said Mykal to Verardian who was the last of those to leave the house. "Go in peace, and one day I am sure we will meet again."

It was three nights later that Verardian stood on a hilltop above the coastal flatlands and watched as the full moon rose over the distant ocean. The following day they would reach the coast and rejoin what remained of the fleet. Usually he found joy in the rising of the full moon, but this time there was only a hopelessness that would not leave him. Though he felt a great sorrow for his father, he could not help but feel more for Kerran. The young man's life had only just begun, his powers barely touched upon, and now he was gone into an evil darkness from which there could be little hope of escape.

The Black One's Gift

Flindas gazed at the full moon as it shone down through a narrow window high in the stone wall above him. The chain on his leg allowed him to move a little and he had been looking at the cold winter moon for some time. His head had stopped throbbing and the food had been simple but welcome. He had not known how long he was unconscious but his hunger and thirst, and now the moon, told him that it was three nights since they had attempted to escape the city. He felt sure that Darbra, Alarin and Tris must be safe amongst the Southlanders. Of Dantas he could only guess.

It had been a gamble and he had lost. Now the wager must be paid. He could see the gleeful expression that must have come onto his father's face when he had heard that his outlaw son had been captured alive. He knew how his father could hate. Even the threat of Maradass would pale against the joy the Governor must be feeling this evening. Flindas guessed that he would probably be brought before the court the following morning, there could be no doubt of the sentence and Flindas felt little fear at the thought of death. There had been so many times he had expected to die that until the noose was around his neck he would not surrender to it, even then he felt he could face it without fear overcoming him. He had found an understanding in his wandering life, a knowledge of his own mortality. He had done all that he had ever expected of himself, and all that he asked now was that he should not flinch from the hangman's noose.

He rested but slept little that night. A single blanket did not keep out the cold and the scattering of straw did little to soften the stone floor of his cell. The sun had only just risen when a bowl of cold oats was pushed through the gap at the bottom of the door, then a small aperture slid open and a bloodshot eye observed him for a moment. Flindas greeted the guard with steady calm eyes. The small opening was shut hurriedly and heavy footfalls moved away from the door. Flindas ate the gruel and waited for the guards to lead him to the court. The sun was high when they finally came. Flindas heard the bolt being drawn. The door swung back and three large men entered, all dressed in the livery of the City. While two held their spears at his chest the third locked manacles onto the prisoner's wrists and then freed his ankles. They said not a word and Flindas did not recognise any of them as he was led from the cell and taken above.

Flindas looked around as they passed through the well known halls of the castle. The doors of the court were swung back and Flindas was led down the centre of the long, high vaulted chamber. People on either side murmured and clambered for a view. Flindas almost smiled when he saw the ridiculous make up and attire which was the latest in fashion amongst the wealthy of the city. It seemed that blue was the important colour this year. Even their wigs were blue, and larger than anything that Flindas had seen in his youth. There were the same riches dangling from ear and neck, wrist and finger. Flindas saw that his father wore the largest and bluest wig of all, the members of the court being very careful not to look too beautiful compared with the Governor.

Then Flindas noticed that the seat beside his father which had been his mother's was not empty and his heart leapt. Was he to see his mother once more? He had gone another step or two when he saw that the woman who sat at the Governor's left hand was not his mother. As Flindas came closer he could see that she was golden blonde, with no wig to cover this natural beauty. Her gown sparkled with jewels and Flindas saw that she was very young. She held the Governor's hand and looked adoringly at his stern, flabby profile.

Standing beside the empty chair at his father's right stood Jondarl, his younger brother, a permanent sneer disfiguring the almost handsome features. His patience was about to be rewarded. Flindas would surely hang, and then he alone would be heir to the Governorship. He was in well with the black commanders who assured him that Maradass had no intention of ending the governorship, that Maradass was truly a benevolent man and wished only for justice. Flindas could see that his younger brother had become even more of a fool than he had once been.

As he was led to the foot of the raised dais, Flindas turned his gaze to his father's bloated and sickly face. The years of debauchery had altered the man more than Flindas had thought possible. Rolls of fat showed through the elegant clothing that adorned this large sallow man. The brows were heavier. The hooked nose seemed even larger that it had before. The full mouth sucked at a goblet of wine as Flindas was brought to stand before him. The young and beautiful woman turned her eyes on Flindas and he saw pure loathing in her stare. The Governor slowly lowered his goblet and spoke into the deathlike silence, not yet deigning to look at his son.

"Welcome home, Flindas. You have not visited us for so long, dear son," he said with a sickly smile.

He licked his lips as though a wonderfully delicious morsel had been laid before him. Flindas opened his mouth to speak and then regretted it as the man at his back clubbed him to the ground. Flindas took a few moments to recover and began to struggle to his feet, the short manacles making it difficult. He was just straightening when the shaft of a heavy spear smashed into the side of his knee. Flindas cried out in pain and fell to the stone flagging. He remained on his knees and was not hit again.

"Welcome indeed," said his father, looking far out over the

faces of the court, receiving a twittering of expected laughter. "I have waited, oh so long, to have this little talk. There is of course no need for charges and courtly procedures for you are certainly guilty!" He spat these last words, the control in his voice slipping. "Even you cannot deny the heinous crime that you committed."

The Governor shook with rage for a moment and then stood, brushing aside the young woman as she reached to assist him. "You will die and I will not make it quick! You may have imagined an easy hanging. Oh no, I have had many years to think over your punishment. You will plead for death, and yet live on to plead again." His voice calmed a little. "Before all this comes to you I will tell you of the great pain you have caused. To kill your own brother was beyond all possible crimes, and now you have also killed your mother."

Flindas looked up in alarm. "She is dead?" he asked softly.

Then he knew that it must be true for another now sat in his mother's place. The guard was about to hit Flindas again but the Governor stayed his hand with a gesture.

"She is dead indeed," said his father, calm now and calculating. "You killed her as surely as if you had struck her through the heart with your own sword. She died of grief at the loss of two sons, though why she ever grieved for you I do not know. Kinslayer they call you now. You are despised and ridiculed here in this court. Nothing you could possibly have done with your miserable life can ever redeem you." Governor Demsharl called over the heads of the court. "What say you, am I too hard on my wayward son?"

"No!" called back the many voices. "Kill him, flay him, hang him. Kinslayer." The words tangled and reverberated around the court.

When the cries had quietened the Governor looked again at his kneeling son. "Will you beg for your life?" He waited for a reply.

"I will not beg, and I will die with no regrets," said Flindas.

The crowd stirred at these words and waited for the Governor's reply with bated breath.

"No regrets you say," said his father with a sneer. "No regrets when you ruin the family that I loved. Kaylan is gone. Your mother is gone. Jondarl, without the strength and wisdom of his older brother, becomes a wastrel and an indolent fool."

At this Jondarl went pale and his face took on a look of fear at being discovered.

"And Darbra, what of her?' spat the Governor. "Have you sent her to her death too? No I will not allow it. She will be found and that burdensome husband of hers will be taught a lesson."

"He had no part in this," said Flindas from the floor.

At a small gesture from the Governor Flindas was beaten, blows raining down on his back as the guards stood closer, and then too close. The outlaw son rolled quickly and in the same movement one of the guards fell screaming, his leg broken by a blow which none had seen. As the other guard rushed at him Flindas took his spear and smashed it across the man's face. It had happened in moments and both guards lay writhing as Flindas held the shattered spear before him. From alcoves and behind the high thrones came a great many soldiers. They were not the castle guards but were from the Black Army of Maradass. Flindas dropped his weapon and glared up at his father.

"These are your enemies!" he cried, pointing at the soldiers who stood poised, ready to cut him down should he show further signs of attack. "You are a fool to trust this black alliance. You are doomed and cannot see it, or do not want to."

His father had risen again from his seat, his eyes afire with hatred. "Take him to the lower level, down to where I cannot hear his screams," he ordered the soldiers, and several came forward taking Flindas by the arms. "You will die, oh so slowly," his father said with venom.

"No, he will not die!" came a hardened commanding voice from somewhere near the great doors of the court.

There was a cry of astonishment from many, and looking down the length of the hall, Flindas could see a number of dark cloaked figures as they began to approach the thrones. They had entered without being noticed, as all eyes had been fixed on the Governor and his son. Those in the hall shrank back from the very tall and powerful man who strode purposefully towards the Governor's dais.

"Maradass commands that this man be spared," he said for all to hear.

Flindas could see that snow still clung to the Black Knight's cloak. He had always known what Zard would look like, but until now had never realised how mighty a warrior the son of Maradass must be. Zard came towards the dais and amongst the group there was another, a much smaller figure who walked beside the Black Knight. Even though this other man was draped in a dark cloak of the Maradass army, Flindas knew that walk, for he had often studied the young man in their travels together. In astonishment and fear Flindas saw that it was Kerran who strode beside the Black Knight.

Their eyes met and then Flindas was suddenly unsure of his first assessment, the face seemed changed, older perhaps, but it was the young man's eyes that had altered so very much. Where they had once been a soft green, they now shone a sparkling blue, not the mad fire of Maradass which Flindas had seen in the eyes of the Krags and marauders, no; here was a clarity that dazzled. Kerran smiled with a reassurance that confused Flindas. Was the young wizard a captive or not? He was not bound and walked with Zard as though they were equals. When Flindas opened his mouth to speak Kerran shook his head slightly.

It was Zard who spoke again, filling the silence with his compelling voice. "You are forbidden to harm this man lest you wish to forfeit your own lives," he told the entire court.

The Governor turned a ghostly white, then found that his voice was not his own to command. He stammered out a few words then withered under the eyes of Zard.

"He will be given his freedom," the Black Knight commanded. "A full pardon for all that he has done."

There was an astonished murmur amongst those in attendance on the court.

The Governor suddenly found that his rage had overcome his fear. "Freedom?!" he screamed, clutching at his chest as though in pain. "He cannot go free!" The large grotesque man stood and scowled at Zard. "He is kinslayer. He will not go free!" he snarled.

"Will not?" growled Zard angrily back at the fat stupid man. "You say 'will not' to me!"

Zard moved forward and in two strides he stood above the Governor, a long dagger in his hand. The fat blubbering figure seemed to shrink into his throne as the young woman beside him screamed and ran down the steps. Jondarl slunk away behind the high seats and disappeared. Zard grasped the writhing creature, lifting him completely from his seat with just one hand. The other hand held the knife before the Governor's terrified face.

"You will do as I say or die," said the Black Knight. "Now what will it be?" Zard continued to hold the writhing creature in the air, his dark face savage and threatening. Governor Demsharl was totally defeated. His wig fell from his balding head and he went limp in the Black Knight's grasp.

"Quickly, say what you will," said Zard, a deadly coldness in his voice.

"Free," stammered the Governor.

Zard let him fall, and then turned back to his companions. "Come," he said to Flindas. "I have commanded your freedom but I do not recommend that you stay in the city. There are some who would still try to collect the reward."

Flindas said not a word, his astonishment complete, and then he bent to the guard whose leg he had broken. The man pulled back whimpering, perhaps thinking that Flindas intended to do further damage. The key to the manacles hung at the man's belt and Flindas pulled it free, but could not manoeuvre it into the slot which would open the lock at his wrists. Kerran came to him, and without a word he freed his friend, and then together they followed Zard and his commanders from the court of Celisor Castle. They reached the courtyard and Flindas saw that snow had begun to collect around the walls. It was going to be an early cold in these Southlands. He turned to Kerran.

"What happens here?" he asked in a low whisper. "How is it you ride with the Black One?"

"I cannot explain it quickly," replied Kerran. His voice

seemed older, more assured. "I have gone through and beyond the fire. I go with him by choice, to speak with his father, and hopefully to return with Tolth. It is strange to know who I am now, and remember who I once was."

"And who are you now?" asked Flindas, not really knowing what the young man was talking about.

"I do not know it all yet," replied Kerran. "But I know that I am Chelasta the wizard, and I have begun to find powers that have been sleeping, even from before I was born. There is much I could tell you but for now there is little time. I came because I was told that you had been captured."

"You spoke with Tris," Flindas said, sure that he was right.

"No," said Kerran. "I have not seen her. I was told in a dream. I saw you climb down a wall in the night. There was swordplay above. I saw the stone hit you and you fell. I saw it, Flindas, just as I have seen other happenings that have come to pass"

Many things had amazed Flindas that morning and this not the least. He was silent for a time, and as they passed through the castle gate he found that a horse had been provided for him amongst the others that stood about the roadway. He mounted the tall war horse. Zard and his commanders were quick into the saddle and they descended the roadway. Zard was not pausing in the city and they rode quickly through the noisy streets, and passed through the gate in the city wall as the guards fell back, daring not his wrath. Zard reined in his horse beyond the gate and turned to Flindas.

"We will meet again I think," he said knowingly. "You are free to go where you will in the land. No black soldier will harm you if you take this."

Zard removed the ornate dagger and sheath that hung from his belt and held it out to Flindas, on the hilt was set the emblem of Maradass, the white dog's skull. Flindas looked at the knife but did not take it.

"I will not need protection from your father's men," he told the Black Knight. "I would destroy them all if I could. It is they who need protection."

Zard laughed and Flindas wondered at the open humour of this man who was said to be so cold. "Yes," agreed Zard still smiling. "I know you do not need my help, but take it all the same. You are a man of blades I believe and there are qualities in this blade which you may find amusing." He looked into the eyes of Flindas for a moment as he placed the heavy knife into the outlaw's hand. "We will meet again Flindas Demsharl," he said deliberately. "But go now, where you will."

"And what of Kerran?" said Flindas turning to his young friend. "Is he also free to go where he will?"

"Yes," said Zard, a smile still flickering from his eyes. "He is free to go where he will, as none can now say him nay, but I think you will find that my steed and his will travel the same road for a time."

"You truly go with him by choice?" asked Flindas as he turned to Kerran with a look of great concern.

"Yes," replied Kerran. "I go with Zard to Mendan Maradass. I would talk with this one they call Evil, and perhaps I can change him." He smiled at the look on his friend's face. "Tell everyone where I am going," said Kerran. "Tell them that all is not as it seems, and all is not yet lost, for I go by choice and I will return." He rose in the saddle and a faraway look came into his eyes, then his voice came with power. "All is not yet known, but if I can do anything to help the lands and its people I will," he said. "Not by oath or by duty, but because in this I truly have no choice"

His eyes sparkled and he gazed at Flindas for a moment with a magical look. Flindas thought that he saw a glow of white light emanate from Kerran, then it was gone.

"It is time to go," said Kerran, again the young man of Westerval. He clasped Flindas by the hand then rode away from the castle gate to join Zard as he and his commanders cantered ahead.

Flindas looked behind him and thought it best that he depart also. A cold wind blew from the west as he spurred his horse down the road, snowflakes pattering against his face. He could see the dark group ahead as they reached the place where the roadway turned beneath the castle walls. They were passing the last tower when Flindas saw movement beside the road. There was sudden confusion as a man fell from his horse. Flindas spurred on quickly as he saw the huge mountain dog leap upon the other horsemen. Another man fell to the ground stunned. Flindas heard the metallic sound as the stone hit a black commander's helmet and he knew that Tris must be somewhere in the shadows of the city walls. In fear for his friends he beat his mount into a gallop.

Men rode quickly from the highroad, and then a great howl was heard from Rark. Confusion seemed to reign amongst the group ahead, but as Flindas rode up their mounts had quietened and they had formed a circle around a figure which lay in the roadway. Two of there number were in pursuit of Tris though it was obvious that they were not trying to harm her. Flindas leapt from his saddle and tears came rushing to his eyes as he knelt beside Rark. The spear still remained in the great dog's body. It had gone in behind the shoulders and protruded from Rark's chest. Flindas could see that there was no hope for his friend who lay motionless. The mountain dog's eyes flickered a moment then closed. Suddenly Kerran was at his side, and taking his friend by the arm the young wizard shook away his grief.

"Pull out the spear quickly," he said into his friend's pain. "Do it now!"

In a daze Flindas took hold of the shaft and with a sudden movement, drew it from the dog's back. Kerran clasped his two hands over the wounds, one forced under the body until he found the warmth of the blood. Flindas stood back as Kerran held Rark, blood pulsing between his fingers as a flickering white light crackled in the air around the two motionless figures.

It was a long time that Kerran knelt there. At first Rark seemed as if dead, and then slowly the blood ceased to flow. Flindas saw the strange white light again shine around Kerran then pass away. There was a whimper, then a gruff deep throated sound as Rark moved a little and raised his head. Kerran continued to kneel beside the mountain dog with his hands gently laid on the large hairy body. Finally Kerran smiled and gave Rark a friendly scratch behind his ears. The dog got slowly to his feet as Flindas stood there, rooted to the ground, his wonderment complete. Rark licked his hand which seemed to break the spell.

"He will be weak for a time," said Kerran, his own voice sounding weary and spent. "He is healed, but he has lost much blood." Then Kerran slumped against his horse and would have fallen if Zard had not reached out and grasped him by the shoulder. "I must go now," said Kerran, and he got slowly into his saddle as Zard looked at him with curiosity.

"For a beast you would drain yourself as you have," said the Black Knight. "You are more vulnerable now. Perhaps I could win if I chose to try."

"If you chose," said Kerran, aching with a strange pain.

"Yes," agreed Zard and he laughed aloud.

With a gesture of his hand Zard had Tris freed, and she watched in wonder as Kerran smiled at her, then rode off with the Black Knight.

"This I surely do not understand," said Tris as she looked at Flindas and shook her head. "How is it that you are free?" The wonder of his presence was as amazing to her as the living dog beside him.

"I am not sure of that either," said Flindas as he knelt beside Rark who seemed a little bewildered himself. Flindas found no wounds, and his thoughts went out to the young wizard as he stroked the thick matted coat. "What of Darbra and Alarin?" he asked turning to Tris.So much had happened that he had forgotten them and their father's threat to bring her home, perhaps his men were on her trail this moment.

"They are safe," replied Tris. "They are with the Southlanders and are being taken to join their children."

"And Dantas?" asked Flindas, though he feared he already knew the answer.

Tris shook her head. "He did not leave the walls," she said looking above at the guards who peered down on them. "There was a cry of pain that was his voice. He could not have fought them all and survived, I think he intended it that way."

Flindas felt a great sadness enter his heart and then his thoughts came back to the present. "You could have been killed here," he said, and then rested his hand on the shoulders of

Rark. "Rark was killed!" his astonishment remained with him.

Tris began to explain but Flindas stopped her.

"Let us go from here," he said looking up the roadway to the gate.

Many people had collected in groups and the ones who had seen the action were telling others about the strange happening at their very doorstep. City guards were now looking towards them and Flindas had no great trust that they would not decide to confront him. Rark could move at a walk, so Flindas mounted the war horse. "Get up behind," he said to Tris who swung up easily and held on as Flindas turned and rode away from the city.

Soon they were travelling south, and though they encountered black soldiers at times, somehow they seemed to know that Flindas and those with him were free to pass. He did not even need to show the dagger, which he had pushed into a deep pocket of the horse's saddlebags.

That evening they camped in a small wooded valley which sloped towards the eastern ocean. Food had been crammed into the saddlebags and Rark was happy with the dried strips of goat's meat. The strangeness of seeing him alive had not left Flindas. Caked blood still showed on his back, yet no wound could now be seen. Tris told of their intent when she and Rark had attacked the horsemen. On the road into the city Tris had seen Kerran riding with Zard. Thinking that he was captive she had waited, not knowing what to do, but knowing that she must try something. She had been prepared to die in her attempt to free Kerran. Rark had attacked without any sign from her. She told Flindas that the mountain dog had found her the night that they had left the city.

"There was a time that I believed in magic," said Flindas. "I may have been eight or nine years old and I believed all of the old tales, until my older brother shattered my belief in them. He did have a great many strange beliefs of his own but magic and wizardry were not a part of them. The old tales now come alive and suddenly I believe in magic again."

He stared into the fire, shaking his head a little and smiling. "It is good to have seen such a thing," he said. "Even though

Kerran now rides into the heart of the magic that is not good. I wonder how strong he might be. He can heal but can he destroy?"

The night was cold, but with a fire and the blanket from the saddle, they lay sheltered beneath an old overhanging tree, Rark lay with his two friends and they were warmed by him. Sleep came slowly, but when they had finally drifted into that magic realm a dream came to them. It was so vivid in their memories the next morning that they both wished to tell the other, then realised that they had both had similar dreams. Kerran had walked in a soft mist, he had beckoned and they had followed, yet neither saw the other in that dream world. Kerran had shown them the city of Mendan Maradass. It lay beyond the mist and above it stood the dark castle which had lain in ruins the last time Flindas had seen it some years before. Tris knew it for what it was. There could be no other place as dark and forbidding as the ancestral home of the Maradass family. They were both totally aware of themselves during the vision which seemed less like a dream than reality.

Kerran walked before them and then he was gone, fading into early morning light, leaving them both alone to look in awe on the tall, grim castle. The Black Army lay in camp, smoke rose wafting on the air and soldiers moved about, going to the camp kitchens for their morning meal. There was no rush or bustle. The army lay at ease, the war in the south far away and of little consequence. Further to the east and nearer to the castle lay an area of flat, cleared land. It spread beneath a rocky outcrop and sloping hillside which formed a natural arena. There was more activity there than anywhere else in the camp. It appeared that it was being prepared for a show of some sort. Dark tents were being pitched in a half circle facing the cleared area. One large ornate tent had been raised on an outcrop. Its view of the coming event could not have been better.

Both Flindas and Tris had known that they were not within their actual bodies for they floated, suspended high above the land, though all physical perception had remained with them. The smells and sounds of the camp came wafting to them from below, all was seen, and nothing missed. At this point their stories diverged. Flindas, within his shadow, flew slowly across the land until he looked directly down on the cleared place below. All obstructions had been removed, and rocks and large boulders had been rolled away to form a long oval area. The sloping hill would allow many to see the coming action, whatever it might be.

Tris's shadow took her across the intervening space to look down upon the castle. There were people on the battlements. Soldiers stood there as well as a group who were distinguished by the great differences in their appearance. Tris recognised Maradass, the wizened and bent creature whom she had last seen screaming at them as they passed through the walls of his stronghold with Luista as their captive. Luista too stood on the castle walls, the first sun's rays lighting her stone like beauty. She had a baby in her arms, and beside her stood her dark gaunt son Mindis. Zard was also there. He stood with his hands on the battlements, looking far out towards the arena that was being prepared. He no longer wore his armour but was dressed in dark clothing covered over by a deep blood red cloak. Tris observed for a time, yet she was too high to hear if anything was being said. A flash of light caught her attention, somewhere far below and beyond the castle walls the sunlight was reflecting off a shiny object amongst the tufted grass.

Without thought Tris's shadow took her plummeting towards the place. As she approached the ground the sparkling light faded and was gone. When she saw what must have been the unnaturally reflective object, she felt surprise. It was only a simple shiny rock, smooth and rounded. Amongst the deep grass of the bank beneath the castle wall were many other such stones, large and small, but nothing else of interest. Confused as to the meaning of this, Tris could remember no more of her dream and had drifted into an unquiet sleep. Flindas too had eventually found sleep, and he had woken with the memory of the dream flooding back into his waking mind.

"It was so vivid," he said when they had both told their dreams to each other. "I know not the purpose for the arena yet I feel that it is important."

"Yes," said Tris. "Tis a pity that Kerran could not show us more. I feel I am supposed to understand something in this and yet I do not."

Flindas nodded in agreement. "I think perhaps it is a time yet to come," he said. "You say that Zard was there on the battlements, though he and Kerran must still be far from Mendan Maradass. Perhaps it is the recent past but I did not feel it so. Seeing the arena was a glimpse of the future I think."

Tris agreed as she stood and stretched, the cold of the night having seeped into her small frame. Rark was nowhere to be seen but returned before they prepared to leave. He looked stronger, a splatter of blood on his coat which was not his own told Flindas that the dog could now hunt and feed himself. They planned to travel the South Coast until they could rejoin the army of Zeta, and Flindas hoped to find Darbra there with her family.

During the day they saw many black troops marching to the north, while none now moved south to replace them. The supply lines had stopped coming down the road, and after a time Flindas was convinced that Zard had ordered the battle to cease, and the troops to leave the deeper Southlands. After another two days they came upon Elbrand scouts and heard how, after a night battle of blue and white fire and light in a snow clad valley, the Black Army had turned away from the battle. They also heard that Kerran had been captured and Mantris had ordered the army of Zeta to the ships. Flindas held his tongue on the knowledge they carried. From the Elbrand they were able to secure another horse and so travelled quickly to join the army on the coast. The fleet stood off from shore and many of the troops seemed to be already aboard. Much of their stores were being left behind for the Southlanders. There was a quietness about the camp as Flindas and Tris rode through the army to the tent where flew the Amitarl standard. Few acknowledged them. A great feeling of despondency overshadowed the camp, a feeling of sadness and defeat. The Amitarl tent was also a tent for the wounded where Verardian and Leana attended to the casualties until they could be taken aboard a ship. Flindas dismounted as Verardian appeared from the tent.

"Flindas!" exclaimed the healer, taking his hand. "I am glad to see you safe. Your sister and her family arrived some days ago and said that you had been captured. I am so pleased it was not so."

"It is something of a story," said Flindas, pleased to see the healer again. "I would see my sister and her family soon but first I must speak with Mantris. I have news that he and yourself must hear."

"I too wish to see Mantris," said Verardian. "Is your news something that will lift his heart? He is not himself and there is little that I can do to cure him. He burns with disappointment and the thought of failure."

Verardian led the way and Flindas told him briefly of how Zard had freed him, and how Kerran had gone to the north of his own free will.

"It is indeed strange," said Verardian walking beside the tall warrior, leading the way to where Mantris had made his council fire.

The commander was there, sitting above the shore, watching the movement from beach to ship. Several of his captains sat around and spoke in low tones. They welcomed Flindas and Tris into their midst, though a feeling of despair hung about them. Flindas told them his strange tale with great detail, trying to remember everything in an attempt to convey the extraordinary truth to them. Mantris was puzzled by his words yet they seemed to lighten his mood. Flindas told of Kerran's astonishing healing powers and Verardian felt his own heart lift in response to the news.

"He travels with Zard freely," Flindas said again and finally ended his telling. "He said that he goes to speak with Maradass, to try and change him."

Mantris sat thoughtfully for long moments then stood slowly. "This is strange news you bring," he said. "If it is indeed the truth that Kerran has found a greater power than Zard, and cannot be harmed, then all is not yet lost." A light came into his eyes and he smiled for the first time in many days. "If the army of Maradass continues to leave the south there is no need for us to hurry from the Regions."

Several captains agreed loudly and others about the hilltop began to understand the news that had been brought by Flindas. Soon it had spread through the camp that the loading of the troops would cease. Only a ship of wounded would sail on the morrow's tide, when Mantris had thought most of the fleet would depart.

When Leana heard she came quickly to the council fire where Flindas again told his tale. Her face lit up. She could not contain her gladness and laughed aloud.

"It is not over yet!" she cried out to the sky, then grew silent as Flindas finished telling all that he knew.

Her eyes grew wide when she heard that Kerran would try to free Tolth from the clutches of the Evil One. There was now an air of expectancy about the camp. Each runner who arrived from the north was swamped by many who wished to hear the latest news. The Elbrand scouts and runners began to use horses now that the Black Army had withdrawn far to the north.

That evening Flindas spent much time amongst the Southlanders where Darbra and her family had taken sanctuary. It was a tearful greeting, for Darbra had never expected to see Flindas again. Her three children were glad to see their uncle, though the youngest child, and only daughter, could barely remember him from his last visit. Flindas remained in camp with them and it was three days later, with the army huddled low against a bitter southerly wind that a runner came with strange and wondrous news. The Black Army had withdrawn from the City Amitarl and the many Stone soldiers and horse troops were now marching to the north on the City Highroad. The entire army was on the move and appeared to be leaving Andrian and the Southlands. Marauders no longer roamed the plains and so mounted scouts were sent to gather news of Brook and his command.

Mantris called a council of Captains to discuss the new developments. It was Leana who first suggested that the City Amitarl and Celisor Castle should now be secured against the Black Army's return.

"The Governor and his men could not hold it against us," she told them. "We should go there and demand that they let us enter, so as to aid the people and the lands. Tolth did not want to usurp the Governor's power but things have changed. I say the Governor has little power now, and none to repel Maradass should he wish to regain the city."

"It is true that Tolth did not wish to take the city by force," said Mantris, who had been quiet for some time. "I agree that much has changed and the Governor along with his guard should go, but I will not make this decision alone, I ask for your words."

He turned then to his captains and there was much discussion into the evening. Some were still in favour of leaving the Regions completely and returning to Zeta, while others feared that they could be trapped in the city, though the fleet should remain at anchor in the harbour as a means of final escape. Maradass had as yet to show a liking for the ocean and tall ships. Verardian spoke against entering the city but could not say from whence his misgivings came, except that this had been his father's wish.

It was Leana who argued strongly with those who spoke against her desire to return the white hawk standard of Amitarl to the city. She spoke of history and heritage, and finally when all had said what they wished a decision was made. The army of Zeta would go to the City Amitarl and ask to enter as protectors of all those within. If the Governor and his guards refused them entry then the city would be taken by force. They would try to do it quickly, without loss of life on either side. There were less than a thousand men in the city guard. Hopefully they would see the futility of resistance and allow the army to enter the city. If not, the walls would be stormed and taken.

The castle itself would be a more difficult prospect. It could be defended by a small number of men, and its gate beyond the deep chasm was of iron, and could never be broken, except perhaps by magic. The walls too were impregnable, only by scaling the walls could the troops of Zeta enter the castle, should those within decide to remain behind the closed gate.

This would be most dangerous and many could die before others reached the battlements. To starve the Governor out would take a long time. As well as the dungeons beneath the castle there were storerooms of food and many other plundered things. Flindas told the gathering that he thought the Governor and his court could last a year or more before they would even grow a little hungry. The city must come first they decided. The Governor and the castle would have to wait.

The following morning two thousand mounted Elbrand and soldiers rode north for the City Amitarl. With them went Leana and Verardian, riding beneath the green and white standard of Amitarl. Mantris rode at the head of the mounted army, and with him went Flindas and Tris, while Rark loped along ahead of them all, showing no sign now of his encounter with death. The days hung grey with winter cloud and the hills near the coast were sprinkled with a light cover of snow. They did not push their mounts. If it was all an elaborate trap, they wished their horses to be strong enough for a rapid escape to the south. Word came to them on the road, and it was news from the city where all seemed to have returned to the way it had been before the Black Army had come from the north. It was easy now for the Southlanders to enter the city and they reported that not one black soldier remained within the walls. Flindas sought news of Dantas but no one had seen him. Word had not come down from the castle of his capture and Flindas remained in hope of finding the old warrior alive.

The Return of Amitarl

The army of horsemen from Zeta lay at camp beneath the trees, not far from the City Amitarl. All those within the city had noted their arrival and the gates remained closed. No one had entered or departed since they had arrived in the mid-afternoon. An envoy had approached the walls requesting that the Governor speak with the Family Amitarl. After a long wait the messenger had been told that the Governor would receive a small delegation the following morning. Around the council fire there was much talk that night of what the morrow might bring.

"Only one of you should go," Mantris was saying as he looked at Verardian and Leana, who sat together near the fire.

"I agree," said Leana. "And it is I who should go."

Verardian shook his head a little wearily. She had argued this way all evening but he did not want to let her enter the city. There may be treachery in the Governor's mind and he did not wish his sister to face that danger, but he finally surrendered to her determined stand. Leana would go into the city with eight Elbrand, and speak for them all. She would ask for cooperation between the court and the army of Zeta. There would be no threats but the Elbrand at her side would be the best. Should the Governor try to hold them, he would learn at first hand how hard it was to overcome such warriors. Several knives would be carefully hidden about their bodies, and they would take great care not to enter the castle at all. This was agreed by all. If the Governor would not speak from the castle walls then it must be done by messenger.

Flindas wished to go too. He still felt protective towards Leana, yet he knew that his presence would surely antagonise his father. The following morning he watched Leana and the Elbrand depart. Flindas knew his father and he was worried that he may see a great advantage in capturing one of the Amitarl family. Scouts came back to report that Leana and the Elbrand had entered the city.

Leana and her warrior companions were led through the streets to the castle high on the cliff. Though Leana had never been to the City Amitarl, she felt that she knew it well, mostly from old picture books in the library on Zeta. She had learned much about her family history and now stood in awe of the tall castle which hung above them. There was consternation amongst the guards when Leana and the Elbrand would go no further than the castle gates. Though the guards were numerous, their captain's strict orders were to cause the visitors no harm, and to bring them to the court. A messenger was quickly sent, and for some time Leana and the Elbrand stood against the castle wall, sheltering from the cold southerly wind. The numerous guards took little notice of them, having begun to throw dice to pass the time. Finally the messenger returned and spoke with the captain who turned to Leana.

"The Governor will have none of this," he told her, and leered at her as though she were some street girl. "You must enter the court or leave,"

"We will leave," said Leana defiantly, and with the Elbrand she began to descend the roadway.

"Wait!" called the powerfully built warrior, and at a signal from him his men moved to bar their way. "The Governor is a reasonable man," he sneered, his manner insolent and threatening. More guards then came from the castle and moved to a position on the bridge which crossed the deep chasm. The captain turned with a twisted smirk on his lips. "The Governor is a reasonable man as I have said and will allow all of you to depart, but only after he has spoken to you."

He looked directly at Leana, her beauty stirred him and he wished to crush her pride. The warrior captain's name was Marlto and he had sworn to cause Amitarl as much grief as he could. His escape from the Southlanders had been an easy task for one trained by Dantas. Once again he had gained much power amongst the Governor's guard. He was a favourite of the Governor and even though he seemed to have joined the Black Army for a time he had been able to explain it away. The Elbrand stood poised for a fight and Marlto mocked them, though he remained well away and let his men stand between him and these warriors of Zeta. Once already he had met and been bested by an Elbrand, and he was taking no more chances.

"You cannot think that your fancy warriors can kill us all," he said smiling with derision at Leana. "You are but a handful."

"You would be foolish to harm us," replied Leana, her voice steady, the air as tense as a drawn bowstring.

Marlto was about to draw his sword as a signal for his men to attack, when a second messenger came rushing from the castle and spoke quietly with him. Marlto scowled and then turned to Leana.

"You can go," he spat the words in disappointment for he had wanted the fight. He longed to see this haughty spirited woman grovel for her life. The green and brown warriors had been as good as dead. "The Governor will see you tomorrow at the same time should you choose," said Marlto. "But he will not come to the gate. You must enter the castle."

Leana thought for a moment. "I will see him now," she said resolutely, the Elbrand protested but she had decided.

"We are here to guard you," one of them said. "We too must enter."

Marlto was pleased. He may yet have the chance to subdue this proud Amitarl beauty, and her warrior companions. "Your weapons must remain here," he said and was surprised that there was no argument. He observed as the Elbrand let fall their array of blades, and watched closely as his men searched the Elbrand, though not all their weapons were eventually discovered. "Come," he said with a mocking gracious bow and led them beneath the castle walls.

The guards in the courtyard were many and Leana did not turn when she heard the gate closing behind them. On entering the court, Leana was shocked by the gaudy, rich surroundings, and the strange people in their garish costumes, twittering stupidly. Many, and not only the men, were silenced by her proud beauty. She was Amitarl and walked with a strength empowered by hereditary magic. The guards spread along the columned walls, while Marlto led the group to the dais where sat the Governor and his new bride. Marlto stood to one side as Leana and the Elbrand slowed and then stopped before the high seats.

"I bid you greetings from the Family Amitarl," said Leana so that all could hear. "We come in peace."

"You come in peace!" scoffed the Governor, but his anger rang with an undisguised theatrical note. The court murmured and laughed just a little as he continued. "In peace you come but you bring an army. Do you take me for a fool? Tell me, is it not your plan to capture the city and castle? Can you deny it?"

"No," replied Leana. "I cannot deny it."

This caused much surprise amongst the court. They were not used to such truthfulness.

"I am here, as my father came before me," said Leana for all to hear. "I have come to ask that you let our army enter the city for its defence."

"What need of defence?" came the reply. The Governor was more restrained now, playing to his audience. "There is no war here. Look around you. Does it appear that we are under threat?"

"You do not realise the danger," Leana replied. "You do not understand that Maradass plays a game, a perilous game that includes your death. He toys with the lands before he crushes it. All will die if Maradass himself is not destroyed."

"It is you who are now the fool," laughed the Governor. "Maradass needs Andrian to feed his people, and we have a contract."

He indicated one of the foolishly attired men of the court who stood up and waved a piece of paper before him. "Maradass has withdrawn to the north and the Southlands are free of his armies," said the Governor haughtily. "It is you who are the real invader here."

Leana became angry. "His contract means nothing," she said with great scorn. "Your only hope is to allow us to enter the city."

"No!" screamed the Governor, his anger very real this time. "You come here and threaten me in my own home and say you come in peace. I will not turn the city over to you, even if your name be Amitarl. None in the land want you here."

"You are wrong," replied Leana, calmer now, her words coming with great conviction. "There are many in the land that want us to remain, and would thrive under our leadership, as few have under yours." She opened her arms towards the court. "All this stupid finery," she said. "When people in your care go hungry, people of the land who you strip of the little they have to feed your own greed."

The bloated face of the Governor had become red with mounting rage. "A curse on all Amitarl!" he spat the words as he came to his feet. "Seize them!" he screamed.

The words had barely left his lips when two Elbrand, eluding reaching hands, leapt up the steps to the throne. Small glittering knives sparkled in the torchlight and were held at the throat of the suddenly quaking governor. His young wife screamed. It had happened so quickly that it took some moments for those in the court to react. There was a stunned silence and then people were leaping to their feet, crying out to the guards to save their beloved governor. Marlto and his men rushed upon Leana and the remaining Elbrand but a strangled, high pitch scream from their governor stopped them.

"No!" came the terrified cry. "No! They will kill me." The fear in his voice seemed to pierce all other sounds and bring the rest to silence.

"We will not kill you unless you continue to act foolishly," said Leana, backing away from the guards. "We will have safe passage from here, or your blood will be the first that is spilt. I warn you now, here amongst your court, that we will be back. The City Amitarl will return to the governorship of our family one way or yet another. My father let you remain here, but now I am the Amitarl with whom you must deal. He would have let you stay in a position of some power, but I see you for what you are and your governorship will not stand."

She climbed the steps and stood beside the fat terrified man, looking out upon the court, the Elbrand standing motionless, ready for any attack. "Soon I will return," she said. "Amitarl will rule here and bring a better life to those who struggle under your domination. Come, tell your men to open the way to the castle gate."

"Do it!" screamed the Governor and there was a parting of the guards.

Slowly the Elbrand led the Governor towards the hallway and courtyard beyond, their small knives held hard against the aging man's throat, drawing just a little blood. The young bride wept and huddled into her throne, but none took notice of her, all eyes in the court were upon the slowly moving band of green and brown warriors. There was a rush of people to the battlements above, while many followed as though in procession. The gates now hung open as the Elbrand reached the courtyard and retrieved their weapons, then they were out on the roadway which led to the city below.

"We will return," Leana again said to the Governor whose brow dripped with sweat, though the day was cool. "When we come back it would be best for you that the gates of the city open to welcome us. The people of the lands are against you and your time is short, retire now and enjoy what life remains to you."

With these words she broke away running, the Elbrand on her heels. For a moment all at the gate stood dumbfounded. They had expected the Governor to remain a hostage at least until they reached the city gate. The Governor spluttered, and then found his voice.

"After them!" he cried and the guards began the pursuit, but were soon left far behind.

The running group caused much attention as they sped

across the city, a high trumpet call from the castle told Leana that they should not expect the guards at the gate to be unaware of their imminent arrival. There had been no more than ten or twelve of the Governor's men lounging at the entrance when they had arrived, and Leana's only concern was that they may have had the forethought to close the gate.

They had far outdistanced the pursuit when the gate came in sight and Leana smiled. The way remained open and the green and brown of Zeta could be seen all about the gate and on the battlements. Mantris had not trusted to the goodwill of the Governor, and the commander himself was amongst those at the entrance who had taken the gate without a fight. Even the city guards could now see that Amitarl would soon rule the city. At the sight of Leana, the Elbrand warriors left their positions on the walls and she was escorted safely from the city by several hundred warriors of Zeta. They did not go far. A signal to the woods brought the remainder of the army onto the narrow plain. It was a show of force which none in the city could miss. Southlanders, men who had fought Maradass and the governorship equally, had now joined forces. An army of three thousand men had been formed, and they too joined in the open threat to the Governor's court.

A large camp with many fires was made that night. There was no danger of attack, and by morning many of those in the city had openly decided that they would rather have the Amitarl family than the Governor. When the gates opened, a great throng of people left the city to join those around the cooking fires, and amongst them were not a few of the city guards. During the day, men of the Southlands army entered the city freely and spoke with the people there. The gate remained open into the evening, and soon it was obvious that the city was no longer under the sway of the Governor, who sat locked in his castle, surrounded by those that remained loyal to his court. The streets of the city were filled with people. A huge fire had been lit in the market place where many gathered to talk and wonder.

Flindas, Tris and Rark entered the city with no sense of danger. People seemed to rejoice in the change that was coming. Storehouses in the city had been plundered and suddenly everyone had enough to eat. Drink too was found aplenty and a party mood soon pervaded the streets. Three or four impromptu music bands competed for dancers around the square and Flindas was surprised and pleased to see amongst the throng a number of those who had been in his father's court, their wigs and ornaments now gone.

"A well fed man is a rich man," said Flindas to Tris as he ate a strange but pleasant tasting stew from a communal pot.

"And woman" said Tris as she lifted her bowl and drank from its contents. "What sort of music do they call that?" she asked, pointing towards a group which was playing a vigorous dance tune.

"I do not know," he replied. "The music is much different from my youth. Best call it a dance I think."

"That I will," said Tris in glee and leapt into the throng of people.

Her love of dance was something that he had seen before, and he knew that it would be a long time before she would emerge exhausted, revelling in the joy of it. Flindas walked about the square. It felt strange to be able to do so. He knew it so well and yet was surprised each time that he saw something that he had forgotten. Amongst the revelry a strange feeling of melancholy wrapped itself around him. He wandered with Rark to lonelier parts of the city, finally making his way to the harbour where the fleet of Zeta would soon find a safe harbour. He looked up to the castle and picked out the light which came from his father's chambers. There were few torches showing on the castle walls tonight, where in the past it had blazed with light. A cool breeze came off the sea and all was darkness beyond the few small ships and fishing boats moored alongside the stone docks.

Flindas returned to the present as Rark gave a low growl. Flindas sensed that someone observed him from the dark shadows. He stood still, his hand reaching down to a throwing knife at his waist.

"No need for that," said a voice from the shadows. "If I wanted to kill you I would have done it by now."

Into the light stepped Marlto, his dark smile flashing as he faced Flindas. Rark moved forward and smelt the stranger who understood dogs and stood still, allowing the inspection.

"Yes, tis I, your old friend Marlto," said the dark warrior. "Did you expect those Southlanders to hold me for long?" He laughed as though he had made a marvellous jest. "I was in the city less than a day after you," he said. "It was I who kindly informed the Governor of your arrival, and for a short time I was back in favour, but Amitarl has gone and spoilt all that now." Marlto had come into the light and Flindas could see no weapon of any sort, but he remained at a distance, silently watchful as Marlto continued. "Could have made my fortune but for the unexpected arrival of that cursed Zard," he spat. "Why did he set you free I wonder? That surprised us all, and the young wizard as they call him, what part does he play I wonder."

"Why do you seek me out?" asked Flindas roughly. "It is not by chance that you have found me I think."

"Indeed not," said Marlto, coming closer, his hands held out to show his lack of weapons. "I sought you out because I can help you, and you can help me."

"What is it you want?" Flindas asked the older warrior.

"What I want is to live," replied Marlto. "When I escaped the cursed Southlanders I had to kill a few of them. They would have killed me, given a chance. What I want is a pardon for their deaths, and any of my past deeds that may in time come to light. I want to remain here in the city a free man."

"What of your black friends?" said Flindas. "It is not so long ago that you wore dark armour and a dog's skull at your shoulder."

Marlto spat again. "Maradass and his Black Son," he sneered. "I rode with the Black Army but I was never with them. You know me Flindas, always for myself. There was gold in it, being one of them. Trouble was your cursed Southlanders. My first responsible task and you have to go and attack us and take our wagons." He spat once more and was silent.

"And what do you offer in return?" asked Flindas. "How can you help us?"

"I can get you into the castle," replied Marlto. "I can convince the rest of the guards up there to throw in their lot with you. Just open up the gates and tis all yours. Maradass, when he sends his army back will take the city, but even his magic would have trouble with that castle."

"The Elbrand of Zeta could take the castle now with little trouble," replied Flindas. "Why should I bother with you?"

"Because even if one of your men dies in the attack it will be a life wasted," Marlto replied. "Why risk any when you can have it without a battle? The guard wavers. There is a great store of food up there but they do not like the idea of a long siege. They will come down if I lead them." He paused a moment and looked at Flindas slyly. "There is one other reason for you to go quickly to the castle." He paused again, relishing the suspense.

"What is it?" demanded Flindas, disliking the man's presence and wishing to be done with him.

"Tis your old friend," said Marlto finally. "Our warrior master."

"Dantas!" exclaimed Flindas. He had sought word of the old warrior in vain.

"Yes," said Marlto. "Your old man governor has him in the dungeons. None too well he is, or so I believe, maybe dead already, who knows? So what do you think? Do we deal, or do I go and make the best of it with your father? I have no plans of becoming an outlaw as you did."

Flindas thought for a while, undecided as to the best move. "I cannot say," he replied. "It is not my place to decide. Come tomorrow to the tent where the Amitarl standard flies. You will be given safe passage. You can take my word."

"Yes," replied Marlto. "You always did keep your word, and it is a failing you may rue some day. Can a man really be trusted who keeps his word and yet will kill his own brother and ruin a friend's life, my life? Do you not remember that we were once friends? Ah, so be it, I will come in the early morning before the city wakes." Then Marlto stepped back into the darkness and was gone.

Flindas began to walk from the docks. He wished to find Mantris and the two Amitarl. The city was alive with the soldiers of Zeta. All danger was gone and for the first time since they had arrived on the shores of Andrian the army danced and enjoyed themselves. The square was even more crowded than before, and it was sometime before Flindas reached the other side and made his way to the main gate. Beyond lay the encampment of Zeta where fires burned low. It seemed that even the guards had entered the city.

When he reached the Amitarl tent he found Mantris and several captains around the fire. Verardian was also there and in deep conversation with the Elbrand commander. As Flindas began to tell them of Marlto's plan, Leana came from the tent and listened quietly.

When Flindas was finished she spoke into the silence. "This man Marlto, he is a traitor to Andrian," she said. "He rode with the Black Army and killed Southlanders. If he can bring out the castle guard without a fight then it must be done that way, but to have such a man in the city could be dangerous. A clever traitor in our midst is something I would rather be without. Let us see if Marlto can open the castle gates, then if he does we must watch him carefully."

The others agreed as Flindas had expected they would. All who held command amongst the army of Zeta thought of their troops safety above all else. No warrior should die needlessly when there was any chance of another way. Flindas slept that night by the Amitarl fire; though he was offered a warmer bed within the tent he preferred the open sky and the silence of the night. Rark lay beside him, and with a heavy woven blanket, Flindas slept without discomfort through the winter darkness. By first light he was awake and watching as Marlto left the city gates escorted by several Elbrand. He was brought to the tent as Verardian and Leana came out to hear what they had already agreed upon.

"You are sure that you can do this?" asked Leana after hearing again what Flindas had first told.

"Yes," Marlto replied, his manner confident, arrogant. "I tell no falsehood here, for what would I gain? I could have disappeared last night or before and not endangered myself. Indeed, the guard will follow me and all I want in return is my freedom. How many would you lose taking the castle? Too many I reckon. One life, my own, tis all I ask. I can do it where you could not. The guard would not trust you to keep your word, but I know they will believe me."

"When can it be done?" asked Mantris.

Marlto recognised this man as the one who had bested him in the courtyard of the castle when he had first entered the city with Tolth and Kerran. Marlto turned to him, a look of hatred barely hidden beneath his heavy brows. "I will go this morning and I will go alone. It cannot be otherwise. They will come, though it may take some talk."

It was agreed and Marlto was led back to the city where the gates stood wide, allowing all to pass freely. Leana and Verardian would not enter the city, for neither seemed inclined to claim it without the surrender of the castle. By noon word came to them, the castle guard, with Marlto at their head, had left the fortress and dispersed safely into the city, though there were many amongst the Southlanders who held great hatred for these men. Elbrand, who had waited at the foot of the roadway leading to the castle had moved quickly to secure the gate. Not one guardsman was left it seemed and a great many of the court had also seen fit to leave. How long these protected fools would remain rich men and women was not known. They were the pampered few who must learn now to live amongst the city people without their ruffians to protect them.

There was a cheer from the army and a great many of the city folk as the standard of Amitarl was carried into the city. Leana and Verardian rode at the head and there were tears in their eyes when they saw the gratitude of the city dwellers. The people clustered about them, welcoming them both into what was their ancestral home, and a way was cleared as far as the road to the castle. Flindas too had come home. He rode with Tris and there were many who knew him. Some felt uncomfortable and looked away, but most, who knew something of his later deeds, welcomed him as a hero. There was an air of joy amongst the people which the gloomy winter's morning could not dispel. Leana and Verardian Amitarl rode with many Elbrand up to the castle, and then Mantris led the way through the gates towards the great hall where the Governor held court. Green and brown warriors entered all doorways and searched the castle for defenders, but there were none. When they reached the court the high doors were locked and barred from within. All other entrances were found to be secured as well and the doors of Celisor Castle were not made to be forced easily. Mantris pounded on the door but there was no sound from within.

"I know of a way," said Flindas. "It was shown to me by Dantas years ago. The hall was thought to be impossible to enter without keys or force, but high on the west wall is a place where all that is needed is a short length of rope. There is just one small window that remains unbarred."

There was rope amongst the Elbrand, and soon Flindas and a number of the elite had reached the upper battlements where it took only moments for Flindas to drop to a narrow ledge. Using the rope, which was fastened above, he swung across to the high window, landing with ease on the sill.

Flindas peered into the gloom of the unlit hall and as he began to make out details in the darkness, a feeling of horror clutched him. Strewn about the court like windblown leaves were the bodies of many members of the court. Some appeared alive, sitting as they were in their seats, but their total stillness and silence told Flindas that they were dead. He could only see the back of the thrones, and with another rope he dropped into the hall, followed by several Elbrand.

Flindas walked slowly towards the high dais. Amongst the scattered bodies he could see gold and silver goblets fallen from dying hands. Flindas knew of many poisons and found his mind already guessing at what they had used. He climbed the steps at an angle, and beside what had once been his mother's seat he saw the sprawled figure of the Governor's young bride. As he came up beside her and looked, expecting to find his father's dead form, his eyes met the scowling hateful glare of the Governor Demsharl. A goblet of dark liquid was held in his hand but he was very much alive.

"You!" he screamed uncontrollably and tried to rise, but either drink or his great girth held him in his seat and he failed to reach his feet. He made to throw the goblet at Flindas then suddenly stopped. "No," he said, an evil insanity twisting within his voice. "No, this is far too good for you." He smiled at the goblet then, as though it were alive. "So you come now when all is over to gloat over me," he said, not looking at his son.

"I do not come to gloat father," replied Flindas. "Our ways are too different for you to ever understand me. I am not like you nor ever have been. I do not gloat."

"Kinslayer!" his father cursed him. "What do you say to that? If you are so wonderful and I so despicable, how is it that you are the one who killed his brother? You are a fool as well as a murderer. You take up with this Amitarl rabble when it is they who are the truly evil ones!" His eyes were wide, his mouth slobbering as he screeched the words."Look about you!" he continued wildly. "There are people here that you once knew, perhaps even liked! They died rather than lose all they had to your ill bred usurpers. Even she!" He turned and looked sadly at the still form of his young bride. "What do you want here?" he said with a bitter snarl. "Is it not enough that you have the castle? Must I vacate my seat and take to the dungeons?" At these words he suddenly smiled. "Yes, the dungeons," he said slyly. "You will find them interesting yourself I think."

The Elbrand had opened the great doors now and as those outside were able to enter they walked slowly down the length of the court, taking in the horror.

"Come in!" screamed the Governor. "Come, take what you will. I will drink you a toast. I drink to your great deaths at the hands of Maradass."

Flindas was not yet close enough to his father to prevent him taking a drink of the poisoned wine, but he did not have to try. The Governor paused with the goblet almost touching his lips. A shudder went through him and violently he cast the goblet down the stairs. "I cannot do it!" he cried. "These fools of my court said they would rather die with me than leave the castle. We all drank together." He suddenly burst out laughing. "All except me," he sniggered. "They died, and as they did so they all knew that I had not drunk of my cup. Some tried to reach me but it works fast this poison. I will take what freedom you will give me and I will go cursing you all." His voice had ceased its raving. It was now broken, crushed.

"Go," said Flindas. "Take what you will and leave the castle. You will not be harmed, and will be housed in the city if you wish. There are healers amongst us who could help you."

"Help!" snarled his father. "I need no help from you." He lifted his great frame, and without a backward look slowly made his way down the steps, he left the hall by a side door which led to his private chambers.

"Indeed I could help him," said Verardian, a look of great concern on his face. "I know what burdens him and could ease his torment with time."

"He will not give you time," said Flindas. "He would have no faith in your ways and would only laugh at your offer. No, it is best that he take his madness and pain with him."

"No one should carry madness when they do not need to," said Verardian as he looked around at the dead, a haunted sadness on his face.

Already there were many soldiers of Zeta in the great hall and they had begun to remove the dead. Flindas was about to go in search of Dantas when one of the Elbrand who had been sent with the Governor returned hurriedly to the hall. He spoke with Mantris who stood surveying the dreadfulness that the Governor had wrought. The Elbrand commander listened attentively to the man and then came quickly to where Verardian and Flindas stood.

"It is the Governor," said Mantris interrupting their quiet conversation. "He has fallen as he entered his bed chamber."

Flindas moved quickly across the floor of the hall and made his way along the passage that would lead to his father's rooms. When Verardian and Mantris arrived they found Flindas kneeling beside the still and lifeless body of Governor Demsharl. Verardian examined him and found no signs of life.

"It was not poison," he told the others. "His heart could take no more I believe." He stood and looked down at the body. "His madness I could have healed," he said. "But his heart I think has been overburdened for a very long time."

Flindas felt nothing. When a father dies one was supposed

to feel something, even relief, but the body stretched upon the floor seemed to have no connection with him at all. Suddenly thoughts for Dantas came to him and he began looking about the room. His father had always kept a set of keys somewhere in his chambers. The way to the dungeons was locked and the gaolers now gone. In a small chest on the wide mantelpiece he found what he sought.

"I go below to the dungeons," he said to the others. "There is one down there who I must find."

It took Flindas some time to seek out his old teacher. There were many prisoners and they were hungry and thirsty, for no one had bothered with them in the last few days. Elbrand began to lead them into the daylight above as Flindas, torch in hand, eventually found his way to a small dark cell where Dantas lay dying. Water was brought quickly and Flindas eased the old man's head into his lap, touching water to the cracked and bloodied lips. Dantas was able to swallow and in the torchlight he smiled.

"I am glad to see you Flindas," his words came slow and faltering.

"You should not speak," said Flindas. "The healers will come soon."

"Tis too late for healers," said Dantas, coughing suddenly, a small fleck of blood spraying across his lips. "All broken inside," he said as the coughing eased. "Did just enough to kill me slow." He paused, gasping. "Glad you found me," he said softly. "Some things you should know."

"It brings you pain to speak," said Flindas stroking the old warrior's head, he felt tears welling at the thought that his old friend would die. "Ease yourself. There is no need to tell me anything."

A light came to the eyes of Dantas and his voice was suddenly strong. "You will listen, as I taught you to listen!" he growled.

It was an old command and Flindas remained silent.

Dantas breathed heavily for a moment, gathering the last of his strength. "You wondered when you were young why I took so much time with you," said the old warrior. "When your brothers received as little time as they wished. I told you that they could never be warriors but that you could. Though this was the truth you wondered at it. I remember well." Dantas smiled then at the memory. "Tis true that I took special care with you over all others," he said his voice almost a whisper now. "I saw great potential, but there was more than that. It was a promise that I would not break." Dantas was again racked with coughing and it was some time before he could continue. "It was a promise to your mother," he said, and then was silent, letting Flindas wonder at his meaning.

"I do not understand," the younger man said. "What sort of promise could you have sworn to my mother, and why?"

"You do not yet understand," chuckled Dantas through his pain. "Sometimes I despaired for you even then. The obvious often eluded you in your youth, as it does now."

Flindas was puzzled but said nothing. He wondered if Dantas was beginning to lose his senses.

"No," said Dantas into his thoughts. "I am not raving, but it is something difficult to tell. I promised Jahna never to reveal it, but she is gone now and no more harm can come to her."

At the mention of his mother's name Flindas felt the beginnings of an understanding. "My mother and you," he said hesitating. "You were friends, I remember well. Are you saying that you were more than that to each other?"

"I loved Jahna as much as I loved life," replied Dantas. "And she in her turn loved me, though I could never understand why."

"Now I see," said Flindas, but was interrupted by Dantas whose laughter suddenly turned into another coughing fit.

"I am going soon," said the old warrior, pain twisting his features. "You still do not understand and I wonder if I should not keep the secret which I promised to your mother." He looked up into the younger man's eyes. "It was more than love which bound your mother and me," he said softly. He paused, a questioning look in his eyes, and then he continued. "Your mother and I had a child together, a son. Now do you understand?"

It came upon Flindas like a sudden heavy wave and he looked with wonder into the face cradled in his lap.

Dantas nodded and smiled. "Now you know," he said with a smile. "Bit of a fall to find you are no Governor's offspring, but sired by some homeless coward from Zeta." He chuckled softly and then looked up into his son's face. "I did all that I could for you in my own way," he said. "I wanted so much to call you son but I would not go against your mother's wishes. She feared the Governor more than death itself, and yet she never denied that I was her only love, and you the son she so much wished for. That fool governor never understood the precious flower he held, and eventually he crushed."

Flindas remained silent, turbulent memories and emotions fought with each other, all his concepts of who he thought he had been suddenly shattered.

"It is good that you finally know," said Dantas, his speech becoming fainter. "She never wanted me to tell." His voice was now a whisper. "Goodbye my son." These were the last words that Dantas spoke.

Flindas sat and cradled his father's head far into the night. Elbrand would come and replace the torch and ask if he wished for anything, but Flindas remained in the small cell in silence. By dawn, when all had been thought through and wondered at, Flindas allowed the Elbrand to take his father's body away. He climbed to the high tower and from the stone battlements he looked out upon the walled city and the countryside beyond. Flindas breathed deeply, and after a time felt as though a great weight was lifted from him. Sadness was left behind to be replaced by a feeling of wonder and gratitude to the man he would always think of now as his father. Flindas took a long breath of the crisp winter dawn as he looked to the north, and his thoughts flew to Kerran. If the young wizard remained alive he would have reached Mendan Maradass by now. Then his mind returned to further memories of his father and the distant threat of the Evil One seemed far off and unimportant for a time.

The Wager of Maradass

The dark stone walls of Maradass castle loomed above them against the grey, sunless sky. Kerran wondered again if he had made the right decision to face Maradass. Perhaps he was underestimating the Evil One's power. The castle must have taken a great magic to reconstruct in so short a time. Maradass was no wizard by birth, but he wielded unknown forces. Kerran knew that the magical strengths of wizards had varied, but there was one important fact that he could not deny and which set him apart from the wizards of the past. No matter how potent his own magic was, he understood that he could never use it to harm another being. In earlier times most of the wizards had fought and killed, but Kerran's knowledge of the past and the ways of the family Chelasta had told him that he could not be as the other wizards had been; he could build but never destroy.

Zard rode beside Kerran as they mounted the straight, narrow roadway which led to the castle gates. The last few days, in the company of this dark son of Maradass had surprised Kerran. Though Zard was new in the world he carried a great inner knowledge from his past lives. Maradass had tried to control his son's nature, trying to mould him into an unthinking follower, but this Zard was a strange mixture of his two previous selves. There was conflict within him that Kerran had tried to uncover during their days on the road. Zard had showed no great hurry to reach Mendan Maradass and he had listened intently to Kerran as they had moved slowly along the Highroads.

Kerran had told Zard of what he knew and had recently discovered. Zard had learned much in a short time about the old times of the wizards, which Kerran had explored through what now seemed many lifetimes. He told Zard of the wizards' game and how he had discovered its uses and dangers. Zard had listened enthralled while the young Wizard Chelasta told him of these many mysterious things. More and more his dark side had become subdued, until Kerran felt that the two of them were almost friends. It would have seemed a strange alliance to him just one year before. Zard though knowledgeable, was ignorant of the many things which told of goodness in people's lives. Maradass had taught him nothing of this, encouraging and nurturing only his son's dark side. Now it was time to meet the father, though Kerran felt that he already knew Maradass well. They had fought within the realm of dreams for what seemed lifetimes, and they had battled in the waking world also. Kerran had almost been consumed by the blue fire but now believed he was beyond its reach.

As Kerran passed under the dark arch of stone he shuddered a little, and deep within he wondered again if he had not made a mistake. He had now entered not only the castle, but also the lines of the Wizards Way. He felt a brooding, expectant presence deep within the stone. They dismounted in the outer courtyard where a large steel door stood open but uninviting. They entered and Kerran walked with Zard through a series of hallways and barely lit chambers. The gloom was oppressive.

"Maradass is expecting us," said Zard as he strode across an inner courtyard which lay barren of colour or ornament.

Dark sentries stood on the damp flagstones and guarded the emptiness, and it was there that Kerran saw what he had long suspected. Sunk into the centre of the courtyard were a number of ancient, weathered stones. They formed a circle several paces across. He paused to look at the familiar pattern of lines carved into their surface.

"It should never have been brought here," he said as though to himself.

"It is the game as you described it," said the dark knight by his side, looking down at the eight pointed star. "Do you know which wizard it was who once used these stones?"

"She was Drinda-mira-Sta," replied Kerran. "The ruins of her ancient home can still be found on the secret Isle of Marl. I have seen it, though little now remains of its splendour. Your father's father brought the stones here. I guessed this before, but now I know. Your own father has found a great and terrible use for it I think."

"You wish to change him," said Zard, turning to his young companion. "And you hope to use me in this. Speaking with you, and listening to your words, I cannot help but see that you are truthful, and that my father has lied. It was his father that began the madness, but he now perpetuates it. There is true madness in this war when there could be a real peace."

Kerran gave an audible sigh, his plan was succeeding. Zard had seen the evil of his father and now the battle with Maradass would be easier. Reason and truth had worked with Zard, but could the father be swayed? Kerran felt that there could be but a faint chance of this, but he also felt that he must try.

"Perhaps he will listen," the words came from Zard, tinged with much doubt. "He will be expecting us. Come, I have tarried too long."

Zard walked quickly into a long hallway and then ascended a flight of stairs. He stood briefly before a tall wooden door as though preparing himself for an ordeal, there were many guards but none dared challenge the son of Maradass as he swung the door back and entered with Kerran at his side.

The heat in the room was almost unbearable after the cold of the outer castle; Kerran looked around the chamber which he knew so well. Even the people were exactly where he thought they would be. Luista was seated by the fire with the baby Darss in her arms. Mindis sat almost opposite her staring into the fire and did not look up when Kerran entered.

On his High Seat, several steps above the floor, was Maradass. He sat with dark thoughts creasing his aged brow, tapping his narrow hooked nose with a bony forefinger as though puzzled by something. Luista turned to Zard and showed no surprise at his companion.

"You have been gone a long time, my son," her voice sounded of sorrow, as though he were at fault in some way for her sadness.

"I have returned," said Zard. "Now you need no longer be unhappy."

She did not appear to hear him and turned her attention back to the child in her arms.

"Why is he not in chains?" said Maradass leaning forward and eyeing Kerran with great distaste.

"I think you know the answer to that question," replied Zard. "He is not in chains because there is now no one in the land who could bind him."

"Are you telling me that the mighty Zard cannot overpower a mere boy?" Maradass sneered. "You are no longer the one who was my brother. Though I hated that Zard, I feared him more. You are but a pale shadow of him. I see that now. You have been gone from your home for too long. Your loyalty weakens, and I will restore that after I deal with this pretender to wizardry."

He turned his baleful eyes upon Kerran, a sneer twisting his lips. "So we meet at last, Chelasta,' he said with disdain. "You come here with great confidence for one who has only just begun to delve into wizardry. Do you really think that you can conquer me?"

"Not conquer," replied Kerran walking forward until he stood at the centre of the luxurious chamber. "I have not come here to conquer, but to make peace."

"Peace?" questioned Maradass. "How can there ever be peace between Amitarl and Maradass? They forced us to leave the south and to abide in the Broken Lands, far from our ancestral home. Amitarl deserve what comes to them. History does not lie."

"Let history, whether true or false, not cloud your thoughts of what is now," said Kerran. "You wish to destroy everything for the hate of one family. The world beyond the boundaries of the Regions is bleak. The lands which we now fight for may well be the very last refuge of humanity. I have looked to the north and yet I see nothing but barren lands and poisoned oceans. It is in your power to do a great good for the Regions should you choose a path of peace."

"Good!" exclaimed Maradass loudly. "Good! What good has anyone ever done for the Maradass household? No, young Chelasta, descendant of wizards, you will not talk me into peace. I will have war on the Southlands until all Amitarl are gone. The lands will die including your precious Magical Isles, and then there will be only Maradass. We will own it all for ever and then ever again."

"I have withdrawn the army from the Southlands," said Zard as his father finished speaking.

Maradass turned on his son. "Yes I know," he muttered. "A son turned traitor is a thing that cannot be hidden, but there are many ways of fighting a war." Maradass leaned forward in his High Seat and leered with evil madness at Kerran. "You will not stop me!" he screeched violently and then his words came softer. "Descendant of wizards you may be," he said. "But I have had a thousand years to learn the arts and I could crush you like a bug."

"You cannot touch me," said Kerran, yet still there remained a little doubt. "I have come in peace and will go as I choose. Listen to me now."

"Listen!" screamed Maradass who was now on his feet.

Darss cried out and Luista bent low to comfort the child.

"I will listen to you when you cry for mercy and death!" snarled the evil One. Maradass lifted his hands above his head, but his threatened burst of blue fire did not come. He stood aghast at the lack of a thing he felt as a natural part of himself. Again he tried but failed.

"What have you done?" he screamed, which brought another wail from the baby.

"As I have said, you cannot harm me," replied Kerran. "It is you who do not understand. While I am in your presence you are powerless, a mere mortal that can die as any other can. Ancient oaths at the Crossroads do not bind my powers, for I am older than them."

"The oath was sworn on the Seacrest," Maradass spat back at him. "I have half and you the other. I think you are mistaken, young Chelasta. The Seacrest was made by Rishtan-Sta and I doubt that you, a mere descendant of a Lesser Wizard could ever truly wield it. I am even protected by his words at the Crossroads. Zard is my true protection and he will not die in combat with any man. Of this even you must be certain."

"Be not so sure of the magic or the man," said Kerran. "I do not yet understand all of my powers, but believe me, they can only grow with time. I talk of peace and look for a time of prosperity in the Regions. Give up your dreams of conquest and join with the peoples of the land. We could turn the Regions into a place of wonder, as it was when the Philosopher ruled in Mendan Maradass and his wise son in Crysta-Sha."

"A time of softness and decadence," Maradass said hatefully. "I have no desire to see people happy and contented. They are vermin and I will see them burned and destroyed, over and over again."

"You cannot destroy them without an army," said Kerran. "Zard is the commander of the army and he too looks for peace."

Zard stood stern and silent under his father's wrathful gaze.

"Now I see how much you have turned my son against me, but tis I who command the army," said Maradass. "They will take orders from me, not my traitor son. Guards!" he called out, and the room was suddenly filled with armed men. "You will seize Zard and take him to the dungeons."

The men looked at each other in surprise but did not move.

"I command it," screamed Maradass.

One man stepped forward but when his companions did not follow he advanced no further.

Kerran turned back to Maradass.

"It is not only fear which keeps them from doing your will," he said. "For a thousand years, Zard, the one who was your brother, commanded the Black Army. Though your son here is not the dark hearted Zard of old, he is still looked upon as the traditional commander. Not even your binding spells will hold them, or turn them against your son. No, Maradass, I think you underestimate the son, and have now lost your army, unless you can find the magic to turn Zard against his own true nature. Only with magic could you change him now that he has heard the truth, and even then you could not completely trust that your spells would hold him for long. We both know that once we are beyond the Wizard Lines all of our powers are greatly diminished. That was why I chose to meet Zard where I did. You must have felt my presence in the game. I spoke to him of peace as once again I speak to you. Will you not choose peace over destruction?"

Maradass waved a hand to dismiss the ineffectual guards, who departed looking wonderingly at each other. "Peace is something I have never really considered," said Maradass as he returned to his seat. "What advantages are possible with peace I wonder?" The words came softly, mocking.

"Perhaps no advantage at all," replied Kerran. "Not for you. But there are many people who crave harmony and friendship, and food in their stomachs."

"I do not think well of people," said Maradass fuming. "Only the selected ones should live. The rest must be doomed and destroyed." Maradass rose in anger from his seat again where he had sat only momentarily. "I will not have this!" his shrieking voice hovered on the edge of insanity. "I am Maradass, and you will not stand in my way!"

He raised an arm, but instead of attempting to cast fire at his enemy, Maradass sent a four bladed throwing knife whistling on a deadly course towards Kerran. There was a searing flash which brought a scream from Luista as well as the baby Darss. The knife burned and was gone and Maradass slunk back in muttering surprise and disappointment.

"Not with magic or mortal weapon," said Kerran moving now towards the dais and the single High Seat where Maradass brooded. "Cease your attacks on the Southlands. Amitarl would wish you driven from the lands, but I suggest a compromise, the Regions be divided up as of old. Amitarl to retain Rianodar and Andrian while you hold Mendan Maradass and Zard again becomes Governor of Glandrin."

Maradass laughed, an evil mocking sound. "You think I am so blind," he said glaring at Kerran. "You have turned Zard against me, yet you are so naive. You do not see that you are but a pawn in the Amitarl game. They are ambitious and wish to govern all. I will not allow it!" His voice had slowly risen until it again became a high pitched screech. "No, I will not allow it! You may be able to overcome my powers for now, but you will not stay here forever."

"And why not?" asked Kerran. "If that be the price of peace I would pay it gladly, but it need not be so. In time, even you could find happiness in a peaceful world. Do not make the same mistakes as your father."

Maradass laughed again. "The only mistake he made was to let *him* carry a piece of the Seacrest," snarled the wizened creature pointing at Zard. "He lost it, and then he lost the war. Had it not been that way, Amitarl and Chelasta would both now be dead and fallen to dust. Nevertheless I will see my father's work finished."

"It is finished now," said Kerran, a confident note in his voice. "In time, as I gain in power, I will not have to remain here. Soon I will be able to bind you and all of your magic. Be sure that I speak the truth. I give you this choice, your freedom in a harmonious land, or to be bound forever by my magic, and perhaps never to find your own peace."

Maradass was quiet for a time. He sat in deep thought, a hand to his chin and a distant look on his face. Finally he turned to Kerran. "You would trust me to keep the peace?" he said in mock surprise. "I know you are young but you are not fool enough to expect me to change my ways so quickly."

"That is true," replied Kerran. "What I propose is that you disband your armies and remove the spells you have on them, though it appears that Zard could do that in your stead. This is something I did not foresee, though I had thought it possible. You must destroy the Stone Army and the Wizard Stones in the courtyard must be returned to where they were found. Then I would trust that you could not easily bring an attacking force or high magic against the Regions."

"Is that all," sneered Maradass. "You would take everything from me then say, 'Go in peace.' I am sickened by this talk. Do as you will." He slumped into his seat. "Disband the army, take the stones! I have no need any more for them it seems."

"There is one other thing," said Kerran, though he saw Maradass already squirming in his seat.

"What now?" the question came as though a curse. "What else will you take that you have not already?"

"It is someone who you must return to us," said Kerran quietly. "You know who I mean."

"No!" came a high pitched voice, but it did not come from Maradass.

All turned to where Mindis sat near Luista, his face now contorted with rage. "You will not have him!" the boy screamed. The dark features twisted with blind hate. All but Luista seemed surprised at the sudden outburst. Mindis slowly stood, trembling, his eyes never leaving Kerran's.

"This cannot be. He is mine," said Mindis. The words came with a bitterness that touched Kerran as no spell could.

"He must be freed," said Kerran. "Why do you hate him so?"

But there was no reply. Mindis sat abruptly and said no more, returning again to his silent world.

"I will bring him here," said Zard simply, and under his father's hateful glare he left the chamber by a side door.

"You have won," said Maradass sneering. "You have even taken my son, yet perhaps not all is lost for me. Do you think that you can truly trust my black hearted son? As once he was, so he can become again. I know that Zard will return to me. You will never be able to hold him completely."

"That may be so," said Kerran. "I cannot claim to know all things, but I know your son now better than you do. He would lay down his life now to protect a peaceful land."

"You are a fool," scoffed Maradass contemptuously. "You may have won him to your cause for a time, but there is one thing that he cannot do. He could never 'lay down his life.' He will never die and nor will I, and perhaps in another thousand years I will be able to take from you the pieces you possess. I have time."

Maradass paused, a thought gleaming in his wicked eyes. "What say you to a wager?" he said quietly. The tone in the Evil One's voice had suddenly changed to a friendly tone, but he could hide nothing of his dark intent. "Zard you say is now for peace and I say he is still his father's son. If you trust him so much, give to him the two pieces you hold and I will do the same. Then when he has all four pieces in his hands let him decide who he passes them to. If you hold so much trust in him, you could then easily take all the power for yourself. I am a gambler, are you? Do you really trust your so called wizardry and apparent deep understanding of one I call my son? I think there is still doubt in you of your own wizard nature."

Kerran stood silently pondering the strange suggestion. He knew that Maradass now played a most dangerous game. Zard was no longer under his influence and was for peace in the lands. Kerran was sure of this. Maradass was mistaken thought Kerran, but he could not truly see into the mind of the wizened creature upon the High Seat, who waited apprehensively upon his reply.

Maradass was surely misjudging his son and Kerran could not see any possibility that Zard would give the pieces to his father, should he actually hold them all. There was something else, thought Kerran, Maradass seemed not to realise that Kerran's own powers came not from the Seacrest but from his own hereditary. If Zard held all four pieces, Kerran knew that he could hold Maradass at bay. Zard could also be spellbound and Kerran could simply take the pieces from him. Kerran remembered the dream of Manzanee and recalled the words from the ancient book of wizards.

IN A TIME TO COME A CHILD OF CHELASTA BLOOD
MAY UNITE THE WIZARD'S BANE.

The old Black Wizard's voice returned to him as though from the ancient past. *A time will come when you must place your life into the Black One's hands. Do not be afraid of it. Remember this when the time comes.*

The dream had come to him and he knew that he could not be mistaken. By giving up his pieces of the Seacrest he would truly be placing his life into the hands of Zard. Maradass was about to gamble on the loyalty of his dark son, but he did not understand that Zard was now far beyond his control. Kerran tried to see if there was any flaw in his thoughts but saw nothing that could prevent him from soon possessing the four pieces of Ma-Zurin-Bidar and bringing the war to an end.

Maradass laughed suddenly but the sound held neither mirth nor joy. "Come, take this wager if you believe in him so much," said Maradass submissively. "You have me powerless and you stand assured of my son's fealty to you. I think you are wrong in this and I will trust in the power of family over all else. If you win, my time of power is done and I am banished." His mannerisms had become pronounced, his hands reaching out towards Kerran as though to draw the desired answer from the young wizard.

"What indeed can I lose?" Kerran asked himself again. Maradass could do nothing if Kerran remained watchful and steadfast.

"Come!" cried Maradass again. "Are you afraid? I am willing to risk all. What can I do? You have me helpless, my magic destroyed."

"I will take the wager," said Kerran suddenly and saw the face of Maradass become rigid as if turned to stone.

His ancient body leaned forward from his High Seat, his hands clasping its carved wooden arms. The silence of Maradass was chilling. Was there something he had missed? What could Maradass possibly do to bring about his own possession of the Seacrest? Kerran could see nothing, nothing. Zard now had free will and had turned from his dark ways. The Evil One was powerless and held no magic that could touch Kerran. Just at that moment Zard returned and beside him came Tolth. Kerran hardly recognised this bent limping creature in a tattered robe as the tall and proud head of the Amitarl family. When Tolth's eyes fell upon Kerran, the look of surprise almost made Kerran laugh.

"Yes, Tolth, I have come to take you away from here," said

Kerran.

"You have changed," said Tolth looking intently at Kerran with his clear, soft eyes. There was much strength in them still, though his face was battered and scarred. One hand seemed to be broken.

"I could not return to you in recent times but I am here now," said Kerran. "It is time for a new beginning and for many things to come to an end."

"I will be silent and observe," said Tolth leaning against a stone pillar, "I see you have gone beyond any advice that I can give."

Just as Kerran turned back to Maradass there was a sudden fluttering of wings, all looked up to see Storm fly from a narrow window and alight on a narrow ledge high up on a wall.

"Yet another of your allies come to observe my demise," spat Maradass. "Bring them all. What of the old Black Wizard, this Manzanee? Why is he not here?" He did not wait for a reply. " Quickly, let us have our wager and be done," he snarled.

"What is this wager?" asked Zard, turning to Kerran.

"I am to give you the two pieces of the Seacrest in my possession," said Kerran simply. "Your father will also give you his two pieces, and then you must choose which of us you wish to give them to."

Zard looked aghast. "Only a moon ago we were the darkest of enemies," he said in amazement. "I would have killed you if I could. Now you trust me with this? How do you know that he is so helpless against you? He connives, and does little for no profit."

"It is my faith in you that makes me take the wager," replied Kerran, reaching out and holding Zard by the arm. "You know as much as I do the value of peace. He can no longer turn you from the truth. It is his last gambit and we both know that it will fail. Though he still appears to hold out some hope that family will triumph over all else. Come, take these pieces and put them in your hand."

Kerran had reached into the pouch at his hip and held in his hands the two fragments of the Seacrest, but Zard seemed loathe to touch them.

"He cannot harm you, or me," said Kerran placing the Seacrest pieces into the large left hand of the Black Knight.

He looked deep into Zard's eyes and saw there a look of gratitude for the great trust that Kerran had placed in him. Kerran himself felt no difference as he gave up the fragments. The Seacrest had its own powers, wrought by the White and Black Wizards. They had been useful to him at times but now it was from his own ancestral line of Chelasta that Kerran drew his greatest strength and high magic. Maradass had been watching intently from his seat, and now began, in a slow lurching walk, to descend the steps from above them. He came close to his tall son, eyeing with undisguised greed Zard's left hand and its contents. Maradass then drew forth the two remaining pieces of the Seacrest.

"You are my son," he said quietly, looking into Zard's eyes. "All else must come second to family, though to preserve one's family there are some who must slay their own father."

Kerran wondered at these last words for they seemed to have no great meaning, then Maradass continued.

"To hate one's father can be almost natural," he said knowingly as he glanced towards the fire. "But between us there is no such enmity," he said as he smiled and looked up at his tall dark son. "All else comes second to family in our household. I am your father and I will be obeyed. When you hold the four pieces you will understand the meaning of power, and you will pass to me that power as you know you must." Maradass reached forward, his eyes never leaving those of his son, and he placed the two pieces into Zard's right hand. Immediately Kerran laid a protection on the Black Knight. Nothing could touch him, nor harm him, so long as Kerran's hold on that protection was unwavering and strong. Zard looked at the contents of his open hands and for some time showed no signs of movement. Maradass stood by, almost drooling at the sight, and then his face grew pale as Zard very slowly began to turn towards Kerran.

From above there was a sudden echoing screech from Storm, and involuntarily Kerran's eyes were drawn away for a moment, his protection faltered. The hawk was diving swiftly across the chamber and then Kerran saw the cause of Storm's flight. Tolth stood looking up as the hawk flew towards him, unaware of the danger that had crept up on him from behind. Mindis had left the fireside and moved silently across the room, and in horror Kerran saw the shining raised dagger. In a fleeting moment he recognised the wicked blade. It was the same which had come near to taking his own life on Zeta in what seemed an age past. It was the same knife which had been under lock and key in Captain Ronsarl's cabin on the ship Moonchaser.

All this passed in the brief blink of an eye. Time seemed to have slowed as Kerran watched the dagger plunging downward towards the back of the old Amitarl, who was still unaware of the danger. Unable to destroy the knife for fear of harming Tolth with blazing power, Kerran rediscovered one of the first things he had learned about his hidden wizardry. The blade was about to enter the old Amitarl's back when the knife suddenly vanished. Mindis fell against his father, a look of surprise on his face. He screamed in an unearthly voice, and then Kerran was suddenly aware of another sound, a dull roar was quickening like distant thunder. He turned back and watched in fear and horror as the stone floor quickly closed over the place where Zard and Maradass had stood. The castle had swallowed them both along with all four pieces of the Seacrest.

For just a few brief moments Kerran's protection had faltered and the Evil One had taken his chance. It flashed through Kerran's mind that it had been a plan all along. One that involved a player that Kerran had not realised was even in the game, Mindis. From all around the high chamber cackling laughter broke out, but it was not from the Evil One. Kerran knew the gleeful sound well, for it belonged to Manzanee. For a moment Kerran thought that he saw the Black Wizard in the darkest shadows behind the high dais, and then the floor of the castle began to tilt and turn sideways. Luista screamed and clutched Darss to her breast as Mindis fell, and then the room began to grow dark.

Kerran heard the laughter again as he lunged for Tolth, who was falling with the fearsome turbulent movements of the solid stone of the castle. All went black as Kerran reached his old friend and clung to him. A violent storm crashed around them. A wind seemed to blow from all sides and there was the crushing roar of falling stone. Then all of a sudden there was silence, as they knelt together and felt fine dust beneath their knees. The air seemed changed and moving. Kerran looked towards the shifting airs and saw a patch of starlight, and instantly he knew where they were, although he had not commanded it so.

"It is Manzanee's cave," he said as he helped Tolth to his feet.

"What has happened?" asked Tolth. "The Seacrest is gone. How can this be?"

"Maradass deceived me with the help of Mindis," replied Kerran surprised at his calmness. "I was not vigilant, and now he has them all. It is strange though, I do not fear it as I might. Manzanee was there. Did you hear his laughter?"

"I heard no laughter," said Tolth despondently. "Maradass has it all. What can be done to stop him now?"

"I do not know," replied Kerran as he kindled a small fire where he had so often before. "Perhaps I was a fool to take the wager, but the dream of Manzanee told me that I must surrender the Seacrest to Zard. It was no mistake, but how it will end I do not know. I have learned much, Tolth. I am not as I was, yet the more that I understand the more I realise that there is so much more to learn. The way ahead still remains difficult and the outcome unclear, but Maradass does not hold all of the magic."

By the light of the fire Kerran began to tell Tolth of all that had happened to him since the last time his shadow had entered Maradass castle. There was much to tell and it was early morning when finally they lay down beside the fire to sleep. For mid winter the cave was surprisingly warm, ancient magical powers still holding the elements at bay. Kerran had barely slipped into sleep when a dream came to him, if truly a dream it was. He woke beside the fire and Manzanee sat in silence opposite him. Tolth lay in sleep and Kerran saw his great age more clearly than at any time before. The Black

Wizard leaned forward over the fire.

"It is not a gift I care for," said the Black Wizard and he indicated the curved dagger of Maradass which lay before him by the fire. "There was great danger in what you attempted to do and yet it had to be so," said the Black Wizard. "None can see the end of this now that Maradass has all pieces of Ma-Zurin-Bidar but this is the way it is and cannot be otherwise. Perhaps he will learn some much deeper magic. He may even be able to draw something unexpected from Ma-Zurin-Bidar that none can foresee, so be it. There is one thing that he cannot do and that is to unite the old wizards' magic.

"No, do not speak," said Manzanee as Kerran was about to ask a question. "Hear me first for there is little time now. Hear this well and make of it what you will for I cannot say more. To unite the magic talisman which you call the Seacrest, all four pieces must be brought together in a certain manner. There is one last element that Maradass does not possess to bring about this bonding, but you do, young Chelasta. The intriguing irony of this is that Maradass knows of this element and yet you do not, and of course I cannot tell you."

Manzanee's face broke into a broad grin. "If you had taken the four pieces and brought them together yourself," said Manzanee. "You would have certainly died and Maradass suspected this I believe. For a time he was prepared to see you take them, and yet it is fortunate for both of you that you did not. There are things which neither of you can know, nor am I able to tell of this, but if Maradass had allowed you to hold all four pieces of the Seacrest, he too would certainly have died."

Again Manzanee leaned forward across the fire, the flames almost licking his chin. "Should you now approach Maradass," said Manzanee. "Or even use the Wizards Way to try to overcome him, you will do so at your own great peril. He holds all of the pieces and it is possible that he could bind some of them, but as I say, only you hold the last ingredient that can complete that binding. Learn your own ways well, Chelasta, and protect all of the life that flows within you. The road ahead may have great difficulties, but your powers of protection are strong." Manzanee smiled broadly and leaned back quickly as the fire burst into brighter flame.

"What of Zard?" asked Kerran. He felt that in some way he had betrayed the Black Knight.

"Of him I cannot tell," replied Manzanee, the smile disappearing from his lips. "He is his father's captive. What future part he may have to play in this must await a future time." Manzanee had become serious again. "Do not approach Maradass," he said. "Not unless you are absolutely sure. Beware of the Wizard Lines for he will entrap you there if he can. He has much power in the game now, but all is not yet lost. Go now, beyond the cave. There is something there which does not come by chance."

Kerran rose, and on turning to the cave mouth he found that early dawn was lighting the sky. He walked into the chill beyond the cave and on looking above he saw figures standing at the cliff's edge. Brown and green warriors stood looking out across the land and Kerran called out but they did not hear. Leaping up the pathway, splashed by the swollen winter stream, he swung around the trunk of the old tree to the great surprise of the Elbrand. They drew their swords at the sight of Kerran who was still dressed in the dark cloak of the Maradass army, but he was quickly able to assure them that this was not a black soldier lost in the forest. All knew his features and could only gape when he told them that Tolth Amitarl lay in a cave below. They looked but saw only a sheer cliff face. Kerran was not surprised.

"I will bring him," he said, and to their astonishment the young wizard vanished before their eyes.

Tolth was awake and there was no longer any sign of Manzanee. The old Amitarl learned with some joy of the sudden appearance of Elbrand, and soon he was united with his fellow countrymen. The soldiers were battle weary, and Kerran learned that they were a small band sent ahead by Brook to spy out the land. The remnants of the one thousand strong force that had fought at the Crossroads had begun its long march to the south. Less than half their number remained. Brook was with the main party still to the north and by nightfall they had joined the battered army. Nothing else could have lifted the soldier's hearts more than the sight of Tolth and the young wizard amongst them. That evening was spent with Brook beside his fire and many sat about and listened to their stories. Kerran's tale was most sort after. His news of the happenings in the south brought many a smile to those who heard it. Andrian and the city were now in the hands of Amitarl, its ancestral rulers.

"I do not know what Maradass will do now," said Kerran in reply to a question. "He has the Seacrest but much depends on the Black Army. Zard has no respect for his father and so I think Maradass will not allow him his freedom, not unless he can truly enslave his son's mind. I think this may not be possible now as Zard knows his own mind and has much magical influence of his own. If Maradass holds his son captive he may even find revolt amongst his own troops. He will surely try to sway his son back to him but if he does not succeed the army may remain loyal to Zard, even though they are still under the Evil One's binding spells. Maradass has magical powers which can sway the minds of men but as they move away from the Wizard Lines. I know that his spells must grow weaker. Maradass has underestimated his son and this may bring about his downfall."

Brook gazed at the young wizard with new respect. There was a quiet confidence in Kerran's manner and speech that told of his newly woken magical powers.

"The commanders of the Black Army, with whom I rode, held Zard in reverence, as though he were more than a man, which of course he is. Over twenty centuries he has absorbed the magic around him, but even if Maradass cannot command the absolute loyalty of his army in time he will still strike south again and he will use the Stone Army."

A murmur came from those around the fire. It was the Stone Army which had finally pushed them from the Refuge and driven them deeper into Dreardim Forest. Many of Brook's command had died at the hands of the overwhelming Maradass forces, but not a few had been taken later by the forest. Weariness had been their greatest enemy.

"The Stone Army cannot come against me," said Kerran

with assurance. "I am beyond their reach, though the very land on which they march remains in great danger from them. If I was in Celisor Castle they could not come against the city. This I understand as a certainty, though there is much else that I can only guess at. I begin to understand Maradass, and though I do not know his thoughts I start to know how he thinks. He has now what he most craved and I think that he may become absorbed by the Seacrest and forget the Southlands for a time. I do not know this but I feel it. We will have to wait in readiness. One day he will return, of that there can be little doubt."

Later, when the others slept, Tolth and Kerran sat up talking. Tolth learned of Kerran's dream of the previous night and wanted to know everything that Manzanee had said.

"There is something that I do not understand," said Tolth when Kerran had finished. "You say that you would have died had you brought the pieces together. Also you say that Maradass would have died. This is something of a wonder to me." Tolth pulled at his beard for a time in deep thought, and then he spoke further. "The old words from history tell it clearly," he said. "Anyone, wizard or not, who has any part in the death of a High Wizard are themselves doomed to die. This I believe is what Manzanee was speaking of, but I have only ever heard it in regard to High Wizards and not the Lesser Fourteen."

"It has puzzled me also for this has been shown to me to be truth," said Kerran. "I have seen my ancestral past and Chelasta was surely not of the seven. He was shown to be one of the fourteen and my ancient visions and dreams do not lie. I have watched as they were written, heard them as they were spoken, seen them as they came about. No! I do not understand what Manzanee could have meant even though I believe him. This was not one of his jests." Kerran smiled then at the thought of the Black Wizard. "Not all is revealed," he said to Tolth. "And even wizards must sleep." He rolled further into his blanket. "It is good to talk with you again," he said to the old man beside him. "Much has happened but there is much I still would learn."

Tolth turned towards him in the darkness. "You have gone beyond me now, Kerran," he said. "You came to Zeta as an unknowing young hero in a smelly rabbit-skin jacket. You are now a true wizard and you will go your own way. Trust in your true self and follow the path that seems wisest to you. It will lead you to where you must be."

They spoke no more and there was silence about the camp as the two friends slipped into untroubled sleep.

It was the day before midwinter when Brook's command rode into the city Amitarl to a happy welcome. For the last days they had all ridden, as horses had been sent from the city as soon as news had arrived of their emergence from the Forest. There was a wonderful gladness amongst the troops of Zeta when they saw Tolth riding into their midst. He looked pale and much thinner, but he had healed well during the journey, except that his damaged hand still remained in bandages. In the city square there was an even greater welcome. A feast had been prepared, and old friends and family came together once again. For a long time the three Amitarl stood in a tearful embrace.

"Learned any good spells lately?" asked Tris poking Kerran in the ribs as she and Flindas came upon him from behind.

"If you wish to become a toad I would gladly demonstrate," said Kerran laughing, glad to see his friends again.

They joined the festivities and it was a night that many would remember as a changing of the times. Snow fell lightly but did nothing to dampen the high spirits of those in the square. The many storehouses of the city had revealed an abundance of food to last well into the spring. The following day was truly the traditional time of feasting but none cared that they were a day early, and most agreed that two celebrations were better than one anyway.

During the afternoon Verardian remained at Tolth's side, his healing powers directed into his father's hand. By evening the healer had straightened the bones and mended the damaged flesh. Leana barely left Tolth's side as the day had passed. All seemed well, even the knowledge that the Seacrest had gone did not dull her enjoyment of having her beloved father returned to them. It was dusk and the fires were being built up against the cold and darkness of night when Kerran looked up, sensing that someone studied him. Piata's questioning eyes looked into his own. He had thought it a dream when she had sat by his bed as he had fought with Maradass; he realised now that it had been no dream. Confusion suddenly ran through his mind and body. He had changed. There was so much that was now different, and yet he suddenly knew that some things would never alter. He remembered waking from his frightful battle at times and feeling the softness of her fingers entwined with his, a soft smile came to Piata's face as Kerran took her hands and drew her close.

The Warrior's Choice

Sunlight speckled the ocean where Flindas sat on the dock and watched the many ships of Zeta which now lay at anchor there. The soft lapping of the water against the old stonework was soothing, the cry of gulls bringing a comfortable warmth to his heart. Two moons had passed since the celebrations of mid winter and Tolth's return. Spring was beginning to warm the lands and Flindas wondered at the peace which now pervaded the city and its inhabitants. From the north there was no rumour of war. The Black Army had withdrawn to Mendan-Var and even Rianodar seemed clear of the enemy. Kerran had been right it seemed. The young wizard had said in Council that he thought Maradass would not come for a time. He held back his forces as he tried to understand the nature of the Seacrest, and so the people of Andrian were able to tend their fields and begin to grow their spring crops. Flindas looked up at the clear sky, a few pale streaks of cloud catching the sunlight. It was warm and he knew it would be a good season for growth.

Of Kerran he did not see a lot. Each fourth day a Council was held in the great hall of Celisor Castle, where the high dais and thrones had been removed and now all who would attend sat in a large circle of benches as different speakers held the floor. Kerran spoke there at the request of many. He told of the ancient past and the time of the wizards. Flindas learned much at these Councils but he knew that only a true historian and scholar could ever absorb the many names of ancient people and places that the young wizard spoke of. Tolth always attended these meetings and had been given a seat of honour, though he had said to all that Amitarl would not claim the Governorship of Andrian until all Four Regions were again at peace. Spies infiltrated Mendan-Var, even into the old city where life for the people was still hard. The Black Army would be fed at all cost.

Leana and Verardian would also attend the meetings, as did Mantris and as many captains as could be spared. Brook retained the rank of commander and he was most often far to the north watching the Crossroads. Any who wished to attend the council could do so. None were barred, and it was the presence of Marlto which often caused Flindas some doubts about this open system of council and debate. This day was one on which the council met but Flindas had decided not to go. Any urgent or important news was usually soon known by those in the city without the need to attend meetings. Sitting on the dock with Rark at his side, Flindas thought of his own family. Though Darbra was now less than a full sister, it had not changed their feelings in any way. She had thought it a great jest when she heard the news of her mother's infidelity. *I would not have believed it*, she had kept saying, chuckling to herself.

Of Jondarl there was no sign. It seemed he had robbed much from his father's treasures and had fled the city. The man whom Flindas had always thought to be his father had been laid in the family tomb, while Flindas had himself seen to his true father's end. Many years before, when Dantas had been teaching Flindas the art of climbing, they had come to a ledge high above the ocean. To the south and west lay the city, and Dantas had gloried in the sight of the ocean, sky and land. Flindas had carried his father to that place and built a tomb of stones where he had laid the old warrior amongst his weapons.

Looking up, Flindas saw Tris walking quickly towards him from along the harbour side. He remembered that he had promised to teach her to sail and he expected a friendly scolding from her, but it was tidings from the council which had brought Tris in search of him.

"There is news from Mendan Maradass," she said as she sat down beside him on the stonework. "Remember our dream, the one with the tournament field?"

"I remember," he replied.

"Scouts came back and described it just as we said, yes?"

He turned to her, not quite understanding as she continued.

"Maradass has begun to hold tournaments to entertain his troops," she said. "Sometimes they use people from the city who are forced to fight and kill each other. Other times his own men battle against each other to the death, even stone soldiers and marauders."

Flindas wondered at the dark news. "What did Kerran say when he heard?" he asked.

"I was not at the Council," replied Tris. "I got it from Mantris. The Council has ended."

Flindas came to his feet. "There is something important here and Kerran may be able to give it light," he said and began striding towards the castle, Tris and Rark at his side.

When they reached the great hall a few people remained in discussion. Kerran and Tolth were poring over an old book. They both looked up and smiled as their friends joined them.

"I have heard the news of the tournament field," said Flindas as he sank onto a wooden bench. "I dreamed of such a thing but had almost forgotten it."

"I too dreamed that night," said Tris. "At the time it seemed most important, but so much has happened since, and dreams are but dreams after all."

Kerran was silent for a moment, a look of puzzlement on his face. At his request they each told their stories more fully, but the slight frown remained on the young man's brow.

"I cannot say what it means," he said when they were done. "The first knowledge I had of the tournaments was when the scout reported it today at Council. Maradass is having trouble holding his army together I think, and he uses the brutal tournaments to keep his soldiers amused." He smiled sadly. "I may be a wizard but not all is clear to me," he said. "Yet you both had this dream together and so I too feel its importance."

As time passed further news of the tournaments came from the north as they became more elaborate and bloody. The audience of black soldiers cheered as their own comrades slaughtered each other and the inhabitants of Mendan-Var for entertainment. The scouts of Zeta were clever, their disguises authentic. The most daring had learned the accent of the north and spoke with others in the black livery. The army of Maradass, though surely under binding spells, had nevertheless refused to march without Zard. It was the commanders, strong minded wilful men, who had stood against Maradass.

"He could have them killed," said Kerran when he heard the news. "He could have but chose not to. Maradass holds the Seacrest and feels that he need not hurry now. The longer he holds the pieces, the more power he may be able to draw from them. I wonder greatly about Zard. He was bending to our ways, but I am not with him and his father may have more control now than he ever had before."

It was said amongst the black troops that Zard was held captive in the castle, and though the magic of Maradass could not yet sway the entire army, he could bind those whom he chose of his weaker troops. These would be the ones who fought in the tournaments and so diverted the thoughts and tendencies of the others. Time passed and further news brought more knowledge. Zard had eventually been seen at the arena, sitting between his father and mother as the troops battered and hacked at friend and stranger alike. Zard had been silent, though it was said that he took great interest in the fighting. Kerran heard the news with sadness.

"The power of Maradass need not enthral the army. He need only bind Zard, and the army will do his bidding. Maradass may soon be able to bring his son into war once again. I thought, or perhaps hoped that Zard would have the strength to withstand his father. It may still prove to be so in time but I cannot say what will be."

It was only a few days later that Kerran's worst fears were realised, a scout had arrived in the early dawn and Mantris woke Tolth and Kerran with the news that Zard had donned his black armour and entered the tournament. A whole troop of soldiers had fallen to his sword, the dead lying in mounds while the Black Knight had shouted a mighty battle cry to the roar of the jubilant army. That morning, though it was a day that the Council would meet, Kerran was not to be seen in the lower castle or its grounds. Alone for a time he stood on the topmost tower, the guards being asked to retire below. Maradass had challenged him, this he knew. To reach Zard and to perhaps turn him away from war, Kerran entered the Wizards Way. Much had come to pass in the previous moons and Kerran no longer needed to go to Manzanee's cave. Instead his body remained standing against the high stone battlements as his shadow flew to the north. Time did not pass more than a few moments before Kerran's shadow floated above the castle of Maradass. The presence of the Seacrest hung about the stonework, and the evil of Maradass burned deep within.

"Come to me," the words raked across his hearing, a chilling threat.

He entered the castle and the wicked laughter of Maradass echoed around him. "Come to me," and Kerran entered the familiar chamber of the Evil One.

Little had changed. There was no sign of the tempest which had thrown him and Tolth into the game, and to the safety of Manzanee's cave. Luista sat as always by the fire with Darss asleep in her arms. Mindis was near her, staring into the fire. Zard was not to be seen and Maradass sat smiling, crouched deep into his chair.

"Greetings once again," sneered Maradass, looking directly at Kerran's shadow. "What have you come for this time? No! Let me guess. You have come to persuade my dutiful son to forgo his plans of war in exchange for a life of peace." Maradass laughed until his voice reached a high pitched cackle. Tears came to his eyes as his mirth took control of him.

Kerran spoke into his thoughts and Maradass was surprised at the intrusion, and he became suddenly quiet. "That is indeed my reason for coming," Kerran told him. "Zard cannot be held by you forever. He understands his past. One day he will certainly find himself."

"Find himself!" scoffed Maradass. "Find himself! When was he ever lost? You wish to see him, persuade him, so be it. Look upon my power and influence and tremble." Maradass spread his arms wide and from the solid floor the Black Knight rose through the stonework, his helmet closed, sword in hand. "There!" cried Maradass. "Do as you will, but know that you have already lost. He is mine, just as you will be."

"I will never be yours," said Kerran into the mind of Maradass. "Even should you succeed over Amitarl and the Southlands, you will never bind me."

"We shall see," mocked Maradass as Zard stood silent, unmoving.

Kerran touched on the Black Knight's thoughts and was met by an impenetrable darkness. It was as though Zard had no mind, no shred of consciousness left. Maradass left his seat, and chuckling he moved down the steps to the side of his dark son.

"You see now," said Maradass. "He is truly mine and you cannot touch him." Maradass reached into his gown and drew forth a piece of the Seacrest. It was a full half of the talisman and there was no sign that it had ever been two fragments. Maradass held it for a moment before Zard, then he spoke an ancient word and a streak of blue flame flew from his uplifted hand to surround Zard, his dark armour glowing eerily. Kerran attempted to touch on Zard's thoughts again, searching the warrior's mind, and was burned. His physical self, far away on the castle tower screamed. There were some in the castle who heard his cry and came running. Two guards of Zeta ran bounding up the stairs but were met by a dense white light which forced them below. Kerran's shadow, his consciousness, would not yet let go of Zard. Maradass was smirking, obviously aware of Kerran's pain. Once more Kerran delved into the Black Knight's mind. He held it in pain, grasping, and found the centre of Zard's awareness. He clung to it though his own consciousness burned.

At the castle of Celisor there were many now who were trying to come to Kerran's aid. His cries of agony could be heard across the city. None who heard it could believe that a man would survive such pain. Flindas was amongst those who attempted to reach the upper level of the tower. He had returned to his old room in the castle and had been resting when he heard the cries from above. He reached the sunlight but could go no further. Others stood beside him and looked at the figure of Kerran whose hands gripping the stonework, his body glowing with blue fire.

The screams died after a time for there was no longer strength in the young wizard's voice, and then as Flindas watched, Kerran suddenly collapsed. At the same moment the blue fire departed his body and the force which had held Flindas back was gone. He lurched forward as the spell was broken and had taken another step when, from the clear sky above, there came a flash of white wings. Storm swooped down upon him talons raking the air, forcing Flindas to evade the attack. Storm returned quickly and attacked a guard who had almost reached Kerran's body. One taloned claw caught at the man and brought a short cry of pain.

"Wait!" cried Flindas as others rushed to assist Kerran. "Do not touch him. The hawk tells us so."

The soldiers of Zeta stood still, a little confused as they watched Storm alight on the parapet above Kerran's prone form. The white hawk screeched at Flindas when he came closer and Flindas waited.

Many had come to the tower. Verardian reached the high place quickly and to the other's surprise the hawk did not object as he came forward and placed a hand on Kerran's chest. For a few moments there was total silence.

"He breathes," said the healer. "Quickly, take him below, he lives but by a thread."

Men picked up Kerran without objection from Storm and the young wizard was carried below to the rooms of the healers. Verardian and Leana both came to the bedside and stayed with Kerran, healing, touching, willing the small flame of life to grow. It was in the darkest of night when Kerran returned. His voice was weak and his body ached as though it had been beaten. Slashes of burning pain streaked his body, he said, though Verardian could see no sign of them. Kerran's whispering voice came to the healer as he bent close to the pain ravaged face.

"Flindas," said the gasping voice. "I must talk with Flindas."

A message was sent and Flindas came quickly. He stooped low over Kerran and listened intently to his words. What Kerran told Flindas no others heard and when Kerran had said all that he wished, he slipped back into a dark world where none could follow. Flindas rose as Verardian came to the bedside.

"He has gone from us again," said the healer, placing his hands on the young man's head and chest. "He spoke much with you, Flindas. I think his words weigh heavy on your thoughts."

Flindas looked at Verardian, a strange dark smile coming to his lips. "I must take thought before I can burden any with what he has told me," said the tall warrior. "Though truly it can weigh only on myself alone."

"Your words are mysterious," said Verardian. "When the time comes to reveal what you have learned, perhaps you will find it easier when carried by others."

Flindas smiled a little, though his eyes held something that Verardian had never expected to see in the man, for Flindas was afraid. Verardian could not be mistaken.

"I will speak when it is time," said Flindas and he left the healers' rooms, finding some solace for his thoughts in the clear morning air.

Tris was bored. The city at first had enthralled her, but the idle life did not now rest well with her. She had not taken to sailing. The unknown depths beneath the small craft had frightened her more than she could say. People had suggested several occupations which she might learn, but none held her more than her times alone in the countryside, her sling ever finding a mark. One day she knew that she would again return to the north and seek out the Place of Puzzles, but it was not yet time. There was more to be done, though she had no idea of what her part may be in the times to come.

She thought on those she had met in the city. Piata was near her own age and they had become friends, though the young runner of Zeta was now somewhere on the Highroad as a link between the Crossroads and the City Amitarl. It was obvious to Tris that Piata loved the young wizard with all her heart, and often she wondered how the future might treat her two young friends. The warmth of Darbra's household was where Tris liked to spend much of her time. It was a happy home amongst the children and it was made more enjoyable by the presence of Kerran's mother. She had come to the city with great doubt in her mind, but had found it not such an unpleasant place as she had thought it might be, and being near Kerran was all she truly asked for.

Tris returned to the city having spent a night sleeping in the woods, a number of long eared rabbits hanging from her shoulders as she entered the gate. The evening air smelled of wood smoke and food and Tris found she was hungry. In the city square communal fires continually cooked meat and fish. She gave her rabbits to the preparers who made jokes about her catch. There were others who liked the strong taste of rabbit and she found where several roasted over low embers. Stretching her legs out by the fire, she was soon in conversation with a wiry old soldier from Zeta who seemed to hold court amongst his much younger fellows.

"Name be Banda," he said introducing himself. "You be Tris I think, young friend of Flindas and the wizard."

Tris nodded.

"You been away from the city yesterday," continued Banda. "Must have missed the young wizard's pain."

"What pain?" asked Tris, forgetting her food.

"Screaming, and near dead, so I heard," said Banda. "Way up top of castle and such pain you never heard. Made grown men cover their ears. Hear tell your friend Flindas has been told some dreadful news by the young hero but keeps it to himself, so we hear. Up on top himself all day this day, thinking, they say." Banda pointed to the towers of Celisor Castle. "Went up this morning," he told her. "Sits on the top tower, or keeps pacing the stones. Just pacing and looking north sometimes."

Tris grew quiet and thoughtful, and the talk around the fire drifted to other things. After she had eaten and rested for a time she went in search of Flindas. Torches burning in the castle walls lit her way as she climbed the many steps of the tall northern tower. Flindas was there, leaning on the parapet and looking to the lands beyond. It was not yet completely dark and Tris could see the untouched plate of food and the dark thoughtful expression on her friend's face. At times such as these she was want to make light of another's problems but something told her that this should not be one of those times. She said nothing as she came to stand near the sombre thoughtful man. They did not speak for a while and Flindas seemed to appreciate her quiet presence. Finally he sighed heavily and turned to her.

"It is a fearful decision I must make," he said to her. "Kerran has told me the day of my probable death, if I choose it to be so that is."

"Then choose it not to be so," said Tris to his strange words. "If you would rather live, and the choice is yours, only a fool would choose to die."

"It is only 'probable' that I will die," said Flindas smiling. "There is a small chance, just a very small chance that I would survive."

"What is this?" asked Tris, not liking his shadowed words. "Choose life above all else. What is this thing that Kerran asks of you?"

Flindas was silent for some time, though he knew that his decision had already been made. He would not step aside from the path that had been laid out before him. "I must choose of my own free will," he said. "That is what Kerran told me. He said that I may be the only man who could kill Zard in combat."

Tris gasped.

"Remember our dreams?" he continued. "I know that I was drawn to this thing, though it was not until Kerran told me of it that I understood. He said that through his pain he was able to touch Zard's mind, and there is still conflict within the man. He has not fully submitted to his father's desires. Zard cannot choose to die and thus end his dark family's influence in the north, but a part of him would have it so."

"Kerran has asked you to fight Zard?" exclaimed Tris grasping his arm. She looked into his face and then drew back. "You have decided already, I see that." She clenched his wrist in her small but strong hand and looked imploringly at her friend. She saw a resolve there that would not be shaken. "Remember the dream," she said as a look of surprise came into her face. "I must come too if you are so decided."

"Yes," said Flindas looking into her wide, fearful eyes. "This must include you also. Kerran still had no thought on the meaning of the dream, but he told me that you and he must go north when I do."

"I heard that Kerran was almost dead," said Tris. "Will he be able to travel?"

"He will travel," said Flindas with assurance. "He will recover soon. This he also told me. He wished me to tell only you. Our plans must remain a secret until he recovers and tells us what must be done. Several times he told me not to tell any but you, for he fears loose tongues or betrayal."

"I will be silent," said Tris. "Though I wish I knew my part in it. You can still change your mind," there was concern in her voice. "How can Zard ever be conquered by one man?"

"That is the question I have asked myself all this day," smiled Flindas.

He seemed to notice the plate of food for the first time and began to eat, now that he had spoken his thoughts he felt more at ease. The decision was made. On the day of the next new moon he must challenge Zard to battle. For a moment the food caught in his throat. He swallowed hard and took another bite.

Kerran recovered slowly and several days passed before he was strong enough to walk from his sick bed and return to his chamber in the castle. Time he knew grew short, and he willed his physical self to heal quickly. He must be strong and for the sake of all the lands he must not fail. He sent a message to Flindas and Tris, and that evening they met in his room. Kerran did not look well. His voice had lost its confidence as he spoke of his fears.

"If you are sure of your decision then it must be this coming new moon as I told you," Kerran said to Flindas. "Maradass has made two fragments into one and soon he may be able to join the other two quarters. With two full halves I cannot say what powers may come to him." His pale face turned to Flindas and he studied his friend for a moment.

"I am sure," said Flindas answering the unspoken question.

Kerran nodded and turned to Tris.

"Whatever my part may be, I too am sure," she spoke with a certainty in her voice that both men knew was there to cover her fears.

"I will have until we reach the Crossroads to regain my strength," said Kerran, continuing to tell them his plan. "After that I will have to protect us all, and this may deplete my powers, though I see no alternative. I can keep the eyes of Maradass from us as we travel the Philosopher's Road. Of this I am sure. He may be able to guess at our presence, but he will not be able to find us until we reach Mendan Maradass."

"How do you know that my challenge will be accepted?" asked Flindas. "Maradass may just turn the army on us. You may survive but I doubt that I could overcome the entire Black Army."

"I could help," smiled Tris, twirling her sling, the gravity of the moment was lost for a time as they laughed together.

"There is a way of escape," continued Kerran. "From your descriptions and those of the scouts, I believe that the tournament field has been made within the Wizard Lines to the north of the city. Maradass has placed it there by no accident, though it could serve us as well as him. I dare not take us there through the Wizards Way, but if the need is great I believe that I could get us all to safety away from the Evil One's power. I do not think that Maradass will refuse a challenge. In fact I believe that he looks for it. The Maradass family is vulnerable for a short length of time. So yes, he will expect a challenge soon. Above all else he wishes to draw me into his net once again, for he needs me, or something that I have though I cannot say what that may be. It may be the small sculpture that was Rishtan-sta's. If it was indeed made by the White Wizard there may be some power within it that will finally unite the Seacrest. I have seen none of this in my travels through the Way. There are things within the history of the wizards that still remained closed to me."

"You could leave it here," said Tris. "If he needs the sculpture then that might ruin his plans, at least for a while."

"I cannot leave it here for I do not have it," Kerran replied with a smile. "If he does need it, then he will never find it I think, for it remains under a rock in Manzanee's cave where it can remain forever unless we have need of it. I believe that Maradass could never find the Black Wizards cave, and if he did I do not think he could enter."

He turned to Flindas. "As I said I am sure that the challenge will be accepted," he said "Maradass has no fear that any could destroy his dark son in single combat. I think only the presence of Elfhand in the lands stayed his hand for so long. Zard is the strongest man alive. There are magical forces running through him and there is also a powerful protection within his armour. Furthermore Maradass has not forgotten either of you and will be hoping, and probably expecting that Flindas Demsharl will be the one to eventually challenge Zard. You ruined his plans when you escaped his clutches with Leana.

"I understand Maradass much better now and believe he would enjoy the encounter. Knowing I am there he will want to entrap me, and that I will not allow. I truly do not know my own strengths in this coming encounter. There is a possibility that I could just take the Seacrest from Maradass. I have felt his fire and my ancestral powers have overcome them before. There is still great danger for us all in this. I do not know if I can truly confront Maradass and win, for my powers are not of that kind. I am strong but there is no violence within me." He paused for a time, pondering. "There is only one thing that remains to be determined, and all else balances on it," he said looking at Flindas, his eyes more like those of an old wise seer than of a young man not yet twenty. "Can you kill him?" he asked. "Can you kill Zard?"

Flindas did not answer immediately, instead he stood and went to the narrow window and gazed out upon the city. "I have thought much on how it might be done," he said finally. "Every suit of armour can be penetrated, but I saw Zard, and studied his defences. He is indeed incredibly strong to be able to carry such weight, and the workmanship is the finest I have seen. You tell me that his armour holds magical powers. I do not know anything of this and perhaps he is truly impossible to defeat. My best hope is to attack his visor where a slim knife may penetrate. To fight him with my sword would not be enough. I would not wear armour as I have always found it a hindrance, and so I must rely on speed. Yes, I may be able to kill him, but it is still more probable that he will kill me."

"I would not wish that you die on an impossible task," said Kerran. "We will be separated if you are to fight Zard in the arena, and if there is even but a little time, I will be able to save you. If you are wounded to the death I could even heal you." Flindas remembered the remarkable incident at the city gates when he had been sure that Rark had died. The tall warrior looked at his young friend, knowing that this would be his last chance to turn from the almost impossible task. In silence his answer was given.

"So be it," said Kerran. "When we depart, none must note our passing. The less time that Maradass has to plan the better it will be for us. I would like to arrive on the day of the new moon without his prior knowledge. If Zard should die that day then according to the history of Maradass, at sundown the family of Maradass will cease to be, all except Darss the child, so let us hope that this will come to pass. Remember, tell no one of this, only Tolth and a very few others must know of our plans."

Flindas and Tris left him to rest, and it was only moments after they had gone that Kerran heard the clatter of a small stone falling. It was strange, for the sound had appeared to come from within the solid wall. Then he remembered being told that the castle had once been connected with the Underways, until the water system had failed from neglect. The long shafts to the tunnels far below had been closed, as the stench had threatened to make the castle an uninhabitable place. Just a falling stone within the shaft thought Kerran, dislodged by a rat perhaps. He was weary. His powers were subdued, and he closed his eyes and slept.

Marlto clung to the sides of the dark stone shaft and silently cursed himself. So eager had he been to hear every last word that he had leaned too far and dislodged the small piece of stone which had fallen, and had echoed so loudly. He waited in silence, the narrow gap between two stones at his ear. Kerran had not heard it seemed, or taken little notice of the sound. Slowly and silently Marlto made his way down the shaft, it was a long time since he had needed to use this means to discover what he wanted to know. None other than Marlto knew of this dark entrance to Celisor Castle. When he had discovered it many years before, he had told no one, not even Dantas, or Flindas his close friend. It was thought to be filled in as all the other shafts had been in a much earlier time, but it had not been done. From the one dark narrow entrance that remained, it was possible to reach many parts of the castle far above. Marlto smiled as he continued his descent, for he planned to make a great deal of gold with the information that he now carried.

Marlto reached the dark tunnels below and made his way beneath the city until he emerged near the main gate. There was a stable there where he always kept a strong horse and saddle. The old man who ran the stalls was surprised when Marlto summoned him from his bed to demand the mount. By dawn Marlto was well on his way to the boat which awaited him on the southern coast of the Sea of Shardis. He laughed when he thought of the incredible wealth that must come to him. He would be rich, and he would have the great pleasure of seeing Flindas, his despised enemy, cut to pieces by the Black Knight.

A meeting was held in Kerran's chamber two evenings later, there were the three members of the Amitarl family, as well as Mantris, Tris, Flindas and Kerran himself. Briefly, for it took not so many words to explain, Kerran told them of his plan. Tolth and Verardian were instantly against it.

"I cannot condone this," said Tolth. "The danger is too great for all of you. Zard cannot be conquered, you would be defeated, Flindas, and perhaps lose your life for nothing." He turned to Kerran. "Your powers are as yet new-found," he said solemnly. "I hear the doubt and fear in your own words. You are far from sure of this, and may throw away your gift too soon."

"It may already be too late," said Kerran quietly. "Should Maradass join more pieces of the Seacrest, all may be in vain. The reign of Maradass must end soon or everything will be lost."

Leana spoke then, and the others were surprised when she favoured the plan. "If Zard can be killed then Flindas is the only man, other than Landin, who could achieve this," she said. "If Kerran can save them should the danger be too great then why not try? There may be little hope in this but if these three great friends of ours would attempt this heroic thing then none should stand in their way."

"What of you, Tris?" asked Verardian. "You go because you had a dream. I know that dreams are powerful and that this one may have been magical, but how do you know that means you should go? It may be your own grave marker which you seek amongst those stones below the castle wall that you have told us of."

"Perhaps," replied Tris, her voice solemn, determined. "I cannot say, but I will go nevertheless."

Mantris had been silent as the others had spoken their thoughts. "You are determined in this," he said finally, speaking to Kerran. "I think there is little that could be said to dissuade you and we will of course heed your wish for a secret departure. Is there anything else that we can do to aid you?"

"No, there is nothing," replied Kerran. "I can protect us three. If there were more in our party I would lose my powers more quickly. Three on horseback that is all. My hope is to surprise Maradass. If he knows we are coming he may have time to prepare a trap. As it is now, his magic cannot hold me, but given time he may in some way strengthen himself. He has joined two of the fragments. Should he bring three pieces together, or the other two into one, I cannot say what might happen, though I know that time is short. I cannot destroy

Maradass, for my powers do not allow it, but I will do all that I am able to protect my dear friends here. I cannot foresee the outcome of this endeavour, but we must attempt it. The family of Maradass must be destroyed before it can destroy all else."

There was a long silence, though Tolth would have argued further had he thought they might change their minds. They would succeed or perhaps perish. The fate of all things now hung in the balance. "It may be the last throw in this century's long game," said Tolth with a wry smile. "After all these years of struggle, it may come down to the skill of just one warrior."

He looked at Flindas who had said little that evening. He had sat by the narrow window and was now looking out at the near full moon hanging in the clear starry sky. Beside the mighty Zard Maradass, this tall warrior seemed small and powerless. Tolth hoped that he was wrong.

The day before their intended departure Flindas was in his room selecting and sharpening the weapons he would take. Rark lay sprawled in a slowly moving band of sunshine that stretched its light and heat across the carpeted floor. Again Flindas knew that he must leave his companion behind. Darbra would look after him as she did with other creatures and people in need. Her large house was full and he could see that many, including Kerran's mother, were enjoying their stay under his sister's generous roof.

Flindas reached deep into his pack. There were still a few almost forgotten things left at the bottom. When his hand came upon an unfamiliar hilt he drew it forth. Then he remembered the dark weapon. It was the dagger which Zard had given him as safe passage in the Southlands. He doubted that it could have any value now and was about to put it aside when he remembered that the Black Knight had spoken about some 'amusing quality' of the blade. He turned it over in his hand, the dog skull leering at him. He had only ever drawn the blade once and wondered if there could be more to this knife now that he was probably going to face its previous owner in battle.

Flindas slipped the gleaming blade from its sheath, and wondered again at Zard's words as he turned it slowly in his hand. He tested its weight and found that it was made for hand or flight, and with an almost unconscious throw he sent the blade spinning across the room to sink into one of the large wooden beams which were part of the castle's construction. It went deep into the dense wood, but as Flindas rose to retrieve it, the dagger faded and vanished. In astonishment Flindas quickly crossed the room. The wood showed clearly where the blade had penetrated. The beam had been wounded deeply, but there was no sign of the black knife.

Puzzled, Flindas looked about the floor, not quite believing what he had seen. It was when he returned to his seat that he saw the hilt of the knife protruding from within its scabbard. He gave a surprised grunt and again drew the blade. It shone clean and sharp. Flindas threw again while holding the sheath in his hand. The blade sank into the beam as before and then vanished, to reappear almost immediately within the sheath.

"An amusing quality indeed," chuckled Flindas and returned to his seat.

The dagger he found could not be separated from its sheath even should he simply lay it aside. He smiled at the thought of a knife which could kill and then return to its owner. Flindas looked over the various blades he had so far selected. He knew that Zard would fight with two blades of his own for he had never been seen to vary. The Black Knight had never been seen to carry throwing knives. In his right hand would be his sword, which was much heavier than the usual one handed blades, and in his left hand he would carry a shorter thrusting sword. It was said that most of his opponents died by this blade, while under attack from the other.

Flindas himself would take many weapons, including his bow, but he planned to meet Zard with knives only. His sword he would lay aside as well as his shorter blades and heavier knives. He did not plan to meet Zard blade to blade. Of his throwing knives he kept six that were slim and narrow, so as to be able to cast them through visor slits should the throw be exact. Beside these he put two long slim bladed daggers, for if the fight were to close he would perhaps be able to thrust either one between the steel plates, or again through the narrow visor slits of Zard's dark helmet.

One other weapon he put with these, but it was not a blade. To any that did not know, it looked like a small white harmless tube. Beside it were three tiny darts in a small package. The least blood letting from their tips would bring death quickly, though he did not really expect to use them, for only at very close quarters could their flight be guided well, and also he somehow doubted that mere mortal poison would work on the black son of Maradass. Flindas looked at the array and then balanced Zard's dagger in his hand. He thought of the irony should he manage to kill the Black Knight with the man's own blade. It was an impractical weapon because of its size, but with a thoughtful smile, he placed it amongst the others that he would take to the north.

Entering the Fire

In the early dawn few took note of the three Elbrand who left the city gates and cantered along the Highroad to the north. They did not push their mounts, having allowed several extra days to reach Mendan Maradass. The air was warm and moist with spring rain. The growing lands of Andrian showed that there would be excess this year should war not return to the Southlands. Blossoming fruit trees and the beginnings of the summer crops spread across the land to the north of the city. There could also be seen the signs of the Black Army's invasion. Occasionally they would pass through a village that had tried to defy the Army of Maradass and had been burned, its people put to the sword, and they passed by newly raised earth mounds where the Southlanders had buried their dead.

After several days they left the green fields of eastern Andrian, the country becoming wilder and more open as they passed beyond the River Lanstra-Dar and onto the Central Plains. They met a number of mounted scouts of Zeta, and those who paused to talk recognised them and were asked not to speak to anyone of their presence on the road. Kerran still held great fear for them should Maradass discover they were coming, and through his strengthening powers be able to entrap them.

They rode three abreast on the Highroad, which, though broken at times along its edges, was still wide. It was only when a wagon trundled by towards the city that they had to make way. Kerran looked up into the clear evening light and smiled when he saw the spread white wings of Storm. The white hawk continued to shadow them as it had over the last days, staying very high where only one who was looking keenly into the sky could observe him. Neither Tris nor Flindas saw the hawk. Something that Kerran was finding since his wizardry had further revealed itself, was that his eyesight was becoming more acute, slowly increasing in strength. Deep within he knew that there was much more to come. At twenty years of age he felt that he may be but a small part of the way towards attaining his full powers of wizardry.

The Crossroads could be seen in the distance, when they were hailed by the Elbrand captain. He and others of the army appeared as if from the earth and came to the road. The captain recognised all three and was surprised to find them on the way north.

"We did not expect you," he said. "Brook will be pleased with your visit."

The captain walked with them and they were soon climbing the slope that led to the ancient ruins. Brook greeted them warmly though he too was greatly surprised at their presence. He led them to a fire in the camp which lay within the ruins. When Kerran told him that the three of them intended to travel into Mendan-Var, Brook tried to dissuade them. When he heard their reason, he looked at Flindas aghast.

"He will kill you," Brook told his friend. "The Black One can be faced only by he who has chosen to die. It cannot be done."

"We will try," replied Flindas with a wry smile.

They stayed the night in the Elbrand camp and in the early dawn prepared to leave the Crossroads. Brook had told them that his scouts had seen no black horsemen or marauders anywhere along the Philosopher's Road except close to Mendan Maradass. Mendan-Var seemed almost empty of the enemy, and villages on the coast of the inland sea were still occupied by fisher folk and simple farmers. The three companions now clothed themselves in the black of Maradass. Should his wizardry fail, Kerran wished for them to still have some hope of concealment. The powers of Maradass were unknown and for the last time Kerran thought of abandoning the venture. He stood for a while on the old broken walls and looked across the lands to the north and east. Nothing moved. All was still as if pausing for a final breath. Fear clutched at Kerran's heart but he would not allow it to take hold. He watched as Storm flew low across the land to the north as if searching, then Kerran climbed down from the wall and rejoined his companions who stood waiting by their mounts. They set out into a thin mist which came from the marshlands at the wide spreading mouth of the River Glandrin-dar.

Noon had passed when they rode down the easy slope which led to the old stone bridge that crossed the wide, slow moving river. Here they were met by more Elbrand who reported that the road ahead remained clear of enemy. The three riders began to cross the bridge and they had not gone far when Kerran felt a shudder of warning pass through him, though he could see no danger. He looked back and the Elbrand waved to him, then the feeling rose in Kerran.

"Turn back!" he cried to the others. "There is danger here!"

He spun his horse, only in time to see the southern end of the bridge begin to collapse and fall into the dark river. The Elbrand leapt back and watched helplessly as another section of the bridge fell.

"Ride!" Kerran called to the others and they forced their mounts to a gallop. The bridge fell, sending plumes of water into the air, though there was little sound that could be heard above the clatter of their horse's hooves. Kerran looked back to see that the bridge fell at the same speed as their mounts were galloping, and they reached the north end well before the last section plunged into the sluggish river.

"Maradass!" spat Tris as they sat on their mounts looking at the wreckage of the bridge.

"He knows we are coming," said Kerran, a fateful note in his voice. "We are not trapped here so I do not understand why he has done this." He remained looking across the river, deep in thought. "What is that?" he asked himself, straining his eyes. The far hillside beyond the river seemed to ripple and sway. There was movement everywhere, and then he understood. "Do you see?" he cried with horror in his voice and pointed to the south. "The Stone Army!"

Flindas and Tris could also see it now, troop upon troop of the powerful spearmen were emerging from the earth that the three companions had just passed over. The distant Elbrand saw them too and as the earth began to move beneath their very feet they leapt into the river, their heads bobbing on the stream as they escaped into the marshland. Flindas looked around, expecting the stone troops to emerge on this side of the river, but they did not. A vast army, greater than any imagined, had now spread across the distant hillside as far as eye could see.

"He will destroy the land!" cried Tris in anguish as the Stone Army began to march south.

"It has always been his intent," said Kerran, his voice like stone itself. "We cannot return. The Southlands would fall now even if I went back. There are more of them than I could ever resist. Maradass expects us and probably knows our purpose. He has planned it that way. It may already be too late for the Southlands." He turned to his companions. "I go to Mendan Maradass," he told them. "It is your choice now. If you go to the west you can escape for a time. I know not what to expect now that he knows of our presence here but I cannot depart from this venture, I will face Maradass, time is short and vanishes quickly."

"I am still with you," said Flindas, a resolute look in his eyes.

"I too," said Tris, and as one they turned their mounts to the east along the Philosopher's Road.

The three riders kept a very watchful eye on the country around them, but they were unaware of the two Elbrand scouts who lay hidden not far from the road and who watched the dark riders approach. The scouts had been told by a runner to expect them. The horses shied a little as the Elbrand suddenly appeared from the grass to the north of the road. Quickly

Kerran told them of the collapsed bridge and the emergence of the Stone Army.

"The South is under attack and you are cut off," he told them. "Tell all your comrades that they must escape from Mendan-Var."

"We have boats," replied one of the scouts, a dark and worried look on her face. "Will you not return to the South with us?" she said.

"No," replied Kerran. "We go to Mendan Maradass, and may all that is good travel with us."

"You will need all the luck you can gather," said the scout, looking eastward along the stone paved road.

"Not luck," replied Kerran as he urged his horse away. "Luck is something that none can expect to help them in these times."

The three riders then rode quickly to the east.

In the Southlands, along many of the Wizard's Lines, the vast Stone Army appeared, the countless marching soldiers invading the Regions of Glandrin and Andrian. The countryside was in panic. The Highroads to the city became choked with wagons and thousands of fearful people. The Stone Army marched relentlessly, and with them they carried blue fire. The grasslands where they walked shrivelled and the land began to die.

"Marauders!" said Tris, standing and sniffing the night air.

They had camped on a tree covered hillside well away from the road and even Kerran's heightened awareness had not sensed the black dogs before she had. They remained in camp, alert to attack but none came. Kerran had decided not to protect them as they had ridden to the east. Maradass knew of their presence in the region and yet had not attacked. The Evil One sat and waited for them, knowing that they would not turn back.

Kerran felt the dark, gloating presence of Maradass to the south and east. They were within a half-day's ride of Mendan Maradass and the following day there would be no moon. The three companions mounted before sunrise and returned to the road. As the light improved they could see a great number of marauders. The dogs came from behind along the road, keeping pace with the cantering horses, their tongues hanging, their hungry eyes never leaving the three riders. By noon the companions had reached a small rise, and not far ahead, its dark towers silhouetted against sky and sea, stood Maradass Castle. Before it, on flat cleared land lay the crowded pavilions and tents that surrounded the field of battle. The dogs pressed in on them as they paused and Flindas strung his bow.

"They cannot come at us," said Kerran, and indeed the dogs seemed to reach a point where they could advance no further. In frustration they howled and pawed at an unseen barrier.

"Neither creatures nor weapons can reach us now," Kerran told his friends. "Only when we separate will there be danger. Tris, I do not yet understand your part in this but I think you must stay by me. If Maradass accepts this challenge I may not be able to help Flindas, but stay close and you will be safe."

The companions left the small hill and rode towards the tournament ground. Kerran felt a familiar tingling sensation as they reached and entered the Wizard Line north of the castle. A roar went up from the massed throng of black soldiers, but it was not their presence which had caused the cheers. On the battlefield man fought against man and there were few who had eyes for those who approached from the highroad, though there was one who saw them clearly.

Maradass smiled as he sat on a high seat overlooking the field and saw from afar the approaching riders, hemmed in by the large pack of black dogs. Soon they would be within his power. His plan had worked as he knew it would, the news from Marlto had only confirmed it. Kerran had come because there was nowhere else to go. The fate of the lands would be decided here, this very day, and Maradass knew that he had won already. He reached into a small pouch within his robes and touched the two fragments of the Seacrest. Where before there had been four separate quarters, now there were two halves, and his power had grown with their joining. The Evil One laughed to himself as he thought of the coming entertainment. Luista sat cradling Darss beside him and Maradass looked down with admiration on his other son, Zard, who stood below on the edge of the battlefield in front of his father's high seat. The Black Knight stood unmoving in his dark armour and waited, as did his father, for the three approaching riders.

Maradass had thought long on this meeting and had decided that Zard would not accept the challenge after all. Even though there was no longer the smallest risk of any warrior of the Southlands ever being able to conquer his mighty son. Maradass had worked his magic and the newly enhanced powers of his son's magical armour could never be pierced, not by any weapon, even the visor slits were impenetrable. Maradass had heard from Marlto the identity of the one who would seek the challenge and he had suddenly wanted to see Zard humiliate and then kill the outlaw warrior. Chelasta and the house of Amitarl were the deaths he prized above all others but the name of Flindas Demsharl still brought angry fire to his thoughts. The death of the girl would also be an unexpected pleasure, for both she and Demsharl had once threatened his beloved Luista. Maradass reached out his wrinkled fingers and squeezed his wife's perfect, delicate hand. She smiled, for she too had won. Demsharl would die and so would Chelasta, and then in time the remainder of the family Amitarl. The House of Maradass would no longer have enemies in the land, and she would live forever in perfection.

Maradass had lost interest in the battle before him. Most of the men from the city had not put up much of a fight against the ten horse soldiers sent against them. One had fought bravely but a spear had ended his useless life too quickly. Even before the battle was over horse drawn wagons trundled onto the field and the bodies began to be loaded on to them by women and youths to be eventually fed to the dogs. The many thousand voices roared again as the last man fell to a blow which separated his head from his shoulders. Maradass took no notice, his eyes fixed to the approaching prize that had now been seen by many in the crowd.

Soon all eyes were turned to the south as the three riders walked their horses onto the battlefield. Those of the Black Army who were closest to them fell back as though pushed away. The crowd of soldiers became hushed. None knew the mind or plans of Maradass but it had been whispered that the young wizard would come, and so it was. Kerran rode, flanked by Tris and Flindas, to the flat ground before the seat of Maradass. Zard stood unmoving and watched their approach. His head was bare, the tall dark helmet resting in the crook of his arm. The three riders brought their mounts to a halt before him and it was then that Kerran saw the lustreless and empty look in the Black Knight's eyes. For a moment he touched on Zard's mind and found only cold blue fire.

"You have finally proven to be the fool I thought you were," said Maradass contemptuously, leaning forward, his eyes gloating. Though he spoke quietly all those present around the arena could hear his words. "I am the spider and, you the stupid flies who come blundering into my web. So be it. You come to end the line of Maradass on this day without moon by challenging Zard to single combat, or so I have been told."

Maradass was looking at Flindas now who had great difficulty in holding the powerful gaze of the Evil One.

"That is why I have come," said Flindas with a steady voice, though in truth he knew that he had never felt such fear in all his life.

The stern face of Zard turned to him, his dark eyes strange and foreboding.

"Another fool!" laughed Maradass. There was laughter amongst those who listened as Maradass leaned down, spitting out his words. "You are all about to die and you do not yet understand that you are already vanquished," he said with a cruel smile. With slow deliberate pleasure he held the two pieces of the Seacrest before him and Kerran felt an almost overwhelming fear. "I see doubt in your eyes, Wizard Chelasta," mocked Maradass. "Not what you expected I think."

What it meant Kerran could not yet know.

"I am beyond you now," said Maradass. "Ancient oaths are beginning to crumble, and when the Seacrest is again whole there will be nothing that can destroy me, not even the death of Zard should that ever be possible. No, it is too late for you now, oh so very late indeed." His evil laugh rose high and demented. "Perhaps I will allow this challenge, then perhaps not," he spoke to the crowd. "But for now I think it is time to play a little. Let us see what this young wizard can do."

Blue fire suddenly leapt from his hands and its ferocity broke through Kerran's protection. There was a flash as of lightning and Kerran was thrown from his horse. The mount screamed and bolted. Tris too slipped from her saddle, stunned by the explosion.

Flindas leapt to the ground and in the same movement sent a throwing knife in a deadly arc towards Maradass. There was a blue flash and the knife vanished in flight. Kerran was on his feet quickly and the young wizard held his ground as yet another bolt of flame enveloped him, but this time his protection held. There was a shattering, tearing sound and the blue fire leapt into the air and was gone.

Maradass seemed surprised, though he covered it quickly. A hush had fallen on the soldiers. None had before seen the full power of Maradass and they waited with gleeful anticipation for him to finish the three. The Evil One leaned back, his heavy lidded eyes watching carefully the scene before him. Kerran stood tall and resolute. Maradass would not catch him unawares again. Flindas was beside Tris and helping her to her feet. She seemed dazed but otherwise unharmed. Zard had not moved during the exchange of fire, though Kerran became aware that the Black Knight no longer seemed as rigid as he had been. Zard's eyes were not quite as dead as they had been before.

Kerran looked up at Maradass and began to play a deadly game of his own. He could have retreated, taking Flindas and Tris into the game and to Manzanee's cave, but had decided that he need not do this yet. His protection had been weakened by the blasts of fire but Maradass had also lost much. It was Zard who could still be the most important piece of the play.

"It is you who are the fool," said Kerran with a taunting note in his voice. The crowd could hear his clear words and they held their breaths, anticipating the wrath of their ruler.

"How so?" said Maradass, leering at him, untouched by the words.

"You are deluded if you think you can defy me," said the Wizard Chelasta arrogantly.

These words from Kerran caused Flindas to look up quickly at the change in the young wizard's manner. His tone was provoking, as though he wished for Maradass to strike again.

"Move closer to me," called Kerran.

Flindas began to help Tris towards him. She was shaken but her mind had now cleared. Kerran turned his head slightly to see them better, and it was this moment that Maradass had been waiting for. The young fool was distracted by his concern for his friends and would not be prepared for his next attack.

Maradass threw out his arms and blue fire leapt from his hands in which he still held the two pieces of the Seacrest, but it was this moment that Kerran had also anticipated. Blue fire crackled and burned cold about them, closing, as Kerran's protection began to lose its power and burn, and then suddenly there was a shattering explosion that burst outwards, away from the three companions. There was a startled cry from many in the crowd. Blue, bitterly cold fire fell amongst them and there were cries of pain. Luista screamed and with the baby Darss in her arms, she rushed from the high dais, disappearing behind the many folds of dark cloth at the back of the pavilion. Maradass had been thrust back into his seat by the blast which had been his own power turned against him. Zard stood unmoved, but a little more light seemed to shine in his dark eyes. Kerran again spoke savagely to Maradass, pushing the Evil One to anger.

"Your strength diminishes," he called. "You cannot touch me and still I stand and defy you."

"What good is your standing there?" laughed Maradass scornfully. "Stand all day if you wish, you cannot harm me."

"It is not to harm you that I came here," replied Kerran. "I come to take that which does not belong to you. It is Ma-Zurin-Bidar, the Seacrest, talisman of wizards that I seek."

Maradass laughed; a cackling insane sound. "You asked for it like that?" he said in mock surprise. "You are more than a fool than I had thought. Take it if you will, though I know you do not have that power." He held the pieces out to Kerran, a crooked twist to his leering smile.

Kerran called them, though he did not know if he truly could. Maradass grasped the pieces suddenly as he felt them begin to drift away from his open hands. He stared at Kerran with a look of fear and surprise. He had almost lost his most valued of treasures and he quailed at his near escape, then he recovered his composure and smiled. Nothing could harm him. Chelasta was not able, and Demsharl would fail also. He shuddered again at the thought of almost losing the Seacrest, and then he leaned forward, his mind suddenly knowing the solution. Chelasta he knew must be taken for his ultimate plan to succeed, and the young wizard had a great weakness.

"So we are at an impasse," he said. "I am a reasonable man. You come here to challenge Zard in battle, to destroy the line of Maradass, so be it then. Zard will fight your fool hero and I will enjoy seeing him die."

The plan of Maradass was simple. When Zard made the killing blow Chelasta would be his, for in that moment the young wizard would be defenceless. Maradass smiled again. The weakness in Chelasta was that he had a soft heart, and in sudden grief his protection would certainly falter. Maradass looked at the back of his tall dark son and then across at Demsharl. It was impossible that the man, skilled though he may be, could ever get within Zard's defences, for in truth there was now no way in. The Black Knight would not tire and Maradass suddenly wanted to see the blood of the tall dark warrior from the City Amitarl, though he would have no time to gloat as in that moment he must attack the haughty young wizard with all of his fiery magic.

Kerran had repelled the blast at great cost to his own dwindling powers, but he was no longer concerned that Maradass could end his life. He looked into the eyes of Zard and saw recognition. He touched on the Black Knight's mind and they came together for a brief moment. No blue fire intruded as Kerran listened to Zard and watched for a time as the Black Knight's eyes lost their darkness, turning to a clear blue that was not the fire of Maradass. For a moment longer the connection held, and then Zard's mind was again engulfed in cold fire.

"So be it," said Kerran quietly and looked at Flindas, who turned to the dais and called the same words aloud.

"So be it."

"Prepare yourself," Maradass said mockingly.

"I too will prepare," called out Zard, the first words he had spoken since they had arrived.

"What have you to prepare?" called Maradass to his son. "You have everything at hand." There was a worried note in the voice of Maradass, and when Zard turned to face him his father's eyes grew uneasy.

"I will prepare," said Zard again, his voice stern and determined.

Zard then walked from the battlefield, disappearing behind a wall of dark cloth beneath the pavilion. Maradass sat back, a worried frown flickering across his dark brow. He was weakened but still had enough strength to finish Chelasta. He was sure of it. What had Zard meant when he said he must prepare? The look on his dark son's face, it had changed. The eyes were not as dark as they had been.

Flindas did not need long to strip the upper clothing from his tall, long muscled body, he would fight unencumbered by jacket and shirt. At his waist were the two long daggers and the five remaining throwing knives. He laid aside sword and bow, and the crowd murmured. They knew now what was about to happen and were pleased at the new sport. Into his belt at the small of his back, Flindas slipped the magical black knife.

"Maradass is weakened," Kerran was saying to him quietly as he made ready. "I reached Zard for a few moments. Deep within his darkness he truly wants peace. I am sure of this. He is now closed again. The blue fire came, but Zard is no longer totally under his father's power."

"Why does he take so long to prepare?" asked Tris, who had recovered completely and stood watching the dark curtains from which Zard would emerge, the crowd of many thousand soldiers and their women were also wondering this.

"Zard spoke to me for only a few moments," replied Kerran, whose eyes were turned to Flindas, great concern for his friend touching him with doubt. "His few words were, 'Only in single combat,'" said Kerran, wondering. "Only in single combat can he die," Kerran repeated. "He cannot give up his own life. Of this we know, though I believe that Zard, the man I spoke with for much of our ride together, would indeed choose death if it meant peace for the lands. The oath and the old magic spells hold him no matter what his choice. He will fight you to the death Flindas even though he would choose otherwise."

"Be careful," said Tris turning suddenly to Flindas. She was not one for showing her feelings but unfamiliar tears came into her eyes as she reached out and tenderly touched his arm.

"I too am weakened," said Kerran. "But I will get you to Manzanee's cave if I possibly can, though I truly feel that it must end here today."

"You should leave the field now," said Flindas quietly. "Zard will come soon and I must finish my preparations alone."

Chelasta gave a small bow of understanding to his warrior friend. "Good will prevail," he said.

Their eyes held for a moment, and then those of Flindas flickered to Tris. A touch of a smile crossed his lips, then turning quickly he walked away towards the centre of the field. All this time Kerran had held his protection over them all, but now Flindas had gone beyond it.

"Stay close," he said to Tris as he scooped up the discarded weapons and clothing of his friend. "I would be as near to Maradass as possible. If it does not go well you should make your way to the castle. There is much here that I do not yet understand, but your part, if there truly is one for you to play, must be found amongst those stones at the foot of the castle. A secret passageway, a stone for your sling, I cannot guess at what it might be but your dream was important. Go there if you can."

Of Wizard's Blood

Kerran turned from the battlefield and walked towards Maradass who still seemed disturbed at the disappearance of Zard.

"Come sit with me," called the Evil One, hiding his concern. "Luista has abandoned the tournament and it is more fun with some one to talk with."

Maradass was again his mocking self, at least on the outside, and Kerran accepted the invitation. He and Tris made their way up the flight of stairs which led to the seats above. There were several tall ornate chairs which were well spaced, and the guards fell back as Kerran came to the one vacated by Luista. Before he sat, he looked into the baleful eyes of Maradass.

"You have surely lost Chelasta," the soft voice came, more evil than ever. "Zard cannot be conquered, and the Southlands will die under my army's feet. Come, sit and watch the end of all things."

There was a crackle in the air and a shimmering of small blue sparks as Kerran's protection touched against the edge of the Evil One's power. Maradass laughed at it and then leered at Tris who had taken the furthest seat from him.

"We meet again," he almost snarled. "You will be given to

the dogs, as will the body of Demsharl. You defied me once and you will pay for that."

Tris shrank back into her seat, avoiding his gaze. Maradass too sat back in silence, but from the corner of his eye he watched the young wizard carefully. Kerran, though very aware of the power which hung so close to him, could not look anywhere but at the lone figure that stood on the trampled earth of the battlefield.

Flindas was moving and stretching his body after the long ride. His mind had become centred, his heart beat slowed, just as Dantas had taught him when he was still a youth. He heard his father's words once again. *Let the other man use his fire against you*, the old warrior had told him. *Meet it with cold clarity and a minimum of energy. Let him burn and he will tire, and then he is yours.*

Fear welled up in Flindas for a moment and he forced it back into a deep hidden place. He was to meet a man who was said to never weaken. He saw Kerran and Tris seated beside Maradass, the dark guards standing as close to their master as the conflicting forces permitted.

Flindas was still looking in that direction when Zard emerged from beneath the pavilion, the murmur in the crowd turned to a sudden uproar. On the high dais Maradass could not yet see what the great noise in the crowd was about, and then Zard took a few steps further onto the field and Maradass shrieked aloud, a terrified look suddenly coming into his darkly shadowed eyes. His son Zard stood below him but was no longer wearing his dark magical armour. Kerran looked down upon the hard muscular giant who now stood bare to the waist. Held in his left hand was a short stabbing sword and in his right, a small circular shield. Maradass was gasping unable to speak as Zard turned to look at his father.

"I fight in the name of Maradass," he called, his voice reaching to all those in the hushed crowd. "In the name of Maradass, and in the name of honour."

Maradass leapt to his feet. "You will not do this!" he screamed suddenly, finding his voice. "You will return to the castle now!"

"No father," replied Zard. "With honour I will fight, and

if I die, then so be it." Maradass began to lift his hands. The Seacrest would hold his son, filling his mind with numbing blue fire.

"Do it and you have lost," said Kerran. His heart had rejoiced seeing Zard emerge without his dark armour. The son could not let himself die, but there were no rules as to what he should wear.

Maradass turned to Kerran, a wild animal trapped and snarling.

"Your power has been weakened," said Kerran. "Attack me and your strength will diminish, and still your son would fight. Hold Zard, and soon your power will be depleted and I would be able to defeat you, not by force, but simply by willing you to give the Seacrest to me."

Maradass knew that Kerran spoke the truth. The young wizard would engulf him and Ma-Zurin-Bidar would be lost. The Seacrest was a wizard's tool and he was a mere, though powerful, mortal. He knew that he would not be able to resist the demand made by a true wizard, should his own power fade. The Evil One brought his terrified eyes back to Zard, but his son had already turned and was walking towards his opponent who stood motionless, waiting. Maradass screamed Zard's name but his son did not turn back.

"Take him!" the Evil One ordered his elite guards. "Hold him. He knows not what he does."

The guards looked at each other but did not move. Maradass lifted his hands as though to strike them, but he caught Kerran's gaze and stopped. He was like a trapped wild animal and Kerran waited, hoping that he would strike, but he did not. Standing stiff and silent, Maradass looked out upon the tournament field, his face ashen, his hands trembling as they grasped the magic pieces in his bloodless, claw-like fingers.

Flindas watched Zard approach and many conflicting thoughts passed through his mind. For a moment he cursed the lack of his sword, and then looked at the small tube that had appeared in his hand. He could now take Zard without difficulty once they had joined battle. If the poison was effective, Flindas knew that he could win easily. His eyes turned back to Zard, continuing to watch the tall powerfully built man as he came nearer. Only moments ago Zard had spoken of honour and had come to fight Flindas without his black protective armour. Flindas understood that the fate of the lands depended on Zard's death, but he suddenly knew that he could not use the blowpipe to achieve it. Not because the poison might not kill, but because of that word spoken by Zard: honour. Smiling at his own recklessness, Flindas replaced the pipe and dart separately into the small pocket inside his boot. Standing erect, he found that Zard had come to a halt perhaps twenty paces from where he stood.

"Greetings Demsharl," said the hard voice of the Black One. "Today one of us will not leave this field alive. I will fight and kill you if I can, but you must know this before we commence. If I should die, then you will have found the peace you seek for the lands, and if you die then I will take my father's side and destroy all mortal beings in the Regions. The pieces of the game are set and the last play is about to begin. Defend yourself Demsharl for I mean to have your blood."

Zard leapt forward, sword in hand, and there was the ringing sound of steel upon steel as Zard deflected the throwing blade which had come flying towards his chest. The crowd roared with approval and Zard pressed forward, his dark eyes intent upon his prey. Flindas moved to keep a good distance between them. He had seen how easily Zard had turned the throwing blade and the speed of the Black One's defence had shaken him. The knife had seemed unstoppable but at the last moment Zard had sent it spinning into the dust. The Son of Maradass lunged forward, his sword arching with deadly speed, but Flindas was not to be caught. The crowd were contemptuous as he moved away quickly, their howling voices telling of their disapproval.

Flindas watched carefully, waiting for an opening. There was no danger yet. He was strong and would not tire easily, though he wished now for his sword so that he could close with Zard. Dust stirred about their feet as the two protagonists circled, waiting for a chance. Zard suddenly charged as Flindas had expected, and from either hand, in a blur of flickering steel, Flindas sent two blades hurtling towards his adversary. With startling speed the Black Knight deflected one with his shield, the other flying harmlessly by as he twisted away from its flight. He smiled then as he came at Flindas with slow deliberate steps. Where his eyes had been softer before, now they were black again, his mind steeped in darkness and the intention to kill. Flindas moved backwards, one of his last two throwing knives in his hand. The sound of the crowd grew to a wild and violent roar and Flindas looked briefly towards the pavilion.

Maradass had remained standing, his small dark figure bent forward, hands held stiff at his side. Kerran, ever watchful, looked out upon the battle and again felt great fear for his friend, whose lean body was dwarfed by the dark stalking giant. Kerran glanced down beside him at the sword which Flindas must surely wish for, now that Zard had entered the battle without his armour. There was a clash on the field and the sound of another deflected throwing knife as it sang through the air. In a movement which startled Maradass, Kerran stood quickly and drawing the sword, he hurled it far out onto the battlefield. Flindas watched the blade flicker through the air and land some distance away. Zard was not aware of it but stood between Flindas and the sword.

For a long time Flindas continued to evade Zard, his last throwing knife held in his fingertips. The Black One had incredible speed with his hands and Flindas thought that only Landin may have been faster. On his feet the Black Knight was not so strong. Flindas could elude him easily, and after another charge, he leapt sideways and ran quickly towards his sword. There was a sudden flicker of blue fire and the sword burned and was gone. Flindas cursed in frustration and turned again to meet Zard, but a glance at the pavilion told him that a battle had also begun there.

As the sword had burned Kerran spread his protecting power and it had almost engulfed Maradass. There was the crackle of cold fire and an explosion which stopped even Zard, who looked towards his father and the young wizard, watching intently for a few moments. Flindas threw his last knife and

Zard laughed as he easily sent the blade spinning far out into the field. He said not a word but the black smile returned to his lips as he once again began to pursue his prey. Flindas could do nothing for Kerran, and though flashes of blue fire shattered the air, he set his mind back to the dark giant before him.

Zard came at him quickly as Flindas drew the two narrow bladed daggers. They were not weighted for throwing and he thought about the black knife at the small of his back, and then decided he would not use it yet. It had gone through his mind that if the blade had such qualities as returning to its sheath, then could it not be made to do other things? Perhaps Zard retained power over the weapon still, and Flindas regretted once again the loss of his sword.

The day was warm and Flindas, knowing that Zard would not tire, understood that the battle could not last for much longer. He decided that he must close with Zard, even though he held just the two slim daggers. One of his throwing knives he knew was not far away in the dust of the battlefield. He edged towards the place where it had fallen but when Zard next charged he stood his ground and met him. Another fierce explosion came from the high pavilion as Zard bore down upon his warrior opponent.

Kerran had almost been able to will the Seacrest from Maradass but had been repelled. The shattering of the air threw the guards backwards, while Tris was blown from her seat. She rolled away and then leapt for cover, reaching the flight of stairs, to fall tumbling as the air again burned with magical fire. Tris remained on the stairs and in fear watched the two battles which had thrown the large crowd of soldiers into an uproar. The black troops would not be held back and many advanced towards the pavilion and also began to invade the battlefield.

Kerran, in terror, felt the power of Maradass reaching into his mind and suddenly he knew that he had now lost the battle. The power of the Seacrest in the hands of Maradass was more than he could resist. Struggling desperately he began to drown in the chilling fire, his protection weakened and burned. In a haze he saw Flindas and Zard doing battle on the field. His mind began to darken and he fell to the wooden floor of the high pavilion. One last time he looked out upon the field, and then his vision blurred and for an age all was darkness and evil dreams.

Flindas met the charge of Zard as the Black Knight's sword lunged at him. He parried the blow but the slim knife shattered, and he felt Zard's blade cut deep into his left hand. Flindas turned his evasive movement into a desperate roll, but before he could rise, Zard was on him again. The gleaming blood-stained sword struck the earth where Flindas had been but a moment before, and then Zard fell, his legs taken from beneath him by a vicious kick as Flindas swivelled away, rising quickly to his feet. With a roar of frustration Zard crashed to the dusty earth and this time it was his turn to roll away quickly as Flindas pressed his attack. Zard, though a large man, was agile and came to his feet before Flindas could reach him. The crowd roared approval, though few had ever expected to see their dark commander fall.

Flindas did not slow his charge and leapt at Zard before the giant man had quite regained his balance. Holding now just the one dagger in his damaged left hand, Flindas grasped the wrist of Zard's sword hand, lunging then with his own blade. The small shield smashed into his shoulder and Flindas was sent spinning away. The Black Knight slowed then and looked to where the dagger of Flindas had scored deeply across his chest and ribs. He scowled at his foe and, fire burned in his eyes, he came to a standstill. Breathing deeply with unsuppressed anger, his eyes never left the man who had drawn his blood.

Flindas was shaken and in pain, and he saw his own death in Zard's eyes. For a moment he expected the Black Knight to charge, but instead he watched with surprise as Zard turned to the approaching soldiers. They were advancing across the battlefield, and with a terrifying voice that carried the sound of death, Zard roared at them to leave the arena and in a tumbling mass they did his bidding.

Zard turned again to Flindas. Many men talk as they fight, goading their opponent, but Zard remained silent as he again began to stalk his prey across the field. Flindas looked to the pavilion and with great dread he saw that the dais was empty. The seats were pushed back and toppled and Tris was gone from the stairs where she had sheltered. Flindas slipped his last dagger into the sheath at his belt and drew the knife that had been Zard's, while in his left hand he held the scabbard. If the knife was to work its magic, it would do so on the first throw. Zard saw the blade and paused, a look of puzzlement on his face, as if he were trying to remember something that he had forgotten. Flindas threw the knife and at the same moment Zard charged. There was a clash of steel and the thrown blade flew high into the air to land far beyond the battle. In a rolling run Flindas escaped the charge and when he came to his feet the knife was again in its scabbard.

Three times he cast the knife at Zard and three times the Black Knight evaded it, charging often and further tiring Flindas who now thought of using his remaining strength to escape. At a run he could reach the ocean before any would catch him, unless the dogs reacted quickly. As the fight progressed he edged closer to the pavilion. No soldiers remained there. Kerran was gone and perhaps Maradass had overpowered the young wizard. The castle would surely hold the answer and Flindas thought on the choices before him. Escape to the ocean and a long swim, or to hope that the castle gates remained open and he could enter blindly. Both possibilities lay in the same direction but then Flindas realised the hopelessness of it, for there to be escape for any of them Zard must first die. There seemed to be no other choice now. To run would mean only a short delay before the Southlands were engulfed by the marching hoards of Stone Soldiers. It must end here he thought to himself and waited for Zard to attack.

When Zard next charged, Flindas met him with the dark blade in his hand. Zard came quickly, but recklessly it seemed. His guard was open, the small shield held as though he did not expect to have to defend himself against a thrown blade. Flindas did not understand, but in the brief moment of that thought the opportunity was lost. He prepared to defend himself, to deflect the charge. When Zard at the last moment dropped his shield and suddenly his sword was held in his right hand.

Flindas cried out as the blade cut deep into the muscles high on his left shoulder. He spun away in pain, dropping the magical scabbard as he did so. Zard turned and looked at his wounded enemy who could not hope to stem the flow of blood. Zard retrieved his shield slowly, deliberately. There was no need to hurry now. Flindas was becoming weaker by the moment and would not survive another charge. Zard walked towards his opponent and a look of death was about him. The crowd were roaring with blood lust. Here was their commander facing the best warrior of the Southlands, a man who was about to die. They gloried in it as Zard began his charge.

Flindas prepared to meet this last attack, his left arm almost useless. Through his pain he saw the Black Knight bearing down on him, his blade swinging wide to sweep the head from his enemy's shoulders. Flindas did not try to move away to the side and avoid the blow as he had done previously. It was too late for evasion now. Instead, to Zard's surprise, he went quickly into a deep crouch. The Black Knight had not expected such a move. His blade changed quickly to a downward slashing blow but it was too high and passed above the head of his enemy. With all the power left in his legs Flindas lunged upward. Zard's shield smashed into the side of his head but in the same moment Flindas felt the dark blade that he held pass deep into the unprotected body of the Black Knight. Zard shuddered and a gasp came to his throat. He remained standing, his sword lifting high to strike his foe, but it was too late. His fingers went limp, his sword and shield dropping to the ground. Zard's body began to slump as Flindas thrust the blade deeper, knowing that the blow had ended the life of the Black Knight.

For a few moments Zard stood transfixed, his arms around the shoulders of his slayer. With great strength he held himself from falling and looked into the eyes of Flindas as his own eyes lost their dark and empty glare. Flindas looked into clear blue eyes, their brightness something he was always to remember, and then Zard spoke, his last words came in a whisper.

"Tis well done," he said. His lips showed a strange triumphant smile, and then his knees gave way beneath him and Zard, the Black Knight, son of Maradass the Evil One, fell to the dust of the battlefield.

When Kerran had finally succumbed to the power of Maradass, Tris had watched in fear as the Evil One stood over the fallen wizard. The battle continued to rage on the field, the crowd, torn between the happenings there and those on the high dais of the pavilion. Maradass had called his guards. They returned and lifting Kerran who was no longer conscious they began to carry him from the battlefield towards the castle. Maradass had stood for a while watching the contest, his eyes glanced towards where Tris had been, but her instincts for survival heightened, he saw nothing but the empty stairs as she crouched away from his view.

When Tris looked next the dais was empty. Maradass had left his son to live or die, for Kerran was a greater prize. Though it had exhausted Maradass to finally overcome the young wizard. Maradass could no longer help his son, his blue fire had dwindled and almost been extinguished, however with Kerran as his captive he knew that even if Zard should die, he could now break all of the old oaths sworn at the Crossroads. The pieces of the Seacrest, Maradass had learned, could only be completely united by the presence of one last element, and that was wizard's blood. His trap had worked and now, even should Zard die, Maradass would live forever with the Seacrest intact. The blood of Chelasta would unite the two halves of the talisman and Maradass would possess all lands, all people, and the fate of existence itself. He had smiled when he thought of how close the old Amitarl had come to discovering the truth. It had not been that one of Chelasta blood may unite the Seacrest. The correct translation should have been that the actual blood of Chelasta was needed to undo the deed done at the Crossroads two thousand years before.

Tris knelt in confused thought. She could not help Flindas and now Kerran had been taken. She watched the two battling warriors for a few moments and then made her decision. The dream had told her to look amongst the rocks near the castle wall. Whatever was hidden there must be the key to her part in this day's violent drama. Unnoticed she slipped away through the dark curtains of the pavilion. It was not far to the castle and when Tris emerged again into the sunlight, she saw that Maradass and the guards who carried the limp body of Kerran had almost reached the gates. She began to sprint towards the high dark walls at an angle to the curving road. There was a rumbling and grating sound as the gates of the castle fell into place.

Tris reached the high stone walls. She closed her eyes, trying to bring the dream more clearly to mind. To the east she thought, remembering the cast of shadows. Tris was not challenged from above. In fact there seemed to be no guards on the battlements at all. She continued her search but saw nothing peculiar, nor was there anything unusual about the myriad small stones and boulders which covered the slope. Something happened on the distant battlefield. There was a roar from the crowd, and Tris, her stomach in a knot of fear, began to leap blindly amongst the rocks, searching desperately for anything that would give her a clue as to why she had been brought here.

There was a piercing cry from above and Storm fell from the sky to alight on a small mound of stones close by the castle wall. Tris leapt towards the white hawk, sure that the bird was trying to show her something. As she rushed forward the hawk again took to the sky, and Tris, on reaching the piled up stones, quickly began to throw them aside. Beneath them must be the answer. She laboured hard, some of the stones being quite large. When she rolled away the last heavy boulder beneath it she found nothing but bare earth. She cried out in frustration looking above, but Storm was no longer in sight. She was about to look further, though it seemed even more hopeless now, when a very strange thing began to happen. A thing that she had seen before.

Kerran lay on his stomach, chains holding him to the stone floor in the central chamber of Maradass castle, and he became aware of the laughter which echoed around the tapestried walls. The fire flickered in the hearth near Luista who sat as she had so often before, while near her was Mindis who remained in his own strange world. Kerran felt the magic oppression of the Seacrest. He was held to the floor by more than chains. The ancient wizards' magic in the hands of Maradass held him captive, while his own powers were reduced to a quiet murmuring from within. He was unable to penetrate the all encompassing domination of Maradass. There was nothing he could do and despair tore at his mind. Then from beyond the walls a vision came to him. He saw Tris clambering amongst the rocks at the foot of the castle. For a time his thoughts held only confusion. It was like watching a play in which he was but a spectator. He saw Tris pick up yet another stone only to cast it aside, then with all his remaining strength, he turned his mind to what he had suddenly realised was the reason for Tris to be amongst the stones.

Maradass looked to the young wizard. "What are you doing?" he screamed, sensing the change.

Kerran continued to concentrate as Maradass again laughed loudly.

"You have lost Chelasta," he said, coming to stand above him. "Whatever feeble trick you try to play it will certainly fail. Too late, all is mine now. All I need is a little of your blood."

Maradass took a dagger from his robes and cut a deep gash into the back of Kerran's right hand. The young wizard barely felt the pain, concentrated as he was on getting Tris into the castle. It was his last hope, for he understood now that Maradass had the final ingredient to bring together the pieces of the Seacrest. The answer had been so simple and yet Kerran had not known what it could be until now.

Tris watched in surprise as a rock of a size that would fit comfortably into a small hand began to move, then lift from the earth. She saw it stop at the level of her knees. Another and then another began to float upwards. Tris suddenly understood, Kerran, though captured, still retained some of his magical powers and he was making a stairway for her. She looked up as more stones lifted above her head and showed her the way into the dark castle. Tris glanced once towards the battlefield which the crowd had begun to invade, and then she started to ascend the magical ladder.

It was a hard climb, the stones barely big enough to balance on. Tris crept still higher and she was near the battlements of the outer castle wall. Glancing back She had a view over the tournament arena and surrounding land. She saw a lone figure dashing towards the castle, pursued by a great many soldiers. She held her breath a moment. Then her heart lightened as she saw that it was Flindas. He was clutching his blood-soaked shoulder, but alive. Tris called to him but he was too far away. She watched as he paused and looked towards the closed gates, and then changed direction and ran towards the ocean. Flindas was escaping and would surely outdistance his pursuers. With a feeling of relief Tris continued her climb.

As he ran, Flindas grasped his shoulder, trying to stem the flow of blood. The entire army of Maradass seemed to have taken up the chase. He was tired but ran directly towards the castle until he saw that the gates were shut. He turned then to the east, towards the ocean. Marauders howled still far behind him as he saw the sparkling waters ahead. He would win the race. Even the dogs could not catch him now. A sloping cliff led down to the sea and Flindas had almost reached the edge, escape within his grasp, when a heavy throwing knife plunged deep into his thigh.

Flindas cried out in agony and fell heavily to the earth. Clutching at this new wound, he had the strength to draw his last slim dagger, only to have it kicked violently from his hand. Another kick smashed into his ribs and Flindas knew that he was finished as a hand tore the knife from his leg. He lay doubled up on his side and through his pain he became aware of Marlto standing tall and arrogant above him, the bloody knife in his hand.

"Old friends meet again," Marlto said to his fallen enemy. "I have waited a long time for this Demsharl. You ruined my life and now it is time for you to pay. I knew you would make your escape this way, hoping to swim out beyond their reach. Tis too late now, Flindas, and it is time for you to die. Goodbye, Kinslayer."

The victorious face of Marlto came closer as the warrior clenched his victim's hair in one hand, the knife bearing down to slit the exposed throat. Marlto was grinning into his eyes when Flindas lashed out with his right hand and Marlto felt the small sharp pain as the little dart entered the side of his neck, then his blood turned to fire. Screaming he fell to the ground, convulsing in hideous death throes as Flindas became aware of the rush of men and dogs toward the ocean cliffs. They were close. He crawled to the edge and slipped over, then, in a sliding fall, he tumbled to the beach below. When the soldiers and dogs reached the white sands all they found was a trail of blood leading into the sea.

Tris reached the battlements and cautiously looked over the fortifications into the castle. There was no one to be seen. All the soldiery of Maradass seemed to have gone to the tournament, and she guessed that only the bodyguard of Maradass were now within the dark walls. Tris slipped over the battlements and stood on the stonework of Maradass castle. She could not decide what to do. The high towers and inner fortifications loomed above her. She crossed to the nearest wall and stood in the shadows. The castle was vast. How was she to possibly find Kerran? Suddenly Tris felt crushed. Even if she was to find him, what could she do alone against Maradass and his guards? At her belt was her hunting knife, and in the pocket of her tunic she carried her sling and a few selected stones. She was about to begin her hopeless search when Storm swooped from the sky, silently flashing by her, leading her towards Kerran.

Quickly she ran after the bird until the white hawk flew upwards, skimming, almost touching the higher walls of the castle. Then Tris could see the hovering stones, another stairway built for her by the young wizard's magic. If his powers still held, then there must be hope. Tris leapt to the stones and scrambled up them as quickly as she could. Again she came to a high parapet and found no guards. Storm had alighted on a distant wall and Tris had to go down a flight of steps and across a courtyard before she again found more floating stones waiting for her. She climbed again as from above she began to hear a voice, rising and falling, its notes hanging in the air. It could only be Maradass she thought and hoped that she was not too late.

Tris reached a narrow slit window and at first doubted if she could fit through, from within she heard the voice of Maradass chanting in an unknown tongue. Tris lifted her head above the bottom of the window and looked in upon darkness. It took some time for her eyes to adjust to the gloom of the chamber beyond. She was looking down into a large room from well above those within. Luista was by the fireplace with her baby son and Mindis while Kerran lay chained to the stone floor of the large chamber. Maradass stood with his back to her at a wide pedestal of stone over which he passed his hands, chanting all the while. On the pedestal she could just see the Seacrest, the two halves laid together.

Tris decided to try and enter. Maradass would not see her but Luista had a better view. She began to slip her slim body through the window, hoping that there was something to climb down or to at least break her fall, for it was some distance to the floor below. The shadow of her movement gave her away and it was Maradass who turned quickly and saw her already partly through the narrow window.

"So!" cried Maradass. "A final trick from you, Chelasta."

He laughed then and placed one hand on the Seacrest while the other suddenly threw blue fire towards her. Tris tried to escape but was too late. Stone exploded around her and the blast threw her backwards. Maradass continued to laugh as she fell from view. After a few moments of looking at the large hole blasted through the stone wall Maradass returned to the ancient ritual. Absorbed as he was he did not see the two small hands, and then the dark head of Tris appear at the gaping wound in the castle wall.

Luista cowered down on the large comfortable divan, covering her baby son with her body. The explosion had terrified the young child, whose wailing cry filled the air, almost drowning out the chanting of Maradass. Tris had just managed to break her fall by grasping at the stones which still hung suspended above the courtyard. She could hear guards running, and soon they would be in the courtyard looking for her body and they would see her. They would carry black arrows and bows. Below, within the chamber, the voice of Maradass reached a high pitch of powerful, unknown words. Tris watched as he took up a small bowl of dark liquid and poured it over the Seacrest. Fire and light leapt upward from the centre of the pedestal and Maradass was wreathed in a swirling, many coloured wind. The fearful cries of Darss and Luista could be heard amongst the rushing sound of the gale, the chamber more brightly lit than the daylight beyond the castle walls.

Tris felt the suspended stones on which she balanced precariously begin to fall from beneath her. She clung desperately to the edge of the shattered wall as the ladder of stones fell away to clatter on the stonework of the courtyard far below. In fear she could do nothing else but climb into the blasted hole. Light and power played around her, almost throwing her from the wall. There was a shattering sound as though the very air was being torn apart and Luista screamed again, though her voice could barely be heard above the rushing of the wind. The room seemed about to be destroyed. Sparks from the fire swirled through the air, tapestries and furniture falling into tangled disorder against the walls and beginning to smoulder. Then the light appeared to focus itself. It rose upwards to the high ceiling then thrust quickly downwards to be drawn into the Seacrest. The wind died and the light vanished as if it had never been.

The silence and darkness of the chamber seemed almost complete after the terrifying light. Maradass cackled with triumph, the sound high with evil and madness. In the dim light Tris could now see the talisman glowing with a soft flame of all colours. Maradass reached out and lifted it from the pedestal. It was whole, and the talisman's inner fire lit the hand of Maradass as he held it aloft.

"It is done!" he cried with great joy. "It is mine and there are none who can take it from me. Chelasta! It is the end now for you and all of those who would defy me. All will fear the name Maradass before they die. Fear me now, Chelasta, for you are about to be no more."

Maradass began to speak words in a broken, forgotten tongue and the Seacrest began to glow brighter within his bony grasp. Suddenly Kerran cried out in fearful pain and Tris knew that her moment would be lost if she delayed. She stood quickly, encircled by the hole in the ruined wall, her sling already in hand. Maradass sensed her presence and his voice lost some of its power as he began to turn towards her, but before he even saw Tris, there was the sudden loud crack of her sling.

The small stone smashed into the hand of Maradass which held the Seacrest, and though he had for a few moments held all power and true immortality in his grasp, still he was human and he felt the sharp pain as the stone broke his bones. Maradass cried out and the talisman spun from his hand. It fell close to where Kerran lay chained to the floor, but passed beyond his reach and began to roll across the chamber, across the bare stone flagging from where the carpets had been flung by the wind. Maradass in his fear was shuffling quickly across the large chamber to regain his prize, his damaged fingers at his lips. Luista reached out a hand towards the talisman but just before it reached her, the Seacrest bounced in a small groove of the stone floor. The circular piece of almost translucent metal turned, still rolling, finally coming to rest against the foot of Mindis who had remained still and silent throughout the violent joining of the talisman.

Maradass leapt towards Mindis. Kerran's chains shattered. His powers of wizardry returned. He came to his feet and also began to rush towards the fallen talisman. Maradass had almost reached Mindis when the young man bent down and lifted the Seacrest with the tips of his long slim fingers. Kerran felt a burst of power that held him, stopping him from advancing any further. Maradass, who was much closer to Mindis, was thrown to the floor where he crouched, unable to rise.

"Give it to me!" he cried. "It is mine, give it to me!"

Mindis slowly turned the Seacrest in his hands playfully, a strange wistful smile on his face, and then he turned his eyes on Maradass. "It is yours no longer," he said quietly, then became silent once again.

"Give it to him!" Luista suddenly screamed. She remained on the couch and could not move, the whimpering of Darss coming softly into the silence. "Would you kill your own mother?" said Luista, her voice now carefully affectionate and tender. "If Maradass does not hold it then he will die, and if Maradass is to die then I too am lost."

Mindis did not reply as his thoughtful eyes looked towards Kerran, and then to Tris who had almost managed to reach the young wizard's side but could go no further.

"Give it to me!" spat Maradass.

He tried to lunge at Mindis but could not penetrate the magical powers which surrounded the young man.

Mindis smiled almost gently then and turned to Maradass. "You are called the Evil One and there is good reason in that title," his voice was clear and strong, silencing all others. "You would destroy all things to have what you crave. There is no honour or justice in your ways. To entrap the House of Amitarl, Luista was sent to Zeta to bear Tolth a son, and then you used that son as a piece in your evil game. Trapped inside my silent place, none could see how different I really was. I am made of ancient oaths and deceit and the mixed magic of Amitarl, Elveren and Maradass. You held me and used me, all for your own ends."

Maradass was gasping, fear and horror showing on his ancient, lined face. Luista, her beautiful features turning to a vicious snarl, grasped at the air before her, trying to reach her son but the Seacrest held her.

Mindis then turned to her. "You are part of this also," he said and she shrank back from the sudden violence in her dark son's eyes. "To live forever in great beauty you would let nothing stand in your way. You are as evil as Maradass, and so you must die with him."

"No!" shrieked Luista.

Mindis stood. Luista called to him again but there was

nothing she could do, as with slow deliberate steps Mindis approached Kerran, and smiling gently he placed the Seacrest into the young wizard's hands.

Maradass screamed and rushed at Mindis who was no longer protected, but Kerran stepped into his path. Maradass, his clawed hands waving futilely in the air, could advance no further. The terrible cry which burst from his lips was the most ravaged and painful sound that any in the land would ever hear. The elite bodyguard of Maradass heard the cry and in fear they ran from the castle, knowing that their master had lost the game.

"It is near sundown," said Kerran, almost feeling pity for this broken and empty creature before him. "Zard is no more and your own time is short."

Maradass seemed to crumble under the weight of Kerran's words. He had known the exact moment when his black son had died, but until now it had not mattered. Everything he ever desired had now slipped through his grasp and was gone. Luista was broken, her life shattered and passing, yet in her dark scheming heart she still felt love and fear for her youngest son whom she held in her arms.

"What of Darss?" she cried to the young wizard, who looked at her with great compassion in his eyes. "Would you let die an innocent child whose only wrong was to be born of Maradass?"

Pity welled up in Kerran's heart. "Darss will not die," he told her. "This I promise. Give him to me and I will take him to safety."

Luista looked with surprise into the eyes of the young wizard and saw that he did not lie. Gently she handed her young son to Kerran. The baby had been whimpering, but became silent as he looked up into Kerran's face. He smiled a small baby's smile and reached up a hand to try and touch the kind eyes which now looked down upon him. Released now, Maradass turned, silent and broken. He drifted as though he walked in sleep and with slow tired steps he mounted the dais and eased his ancient body into his High Seat.

"You have won," he said into the silence. "Go, and let us die without spectators. You have what you wish, now go."

The look of hate and despair on the shattered face held Kerran for a moment' He looked one last time on the shrunken form of Maradass, then holding the Seacrest in one hand and the child in the crook of his other arm, Kerran led Tris and Mindis from the castle. None could touch or harm them. There was a soft glow around them and the soldiers of Maradass fell back as the group passed through the open gates and came to stand on the roadway facing the Black Army.

"All is now over for you," Kerran said, his words reaching all ears. "Return to the Broken Lands, or lay down your arms and join us in the peace to come. Maradass is no more and as the sun departs this day you will be free from the spells that he enthralled you with." Kerran looked out over the army to the distant sun which was about to set. "Leave this place!" he said to them. "The works of Maradass are about to pass, when the sun sets many things will be at an end."

Kerran turned from the road and walked towards the cliffs above the sea. He had already seen in Tris's mind what she had seen and he wanted very much to find Flindas and heal his wounds. They came to stand at the blood spattered cliff's edge where the body of Marlto lay. On the dead warrior's face was a look of rigid terror. A tremor ran through the ground. Tris almost fell and Kerran pointed to the sun as it slowly disappeared beyond the horizon. The earth shook again and then the army of Maradass began to scatter. Kerran and Tris watched the dark castle. The tallest tower swayed and then toppled in a cascade of dust and stone. A second tower fell in on itself and then a swiftly widening crack ran through the outer walls as they too began to crumble. Splitting and shattering, the stonework of Maradass Castle fell. Fire belched upwards, consuming the woodwork. A dark pall of smoke drifted on the light breeze, stretching out slowly across the darkening sea. Except for the fire, there was silence. The army of Maradass fled in terror, scattering into the north, running from the power of Chelasta.

Flindas lay back, weak and exhausted from the loss of much blood. He strapped his wounds with the material from his breeches but still the redness continued to stain the sand beneath him. When he had swum out to escape the soldiers and the black dogs he did not expect to survive for long in the ocean. Weakness would finally see him drown, or his blood would soon attract flesh-eating creatures from the deep. Moving through the shallows to the north, Flindas had watched marauders searching the coastline, and staying low in the water, it had been some time before he was seen. Though it caused him much pain, he had made his way to deeper water until the soldiers and dogs looked like dark ants crawling along the beach.

For a time he floated and the pain receded a little. Flindas knew the danger of this. He had been weakened and could not have lasted much longer before succumbing to the ocean's depths. Then he had seen his hunters leave the darkening beach and his hopes rose, until he attempted to swim back to the shallows. It was then he realised that his strength was almost gone. He still tried to reach the shore but it was impossible against the slight current. Just keeping afloat was difficult. Then he had seen the head of a large dog coming through the light surf. At first he thought it was a marauder, one solitary beast keen on tasting his blood, and then he had laughed aloud with relief.

Now for a time he was alive and safe. Rark had dragged him to the beach and a small rocky cave close by the shore. The mountain dog was gone now and Flindas wondered at the creature that once again had saved his life. Though the pain in his leg and shoulder was great, Flindas dozed a little until evening, and when he woke it was to the sound of footsteps coming towards the cave. He no longer had any weapons, even his blow pipe was gone for he had kicked away his boots when he entered the ocean. There was no strength left in his body and nothing at hand to fight with, and it was with great relief that he saw the large head of Rark appear against the dimming light. The mountain dog gave a low bark of greeting and then retreated from the cave mouth to make space for Kerran to enter.

"It is over," said the young wizard coming quickly to his

side, and Flindas leaned back with a heavy grateful sigh. Then his mind swam into welcome darkness.

The High Wizards

In the far distance Flindas could see the high walls of Celisor Castle. For some unknown reason the Wizards Way had been closed to them and the road south had taken them many days, but now they had finally reached the City Amitarl. Kerran had healed his wounds, though a deep stiffness remained in his right thigh. Walking was still a little painful and they had been fortunate to find stray horses scattered from the Maradass herd. Kerran had entered the city of Mendan Maradass and told the inhabitants there that peace had come to the land, but most of the people had been suspicious and afraid.

"They have lived under oppressors for centuries," Kerran said. "It will take them time to realise that peace has truly come. Amitarl will govern all the Regions now and they will prosper."

Most of the Black Army had left the Regions for the Broken Lands. Leaderless and with their binding spells broken, they had lost the will to fight now that a wizard's protection hung over the lands. Kerran was sure that many would return to the Regions when they heard that they would not be hunted or singled out for punishment. They had been deluded and held against their will, he told all who he met, and they listened for he was a wizard and a great hero of the times.

Kerran looked at the young baby in his arms. If this Darss, who was now Maradass, was allowed to mature he would eventually wed, and Kerran knew that his wife would bear two sons and then the Maradass family would again enter the land. Without the Seacrest they would hold no great power, but even Kerran did not know how true this may be. There was no longer room for both Amitarl and Maradass in the Regions and the Elbrand who now rode with them had been shocked that Darss still lived.

Tris rode beside Kerran and wondered at the changes that had come over the young wizard. A great compassion and understanding could be seen in his eyes and his manner had become even more calm and gentle than before. She had often held the young Darss as they camped, but always it was Kerran who held the child when they rode. The baby need only whimper and Kerran would sing to him in a strange tongue and the child would grow quiet. There was goat's milk to be had and Darss would gnaw on a crust of bread. Strangely, he had never truly cried when in Kerran's care.

The lands to the south of the Crossroads showed much devastation where the Stone Army had marched. Large tracts of land were dying and all living things in the Krags path had suffered. Even the weeds and small grasses that had grown in the cracks of the City Highroad had turned to dust. The companions had not been long on that road when Elbrand scouts had reached them and told them of the happenings in the south. The Stone Army had appeared in many places along the Lines of the Wizards Way and then pressed towards the City Amitarl. The army of Zeta which was spread throughout the Southlands had rushed to the defence of the city and within days the army of Krags had surrounded the outer walls, but had not taken the harbour where lay the fleet of tall ships.

The Stone Army pressed hard on the city, and as before they showed no fear of death. The defenders defied them by casting stones upon their advancing lines. Many of the old ruins in the city had now disappeared as everyone who could, had been asked to assist in the gathering of stone to throw down upon the enemy. The dead Krags became as piles of rubble themselves and did not turn to dust, slowly mounting higher against the walls. Then all those within the city had been able to see their plan, the Stone Soldiers would keep advancing and dying until they built a ramp of their own dead high enough to pass over the battlements.

Their numbers were vast and they attacked relentlessly, day and night. Tolth had let it be known that the fate of the city would be decided at sundown on the day of the new moon. By that day the mounds of dead were in places within a spear's thrust of the walled battlements. On the day of the new moon, as the sun had set, the Stone Army had faltered, and to the wonder of all within the city, every one of the Krags, living or dead, had crumbled into fine dust and were gone.

Tris looked about at the signs of war. Large areas of land were turning to dust and many trees stood gaunt and grey, their leaves fallen to the earth. Crops and grasslands had lost the green of spring. Ghostly fields, the colour of ash, lay crushed and lifeless, and the plain leading up to the walls of the city was bleak and lifeless. Many thousands of people welcomed them, pouring out from the city and giving some colour to the barren land, for all knew that the Evil One was dead and they rejoiced.

There were many greetings and tears, and it was much later that Kerran went with Flindas and Tris to Darbra's home, where Kerran's mother and now Piata were staying. Kerran had changed greatly but he soon found that his feelings for Piata had not. Now that Maradass was no more, and peace was assured, he felt a yearning to hold her, and when he looked into her eyes, his wizardry seemed to leave him. Darbra was wise, and when she asked if they would like a room together in her home. They nodded, unable in their shy embarrassment to say a word.

As spring turned toward summer, many things came to pass. The harvest would be good it seemed, despite the ashen strips of land. Tolth was made Governor of the Four Regions, while Leana, with a great many Elbrand, was sent to Mendan Maradass to help bring about true peace for those who lived there. It had always been a place of vice and degradation and she saw her work as a great opportunity to help those in need. She was a changed person. There was a bright light in her eyes and rarely was there not a smile on her lips. With her went Verardian for a time, healing those that he could, and bringing hope to many before eventually returning to the Magical Isles. With him went a large number of the Elbrand and soldiers of Zeta, most of them wishing to return to family and loved ones. Amongst them went Brook and Teaker who hoped that Flindas and Tris would one day visit Zeta. Mindis was perhaps the strangest of changes. Though he still remained very quiet he had come alive with a great thirst for knowledge and learning.

"I must make up time," he said to Kerran one afternoon. "There are some things I understand as if I have always known them, but there is much that is a great puzzle to me."

Often they spent days together poring over ancient books that had remained unopened for centuries in the library of Celisor Castle. It seemed that Mindis had picked Kerran to be his first friend. He remembered almost nothing of his previous life and Tolth also spent much time with his son, telling him of his heritage, and his lost eighteen years of life.

Kerran and Piata lived with Darbra and Alarin's family. They had been invited to reside in the castle but preferred the openness of the city. The young baby Darss was also taken into Darbra's home. It was possible that one day he could become an enemy to them all, but for now he was just a smiling and happy child who adored Kerran above all others. Kerran's mother was amazed at her son's story. She became a celebrity herself and was often astonished at the great courtesies shown her by the people of the city. Although Piata had also found a welcoming home amongst the pleasant company of Darbra's household she longed for the Magical Isles and to see her parents again. Both of her brothers had come to the lands and had survived, much to her joy, though now they too had returned to Zeta. There was much movement of ships between the Regions and Zeta, but for now she remained in the city, for she loved Kerran with all her heart and wished to be near him.

They had spoken much of their future, though so much

had changed, it could never be the same again. Kerran was a true wizard and would not die for a great many years, if at all. It was difficult for both of them to contemplate, but at least for a time they were together and that was all that really mattered to them. Kerran had learned much from ancient history, and little was closed to him now if he chose to seek an answer. He was also learning that his powers had limits which he could not go beyond. With the Seacrest in his possession he knew that his wizardry could eventually be boundless, but on this path lay great danger for him and all the lands. He could not hold to the talisman forever. This he knew.

With Ma-Zurin-Bidar he saw all possible futures if he chose, but even with his wizard's capacity for memory and time, he did not delve in that confused direction very often. At anytime he could now travel at ease through the Wizards Way, and if he chose he could take others with him, though it weakened him to take many, or to travel often. Unless it was most expedient he was somewhat loathe to use the ancient game without great cause or purpose. One thing which he had seen in all possible futures had pleased those in the Southlands who had looked with horror on the destruction wrought by the Stone Army. Now that Maradass was no more, the evil magic that had drawn the life from the earth where the Krags had walked would eventually cease to haunt the lands. By the next spring he expected that they would see new green shoots where now lay only barren earth.

There was also something that lay unexplained, a time approached of great importance, yet nowhere in future or past could he find an answer to what it might be. He had told no one of this for there was little to tell, dreams and feelings, a new beginning and a time of ending approached. The mystery of it kept him silent until one evening when he sat with Piata and Tolth by the harbour where they had walked for pleasure and to see the expected arrival of a ship from Zeta. It had been a warm spring day and now as darkness began to gather, Kerran told his two companions of his recent uncertainty.

"It often comes to me in dreams," he told them, gazing out upon the still waters with a puzzled look on his brow. "I see the sun go down over the ocean and I am standing as though on the surface of the water, yet it feels solid underfoot. There is no land to be seen in any direction. The moon rises and it is full and bright and for a long time I seem to be waiting for something, then the moon begins to grow dark."

"Do you remember our discoveries from the old book?" asked Tolth, his own mind winging back to the Magical Isles and his workrooms where he and a young hero had begun to search for answers.

"Yes," replied Kerran. "I am sure of the connection but still I do not understand. Black moons and High Wizards, gifts and warnings, these mean nothing to me. The dream comes to me often of late, almost every night, first there is the fiery sunset and then the darkened moon. Other dreams come less often, but all are important I think, as if laying out a path for me which I must follow. There are times in my dreams that I am in Manzanee's cave and the old wizard is there, but he only smiles and does not speak. Then there is a most powerful vision that I cannot comprehend at all. There is a great light that comes up the Highroad towards the city, we are all there waiting for it and from the light rides a tall woman on a ghostly white horse. At first I thought her to be Leana but it is not she, though there is a likeness."

As the days of late spring became warmer there were a great many in the land that looked forward with happiness to the coming celebrations, which accompanied the first day of summer. Few if any had expected to celebrate this longest day, for less than two moons before Maradass was thought to have the Southlands completely in his grasp. Preparations had begun well in advance for the coming festival, and Kerran was in a light hearted mood when strange news was relayed to the city from the west of Rianodar.

Kerran was sitting with Tolth in the library of Celisor Castle when the message reached them. From the Closed Monastery had come a radiating light which had lit the night sky as though it were day. For leagues around the forest glowed, and the Elbrand scouts who saw it had been forced to withdraw to a great distance, their eyes unable to withstand the glare. Then from the edge of the forest had come a rider who travelled Narinda's road toward the Crossroads. Some of the light went with her, surrounding her unmoving erect figure and the tall mount on which she rode. Upon reaching the Crossroads she had turned south towards the city, and though Elbrand scouts and riders watched from a distance, none could approach or speak with her. She continued towards the city in silence, neither resting her mount nor needing to take nourishment herself.

"She comes," said Kerran as though in relief.

"Who comes?" asked Tolth as the messenger left them.

Kerran thought for a time before answering. "I only guess," replied Kerran thoughtfully. "I believe it is Narinda who rides to us from the past."

"Narinda?" said Tolth in bewilderment. "How can she still live? Amitarl have long lives but two thousand years is impossible."

"Nevertheless I think it can be no one else," said Kerran, and from his dream he once again saw the tall and proud rider. "She brings a message," he continued. "A message for me and for all people of the land. I have been waiting for it, though I know not what it could be."

There were a great many people gathered outside the city gates as Narinda Amitarl drew near, riding her ghostly white steed. A light shone around her yet there was a paleness about her which was likened to the burning of a white candle. It was almost as though she could be seen through, and even her clothes had a strange unreal quality as they wafted gently about this tall and stately woman. As she rode towards the city none who saw her felt anything but promise in the magical ancestor of Amitarl. When Narinda came nigh the gate, she reined in her horse but did not dismount. She looked over those present as though she was recognising people she had once known. When she spoke there was a mysterious air to her voice. It seemed to float on the light breeze and reached all ears equally.

"I greet you Tolth Amitarl of the line of Barthol," she said.

Tolth bowed but could not speak. From surprise or from magic he could not tell.

"I am Narinda," she continued. "Daughter of Barthol the Old, and Keeper of the Closed Monastery. I am pleased to see that our family has won through the evil times that are now passed." She turned to Kerran then and slowly a very faint smile came to her austere face. "Greetings to you, Kerran Chelasta," she spoke softly. "I bring to you a message that has been in my keeping for almost two thousand years. It was given to me by the father and mother of your most ancient family line. You hold the power of all good and evil within your hands, to choose the path of good is most difficult but brings the most reward for yourself and for those about you. To hold this power and to know it well, there is much that you must first do, and become. There is a road laid out before you, though you see it not, and none can show you the way. You must go beyond and seek what has been forgotten, but first you must lose much of that which you now hold.

"Ma-Zurin-Bidar, the wizardry which you call the Seacrest, must be returned to from whence it was found, to the very place where Rishtan-Sta used it for its dire purpose. There comes a time, when time has turned fully two circles, when the day can be no longer and the night holds a full and darkened moon. Tis then that you must go to the ancient High Seat of Rishtan-Sta the White and from there you must cast Ma-Zurin-Bidar to the north into the great depths. The time draws nigh and if this be not done you will hold that power forever. You will never be able to release it and this would lead to the destruction of all. Even Rishtan-Sta dared not do this, to possess it for long. It is more powerful than any wizard can hold. You would be corrupted and lost, and then all would perish under your dominion. The choice remains with you. Choose your path carefully, for if this time is not found then it to will be lost forever. There can be no returning."

The strong and ominous words moved Kerran, though he could not comprehend the entire meaning of the message. As the silence lengthened he began to understand. He looked to the tall silent woman and stood in awe of her majestic presence.

There was a magic about her which was stronger than any he had imagined. He had thought that in the lands only he and Trontar held wizardry, but here was one who could hold him and the Seacrest captive should she wish it. His voice finally came to him as if from a great distance.

"I am but young in the ways of wizardry," he told her. "If I cannot hold Ma-Zurin-Bidar without great danger to the people and the lands then I will surely return it from whence it was found, but might it not be more useful in healing and cleansing the great wounds that the lands have suffered? Will you not take it yourself and bring peace and comfort to all places?"

Narinda looked at him steadily, the faintest expression of surprise on her uplifted brow. "You know me not," she said. "Yet you would give to me the greatest power that can exist in this present time." She paused, smiling. "No, young Chelasta," she finally said. "I could not take it, even if I wished it so. I am from the past and can only remain there in safety if Ma-Zurin-Bidar is returned to the depths. In the deepest part of the ocean its power is no more, for it was made there for one purpose only. If you choose to hold it for yourself then so be it. I can bring you no harm or force you to surrender it. Only Ma-Zurin-Bidar can do that to you. The choice must remain yours."

There was silence for a time and then Narinda spoke again. "There is one other task which I must perform here," she said. "I have come for the boy child of Maradass. He will return with me to the Closed Monastery for he cannot remain amongst you. Should he stay here in this present time he would breed corruption, and this cannot be again. Bring him to me, for my time is short."

A horseman was quickly sent to Darbra's home where Kerran's mother minded the child. She had grown fond of the peaceful and intelligent boy but also knew of the dangers he may pose for the future of the lands. It was done swiftly and all the time Narinda sat in silence, while those who watched her did so as if held in a spell which she had not cast. Kerran knew that he was right in allowing Narinda to take Darss, for the family of Maradass should never return to the lands.

Narinda left as she had come, except she held the boy child before her. The Elbrand scouts, who watched her closely, told how the night sky above the three pinnacles glowed as if it were day until Narinda had re-entered the secret ways. The light had then faded and the last of the Maradass line was taken from the land.

That same evening Kerran sat with Tolth and several others in the library of Celisor Castle.

Tolth, after studying several books and making a great many calculations, told them that the day of summer celebration, which would be with them in a few days, was also the day of the first full moon of summer. Tolth smiled and nodded. "An eclipse of the moon also falls on that day," he said to Kerran, though the young wizard had known that it must be so.

Though Kerran had been able to understand much of what Narinda had said there was one part which puzzled him greatly. He was to stand at the High Seat of Rishtan-Sta and cast the Seacrest to the north and into the great depths.

"How can I stand at the High Seat of Rishtan-Sta if it is not there?" he asked Tolth, but the old scholar could give him no reply.

The Sea of Shardis was so deep to the south and near its centre that no one had ever reached the bottom with line or rope. It was thought that deep currents had brought the Seacrest closer to the surface when it was found again though none could say for certain. It was now only two days to the summer solstice and Kerran decided that he must enter the Wizards Way and again investigate that part of the ocean which had once been the high hilltop from where Rishtan-Sta had brought the Wizard Wars to an end.

He entered the Way within his shadow and was soon poised above the dark and turbulent Sea of Shardis. A strong wind blew, causing waves to crest and tumble. Nowhere within sight was there any sign of land. This was the place. He knew that there could be no other. Within his shadow he descended until he was just above the waves. He had never tried to go beneath the surface of the ocean before but soon found, as with the earth of the land, he could go no further. Feeling frustrated and at a loss, he returned to the library to find that Flindas had joined the company there. It was not often that his friend entered the castle in these days of peace, but he had been told of Kerran's quandary and thought that he may be able to help.

"Show me where the High Seat should be," he said to Kerran as he put a map of the Regions on the heavy wooden table.

Kerran took only a moment to point to a place no more than thirty or forty leagues from the southern coast of Shardis.

Flindas nodded and smiled. "You should not be asking scholars to answer this question for you, especially not ones from Zeta who may not know the oceans. You should ask the fisher folk who live on that coast."

He turned for a time to the many shelves of books and scrolls and eventually found what he looked for. It was not a book which he retrieved from a low shelf. It was another map, except that this one was of an area of coastline, and part of the southern portion of the Sea of Shardis.

"There is a place that for many centuries has been called the Fisherman's Graveyard," said Flindas spreading the map. "The centre of the Sea is indeed so deep that none have found the bottom, but some thirty leagues or so from the southern coast there is one rock shelf that comes near the surface." Flindas pointed to a small circle marked on the map. There was nothing else near it except the ominous name: Fisherman's Graveyard.

"It has that name for good reason," said Flindas as he allowed the map to roll back into itself. "Many fishermen of Andrian have come to grief there," he told them. "The rock is shown on all charts but the fishermen grow careless. There is but one rock in the vastness of the sea that they must guard against, and so few of them ever bother. At the lowest of tides, the rock will lift above the level of the water. I think you will find that you have never visited the High Seat of Rishtan-Sta at the correct time of the tide. My guess is that, should you go on the evening of the full moon, you may only get your feet a little wet."

Flindas smiled at the wondrous look on the young wizard's

face. "It is also said that the Depths begin at the northern edge of that rock," continued Flindas. "A swim in that direction would quickly have you floating over the bottomless part of the sea."

During the next two days Kerran roamed about the city and a feeling of high expectancy went with him. A most important moon was soon to rise and perhaps the last of his questions would then be answered.

"You will be changed when you return," said Piata as they stood together upon the castle walls. It was noon and they had come here to be alone together, away from the festivities below.

"I think so too," he said holding her hand and looking out over the grey land. "It is nothing to fear. Only good can come of it."

Piata turned to him. "Good for some may be difficult for others," she said. "For the last few days I have feared that you will not return at all, or that your path will lead you away from here. I still feel this and I am afraid."

He held her then and for a long time they were silent, when Piata spoke again there was a warm softness in her voice.

"I am glad," she said.

"What are you glad of?" he asked, leaning back and looking into her eyes.

"I am glad that we have had this time together. If you do not return..." she did not finish the sentence.

"I will return," he said and was sure of his words.

Inside his body, Kerran entered the Wizards Way just before dusk of the portentous day and was surprised when he found himself at Manzanee's cave, and not upon a rock shelf in the Sea of Shardis. From where he sat on the Black Wizard's High Seat he could see the sun dipping behind the distant forested hills. From the back of the cave there came the slow laugh of the wizard.

"So, Chelasta, we meet one last time," said Manzanee as he came into the light and looked with quizzical amusement at the young wizard. "You did not expect to come here but there is something you have forgotten, and you will need it soon unless you care to drown." Manzanee leapt nimbly to the rock ledge and, lifting the stone which represented the Crossroads, he took from the recess beneath it the small silver sculpture. "Take it now and go, for you will never return to this place," said the Black Wizard handing it to Kerran. "There are those who await you out there and the moon will soon rise. Goodbye, Chelasta, we may yet meet again somewhere in another time, future or past."

"Goodbye, Manzanee," replied Kerran. "Another time, past or future."

The cave was gone and Kerran felt solid rock beneath his feet, though it was as if he stood upon the very surface of the Sea of Shardis. He felt the wetness coming through his boots and as he looked to the skies he saw, in the last rays of the sun, Storm circling on the wind.

The moon rose golden yellow from the eastern sea and he stood for a while, the Seacrest in his hand, waiting. The light of the moon shimmered on the almost still lapping waters, and the first star appeared in the clear, deep blue sky. After a time Kerran saw that the level of the sea had sunk a little and that he now stood on a flat shelf of rock five or six paces across. It was cracked and worn with time and the relentless sea had smoothed it. However, in the moonlight, he began to make out the faint lines carved into the stone. Here again was the seat of a High Wizard. Rishtan-Sta had stood here on the final day and with his own life had taken the doom of the lands away from his kind.

The moon rode higher into the sky and Kerran saw that the tide again began to lap higher at the rock. Looking one last time at the talisman in his hand he drew back his arm and cast it as far to the north as he could. He watched its flight as it curved glittering through the night, and then with a soft splash it disappeared beneath the surface. A great silence hung in the eerie light around him.

Kerran reached into his pouch and drew forth the silver sculpture and he began tracing the ancient lines on the rock surface. Soon he found the point where the lines came together at the seat of Mar-Dran-Thara and the Crossroads of the land. Placing the sculpture in the slight depression he went to stand at the point south and east of the first. Here Rishtan-Sta would have placed his own High Seat. Kerran was about to sit on the cold wet stone when he saw something fly across the face of the moon. Storm soared through the night sky above and again Kerran saw the white hawk as it glided across the glowing orb. Once again and slower still the hawk returned until the bird was silhouetted clearly against the moon.

The white hawk flew down the moonlight directly towards Kerran, the dark spread of wings growing larger until they blocked out the entire moon. Storm seemed to vanish then, or was transformed, merging with the moon, darkening it until Kerran saw the celestial orb as only a dim shadow against the starlit sky. The eclipse had come about in such a strange way that Kerran stood transfixed, lost in wonder. As he gazed at the moon it began to change, but as yet no light could be seen at its edges. Instead it seemed to grow a darker shadow that was no longer moon or white hawk, then a soft light began to enter the darkness until the shadow and the moon burned with white fire that did not consume.

Kerran held up his hands to shield his eyes from the penetrating light. He could not look into the brightness, but after a short time it began to dim and as he watched he saw two separate lights emerge from the one and begin to float towards him. He saw that two glowing human forms had emerged, drawing nearer until they came to float close to him. They were from an ancient lost time and Kerran shuddered within the power that surrounded them.

The man was old and Kerran knew him from his dreams and visions, for here was Rishtan-Sta the White Wizard. At his side floated the softly glowing figure of a beautiful woman who seemed entwined in the locks of her own silver hair which flowed around her as if it were alive. Rishtan-Sta held a large book in his hands, and as their figures became more tangible, he spoke.

"Tis well done, friend Chelasta, for peace is what all people seek," he said softly. "Your deeds have created a time when all will flourish, tis well done I say again and there is a gift I would give you in return."

Rishtan-Sta held the glowing book before him, and as he lowered his arms the ancient tome floated across the space between them and Kerran received into his trembling hands.

"It is a history of your lineage," continued Rishtan-Sta. "It tells of the Far Northlands from where our people first came. It is the history of all wizardry, and if you can find the deeper understanding within the words, you will learn how you came to return at this darkened time in history, and then you will wish to seek further."

There were a few moments of silence and yet Kerran could not speak. He held the book before him and was dumb in the face of the two glowing figures. Then it was the woman who spoke, her voice soft and kind.

"There is much that you have yet to learn, dear Chelasta," she spoke as a mother to her beloved child. "Much to learn and understand, but there is one thing which we are now free to tell you. Though your ancestor was one of the fourteen and showed no high powers in the times of great wizardry. Know now that he was more than the others, for Chelasta was born of High Wizards. The only child to have ever been conceived by two of our kind. He lived as one with the land and all creatures, choosing not to turn to the governing of people, and he happily relinquished his powers and then slowly he forgot that he was truly a High Wizard himself. Your line comes directly from him, and before that from two of the seven, for I am Orlandi, High Wizard of the Moon, and I was your ancestral mother."

Kerran's eyes widened, always he had found Orlandi to be a mystery, all his time in the Wizards Way had revealed almost nothing of her. Now he thought that he had begun to understand, but the biggest wonder was yet to come.

"There is more," said Rishtan-Sta, reaching out a hand to Orlandi, their lights meeting, entwining. "Tis I who was the father of Chelasta in those ancient times and I am greatly pleased with my son. It is all written in this book, and you will learn much from it. You are born of High Wizards, young

Chelasta, and there is much that you may accomplish if you choose. Go now. Return to the people you now love and do as your heart tells you. Our purpose here is at an end and our time is finally done. Read the book carefully, and perhaps you will find yet another path before you, an unexpected and unlooked for journey to be taken. Farewell, Chelasta, and again I say, tis well done."

"Goodbye," said Orlandi. "Learn, and remember, your life will be long and there is much yet to be done."

The light of their presence began to fade, and when Kerran had rubbed his eyes, all that remained was the beautiful bright full moon hanging amongst the stars.

Kerran returned to the city that same night but he was changed and could not say how. He spoke with Tolth about his ancestry, and then he and Piata sat by the ocean far into the night. By sunrise Kerran was in a small private room of the castle and would not be disturbed as he studied carefully the old book of wizardry. For many days he remained there, taking little food or sleep. Sometimes he would be brought a plate, and though he had not left the room, his seat would often be empty, the book nowhere to be seen.

A moon passed, and then another. Autumn came with chilling winds and Flindas felt restless to his very bones. The city had started to pall on him and he began to long for the open lands and new adventures. His wounds had healed well and when Tris began to talk of her desire to return to Trontar and the Place of Puzzles, he said he would accompany her at least into Rianodar. Though he knew that he would miss his young friend when she returned to the wizard's Castle, Flindas looked forward to the journey. There were a great many sad goodbyes before they left the City Amitarl. The two companions had decided to walk, as both had become a little idle and well fed in the city. As Flindas put it, 'The walk will help to tighten our belts.' They set out under a cold but clear sky with Rark, who seemed greatly pleased with the new adventure. After a great many days of slow leisurely travel they reached the Desert Pass. There was no longer any sign of black soldiers as there had been the last time they had tried to enter the narrow way. Flindas then decided that he would go with Tris to the ring of magical stones.

When they finally stood at one of the narrow gaps between the high stones of the Place of Puzzles neither could say goodbye. They had shared so many dangerous times together that it was going to seem strange not to have the other's company. Tris held Flindas by the hands as tears rolled down her face.

"I will ask the wizard to find you in his blue dome so I can see how you fare," she said, and then she stretched up and kissed him quickly and was gone, sliding quickly through a gap between the wizard's stones.

Flindas stood for a long time looking at the narrow space between the huge rocks. He almost wanted to follow her but no, science and study were not his way, though for the first time in many years a great loneliness settled on his heart. He placed his hand on Rark's shaggy neck and scratched him behind the ears, and then he turned and left the Place of Puzzles. When they had again reached the end of the new road built by Maradass, Flindas stood for a time and looked to the east where the pass narrowed and entered the Regions. He laid a hand on Rark's huge shoulders and the mountain dog looked up at his friend as though he guessed his dilemma.

"Let us go another way," Flindas said to the dog, finally making his decision. He turned then not to the east but to the west, into the dryness of the Outlands. There was a friend that he went in search of and it was some years before Flindas Demsharl was seen in the eastern lands again.

Kerran, the High Wizard Chelasta, had learned of his true ancestry and the nature of the Far Northlands that used to be. With this knowledge came an understanding. The path which Rishtan-Sta had spoken of led to the distant north, to the ancient home of the wizards. Kerran knew with great certainty that he must go to those long forgotten lands, for it had been foretold in the book that a High Wizard would return. He knew that he was that chosen one, and he also knew that he must go alone, for none other than a High Wizard could survive a journey into such corrupted lands.

With sadness Piata returned to Zeta and her home of Felstrar. Her heart was lightened somewhat when she heard from her parents that high above the village, on a rocky ledge, and also in flight, two white hawks had been seen. It was the sign that peace had truly come to all of the lands. Piata remembered the day when Kerran had left the city and Storm had flown with him into the north. Kerran had gone with the promise that he would return.

She stood on the beach and touched with loving hands the slight swelling that told of the child to come, and then she looked across the bay and wondered if she would ever see the father again. She knew that the child of Chelasta would come as a magical boy, but would Kerran ever reach these green shores again to meet his son? She could not guess at the answer, and as the day was growing cooler she turned for home and the warm family hearth where their son would be born.

Flindas nudged the small log further into the fire, sending sparks crackling into the cool night air. Rark opened his eyes a moment then sighed deep in his throat and returned to his dreams. The constellation of the Six Sorcerers hung in the southern sky and Flindas smiled as two glowing stars fell across the moonless night, one after the other.

"It is a good omen to see two stars fall," said Duragor who had also seen the trails of light arc across the darkness. "Tell me," he continued. "Now that all is at peace in the lands, why do you sit here beneath the stars, when you could have all the luxury of a prince? Other men would kill for what you give away."

"Those are other men," said Flindas, a soft peacefulness in his voice. "I have all that I can ever need. To have more would be a burden that I do not wish to carry." He smiled then and turned to his black companion. "You talk this way and yet you own even less than I," he said with a smile.

Duragor chuckled and looked to where the main campfire burned, and his people sat in talk and play. "You are wrong there," he said to Flindas, a warm smile touching his lips. "I own everything and more."